Novels of the Sons of Destiny by Jean Johnson

ROMANCE LOVERS ARE FALLING FOR
THE SONS OF DESTINY

"Jean Johnson's writing is fabulously fresh, thoroughly romantic, and wildly entertaining. Terrific—fast, sexy, charming, and utterly engaging. I loved it!"—*New York Times* bestselling author Jayne Ann Krentz

"Cursed brothers, fated mates, prophecies, yum! A fresh new voice in fantasy romance, Jean Johnson spins an intriguing tale of destiny and magic." —Robin D. Owens, RITA Award–winning author of *Heart Fate*

"What a debut! I have to say it is a must-read for those who enjoy fantasy and romance. I so thoroughly enjoyed [*The Sword*] and eagerly look forward to each of the other brothers' stories. Jean Johnson can't write them fast enough for me!"　　　—*The Best Reviews*

"Enchantments, amusement, and eight hunks and one bewitching woman make for a fun romantic fantasy . . . humorous and magical . . . a delightful charmer."　　　—*Midwest Book Review*

"A paranormal adventure series that will appeal to fantasy and historical fans, plus time-travel lovers as well. Jean Johnson has created a mystical world of lessons taught, very much like the great folktales we love to hear over and over. It's like *Alice in Wonderland* meets the *Knights of the Round Table* and you're never quite sure what's going to happen next. Delightful entertainment . . . An enchanting tale with old-world charm, *The Sword* will leave you dreaming of a sexy mage for yourself."　　　—*Romance Junkies*

continued . . .

"An intriguing new fantasy romance series . . . a welcome addition to the genre. *The Sword* is a unique combination of magic, time travel, and fantasy that will have readers looking toward the next book. Think *Seven Brides for Seven Brothers* but add one more and give them magic, with curses and fantasy thrown in for fun. Cunning . . . creative . . . lovers of magic and fantasy will enjoy this fun, fresh, and very romantic offering."   —*Time Travel Romance Writers*

"I love *The Sword*. The writing is sharp and witty and the story is charming. [Johnson] makes everything perfectly believable. She has created an enchanting situation and characters that are irascible at times and lovable at others. Jean Johnson . . . is off to a flying start. She tells her story with a lively zest that transports a reader to the place of action. I can hardly wait for the next one. It is a must-read."   —*Romance Reviews Today*

"A fun story. I look forward to seeing how these alpha males find their soul mates in the remaining books."   —*The Eternal Night*

"An intriguing world . . . an enjoyable hero . . . an enjoyable show-case for an inventive new author. Jean Johnson brings a welcome voice to the romance genre, and she's assured of a warm welcome."
                                                —*The Romance Reader*

"An intriguing and entertaining tale of another dimension . . . quite entertaining. It will be fun to see how the prophecy turns out for the rest of the brothers."   —*Fresh Fiction*

The MAGE

JEAN JOHNSON

BERKLEY SENSATION, NEW YORK

THE BERKLEY PUBLISHING GROUP
Published by the Penguin Group
Penguin Group (USA) Inc.
375 Hudson Street, New York, New York 10014, USA
Penguin Group (Canada), 90 Eglinton Avenue East, Suite 700, Toronto, Ontario M4P 2Y3, Canada
(a division of Pearson Penguin Canada Inc.)
Penguin Books Ltd., 80 Strand, London WC2R 0RL, England
Penguin Group Ireland, 25 St. Stephen's Green, Dublin 2, Ireland (a division of Penguin Books Ltd.)
Penguin Group (Australia), 250 Camberwell Road, Camberwell, Victoria 3124, Australia
(a division of Pearson Australia Group Pty. Ltd.)
Penguin Books India Pvt. Ltd., 11 Community Centre, Panchsheel Park, New Delhi—110 017, India
Penguin Group (NZ), 67 Apollo Drive, Rosedale, North Shore 0632, New Zealand
(a division of Pearson New Zealand Ltd.)
Penguin Books (South Africa) (Pty.) Ltd., 24 Sturdee Avenue, Rosebank, Johannesburg 2196,
South Africa

Penguin Books Ltd., Registered Offices: 80 Strand, London WC2R 0RL, England

This book is an original publication of The Berkley Publishing Group.

This is a work of fiction. Names, characters, places, and incidents either are the product of the author's imagination or are used fictitiously, and any resemblance to actual persons, living or dead, business establishments, events, or locales is entirely coincidental. The publisher does not have any control over and does not assume any responsibility for author or third-party websites or their content.

PRINTING HISTORY
Berkley Sensation trade paperback edition / April 2009

Library of Congress Cataloging-in-Publication Data

Johnson, Jean, 1972–
    The mage : a novel of the sons of destiny / Jean Johnson.—Berkley Sensation trade pbk. ed.
        p. cm.—(Sons of Destiny; bk. 8)
    ISBN 978-0-425-22594-3
    1. Twins—Fiction. 2. Prophecies—Fiction. I. Title.

PS3610.O355M34 2009
813'.6—dc22
                            2008050462

PRINTED IN THE UNITED STATES OF AMERICA

10 9 8 7 6 5 4 3 2 1

ACKNOWLEDGMENTS

Alas, now we come to the end of this series. I can only hope you've had as much fun reading it as I've had writing it. (Preferably more fun in reading, come to think of it.) This book wouldn't have been nearly so well-polished if it weren't for the efforts of my beta-ladies, Alienor, Alexandra, Stormi, and NotSoSaintly, plus the cold-reading skills of my friend Buzzy. To my friend Effrick for her comment on Internet dating, and my sister Nylima for her knowledge of "espressology." My deepest thanks go to Cindy and Leis at Berkley; without these two lovely ladies, I'd be just another wanna-be. Since I'm now doing what I love to do most in the world—and I'm getting paid for it, squee!—they have my eternal gratitude.

To reassure those interested in reading more of my stories, I do have more coming! While the Sons of Destiny series is drawing to a close with this book, there are still plenty of other stories waiting to be told elsewhere in this particular world. There are also other universes and genres waiting to be explored. (It's actually a good thing this series is coming to an end; I have a ton of new plot-bunnies waiting for me to get around to them . . . and some are running out of patience, eep!)

If you're eighteen or older, come see if the benign mayhem of the Mob of Irate Torch-Wielding Fans is for you, at: http://groups.yahoo.com/group/MoITWF. Or if you are interested in having a random chat with me on the forum boards or want to check the website to look for updates on what's coming out next, all ages can safely visit: www.JeanJohnson.net.

Enjoy,
Jean

ONE

The Eighth Son shall set them free:
Act in Hope and act in love
Draw down your powers from above
Set your Brothers to their call
When Mage has wed, you will be all.

The Portal of Nightfall stood on a flat, pale granite platform on the first of the hills rising up from the harbor. Its posts and lintel were huge, square-cut blocks of dark gray basalt, contrasting against the whitewashed walls and blue-glazed roof tiles of the city. Even the threshold was basalt, though only someone standing on the platform could have seen it easily, since the block had been sunk into the dais, leaving it flush with the weathered, speckled stones.

Within the dark gray frame of stone, a rippling curtain of light was twisting, spiraling outward from a pinpoint at the center. Lines of colors spun and stretched; as soon as they reached the edges and corners, the image twisted itself into alignment. Instead of a faintly watery view of the temple district and the green-forested hills of Nightfall, the square-shaped opening contained the familiar view of the city of Orovalis, as seen from its own Portal doorway.

The dais on that side was filled with a full score of mages. Two heartbeats after the Portal stabilized, half of them came across. As soon as they cleared, the Portal Master in the other city closed the connection; the image of the other harbor city swirled away, restoring the basalt-framed view of the city and the green-cloaked mountains beyond.

"Thank you for coming," Nea told the mages who had stepped across. "If you could shut down the Portal as soon as possible—"

"I'm afraid that's *not* possible," one of the mages stated, interrupting her. His brown hair was cut fashionably short, his knee-length robes bore more elaborately striped trim than the others wore, and his attitude was pure bureaucratic condescension. "At least, not until you have signed this binding Indemnity Scroll. I presume you are the Duchess Haupanea of Nightfall?"

"I am, yes," Nea agreed, nonplussed by his attitude. She gestured at the man to her left, then the two women to her right. "This is my seneschal, Lord Niktor; my Prophecies scribe, Giolana; and our Portal Mistress, Lady Abeyda. If we could get the Portal shut down . . ."

"First things first." Holding out his hand with an expectation of obedience, the mage took the scroll one of the others dutifully pulled out of a satchel.

Niktor intercepted it before Nea could reach for it, untying its ribbons so that he could look at it first. He had the experience of his years as seneschal of the duchy to draw upon, when it came to skimming through legal documents.

"And you are . . . ?" Nea asked the imperious mage, giving Niktor time to read.

"Count Kaidannen of Kairides, *the* Councilor of Portal Management," he proclaimed, looking down his nose at her.

Men whose manners are of the slob
Shall find themselves without a job

The words were smug, sneaking through her thoughts. Nea blinked, then slanted a quick look at Giolana. Her scribe hadn't moved, wasn't recording the silly little verse. *It's just Nauvea, playing Her little tricks on my mind . . . This is not really the best time for You to have a sense of humor, my Goddess. You Yourself said this was a very serious business.*

Niktor finished skimming the scroll and leaned close enough to murmur in her ear. "They're demanding we pay the full cost of lost export/import fees for the entire time all the Portals are shut down, for the inconvenience of it. Milady . . . we don't make that much money in *five years* of desalinating."

The longer you delay
The worse is your dismay

This time, the words were firmer in her mind, and she could feel the Goddess rippling through her thoughts.

"Don't you mean the longer *you* delay?" the Councilor countered, giving her an arch look.

Releasing her portable scribing board to let it hover midair so she could write that down, Giolana opened her mouth to correct the Count. Nea, realizing she had spoken the verse aloud that time, nudged her assistant with an elbow. Such a short little prophecy wasn't important. Getting the Portal closed was. "Give me the scroll, please, and a pen."

Wincing, Niktor handed her the scroll. Giolana surrendered one of her pens. Bracing the scroll on the floating board, Nea skimmed through the legalese herself . . . and scratched out a long line. The Count started and scowled, but Niktor quickly stepped between them. Nea's gray-haired seneschal might not have been in the best of physical shape, but he was loyal and strong-willed. Ignoring the silent stare-down between the two men, Nea wrote her changes onto the parchment, then signed it with a flourish, glad her scribe always kept the ink reservoirs in her pens full.

"There. *If* the closure of the Portals turns out to have been un-necessary, Nightfall will pay *double* the amount of estimated losses in export/import fees to the Empire of Katan . . . but if the closure *is* necessary and this delay of *your* doing damages Nightfall in any tangible way . . . the Empire will pay half those estimated lost import/export costs to the Duchess Haupanea of Nightfall, or to her designated heirs. Copy that, and secure the copies in the usual places," Nea ordered Giolana, passing back the pen and the scroll-draped board. Taking them, her scribe dutifully began enchanting spare sheets of paper into duplicates of the scroll.

Count Kaidannen frowned at her. "Who do you think you are, changing the agreement like that? You cannot do that!"

"I *think* I am the Seer of Nightfall, the Seer who Prophesied a Disaster of unimaginable proportions if those Portals are not shut down!" Nea retorted, hands going to her green-skirted hips. She could feel the tightness of anxiety building up inside of her. "Now, get to work, or *you* will have to explain to your superiors the indem-nity *your* delay is threatening them . . . *if* I am right and you survive the coming calamity."

"You *cannot* change that agreement!" Kaidannen argued as Gio-lana started enchanting two more rolls of parchment extracted from the bag hanging at her side. "That scroll was drawn up by the Council of Mages!"

Nea lifted her chin. "I hardly think the Council would argue the matter, when I have written upon an enchantment-bound scroll to pay *twice* the extortion they have demanded, should there be no le-gitimate reason to close the Portals of Katan . . . but if there really is one, and *your* delay worsens things . . ."

Scowling, the Councilor deliberately delayed a long moment, then spun and snapped orders at his fellow mages. Giolana handed the original to Niktor, who passed it back to the Councilor as soon as his attention was free. The other two, she tucked into scroll cases and chanted over. When she was through, she touched Nea's elbow, murmuring in the younger woman's ear as soon as she had the duchess' attention. "One copy has been sent to the palace archives, the other to the Desalinator office."

"Good—thank you," Nea added, prodded by her anxiety into speaking her thoughts.

Giolana wasn't the strongest of mages; she would never have gotten very far in Katani politics had she moved to the mainland, as the brown-haired young woman didn't have much in the way of magic. But the scribe could craft and cast a modest number of spells. It was far more than Nea could manage. She could only hold and aim magical forces; she could not shape them. Giolana had enough magic to manipulate pens, papers, copying spells, and even minor translocation Artifacts, making her a superb scribe for a Seer's needs. Because they were close in age and temperament, and were in constant proximity, the two of them had become friends.

"I don't say it often enough, but I thank you for all that you've done for me," Nea added, prompted by instinct. That prompting made her feel uneasy. Too much was going on right now to just assume the urge was nothing more than a product of their friendship.

"It's an honor for any scribe to be picked to work for a Seer," Giolana said earnestly. Then she smiled and leaned close enough to bump her elbow gently against Nea's. "But you make it fun."

"We should probably leave the dais to the mages, Your Grace," Niktor told Nea as the men and women from the mainland began their magics.

The thought of leaving the Portal made Nea's skin crawl. In the back of her mind, she could feel Nauvea shaking Her head, and shook her own.

"No. You go. Try and convince more of our people to leave. Being the last to close down is already cutting things too close, and with the delay . . . No, I want Nightfall evacuated, just in case. If something goes wrong, my people shouldn't be here. Giolana, you should step back, too."

"My place is at your side, Your Grace," her scribe argued. "Especially at the moment a Prophecy unfolds."

No—no, You Fool! Do not challenge her! Do not!

Nauvea? Are you talking about Giolana? Nea prodded her thoughts, but the Goddess did not respond. Not that Nauvea had much energy anymore, with only a handful of people on the Isle who still worshipped Her. The Goddess of Dreaming had once been powerful enough to manifest, to appear in a physical form. But over the centuries, immigrants from Katan had brought their worship of Kata and Jinga to the island, slowly supplanting the fading powers of their original Patron.

Long before Nea's time, her family had been forced to accept tacit protection from Katan, becoming a mere duchy instead of a small, independent kingdom, though the rulers of Nightfall never stopped believing in their half-forgotten Goddess. Perhaps She wasn't technically a Patron anymore—Nea didn't even know if Nauvea was still Named at the Convocations—but She was definitely more than a mere spirit.

Beloved Gods never die, Nauvea whispered to her, following Nea's thoughts as only a Goddess or a ghost could. *They just fade away . . . except for This Fool. This will not end well—do not leave the dais. As you love Our People, do not leave this dais!*

Nea didn't budge. Even if Nauvea hadn't spoken to her, she wouldn't have moved; the safety of her people demanded that she personally oversee the closure of the Portal. Something bad was going to happen, something she had personally Foreseen in that half-blind way of Prophecy. No, she remained where she was, standing just beyond the half circle of carefully positioned mages, nine of them chanting in unison, power flowing visibly from their hands to designated points around the square frame of the Portal. The tenth mage, the Count, was chanting a counterpoint spell, with his powers aimed at the center of the opening, where the twisting views of other locations normally originated.

Power exploded off to her left. Nea whipped her head in that direction, but it was soundless, sightless, and entirely in her head. *Nauvea? . . . Goddess?*

Ow—

The Portal buckled. Three of the mages cried out as power crackled *out* of the dark stone structure, snapping into tiny streamers that stretched for the dozen bodies on the platform. Darkness swirled out of the center point of the Portal opening; brightness seeped in from its corners. Even the arrogant Count buckled, body trembling as he fought against the warping energies. Giolana flinched back, ducking behind Nea's body for shelter.

"Oh, Gods!"

"Keep chanting! *Contain* it!" the Councilor of Portal Management ordered through gritted teeth.

They're not going to!—SAVE THEM!

Nea lunged past the startled Councilor. When her Goddess commanded, she obeyed. Flinging herself into the Portalway, Nea grabbed at the energies with her will. She could not *shape* it, but she *could* channel and contain magic. Power rammed into her, vibrating painfully.

Teeth rattling, jaw clenching, she fought to contain it, but it wasn't just the Portal she had to fight. There was energy coming in from something else, something more. Something that felt Godlike. It was worse—a hundred thousand times worse—than wrestling with the power of the Nightfall Fountain, which she had been forced to Guard for the last year. The two energies fought, one assertively defined, the other utterly chaotic.

She couldn't hold it back from pouring across her island for more than a few moments. She couldn't!

Don't contain it, Nea; use it!

I'm a Seer, not a mage, dammit!

USE IT!

Opening her mouth, to scream, to demand *how*, Nea felt Nauvea sweep into her senses, blinding and deafening and dulling the young woman to the fullness of reality, as She had done only a few times before. *This*, at least, was a power that had used her before. Relaxing into the grip of her Goddess relaxed her into the grip of the Portal, turning her into a conduit. *That*, Nea understood. The only thing she *could* understand, as pain and power merged into near madness, blending from skin inward and bone outward, absorbing into her nerves and pouring out of her throat in chanted words.

More power! Tendrils shot out from her nerves, but they weren't under *her* control. Like blind feelers, they skittered across the mountain to the north, seeking a way through the protections guarding the Fountain. Others found a nearer source of power; it wasn't immense like the other, but it *was* large enough that most of that questing need latched onto *it*, draining it. *Yes—yes, enough! Just barely enough—!*

She heard a yell, something about the Portal collapsing, then her world turned upside down.

Light blinded her, sound assaulted her, nausea ambushed her— pain *slammed* into the back of her head. Nea hit something hard, bruising her elbow, hip, and knee. Eyes squeezed shut, she felt herself being pelted by bits of things, some of it cold and wet, a lot of it hard and stinging. Fearing it was the square stones of the Portal arch collapsing around her, she screamed and rolled herself into a ball, trying to get clear. Her shriek was almost lost in the howling of the wind tearing at her clothes. With her hair blown across her eyes, making her flinch and wince from the whipping strands, she could not see where the stones were coming down out of the suddenly leaden sky, and rolled again, trying to at least get off the platform.

Something smacked into her body, making her yelp in fear. It was large, and somewhat heavy, but it did not crush her bones; instead it sheltered her from the worst of the whirling debris even as it pressed her down. Curling up her bruised body, Nea huddled under the broad object, listening to the roaring noise recede into the distance, the clatter and tumble of wind-thrown debris, and the hissing waves of rain.

Slowly, the wind and the rain died down, dropping the grit and other things that had been lofted into the air. Unsqueezing her eyes, Nea cautiously peered at her immediate surroundings. She was covered by a door. A strange, gray-painted, *metal* door. A hollow one, thankfully, but she wouldn't have known what it was, if she hadn't seen a silvery metal knob projecting from midway down the edge, not far from her knee.

It wasn't crushing her because a chunk of furniture and a thick book crammed with thin, yellow and gray pages were holding it up over her body. It was pressing her in place, but a bit of wriggling allowed her to twist onto her back, then work herself free with her heels. Once out from under the door, she rolled onto her knees, grimacing at the mud staining her dress. When she finally looked up at the greater world around her, she froze.

The scene that met her eyes was doubly unimaginable: The first hard-to-grasp aspect was the sheer destruction that surrounded her. Far off to either side were buildings, structures barely visible in the gray twilight of either dawn or dusk . . . instead of the brighter light of the mid-afternoon it should have been. In the mid-ground, half-wrecked ruins of once-intact buildings, their walls and roofs literally ripped apart. In the foreground, for at least a score of body lengths across . . . Nea could see nothing but scattered debris, none of it standing higher than herself, and most of it drenched from the fading rain.

Nothing about this scene could have been foreseen by her, not even in her wildest, Nauvea-worshipped imaginings.

Only the most powerful of spells could have unleashed that much damage, could have scraped buildings down to the very ground. She could see the slabs of what had to be house foundations, mangled stumps of trees, and a strange, grayish, pebbly surface. It formed some sort of broad road ribboning off at an angle to the trail of destruction left by the whirling, twisting thumb of rain and wind dancing in the distance.

No . . . not magic. That was a tornado! But . . . but they don't form on Nightfall, just waterspouts . . . and . . . And this . . . isn't Nightfall . . .

That was the other unimaginable thing: This *wasn't* her home island.

She couldn't even describe half of the things scattered around her: large, glossy white or matte beige boxes with two sets of doors on them, too awkwardly placed to be coffins but too small to be anything else; strange, enclosed, horseless carts, only known by her *as* carts because she could see seats for passengers inside and wheels for rolling on the ground outside. Chunks of glass mingled with strange, glossy, opaque materials that might have been some sort of artistic homage to oil-boiled leather armor, and a broken, fabric-stuffed sofa of foreign design sagged on its back, its cushions long since flung elsewhere by the force of the storm. And on the door that had sheltered her, a bright red sign with white, incised lettering that made her eyes twitch with the effort of translating the words: *Employees Only*.

Not written in Katani, but in some other language, one she had never seen before.

The storm was fading. The thumb of whirling rain and wind withdrew ponderously into the bottom of the clouds. In the distance, strange horns were blaring, and from the buildings that were semi-intact, people were emerging. It was too late to hide herself, though Nea had no clue where she could have hidden. Literally, nothing stood taller than she herself, abandoned by her Goddess in the midst of the tornado's trail, in a kingdom clearly nowhere near her own.

Unsure what to do, Nea tried to gather her wits. Someone shouted, spotting her. They hurried in her direction, having to pick their way carefully past some of the debris. The duchess didn't move. Her head ached, her body hurt, her clothes were soaked and muddied, and she had no clue where she was.

Her ears twitched as the woman, clad in strange blue pants and a sweater that looked warmer than Nea's rain-drenched dress, shouted again. Behind the woman hurried a man. They reached her side within moments, touching her arm, her shoulder; in the babble of the woman's voice, Nea could only feel a deep relief that her dose of Ultra-Tongue potion was still working. Wherever she might be, at least she could speak with everyone.

"Hope? Hope—ohmigod, ohmigod! You're alive! How did you get all the way out here? Ohmigod—where is your *family*? Ger, look for her family!"

"Ann, she's half a mile from home! I doubt they're anywhere nearby. Are you okay?" the man asked Nea gently, touching her shoulder again. He craned his neck, peering at the back of her head. "You're bleeding!"

"I . . . was hit on the head," Nea explained cautiously.

They seemed to recognize her, were calling her by a variant of her full name, but she *knew* she had never been here before. Without knowing where she was, how she had come to be here, or even *why* she was here, caution was her only ally. Inspiration struck, connecting the blow to her head with the confusion over her identity. She didn't *want* to lie to them, but given how vastly different the remnants of objects in the wreckage were from all the furnishings she had known, she didn't think it would be prudent to tell the whole truth, either.

"I don't remember . . . Do I know you?" she asked.

The couple exchanged quick, worried looks, and the blond-haired woman patted her gently on the arm. "Hope, it's *me*, Annette! Annette, from the Middle Ages Society? Annette and Gerald Fortescue?"

"I . . . My head hurts," she managed, trying to portray someone utterly at a loss because of a head injury. "I don't . . . Sorry. I don't know you." Pinching her brow into a frown, she eyed the two. "I take it I'm supposed to?"

"Amnesia?" Annette asked her husband.

"She does look like she was hit pretty hard, though her eyes don't look dilated," Gerald said. "We'd better get her out of here and over to the streets and find a functional *phone*. The hospitals will be full of people with injuries, but head trauma is a serious thing."

Hope didn't know what a *phone* was, maybe the local name for one of those odd, metal-and-glass-cart things. She didn't want to expose her ignorance too quickly, though, even with the handy excuse of head trauma. Still, even if she didn't dare confess who she was without a frame of reference these people could understand—if there was one; this place was *very* strange looking—she wasn't going to be entirely passive about her circumstances.

So, while she didn't resist being guided away from the debris, she did ask plaintively, "Truly, I honestly don't know either of you. Or even where I am. If there's anything you know that you could tell me . . . ?"

Annette gently patted her on the arm again. "Your name is Hope O'Niell, and we're . . . well, we're not *close* friends, but we have met and mingled several weekends a year for the last . . . how long has it been, Ger?"

"Eight years," Gerald said. "I've known your aunt and uncle on your father's side for longer than that—God, Ann, their house could've been in the path of that twister, too!"

"Don't you worry," Annette quickly reassured Nea. "We'll put out the word that we've found you and ask around for any news of your family. You just come with us, and you'll be fine."

Fine, yes . . . except I still don't know where I am, Nea thought, accepting Gerald's help over a stretch of debris in their path. *And what if this Hope woman that I look like is actually found?*

A *boom* in the distance made all three of them flinch. They twisted in its direction, catching sight of a billowing black and red mushroom cloud. Gerald grimaced. "God . . . I think that was the gas station on the corner of Madison and Sixty-third! That's within a block of your house, Hope—if there *was* anything left . . ."

"Think positive, Ger—at least we know Hope is still alive," Annette offered, trying to sound hopeful. Her voice shook, though, and she wasn't very convincing. "The others could . . . you know . . . maybe . . . ?"

Nea didn't bother to try for a hopeful comment of her own. She might remember who she really was, but she was still in shock from suddenly being Elsewhere, far from anything she had known. *These people don't know if this Hope O'Niell's family is still alive . . . and I don't even know if my people are still alive. Goddess of Dreams . . . why did You drop me here, of all places?* How *did You drop me, here, and* where *is here, for that matter?*

Hope O'Niell . . . it sounds vaguely like my name, Haupanea. It's been said that, across the Veils that separate the various worlds, there are certain points of similarity that crop up between two otherwise disparate realms. Is this Hope woman my local counterpart?—Goddess, she didn't get sent across to my world, did she? My world would undoubtedly be just as foreign to her as hers is to me; she'll be just as lost as I am!

For that matter, what am I going to do with myself in this place, if I cannot get back to whatever is left of my duchy?

It was a sobering, unsettling thought.

"But people *do* want to know what happened to you, Miss O'Niell," the man in the long-coat said, his tone coaxing. He was a *reporter*, some sort of news-gathering bard as far as she could tell. Which made her wary of his need to question her. The man tried again, smiling. "Your survival when the rest of your family, well, *didn't*, is a very powerful human-interest story."

The nurse tried to shush him, muttering something about not upsetting her patient about the tragedy. Hope shook her head. "That part's not upsetting, because I do not *remember* anyone. Maybe one day I might know them, but not right now—and I don't feel comfortable about having my story spread around like base gossip. There are people who lost family members out there; loved ones that they *do* remember, and therefore *do* miss severely. *They* should be the ones receiving the sympathy of the people. Not me."

"But what about your own sympathy? You've lost *your* life," Dave

Connor reminded her. "You may still be alive, but you've lost a good portion of who you were. If your story gets out there, people will know you need help rebuilding your life."

"I'll concede that I do need to rebuild my life," Nea agreed. "But I prefer to do so in privacy. I will not be gawked at like some exotic beast in a cage. I thank you for visiting me, but I do not wish to be interviewed."

Another knock interrupted them. This time, it was another of the nurses serving the rooms in this corner of the hospital, a tall, dark-skinned male who looked like he could have come from the northern shores of the mainland, back home. With him came an older man and a woman, both of whom looked like they could have come straight from Nightfall itself, if they hadn't been wearing the fussy, fitted, piecemeal layers of this realm, instead of the flowing lines of the gowns and robes that had been fashionable in Katan.

"Excuse me, Miss O'Niell, but these people are Marco and Mila Gioletto," the new nurse told her, while the couple gave her anxious looks. The woman looked a lot like Nea's own mother had, if her mother had only lived to be about ten years older, rather than having been lost at sea. She had the same tanned skin, the same dark brown waves in her hair, and even the same nose, flat and slightly hooked at the tip. The man looked more like someone transplanted from the west coast of Katan than from the east coast and Nightfall, his hair just as dark, but his skin lighter and his nose sharper.

Holding up her hand before the male nurse could say more, Nea faced the reporter.

"I'm sorry, but I must ask you to leave. This is *my* life, not yours, and it is my decision alone as to whether or not I will share my suffering with the rest of this world. Which I do not choose to do at this time. If you have any sympathy for my suffering, you will respect my decision. I thank you for coming, but please leave now."

Hesitating a moment, the gossip-scribe nodded his head and left, as did the two nurses. They looked determined to escort him out politely, so as not to upset their patient. Once those three were gone, Nea faced the two newcomers. "Thank you for your patience. Now . . . who are you?"

"It's true, isn't it?" the woman breathed. Nea's ears twitched, letting her know the woman was speaking in a different language. The older woman crossed to Nea, stared at her a moment more, then wrapped her arms around the young outworlder. "My baby, you don't remember me!" Pulling back, she held Nea by the shoulders. "You don't remember me, your own aunt Mila?"

From the way the woman addressed her directly, waiting for an answer, Nea guessed she was supposed to know this new language. She shook her head. "I'm sorry. I don't remember you."

"Your aunt Mila is your mother's sister," Marco stated, also using the new language. He scratched nervously at his gray-salted black hair, then shrugged. "The police came and told us we had to identify you, and to try to identify the, ah, remains of your mother, father, and brothers. Or brother. They still haven't found out anything about George, though there were a few who were unidentifiable after the gas-line explosions."

"We drove all the way here from Oklahoma City as soon as we heard what had happened. Though it's very hard to believe you've lost your memory of everything," Mila added, shifting to sit on the edge of the bed. "Even of us!"

Nea shook her head. If she could fool this Hope's own blood relatives, there might be a hope—pun unintended—that she *could* step into the other woman's life. From the looks of things, this strange, magicless realm ran on just as much bureaucracy as the Katani Empire. If not more. Trying to establish a new identity would be far more difficult than stepping into the life of Hope O'Niell. It meant she had to keep lying to everyone, but it was far, far easier than confessing the truth. Which, in a realm with very little obvious magic—if they even had any—might make these people doubt her sanity.

"I'm afraid I really *don't* remember anything from more than two days ago. I don't remember either of you. I wish I did, and it's clear there is some resemblance between us . . . but I don't. I don't even know if I have any means of paying for the care I've been given in this place."

"Well, your mother told me the name of her and Bill's—that's your father, if they haven't told you—lawyer so your uncle and I will start looking into insurance papers and so forth," Mila reassured her. She patted Nea on the knee. "And *you* have been practicing your Spanish. Your accent is very good! Your grandmother would be proud of you for not discarding that quarter of your heritage."

Oops . . . Ultra Tongue may give me the ability to speak and understand, but it does have its drawbacks. I forgot to speak only in the original language, and instinctively used their "accent" to address them. She managed an awkward smile and spoke in the first tongue she had learned in this place, which she still didn't know what to call; probably "American," the name for this land she was now in. "I guess it's one of the few things I do remember . . . even if I don't remember *how* I learned it."

"Well, Bill was very smart and very organized," Marco said, reverting to the first language as she had done. "I know he arranged for life insurance policies for himself and his wife. Possibly more than one. If his lawyer doesn't have copies, then his accountant definitely would; he was very good about handling his money. We'll start looking for all the insurance policies for you: house, *automobile*, life, health, and so forth."

Something within her urged her to trust this couple. It was the same thing, Nea realized, that prodded her to *distrust* that reporter fellow. Since her arrival, Nauvea hadn't whispered in her mind, but Nea didn't expect to hear from her Goddess; she was clearly too far away from her old life. Until those instincts proved unsound . . . well, it was all she had to guide her in this strange new world.

"Now, I won't be able to stay more than a week—I have to get back to my *dental* practice"—*her* uncle continued—"but Mila can stay for as long as you need her." Marco managed a sly smile, glancing at his wife. "I may be forced to eat my own cooking and may

waste away to nothing from the horribleness of it, but your aunt
and I are going to do whatever we can to help you recover your
memories . . . and if not your memories, then at least your life. Or
a life. The house . . . is completely gone. I don't know if anything
can be salvaged. The contents of fourteen houses were shredded and
scattered across several city blocks, plus all the damage from the
gas station explosion."

"The doctor told us under normal circumstances you would be
sent back to your own home, to recover your memories with constant exposure to familiar things," Mila added in American, "but
there isn't anything familiar left. But!" she exclaimed softly, patting
Nea on the knee again. "I have brought several photo albums and
old Christmas letters, and we will try to track down all of your
friends. It would be helpful if we had lived a lot closer and knew all
the same people that you did, but we'll see who we can get to come
meet with you."

"Are you sure you wanted to turn away that reporter? The news-
paper *could* be a great help in rebuilding your life," Marco said.

"Very sure. I could handle a quiet word among the people in
town. But the pity of the whole region?" Nea shook her head. "Thank
you for coming all the way out here for me—I may not remember
either of you, but I do appreciate your help," she told both of them as
candidly as she could. "Aunt Mila" hugged her again, this time cradling the younger woman to her plump chest. Hugging her back,
Nea contemplated her situation.

If they haven't found Hope after two days, alive or dead . . . then she's
probably one of the unidentified bodies he mentioned. Considering this, I
choose to believe that, knowing this disaster would strike these people, Nau-
vea made a bargain with the Gods of this world to fling me into this Hope's
life—She did command me to seize the power of the collapsing Portal and
use it, rather than contain it. She was the one who used that power, sending
me here.

If I'm so much like this Hope that even a blood relative could mistake
me for her . . . then I might as well step into the life of Hope O'Niell, Nea

silently acknowledged. *Without mirror-Gates that can cross the Veils between this world and my own, without magic to open a way, and with no hint of this technology stuff being able to re-create a mirror-Gate, I'm stuck here. At least, if I step into Hope's life, I'll have something to do with myself.*

I certainly don't have a duchy to run anymore . . .

"Her" aunt released her, and Nea—Hope, rather—straightened, ready to ask careful questions about how to go about reclaiming her life, now that they had "identified" her. In the back of her mind, she was concerned about Nightfall, about what the collapse of the Portal might have done to her people, but there was literally nothing she could do about it. Her energy would be better spent learning how to blend into this strange world, while treading carefully enough to hide the fact she wasn't really a part of it. Yet.

"Excuse me, but could you help me find the salad dressing?"

Her contemplation of the various jelly and jam selections interrupted, the young woman now firmly known as Hope glanced over her shoulder. Her questioner was slightly taller, a bit thinner, and definitely paler, though her skin was scattered with freckles. She also had strawberry blonde hair, light blue green eyes, and an accent that had nothing to do with Ultra Tongue, and everything to do with regional dialect.

The aqua-eyed woman smiled self-consciously. "I'm afraid I'm new to the area, and I haven't learned where anything is, yet."

"It does take practice," Hope agreed. Where *she* came from, food was sold from a variety of farmer's stalls in a marketplace. Not crammed into packages and squeezed onto the shelves of a single, oversized shop. "Salad dressings should be one aisle over, to your left."

"Thanks—while I'm at it," the redhead added, "do you know if they have any walnuts here? I was expecting the nuts to be next to the spices, but they're not."

"End of the row, here, by the peanut butter," Hope told her, lifting her chin at the end past the woman and her *plastic* and metal shopping cart.

She needs a friend . . .

It wasn't really the voice of her Goddess talking to her—Nauvea hadn't *spoken* to her directly since those last chaotic seconds Elsewhere—but Hope still had occasional feelings about things. Feelings which, if she followed through on them, invariably came true in some way. Usually a good way; if she didn't follow her feelings, awkward things happened. Sometimes bad things, too. Trusting her instincts, Hope held out her hand. "I'm Hope O'Niell."

The woman smiled and clasped hands. "Kelly Doyle. I'm from the Seattle area. I inherited a house in this neighborhood, and then I got offered a job in the area, a really good one, so I packed up and moved out here. I take it you're a native?"

"You could say that," Hope hedged. She smiled as she said it, making it sound self-depreciative. "I was living in a larger town north of here, but everything got wiped out by a tornado, so I ended up down here where I could afford a new place, rather than rebuilding on the old foundations."

Kelly nodded. "Sorry to hear about the tornado. That's tough, having to rebuild everything . . . I have some questions about the area—the location of certain shops and the like, that sort of thing. Perhaps I could buy you a cup of coffee or something, if you'd be willing to answer a few of them?"

"Well, I just went through the frozen food section," Hope hedged, "but if you're headed up the aisle with me, we can talk as we walk. And if I haven't answered all of your questions by the time we reach the check-out line, then maybe we could meet either later today or maybe tomorrow for that coffee? . . . Though I'm a lot more partial to hot chocolate than coffee."

Chocolate was the one thing that made this bizarre universe worth visiting, in her opinion. Chocolate in any form, really; her first experience had been a scoop of chocolate ice cream in the hospital, and the second a candy bar bought for her by one of the nurses. The third time, she had gone out with her new aunt and uncle to shop for clothes and had been introduced to a chocolate layer cake. Just thinking about it now made Hope's mouth water, and she glanced past the redhead's shoulder to where the jars of chocolate-hazelnut spread sat patiently on their shelves, waiting to be purchased and gastronomically worshipped.

"I don't blame you; chocolate *is* better tasting than coffee," Kelly agreed, smiling. She lifted a scrap of paper she held in her hand. "But I only came in for a few things, and I don't want to delay your shopping, particularly if some of it's frozen. I saw a pastry shop a couple blocks over, and it had one of my own favorites advertised in the front window, cinnamon-apple cookies; perhaps we could meet there?"

"Sure! In about an hour?" Hope offered. "You're talking about the Rafferty Patisserie, right? That should give me enough time to finish shopping and put everything away at home."

"Yes, and I'd like that—Hope, right?" Kelly asked. "I'm not imposing by asking this, am I?"

"Yes, it's Hope, and you're Kelly, and you are *not* imposing," she said, smiling. Again, she felt an inner twinge of awareness. This woman, this meeting, was important. Smiling playfully, Hope added, "Something tells me that you and I will be the best of friends, Kelly Doyle—if you don't mind my presumption?"

Grinning, Kelly shook her head. "I don't mind. In fact, I'm happy enough to meet you simply because I *might* be making a new friend. Assuming we do get along, and all. It's been very hard, starting a new life in a whole new location. My new job pays great, but the workload is so heavy, I haven't even had the time to socialize with my coworkers yet, let alone any of my neighbors."

"Then you've come to the right woman," Hope said confidently. "I know better than most what it's like to be a stranger in a strange land—don't forget, salad dressing is one aisle over, and the nuts are behind you, at the end of the row."

Kelly twisted to look at the shelves behind her, then flashed Hope a mischievous smile. "Funny, the only people in the aisle are you and me!"

Laughing, Hope flapped one of her tanned hands at the other woman. "Go on, find your food—I'll see you at Rafferty's in about an hour."

Kelly sighed and relaxed her head against the back of the couch, her dessert of praline pecan ice cream nothing but pale smears in the dark blue bowl balanced on her lap. "That was good."

"Yes, it was," Hope agreed, licking a bit more fudge from her spoon. "Thanks for coming over and watching a movie with me."

"You're welcome. It's not like I had other plans tonight . . . Speaking of which, town scuttlebutt says you're no longer dating Jim," Kelly offered, glancing at her best friend for the last year. "I thought you liked him? It's been, what, five months since we met him at the county fair?"

"I did . . . until I overheard him telling one of his buddies how much he liked my really big *bank account,*" Hope groused. "Which isn't all *that* big, but he doesn't know that. He just went on about how it didn't hurt that I was 'pretty, as well as loaded with all that insurance money.' As if the deaths of my family and the loss of our home were all arranged for *his* personal plundering.

"Even worse . . . he then made fun of my laughing," she muttered.

"Laughing?" Kelly asked, thrown by the odd segue. "You have a nice laugh. Why would he make fun of it?"

"Not that. During lovemaking."

"Ahhh. Scum," her freckled friend scoffed. She glanced at Hope, aquamarine eyes peering at the other bowl. "Need a refill on your chocolate prescription?"

"Tempting . . . but I'd better not. I might need another dose tomorrow, and the grocer's is out of the kind I want. So, how about you?" Hope asked. "Any prospects on the horizon?"

"No. I've been busy trying to get my little in-home business going. I got rejected by another company. I'm running out of jobs I can apply for that pay more than minimum wage," Kelly said, sighing glumly this time. "Minimum wage won't pay the credit card bill left over from the expense of moving all the way out here."

"Sure *you* don't want a bowl of chocolate fudge ripple chunk, instead of that pecan stuff?" Hope coaxed, scraping up a last bit of ice cream with her finger.

"Tempting . . . but as you said, I'd better not. I have to start getting the garden ready for spring," Kelly added. "That'll work off the praline pecan, but not the ripple chunk. How about you? What'll you do to work off your caloric exuberance?"

"Dog walking. My neighbor twisted her ankle. I promised to walk her three dogs tomorrow morning, so that she could have enough time and energy to hobble off to work."

"What about the tarot shop?" Kelly asked. "And the jewelry sales?"

"The jewelry's doing okay, though I need to get more from my cousin. The shop . . . I worked it out with Carol; she'll take the morning clients if I take the evening ones—it's not as if it's all that difficult to dispense sensible advice to strangers," Hope added lightly. *Or give them instinct-prodded advice . . .* "They want their wisdom wrapped up in a mystical gift bag. The morning regulars, I know how to tailor my advice a bit more, but it's all sound, sensible advice, so I should be fine."

Kelly snorted. "Tell that to the nine hundred number scammers."

"You know very well that Carol is sincerely trying to help people and not scam them," Hope chided. Technically, she was younger than Kelly by about four years, whether it was the original Hope's age or her own chronological one, but both women traded off the roles of elder sister their friendship had evolved into. "It's just like consulting with a Catholic priest for advice, only it's for the Pagan community."

"The Pagan community that's over in the next county. This one's solidly Baptist," Kelly pointed out. "I made the 'mistake' of overhearing Mary Colvers, town gossip, trashing the Lutherans at the bookstore a couple days ago. I stood up for their right to freedom of worship, since no one else was doing it. Which devolved into the rights of other religious beliefs . . . and you know how *that* ends with that woman."

"Which did she call you, 'Satan's Advocate' or 'Godless Heathen'?" Hope quipped.

"Godless Heathen. So I called her a Mindless Parrot, incapable of original thought."

Instinct twinged inside of Hope, but not in the way she would have expected. Rather than cautioning her friend against riling the socially prominent woman, Hope found herself encouraging it. "She *is* one . . . and if you *don't* say something against her, then her narrow, bigoted viewpoints will continue to prevail. Be careful *how* you say things; you do have a temper. But do stand up for what you believe in."

"Good advice—and hey, you didn't even have to read my palm," Kelly quipped.

"I can read anything: palms, tea leaves, tarot cards, and even ice cream smears," Hope joked back. Craning her neck, she peered at Kelly's bowl. "Your smears say . . . ah, yes. It's *your* turn to do the dishes."

"*My* turn? It's *your* house!"

"Yes, and you're family," Hope shot back. "It's like Mrs. Case says: 'First time you're a guest; we'll get it for you. Second time you're a friend, and we'll show you where to find it. Third time, you're family—' "

" '—So get it your damned self,' " Kelly recited with a wry smirk. " 'And fourth time, you're a slave, 'cause you'd better get it for everyone else, too.' My grandmother used to say that, too. You think she's the one who taught it to Mrs. Case?" Hauling herself off the sofa, she plucked Hope's bowl from her grasp and headed toward the kitchen. "Okay, so Jim is out of the picture. Any other prospects on the dating horizon?"

"No . . . but the right man is out there, somewhere. For both of us," Hope added.

"Ever the eternal optimist, just like your name says," Kelly called over her shoulder. "I'll settle for the right clientele for my sewing business."

Roused out of an uneasy slumber by the disorienting sound of the doorbell ringing, Hope stopped fumbling with her alarm clock. Rising from the bed, she dragged a bathrobe over her nightgown, stuffed her feet into slippers, and shuffled through the modest house she had bought with some of the money she had inherited. Technically, it was the real Hope's money to inherit, but the real Hope was dead. Being stranded in this other universe had given her no choice but to accept it, though the lingering guilt did occasionally plague her dreams.

The chimes rang again. Once she rubbed the grit of sleep from her eyes, Hope peered through the peephole in the solid wooden panel. The sight of a uniformed officer reaching over to press the button for the doorbell a third time cleared away the last dregs of sleep. Wide-eyed and unsure what this visit was about, Hope tightened the belt of her dressing gown and opened the door.

"Good morning, sir. How may I help you?" she asked politely. This realm or the other, it always paid to be polite to government officials. *Particularly now that I have no official rank or title to stand on . . .*

Taking off his hat, the deputy officer asked, "Ma'am, are you Hope O'Niell?"

"Yes, sir, I am. Is something wrong?" she asked, wondering what it could possibly be. Usually, her instincts twinged when something unexpected happened, but she'd gone to bed more or less content and had suffered no memorable dreams, unpleasant or otherwise.

He gave her a somber look. "I'm sorry to say, ma'am, that at 2:13 this morning, a house fire at 1217 Beverly Street was reported to Emergency Services."

Her hand flew up to her mouth, muffling the name of her friend. "Kelly . . ."

"Fire station crews subdued the blaze by 5:57 this morning. So far, there has been no sign of the owner, Ms. Kelly Doyle, either on the premises or at the neighbors'. Ms. Doyle had apparently filed several complaints of harassment with the department recently; on one of those forms, she listed you as her emergency contact. Have you been in touch with Ms. Doyle at any point since last night?"

Instinct—thank the Goddess—said that Kelly was alright. But instinct wasn't a fact. "No . . . no, I don't know where she is. She *did* get out, didn't she?"

"I'm afraid that has not yet been determined at this time, ma'am," the deputy hedged. "The fire marshal won't begin his investigation until the remains of the house have cooled sufficiently for an investigation of how the fire started. Now, whether it was a malfunctioning gas line, or the furnace, or bad wiring—"

"—Arson," Hope asserted firmly, folding her arms across her chest. "I know very well that she was being harassed by the closed-minded bigots in this town. She told me that she had told your department that she had received death threats, *and* that you people brushed off her concerns.

"*Your* responsibility is to search for possible signs of arson," Hope ordered him. "If she died in that fire, and it was arson, then you will have one or more murderers to catch. If she didn't die . . . you may still have one or more would-be murderers to catch, because it's still most likely a case of arson. Just make sure you finally do your job."

The deputy gave her a long-suffering look, but merely dug out a business card, offering it to her. "Ma'am, if Ms. Doyle is still alive and she contacts you, please call the department immediately. If not . . . we'll contact you. I'm sorry for the bad news, ma'am."

A polite nod, a replacement of his hat, and the uniformed officer retreated down the porch steps. Hope watched him leave, then closed the door quietly, thoughtful. *If something* has *happened to Kelly . . . surely I'd be getting a twinge of feeling? There's very little magic in this universe, true, but I am still something of a Seer. I've proved that over and over, working for Carol.*

When I think of Kelly right now, all I get is the same contented happiness for our friendship. Nauvea, I know You cannot hear me, lost so far from my home . . . but I'll take that as a sign from You that she's still all right, whatever may have happened. I hope.

Sleep was now impossible. Heading to the bathroom to shower and dress, Hope wondered if she should try Kelly's cell phone. *She might not have grabbed it, if she woke during the fire and had to leave in a hurry. I don't think she would have left the house voluntarily, not overnight, and not with gas prices fluctuating so much . . .*

If only she'd taken some of my money, instead of holding out hope that she could last until the start-up of tourist season. Stubborn fool. Goddess . . . God of this realm, if she's still alive, watch over her? Hope asked, looking up at the ceiling of her bathroom as she removed her nightclothes. *Seers don't usually ask for much, but . . . please?*

"Careful, Miss; the floor over there isn't entirely stable," the fire marshal warned her. "It's been judged solid enough to walk on, but there's no sense in stomping around."

"I'll be careful," Hope agreed. Mostly because medicine on this world was a primitive, mechanical set of contraptions and contrivances that unnerved her, rather than a sensible application of life-giving magic. But something about the area that once was Kelly's bedroom drew her onward. Picking her way carefully across blackened floorboards that creaked underfoot, she stopped at the midpoint in the former room.

Something was there, in the air over the bed. It wasn't strong; in fact, it was very weak, clearly faded with time . . . but at some point in the last three days or so, *someone* had cast magic. Which *shouldn't* have been possible, in this low-magic universe. Then again, just because she hadn't *met* any mages here didn't mean they didn't exist . . . Stepping over a burned bit of wooden bed frame, Hope opened her senses to that tiny bit of faded but still welcome power.

Right . . . *there.* A cautious glance over her shoulder showed the fire marshal examining something off to the side. Quickly, Hope swept her lightly tanned hands—mistaken for the original Hope's Latino-Irish heritage—through the air, seeking the edges of the phenomenon. From the tingling of her skin, she defined an area that was long, somewhat broad, and rectangular.

Something about the size and shape of a standard mirror-Gate.

Oh, Goddess . . . I could be wrong, utterly wrong . . . but this is like a breath of sweet wind blown all the way from home—*a draft cutting through the Veils separating this place from my own world. Or maybe not my world, exactly,* she acknowledged silently, lowering her arms. *Mages have claimed there are thousands of alternate realities out there. Maybe even hundreds of thousands. Some have a lot of magic, some have only a little, and some are reasonably similar while others are very strange. Stranger than even this place . . .*

But the odds are, it could have been an opening from my world. Nauvea, if someone found Kelly's bedroom, and that someone opened a Gate between worlds . . . Maybe that's why her bones weren't found in the rubble of the fire, yet she also hasn't been found anywhere else, either. And if someone from my world found her . . . maybe, just maybe, they might find me, too? Niktor, Giolana, Abeyda . . . if they didn't find my bones in the Portal explosion—presuming they lived—then surely they'd still be looking for me?

As much as she had adapted, as much as she had learned about this place and how to survive in it, even how to enjoy living in such a foreign culture . . . this world wasn't her home. Turning around, mindful of the floor, Hope surveyed the houses to either side, Kelly's vegetable plots, the trees and bushes planted in ornamental, foreign patterns, the chain link fences, and the automobiles and the telephone poles with their wires and their weirdnesses. Though she had grown used to this world, that fading trace of magic made everything look strange again.

Home was an eight-sided, blue-tiled dome flanked by white granite walls and gleaming windowpanes. *Home* was a semitropical, maritime-mild climate. Not this winter-wracked, summer-scorched inland zone. *Home* was where her heart belonged, despite the friends and the life she had managed to make in this place.

Home, unfortunately, was nowhere within her reach . . . save for this one faint piece of faded evidence that she wasn't completely lost.

The voice of the fire marshal called her attention back to her assigned task. "If you'll carefully make your way back over here, miss, we can go fetch that roll of plastic bags you brought and start salvaging a few things. I'm going to have to ask you to stay out of the southwest corner of the house, however. The floor in that corner of the living room might be too weak to support human weight for the length of a salvage operation. The fire was started there with some sort of an accelerant splashed on the outer wall. The labs are still processing which one it was."

"I'll stick to the parts where it's safe to walk," Hope promised, making her way back out of the debris that had once been her best friend's bedroom.

Yes, my instincts are finally speaking to me again . . . and they're telling me that Kelly is safe. Elsewhere, but safe. So I'll not worry too much about her anymore, and just worry about salvaging whatever I can for the day when we meet again, Goddess willing.

Maybe I should've told her about other universes, prepared her somehow?

Since it was too late for that, the transplanted Seer shrugged mentally and started her search for anything of her friend's that wasn't too badly damaged by the fire. She was listed as Kelly's beneficiary as well as her emergency contact, and the local authorities had decided it would be alright for her to try to salvage whatever she could find. The sight of all this damage was depressing, but the thought of another doorway opening to the other world lifted her spirits despite the rubble.

If a door opened once, it can always open again.

Her cell phone rang, startling her. Digging it out of her pocket, Hope flipped open the device. "Hello?"

"Hello, Hope! It's Anita, your cousin."

"Hi, Anita—I'm kind of in the middle of something," Hope warned the other woman, skirting a broken wall timber that looked precariously perched. "If you want that list of the jewelry I sold for you, it's back at the house."

"I won't take too long, but, well, I have something very important to ask you. It's about Carlos and I, and, well, our attempt to have children . . ."

Hope skidded into the kitchen as the bell that hung by the refrigerator finished jingling. *He* was calling again! Ever since Kelly had first reappeared over a year ago with that man, Saber of *Nightfall*, Hope had felt the burst of magic caused by the opening of the Veils between worlds. Like a radiant lamp, only it warmed her very soul instead of merely heated her skin.

From as far away as two blocks, she knew whenever *he* called, whether it was merely a window upon her world and her activities, or a doorway through which he could hear her voice asking him questions and write messages of his own in return. The bell was needed to wake her up, since she didn't always sense a Veil-call when she was asleep, but when she was awake, she could.

He was Morganen. Of *Nightfall.* And the more he communicated with her, the more she was reassured that it was *her* Nightfall. Her duchy . . . or what was left of it.

Her Seer's instinct—stubborn and contrary—had demanded that she *not* reveal she was the Duchess Haupanea of Nightfall. It had turned out to be a good thing, because some careful, cautious questioning had revealed that *two hundred years* had passed since she had been thrown out of her world and dumped into this one. Time didn't always flow the same from universe to universe, but a displacement of two hundred years was highly unusual and would have been too awkward to explain. Particularly since her instincts, capricious and annoying, had insisted that she *stay* in this realm. At least until the time was right.

Staying silent had given her the time to grieve in private. Everyone she had known had long since died. Hope had grown used to the idea that she would never see them again, though for a little while, she had believed she *would* see Niktor and Giolana and all the rest. But they were gone, and she would never see them again.

Nightfall wasn't her duchy anymore; her people had long since abandoned it, for the power to contain the Portal's explosion had been drained from the Desalinator by Nauvea's brief possession of Hope—of Nea, rather. Without freshwater to drink, her people had been forced to relocate to the mainland, and the island had become a place of exile for the politically inconvenient.

Not that she was going to complain. Using her former home as a place of exile was undoubtedly more comfortable than the usual sort of Katani dungeon and a vast distance above and beyond the worst punishments a criminal mage could face. Of course, that was presuming these brothers of County Corvis were criminals, which they definitely weren't. Just victims of a Prophetic misinterpretation.

After his hand emerged through the invisible boundary between their worlds, after she had pressed her flesh against the warmth of his palm and fingers, *feeling* the magic humming beneath his skin, Hope surprised herself with the first words out of her mouth.

"I'm coming across in just over a week. Eight days, your time, minus five hours."

Hearing a soft *clack* behind her, Hope twisted and stared at the whiteboard on the wall next to her fridge. One of the dry-erase pens floated up, uncapping itself. The cap drifted back down to the ledge at the base of the board, and the pen twisted, marking the board in neat English lettering.

Eight days my time, minus five hours? Are you sure? Even after I sent for all that wheat, you put me off for a long time.

"Yes. I'm *very* sure—the shipment of cacao seedlings will be arriving soon, too," she warned him. "I've rented a greenhouse at a farm outside of town, so you'll have to shift the mirror's focus when it comes time to pick them up and take them across. It's very important that they survive the crossing, because the *last* thing I want is to be deprived of chocolate over there."

Understood. I'll see to their transplanting personally.

"Thank you."

The eraser shifted, removing his previous words. Between the two of them, they had figured out that the reason he could hear *her* speak was because the magic in *his* world amplified her words . . . but her—or rather, Kelly's—world had very little to aid in amplifying anything crossing over into this realm. It was magically "dead" and thus muffled Morg's efforts enough that she couldn't hear *him*.

The only part of Morganen of Nightfall which Hope really *knew* was his hand, both its physical manifestation, and the neatness of his scribing abilities. She hadn't seen his face, hadn't heard his voice, didn't know if he was tall or short, fat or thin. In fact, Hope knew more what his brother Saber looked like than what he did. She did know his thoughts; they had gone through several dry-erase pens over the months since Kelly's disappearance, communicating their ideas, likes and dislikes, questions and answers, getting to know each other.

Now Morg wrote a statement on the whiteboard. *If you do come across . . . I would want to keep you at my side. I don't want to be without you, Hope.* He had to pause to erase the words for more room to write, then added, *Not after coming to know you so well. Are you prepared to stay in this other realm?*

Prepared to stay in *her* home, *her* island, *her* world? She couldn't return as the Duchess of Nightfall, but she could and would return

as a citizen of the new kingdom he and his brothers—and Kelly—
were trying to build. Hope nodded firmly. "Yes. I'll start packing up
the things I don't want to be parted from, and we can start sending
them across, along with the seedlings and the supplies I'll need for
making chocolate—it is *totally* the food of the Gods, and I'll make
an absolute fortune as the other world's very first *chocolatier.* Found
only on Nightfall Isle, exclusive to your new kingdom. I promise I
won't be a burden to you."

*No, Hope. I meant, I want to marry you. Will you grant me the op-
portunity to court you fully in person, once you arrive?*

Unbidden, her mouth curved upward in a smile. "It would be my
honor to be courted by you. Provided I could court *you* in return?"

That would be my deepest desire, he wrote. Then added, *I have to go,
sorry. Duty calls.*

The pen lowered to the ledge, where it capped itself. Facing the
intersection plane, Hope held up her hand. He reached through the
nothingness, pressing his palm briefly to hers, then withdrew it.
The radiant warmth of magic slackened, beginning its slow fade.
She didn't let herself bask in it, though. The thought that she *was*
finally going to cross back over the Veils galvanized her into action.

Not only were there seedlings to transport, there were things
like books and clothes and half a ton of chocolates for her personal
enjoyment, some purchased, others made by herself in her classes,
all to be delivered across the Veils. It could take years for her cacao
trees to grow into maturity, *if* they could survive in the other world.
But they have to. They must!

Chocolate was the one thing—aside from Kelly and the kindness of the original Hope's family and friends—that had made life
in this mad, magicless world bearable all these years. Chocolate,
and this last year of courting by her unseen lover. Morganen.

*It's sort of a mixed-up Cupid and Psyche situation, isn't it? He's the
invisible one, yet I'm one with the hidden, secret life that he doesn't know
about.* She grimaced, knowing she would have to confess her true
identity when she returned to her homeworld. *I just hope things don't*

end as badly for Morganen and me as they almost ended for the old legend of those two Greek Gods.

Nauvea, let our friendship be strong enough to survive the shock of the truth, because I do love him. As a dear friend, at the very least . . . though the way his hand makes me tingle, I have strong hopes for the rest of our bodies when we touch!

For that matter . . . what am I going to take across? Oh, and my will needs to be updated. I forgot to do that after Anita's baby shower . . . Mind racing with all she had to do to get ready for going home, she paused at another thought. *There's an idea I haven't considered before— what am I going to call myself, once I go back across? I'm no longer entirely Nea, and after all that's happened over there, I won't be a duchess anymore, but I'm not the real Hope, either . . .* a Hope, *but not* the Hope *everyone thinks I am . . .*

I don't have time for this introspection! I have to pack, first. I'll decide if and when the question comes up, which will be after I've relocated back to the island. Back where I belong, in my own rightful home. I can make amends for my deception after I've come home.

Home . . . Home! I'm finally going home!

TWO

"I'm finally *home!*"

Of all the words Morganen had expected Hope to say, of all the words possibly anticipated once she arrived in this universe . . . those were not the ones. The tears in her eyes, the tremulous emotion in her voice, those had alarmed and worried him, because her arrival was supposed to be a joyous occasion. Of course, there was that whirlwind that had destroyed her home, forcing a hasty exit from the other world. But *this* stunned him. He didn't know what to say.

From the looks on the others' faces, they didn't know what to say, either; his brothers and their brides looked just as shocked as Morg himself felt. Even Kelly, who had known Hope the longest, looked at an absolute loss for words. She blinked her aquamarine eyes several times, visibly struggling to register that simple, shattering statement.

Wiping at the tears that had spilled down her tanned cheeks, Hope O'Niell lowered her gaze from the donjon at the heart of the palace to the men and women gathered around her. Dropping the canvas satchels from her shoulder to the paving stones underfoot, she offered an uncertain, unsteady smile: half apologetic, half coaxing. "I suppose I should explain, shouldn't I?"

"Damn straight, you should!" Kelly snapped, finding her voice.

"*Kelly*," Morganen interjected, automatically playing the mediator. Of anyone gathered in the palace gardens, he and Kelly both had the greatest right to know what Hope meant by that. Kelly as her best friend, and himself as her future husband. But even he was finding it hard to accept. "Hope . . . what do you mean, you're *finally* home?"

"It's . . . well, it's a very complicated story. A short one, but complicated," Hope said, glancing at Morg. Compared to his clothing, a sleeveless, light blue silk tunic and white trousers, semiformal clothes donned to honor her arrival, hers were typical casual wear for her realm: those thick blue trousers called *jeans* and a flower-speckled white blouse, with her feet laced into those strange white shoes they called *sneakers*.

She *looked* like the quintessential outworlder to him. But her words said otherwise. Lifting his eyes from her feet, Morg saw that she was staring at his right hand.

The corner of Hope's mouth curled up, and she lifted her gaze back to his face. "So *that's* what the rest of you looks like. I wondered."

"Stop stalling and get on with the explaining, Hope," Kelly ordered her friend.

"Fine. The woman you know as Hope O'Niell isn't the real Hope O'Niell," Hope told her friend. "The real Hope O'Niell died in a combination of tornado wreckage and *gas-station* explosion. Because her body was damaged beyond recognition, and because I looked so much like her, I was mistaken for her . . . and I *let* that mistaken identity stand, because at the time—and *all* this time—I have had no other choice."

"No other choice, but to impersonate someone whose family

should've been told she was dead?" Kelly scoffed, hands braced on her hips.

Hands going to her own, fuller hips, Hope gave her best friend a pointed look. "Can you *honestly* tell me that if I'd told you I was from an entirely different world than Earth, you would have believed me instantly? Or would you have doubted me, and doubted my sanity, and doubted the value of even being my friend?

"I'll remind you this was *before* Morg rescued you into another universe. Before you even *knew* that such things existed . . . because as far as *your* people know, they *do not*. They have no way of parting the Veils, and no way of observing other realities. If I had told *anyone* I was from another universe, *what* would have happened to me?" she challenged Kelly.

Dropping some of her belligerence, Kelly grudgingly admitted, "If you'd told anyone . . . you probably would've been declared insane. And . . . I wouldn't have believed you, before my trip through the looking glass. But you *could* have told me *after* I came through to this world, when I learned that other universes are indeed real!"

"Well, therein lies the *other* complication," Hope said, spreading her hands. "When I investigated the ruins of your house, I could sense the dissipating magics of this universe coming from the spot where Morg had opened the Veil. But I didn't know *where* in this world you had been taken, or by whom, or even if it *was* my home universe. Nor if you'd ever return. Not until you popped up at that medieval event with *him* in tow. When I met him, that was when I knew."

Saber warily eyed the finger she poked in his direction. "Why me?"

"She introduced you as Saber *of Nightfall* . . . and that's where things became complicated all over again. I didn't know if it was *my* Nightfall, or just a coincidence of names. I had to wait, to find out more information of everything that had happened since I was thrown out of this world and into the other. Living in another universe taught me to be cautious," Hope explained. "It was still more prudent to keep my mouth shut than to open it, given the circumstances."

"How did you *get* to the other world in the first place?" Koranen asked her, sinking back onto the stone bench beside him. The redhead pulled his short bride-to-be back onto his lap, her short auburn hair a match for his longer locks. "Where do you come from?"

"I come from *here*. This island is—or was—my home. I know that Nightfall hasn't been inhabited in over two centuries, and that it's inconceivable that I used to live here. But I did. I don't know why," Hope added, shrugging, "but when I left, or after I left . . . the time synchronization between the two universes was altered. I think it was probably while I was in transit, at the will of the Gods."

"*I* think we need a Truth Stone." That comment came from Morganen's second-eldest brother, Wolfer.

"And I will be *happy* to touch one, now that I'm finally free to speak the truth," Hope agreed firmly.

"Fine. I'm sure you did what you thought was right, all these years. I just want to know *who* you are," Kelly told her friend. "Who I've been friends with all this time. You've lied to me. To all of us. I think we deserve the truth. Who are you supposed to be, in this world?"

Hope grimaced apologetically. "That's also something that's complicated. And best reserved for the Truth Stone, so you'll know it is true. So, if someone would go and fetch one . . . ?"

Hands already digging into the pouch slung at his waist, Morg sighed.

"Considering how much we've been needing them of late, I've taken to carrying one with me at all times." He pulled out the pure white disc, but hesitated a moment before handing it over. Glancing at the woman he had come to know over the last year, he clutched the disc in his fingers. "Part of me wants to believe that I still know you, that the woman you showed me during all our conversations is still *you* . . . but you've shaken my confidence in you. Whoever you are."

Pressing the disc into her hand, the youngest of the brothers waited to hear the truth from the stranger in their midst.

Clutching it, Hope nodded and spoke. "My name is Kelly Doyle."

The others didn't flinch at that; they knew how the Stone worked, and when she displayed the blackened imprint of her fingers and palm against the smooth white marble, they knew the Artifact was functioning properly. Black meant a lie, and gray indicated hesitation. Only pure white would prove her words true. Gripping the Stone again as soon as the darkness faded, Hope breathed deeply before speaking.

"I want to state first and foremost that I *did not* lie in order to hurt anyone. My situation was awkward and perilous. To reveal the truth would not only have been complicated, it might have been even worse than lying to people whose trust I had earned. To protect myself—which I had every right to do—I had to lie." A brief flick of her fingers and a tilt of her palm showed the Stone was unmarred.

Morg folded his arms across his chest. "That's understandable, but it *doesn't* tell us who you are."

Nodding, she gripped the stone. "My original name was Haupanea . . . and I used to be the Duchess of Nightfall, before I was stolen away."

Silence greeted her words, as each set of eyes dropped to the Truth Stone in her hand. The unblemished Truth Stone. Morg struggled to grasp that truth. That, not only had she lied to him all this time, she was the rightful ruler of the Isle . . . from more than two hundred years ago.

"I was born right here on Nightfall Isle, roughly two centuries ago," she continued, unconsciously echoing his thoughts. "When my parents died, I took over the duchy—I even had to take over the Guardianship of the Fountain for about a year, since Lady Abeyda couldn't handle it and still be our Portal Mistress as she aged. Then the Portal Prophecies came along.

"Not just to me, but to other Seers around the world, though I was the first in Katan to Foresee the danger. The Great Portals *had* to be shut down, and shut down by a specific date, to avert an impending Disaster. Unfortunately, the Council, in its infantile wisdom, decided to 'punish' Nightfall by not only insisting that its Portal be closed last, they tried to delay its closing with *paperwork*," she groused. "Because of that delay, the Nightfall Portal was still open when the Disaster struck . . . which I now know was the moment Aiar Shattered. But I didn't even know that much until *you* told me their capital had been destroyed, breaking up the Empire."

The handful of men and women who had gathered to meet her watched in thoughtful silence as she paused, opening and closing her fingers around the Stone to show the truth of her words.

"At the time, all *I* knew was that the Portal was threatening to erupt with uncontrollable power. Energy that had to be contained, but the mages who had come to close the Portal couldn't do it. That's when my Goddess told *me* to contain it, to be Her vessel for the powers involved." Fingers flexing between each statement, she showed them the continuing truth of her words. "So, I flung myself into the Portalway to channel it—which a Seer *can* do, even though we're not mages—and that's when She took all the energies She could grasp and used that to fling me out of my rightful place in the universe.

"*Why* She did so, I still do not know." Again, a truth. Hope curled her fingers around the Stone again and continued.

"I landed in the tail end of the tornado that destroyed the real Hope O'Niell, her life, her home, and her immediate family. I didn't know where I was, or why, and I *certainly* didn't know how to get back home. All I could do was pretend to have lost my memory and to accept the identity mistakenly attributed to me. Given just how complicated Kelly's world is, it was the safest course I could take—and since I looked uncannily like the real Hope, and she had lost her life and her identifying features in the wreckage created by the storm, no one questioned my identity.

"After your disappearance the night of the fire," she added, looking at Kelly, "when I went to the wreckage to salvage whatever could be found, I discovered the Veil-Gate. I was saddened by your absence and nervous at how you'd take being thrust into a world as alien to you as yours was to me . . . but I was deeply reassured that you *were* alive and that I *could* find a way back to my own world. Or at least *a* world of magic," she amended, "until you came through at that Faire with Saber, and I started learning that it was my world you had been transported to. And though I was alone and Godless in your world, I still had my Seer's instincts to guide me. I knew there would come a time when I *could* cross back over. That time has now come . . . and I've come home.

"I *am* Haupanea of Nightfall . . . but it's been so long since I was Nea of Nightfall, I'm not sure if that's the right name for me anymore. Living in a completely different world, a completely different culture . . . it changes a person. But neither am I sure if I should continue to call myself Hope," she murmured, looking down at the unmarred disc in her hand. "After all, I'm not *the* Hope O'Niell, though I have been *a* Hope for several years, now . . .

"Anyway," she finished, attempting a blithe shrug, "that's the truth of who and what I am. Short, as I said, but complicated. I, um, hope this isn't . . . well, unforgivable. It's not as if I had any say in being flung Elsewhere, or a say in the skeptical culture of Kelly's world. I did what I did to protect myself, in the only way that I could."

The silence that followed her words was broken only by the droning of insects flitting among the flowers of the garden.

Kelly studied her friend for a long moment, then glanced at her husband. Saber in turn looked to his brothers and their ladies. They glanced among themselves, then turned their attention to Morganen. Even Kelly looked at him, silently agreeing that this was *his* decision.

Settling his arms across his chest, Morg sighed. "Your reasons are understandable, and valid. We'll acknowledge that it was necessary at the time. And we did offer you a home among us. That offer still stands."

"But . . . ?" she asked, tipping her head. Her dark brown locks slid across her cheek as she did so.

"But you lied to me. And because of it, I don't really know you."

"Everything *else* I told you was the truth," she pointed out quickly. "The person you've interacted with *is* still me. You *do* know me—see?"

Holding out the Truth Stone, she showed him its unblemished sides.

"Hope—*Haupanea*, you left out *most of your life!*" Morg started to say more, but caught sight of the expressions on the others' faces.

As much as he loved them, their avid curiosity wasn't going to help the situation.

"If the rest of you will excuse us, I'll get Hope settled in her quarters. Thank you for being here to welcome her . . . *home*."

The irony of that last word soured the moment, but he couldn't help adding it. Morg scooped up the satchels at her feet and gestured at the palace. Complying, she headed toward the nearest door. Halfway to the nearest wing, she turned and gestured hesitantly at the bags in his hands, made from the same blue twill as her trousers. Morg held out his hand, taking the Truth Stone, but kept hold of her outworlder gear. Just because she wasn't quite the woman she had seemed to be was no reason to rudely make her carry her things.

Morg studied her profile as they walked side by side. She was still beautiful, and all the more real, now that he was seeing her in person instead of through a mirror. And now that he knew she was from his world, he could see the way she shared some of the same eastern Katani facial features as Cari, head of the Companionship Guild: the slightly flattened nose, the broad cheekbones, the firm chin, and the full lips. There, the resemblance ended; Cari had a narrower face overall, with a more slender body, whereas Hope's face and figure were both rounder, fuller.

"So . . . um . . . I'm guessing I probably won't get my old quarters back. Assuming anything might still be salvageable after so many years, of course," Hope added awkwardly, filling some of the silence between them.

"Not unless your quarters were in the northern branch of the east wing. That's where I prepared a suite for you," Morg told her.

"No. The traditional place for the duke or duchess is, or was, the suite above the donjon dome," she said, gesturing vaguely up at the dome off to their right.

"Kelly and Saber occupy that now," he said.

"Ah. Well, I won't intrude without permission, though I wouldn't mind reclaiming a few things, if they're still in existence—if this feels awkward for you, Morg, just remember how much worse it is for me," Hope added.

"How could it be worse for you?" he challenged her.

Her hand swept out, indicating the garden and the castle-like palace. "Because I have lost all the things I knew before? I look at this place, and half the plants are wrong, the walls are missing their whitewash, and I keep expecting to see all the *people* I used to know, but who aren't *there* anymore. Niktor, Giolana—even the new goose-girl whose name I never got around to memorizing! They're all *gone*, Morg," she stressed. "*You* at least can go back to the mainland and return to County Corvis and see all the old servants and retainers, the villagers and craftsmen you once lived among.

"Everyone *I* once knew is dead. Even their *grandchildren* are dead. The only people left in this entire world that I know are you and your family. And of you and your family, until today, I only ever *saw* Kelly, Saber, and your hand," she reminded him, before gesturing again at the group of people still out in the middle of the garden. "While I can guess at their identities, that the big fellow with the gold eyes is Wolfer, and the two redheads are Trevan and Koranen, and so on and so forth, we haven't exactly been formally introduced. Coming *home* isn't exactly what I'd hoped it would be.

"I'm happy to be back in a world that makes *sense* to me . . . but as much as you'll have to adjust to me being from Nightfall, I'll have to adjust to being back on Nightfall, too. And I don't *know* this Nightfall, other than whatever you've told me about it."

"This *isn't* your Nightfall. It's no longer a duchy. It's an incipient kingdom," Morganen reminded her. He reached for the door into the palace, then winced. "Gods . . . if you are the Duchess Haupanea, then you might have a *legal* claim to the rulership of the Isle."

"Hey, I don't want it," she quickly reassured him. "I learned that much about myself in the other realm. Yes, I was born and raised with the thought of being the next duchess, but trust me, I've found my true calling!"

Distracted, Morganen eyed her askance. "And that would be . . . ?"

"All those plants I sent across, and those boxes I asked you to store with a cooling spell? I plan on making chocolate," she stated firmly. At his puzzled look, she grinned. "Wait until you *taste* it. You'll swear there's been a Convocation invoked in your mouth!"

Bemused, Morg finished opening the door for her.

She stepped inside, then stopped abruptly, gasping. "Oh! Oh . . . I'd forgotten about this." Hope blinked at the walls. "Wow . . . that's really, um . . . different. *Completely* different from what I remember . . ."

Since he was half a hand-span taller than she, Morg could see what she saw. At first he didn't know what she meant, then realized she was referring to the walls. Or rather, what was on the walls, one of his creations. Horses bearing slender, colorfully clad riders lined up on either side of the entryway, while the figure of a man farther down the hall held up a pulsing, glowing orb, his long, fluted sleeves draping all the way to the grass at his feet. The color of the orb shifted from red to yellow, then flared white. The horses leaped forward in blurred, slowed motion.

"Of course, the paint," Morg murmured.

"Yes. You mentioned it only once or twice. Something about foiling scryings?" she added over her shoulder, glancing up at him with those lovely brown eyes.

"Scryings and mirror-Gatings of monsters into our home."

Morg watched her nose wrinkle at the thought, and gestured up the hall. "You'll get used to it. Come, we had a room readied for you across the corridor from mine, on the second floor."

"*You* might be used to it, but it totally changes what I was expecting. It makes everything . . . weird-feeling," she muttered, eyeing the walls warily. "Unfamiliar."

That brought their conversation back around again. "You should have expected differences."

"Yes, but I couldn't ask a lot of questions, not without inviting even more," she reminded him.

"True, but it's still a lot to come to terms with. Not only are you *not* from Kelly's world, but you're not even from *my* world, in the sense that you're not from *my* time," Morg pointed out. "You come from a time when Nightfall was prosperous, and the Great Portals still functioned, and the Convocation of the Gods was a common event—we go up these stairs, here."

"The walls haven't thrown me off by *that* much," she muttered wryly. "By a bit, but at least the doors are still in the same places— you know, I pictured your voice being deeper than it is? It's a nice voice, but not quite what I expected."

"Your . . . *Kelly's* world didn't have enough magic for me to project my voice loudly enough to be heard. Otherwise I would have spoken, instead of using that clumsy writing system."

"You do have neat penmanship, though," she offered. "Not quite like Giolana's, but it was always a pleasure to watch you scribe your words on the board in the kitchen."

"Giolana?" Morg asked her.

"My scribe. Once my parents realized I was going off into Seer fits, and not just spouting random bits of poetry, they hired a personal scribe to follow me around and write everything down. Giolana was my primary scribe, and a dear friend. We knew each other from preliminary school. There were also Tomak and Chaiden; they took turns shadowing me in the evenings, and they'd take turns once every four days, so that Giolana could have some time to herself. But mostly it was Giolana by my side. I miss her . . . Which way down the hall?" she asked as they emerged on the third floor.

Morg gestured, and they walked that way. "When you wound up in the other realm . . . you didn't have any translation problems?"

"None, thank the Gods. I was given a dose of Ultra Tongue at the age of ten, when I'd proved in class I had a good enough grasp of grammar and such. Any earlier than that, and my parents didn't think I'd make the transition from language to language with the eloquence required of a future duchess. I'm *very* glad it continued to work in that other world," she added, "though I almost gave myself away a couple of times, knowing languages the original Hope couldn't possibly have known."

The reminder of her namesake made Morg grimace. She caught sight of it and gave him a questioning look. Waving his hand at the door they were approaching, Morg sidestepped the subject for a moment. "This is the suite I readied for you, for, um, while we would be courting. Mine is that one. If you don't like it . . . well, most of the rooms in this wing are empty, and you can always pick another."

"You say that like you're not sure we'll still be courting," Hope said cautiously. "Have you completely changed your mind? Is my sin against you that great?"

He grimaced again, wrinkling his long nose. "Hope . . . Haupanea . . ."

"Hope," she chose. "Just call me Hope. I've grown used to it by now. I'm really not Nea anymore; I've seen too many things and lived too far from home . . . and it's close enough to the first part of my name, Haup, that it's not that far off."

"That's the point. The woman I grew to know, and to *love*," he confessed quietly, "is only a fraction of who you are. And to be presented suddenly with this whole extra dimension to your background, with *this* universe in your background . . . it's pushed us apart by several steps. I feel like I almost have to get to know you all over again."

Tucking her hands into her back pockets, Hope nodded. "That's only fair, I suppose. In fact, one of my friends in the other world said something similar."

Morg lifted his brow skeptically. "I thought you said they don't know anything about alternate realities."

"What? No, nothing like that." She chuckled, flashing white teeth at him in a grin. "No, she was talking about *Internet* dating—it has to do with that computer thing I showed you. It's very complicated, but it's a way of getting to know people without actually meeting them in person," Hope explained briefly. "Anyway, my friend said that the person you meet on the Internet is usually only around ten percent of who they really are. Even if they're being completely honest in their correspondence. The same could be said for courting by sending letters back and forth, except the Internet is a lot faster when it comes to sending and getting responses.

"What *we* did, you and I, is correspond long-distance. So while my 'ninety percent' is admittedly a bit more unsettling to learn . . . at least *you* knew what I looked like. I didn't even know that much about you," she reminded him. Dropping her gaze, she shifted her left hand, almost but not quite touching the fingers supporting her satchels. "Aside from your hand, I didn't know what you looked like, while you could see me each and every time we talked. I didn't know what you sounded like, nor even if you had a second hand.

"You could've been born with only one arm, or lost the other one from some accident that the Healers couldn't fix," she added lightly. "And unless you told me otherwise, I still wouldn't know if you had or not. But the person you *are* is still the same. Just as I am."

"Maybe." Morg sighed. "I had thought we had grown close enough to tell each other anything. I even told you how I messed up trying to match-make Rydan and Rora. Finding out that there's this whole new aspect to your past . . ."

"Well, maybe all we really need is a little more time to get to know each other," Hope offered, clasping both hands behind her back. Her pose was coquettish, her expression wistful, as she rocked on her toes and added, "You *do* still want to get to know me . . . don't you?"

Morg knew she was trying to flirt with him. She was still as lovely as ever—even lovelier, for she was here, in person—but there was a part of him that was still a little hurt by her revelation. A part that wanted coaxing before he'd pull her back into his good graces. Acknowledging it, Morg affected a thoughtful look.

"I don't know . . . I've worked so hard to match-make my brothers, all so that I could look forward to having a love of my own—I think I'm rather tired of doing all the chasing. And since you were *supposed* to be from Kelly's world, I was expecting to be courted by Kelly's ways," he said.

Hope's brows quirked, her expression changing to a bemused one. "What does *that* mean?"

"I want to *be* courted, instead of having to do all the courting myself. Why should women be the only ones who get to sit back and enjoy the attentions of their swains?" he added as she stared at him.

"You *want* me to court you?" she repeated slowly.

"Yes. And bring me flowers," he added on impulse. "Kelly keeps saying how she comes from a world where the genders are equal in all things, and if men can bring women flowers, then surely women can bring men flowers."

"Well, if you want me to court you by Kelly's rules, she comes from a world of equality. That means I'm not going to do *all* of the work. I'll court you enough to hopefully make up for misleading you—however good the reason at the time," Hope amended firmly. "But I will expect you to reciprocate at some point. Particularly since, as this is Kelly's incipient kingdom, she'll still be insisting on everyone being treated equally here on Nightfall, too."

"Alright," he agreed. "You court me, and then I'll court you. And we'll get to know each other better. A lot better."

"Agreed." They stared at each other for a long moment, then Hope cleared her throat. "Um . . . could I have a hug? I *was* kind of hoping for a warmer reception, considering I've gone and lost my old life *twice*, by now."

She did have a point. Even he had expected a warmer reception. It was the directness of her brown eyes, which Morg was used to seeing filled with happiness yet aimed only vaguely in his direction, that made up his mind. Those beautiful brown eyes were finally focused on *him*, not just on the intersection plane formed by his mirrors . . . and her gaze was wistful.

Opening his arms, he let her step into them, wrapping her own around his ribs. Closing the embrace—mindful of the bags still dangling from one hand—Morganen allowed himself to enjoy the feel of her body pressed against his, and not just palm pressed to palm. She was warm, soft, and feminine, smelling of flowers and soap. Hope snuggled against him from chest to thigh and let out a contented sigh.

As comfortable and natural as it felt to hold her in his arms, he couldn't hold her forever. The weather might have cooled from the heat wave of a few days before, but it was still summer, and still warm. There was also the problem that she *was* female, and she *was* his Destined bride . . . or at least, the most likely candidate.

Morganen knew he—*they*—needed time to come to grips with all the unexpected differences in their lives. She needed to grow used to a Nightfall that was very different from the one she had known, and he needed to accept the idea that she was from *his* world originally, for all she had been exiled in another one when they first met.

Easing their bodies apart, Morg opened the door to her suite and handed her satchels to her. She sighed but complied with his movements. Stepping inside, she stared at the autumn leaves slowly drifting down over the walls, then shook her head. Focusing on the rest of the furnishings, her expression became amused, and she twisted to glance back at him.

"Did you cram *everything* I sent across into this suite?" Hope asked, gesturing over her shoulder at the furniture cluttering the sitting room. There was enough room to walk around, but only in paths that wound their way through the various bits of padded furniture and thigh-high stacks of boxes.

"Not everything, but most of it, yes. I didn't know where you'd want everything—as I said, you can claim any room in this branch of the wing," Morg told her.

Her lips quirked up on one side. "And if I wanted to claim *your* room for my own?"

Her lighthearted teasing was appreciated, and very similar to their normal, pre-crossing banter, but Morganen didn't fall for it. "If you wanted to claim it right now, then I'd have to move my own things out first, on principle . . . but if you wanted to claim it later . . . we'd have to see if I *needed* to move, first."

"Morg, I'm quite sure I wasn't thrown across time and space to endure five years in a thoroughly confusing realm, just to be turned down by one of the few men I've considered worthy of me." Turning back to the room, Hope finished stepping inside. "Now, where did you put all my chocolate?"

"In the wardrobes in the dressing room. Through that door and around to the left," Morg directed her. "And yes, I enchanted them for stasis cold-storage, as requested. Though I really don't see what's so special about a bunch of brown lumps."

"You didn't try any?" she asked him, heading toward the door he had indicated.

"Of course not; they're yours. And, well . . . it's just a bunch of brown lumps," Morg said. "They smelled sweet, if strange, but they didn't exactly look all that appealing."

She started to reply, then closed her mouth. A thoughtful look crossed her face, and she quirked one brow. Sighing, Hope shook her head. "No . . . no, if you tried chocolate right now, it just wouldn't be the same. I see I'm going to have to seduce you into the proper mood to enjoy it first, as well as the proper mood to enjoy *me*."

"I look forward to your efforts," Morg agreed solicitously. "Now, who or what is this Nauvea you mentioned?"

"Nauvea . . ."

Pausing midway through the bedchamber, she sighed, then detoured to the cushion-lidded chest at the foot of the bed. This room wasn't quite as cluttered as the other one, but it was still filled half with local furnishings and half with otherworldly goods. Patting the empty spot next to her, Hope coaxed Morg toward the bench-like seat. Thankfully, he didn't hesitate more than a moment before joining her.

"A very long time ago, Nightfall was its own kingdom. A very small kingdom, but independent of all others. And my ancestors worshipped our very own Patron Deity, the Goddess of Dreaming. That was Nauvea," she explained. "But, over time, enough settlers came from the mainland that the worship of Nauvea was slowly replaced by worship of Kata and Jinga. My own family line continued to worship Nauvea, but eventually we had to acknowledge homage to the mainland Gods and mainland rule, with Nightfall becoming a mere duchy."

The way she put that made Morg smile ironically. "I've heard the complaint put the other way, that this island was too small to be something as exalted as a duchy. I certainly never heard a whisper that it used to be its own realm. Of course, if you were planning on everyone on Nightfall worshipping Nauvea, reviving the island's old Patronage . . . Kelly might have something to say about that."

"Yes, well, she *is* an American. And a rabid equalist. No, I know Kelly plans on making *all* the Gods the Patrons of Nightfall, if she can get the Convocation restarted. And I have no problem with that," Hope agreed. "I think it's a wonderful solution to the situation. It's just that Nauvea was *my* Goddess. It was Her voice I heard speaking in my head, the voice that occasionally made *me* speak aloud."

The polite, almost sympathetic curiosity in Morganen's light aqua eyes encouraged her to continue. Hope shrugged, searching for the words to explain herself.

"It was unnerving, in that other world. All those years with only base, raw instinct to guide me and no Voice to comfort me. No touch of divinity, however small and diminished She might have been by my day. Now that I'm back . . . I keep expecting to hear Her, but it's likely that no one has worshipped Her for two hundred years, and I'm terribly afraid that She's gone. And if She *is* gone . . . who else among the Gods will speak with me? I feel like I've been abandoned a second time, though I've known that my absence from this world was by Her choice when She used the energy from the Portal to fling me away, preventing it from destroying the land."

Morg covered her hand with his, wanting to comfort her. She glanced at his fingers and smiled wryly. Turning her palm over, she laced her fingers with his.

"You'd think that I'd be relieved of the burden of being a Seer. But I had that 'relief' for five confusing, lonely years. And She was *my* Goddess. Not many people could ever claim to have a personal Deity. That might be hubris . . . but She was my guide in life," Hope admitted quietly. "And my friend."

"Gods are raised by faith, belief, and the power of prayer," Morganen reminded her. "Maybe all She needs is enough prayers to revive Her from two centuries of . . . slumber? It is said that Gods are not born as men, and so cannot die as men. Either They manifest, or They fade away . . . but surely if They do not die, They can always manifest again? If She was such an important part of your original life, then perhaps you should tell me more about Her. Since you should tell me all the things you *didn't* tell me before," he offered lightly, if pointedly.

Hope rolled her eyes, but began. "Well, Nauvea is, or was, the Goddess of Dreaming."

"Is," Morg asserted, squeezing her fingers. "She *is* the Goddess of Dreaming."

Warmed by his faith, or at least his politeness, Hope smiled. "She *is* the divine wellspring of dreams, both asleep and awake. She gives us the sort of dreams we have when we're sleeping," Hope explained, "but also draws strength from our daydreams. She foments imagination in young children and inspires artists with the visions of the things they create."

"All sorts of dreams? What about nightmares?" Morg asked, curious.

"Those, too. She's also responsible for the visions seen when someone is feverish and hallucinating. Good or bad, frightening or sublime, Nauvea watches over our straying thoughts. She *did* say that the Gods who were loved never truly die," Hope added. "It was right before the Portal collapsed, but I do remember Her saying that. Yet without the power of prayer to sustain Her, without the will of Her people encouraging Her to exist, even if it was only a handful of us at the end . . ."

Morg squeezed her hand again. "Then pray to Her. Restore Her strength. In time, She may speak with you again."

She rolled her eyes. "I'm only one woman, Morg. No matter how great my faith may be—"

"—*One* woman had enough faith in *all* Gods, everywhere, to convince Them to grant her an impending crown," Morg reminded her. "A woman who was strong-willed enough to take on the entire Katani Council—alright, *half* the Council—and do so successfully with no magic of her own. I refuse to believe that someone with enough internal fortitude to be Kelly of Doyle's friend *isn't* strong enough to resurrect a beloved Goddess."

Hope laughed at that. "You make her sound like a force of nature, like a flood or a tornado!"

"*You* said it, not I," Morg quipped.

Hope laughed again, then leaned in close enough to rest her head on his shoulder. She peeked up at him as she did. "I've missed this. The bantering. We've been so busy in this last week or so, arranging for everything to come across the Veils, we didn't have time to just *talk* . . . but it's even better to *hear* you say all the things you would've written."

"I agree," Morg murmured. He wanted to say how much he liked holding her, but his cryslet rang. Pulling his hand free, he flipped open the enchanted bracelet, peering into the mirror installed on the inside of the crystal-topped lid. His twin, Koranen, peered back at him. "Kor?"

"Danau says it's starting to rain down at the harbor, and *you* left your mirror in the courtyard."

Morg grimaced. "I'm on my way. Thank you." Snapping the lid shut, he glanced at Hope. "You can get yourself settled in while I take care of my looking glass, right?"

"Of course. But I hope you'll come back," Hope added. "I may be familiar with the old palace layout, but everything's different, and it's not just the paint. I'd rather have a tour to find out which rooms are being used for what these days, rather than blunder into some formerly public chamber that's been appointed for private use."

"I canceled my evening classes, anticipating you'd need a tour. You can meet everyone at supper, which will be in just under . . . three hours," Morg said, glancing at the milky white gems affixed to the silver that framed the larger milky white crystal embedded in the oval lid. Hesitating, he leaned in close and pressed his lips lightly to her temple. "I *am* glad you're here . . . but I do expect to be courted, to make up for that little secret you've been hiding."

"Go rescue your mirror. And prepare to be seduced, Morg," she added as he rose to leave her quarters. "Maybe *you* should pray to Nauvea that I actually can fulfill your wildest dreams with all that kinky, otherworldly stuff I might've learned while in another universe. After all, five years is a very long time to have immersed myself in their lascivious, decadent culture."

Unsure whether he should be amused or alarmed by that idea, Morg merely smiled, bowed politely to her, and left. As he walked away, doubts and discomforts rose up within him. All this time, his best friend wasn't who he had thought she was, and he wasn't quite sure how he was going to handle that fact. But he did know that he needed to. What he needed now was a way to clarify his thoughts by talking them through. If Hope herself was the source of his confusion, there was only one other person he could go to.

"All this time, we've been talking and conversing, and she never once told me that she's the *lost duchess* of my new home." Pacing around the area between the tables in the tiling workshop, Morganen raked his hands through his hair, scraping back the light brown locks from his brow. "I thought she was someone just like Kelly—well, not *just* like Kelly, for which I thank the Gods, since she's her own woman—but I thought she was something special and exotic, and she's a fellow Katani!"

"A fellow Katani from over two hundred years ago," Koranen pointed out reasonably. "Time travel is exceedingly rare, which would definitely make her special. And she *did* live in another universe for several years. If that's not exotic enough, then there's no pleasing you, Brother."

Less than half of the redhead's attention was on his twin. The rest was focused on the large kiln stuffed with faience roofing tiles. Koranen only needed to visit the kiln three times a week for a couple of hours each. That was after the manual laborers had mixed, shaped, and stacked enough new tiles into the kiln.

Without Rydan's enchanted grinding and sifting of the quartz that was the base material, without Koranen's pyromantic magic to concentrate the heat needed to fuse the gritty particles into watertight, weather-resistant tiles, what only took a handful of days from start to finish would have taken two weeks or more. Now that Hope had arrived—disrupting everyone's schedule, as well as their preconceived notions about her—Kor had gone back to work.

"Yes, but . . . she's from *this* universe. And not just the one that you and I know, but a bygone era!" Morg slumped against the edge of one of the tables, ignoring the bemused look of the woman measuring proportions of powdered minerals into a large cauldron on the other side. "It's not at all what I expected . . ."

"What, like Danau was?" Kor snorted.

"You didn't *have* any expectations where your woman was concerned," Morg shot back.

"Of course I did! I expected her to be taller, and to have longer hair—*much* longer—and I expected her to welcome me with open arms," Koranen told his twin. "I also expected the two of us to continue living here. But we're not going to."

That pulled Morg out of his fretting. He frowned at his twin. "You're not? What do you mean?"

"Danau came here to study, repair, and learn how to replicate the Desalinator. Once she does, she can go back to Menomon to construct their own version. For obvious reasons, I have to go with her"—he added, pausing to flex his fingers and mutter a spellword to intensify the heat inside the already blazing kiln—"because without me, she doesn't have enough power to fix our version, let alone construct one of her own. Together, we do."

"So, what, after our Desalinator is up and running, you'll take off for a year or so until you've constructed one for Menomon?" Morg asked, calculating the time that would be needed. "Permanent Magics only take around a year to erect, but usually not much more than a year or two. They do have an Aquamancy Guild, so I'd think you'd have plenty of helping hands. And a thirst-motivated populace."

"Yes, but if those hands are Reuen's or Chana's, they can go help *elsewhere*," Kor muttered.

Morg tipped his head, conceding his brother's point. The petite, redheaded Aquamancer had not arrived alone. But while the woman named Ama-ti was sweet-natured, the other two weren't nearly as kind. Particularly toward Danau, whom they had considered to be defective as a woman, simply because she literally froze when touched by most men.

"Fine. We'll all miss you terribly, but you'll only be a mirror-call away. If we can make twinned mirrors that can reach into the heart of Natallia and communicate with the Nuns of Koral-tai, we can make twinned mirrors that can contact you when you're in Menomon. And then, once the Desalinator is made, you'll come back, right?"

"We probably *won't* come back. Danau is pressing for the two of us to take over Guardian Sheren's job. Together, we're strong enough for that task, as well. No one else is, in Menomon."

Kor didn't say more than that, but he didn't have to. Sheren was the Guardian of Menomon City. Guardians were interpreted by most people to be the magical champions and defenders of a particular place, but in truth, many of them were also the protectors of Fountains. Such wellsprings of magic were rare; they were scattered raggedly across the world, and they were carefully guarded against misuse. In fact, Fountains were so carefully and closely guarded, it was only within the last year that Morganen and his family had learned that Nightfall itself hosted one.

Considering that the Fountain of Menomon allowed the hidden, underwater city to exist without its inhabitants drowning, Morganen could see how someone who was both powerful and trustworthy enough to safeguard a Fountain could not turn down the task lightly.

"Yes, well, there is that, but you'll still only be a mirror away," Morganen said, as much to convince himself as to remind his brother of that possibility. He would've said more, about using the Fountains to travel swiftly between the two locations, but a voice interrupted him.

"Pardon, milords," the other occupant of the kiln shop said, "but I'm almost done tidying up for the day. Are you going to be much longer?"

Kor shook his head. "No, I'm done. Let the kiln cool on its own for a full day," he instructed her. "These won't be quite as gray as the last batch, since we're not in a heat wave anymore, but I do think they'll be a little greener than usual."

The woman nodded. "If I remember right, there's a request for greenish tiles down in the shipyard area, milord; I'll see if they're suitable for the client. If not, we just received some extra copper oxide that could be mixed into the next batch. Now, um . . . if you're done in here, mind if I lock up and go somewhere cooler?"

"Like everyone else did?" Kor asked wryly, shrugging back into his tunic. He hadn't stripped down to his loincloth, as he often did when working in his forge, but he had removed his shirt before concentrating on the kiln-fire.

Morg mock-sighed at his twin. "Poor Kor, wildly popular *only* in the depths of winter."

The auburn-haired mage mock-glared back. "Careful, or I'll sic my wife on you."

"You haven't married her yet . . . and *that* threat would be far more effective in winter. Right now, I'd actually welcome her icy-cold fingers on the back of my neck," Morg joked.

"True." Buckling his belt and pouch in place, Kor joined his twin, heading for the workshop door. "We were thinking of getting married in the next few days, something quiet and quick, rather than a big production. After all, Hope is here, and I do need to be married before you, if that last line in your verse of the Prophecy is to come true. Better to do it before we restart the Desalinator than afterward, since who knows what sort of chaos will happen once we try resurrecting the Convocation."

"I have to resolve a different sort of chaos, first. Your woman may be different than what you imagined, and you've accepted that, but I'm still struggling with the fact that Hope is different than what she *told* me she was," Morg muttered as they approached the wagons parked in the lot next to the workshop.

"Is she *really* all that different, Morg?" Kor prodded him. "Everything she has done, she did *while* she was the last, lost Duchess of Nightfall, deep down inside. Nothing about *her* has actually changed. Only your perception of her has . . . and that's *your* problem, not hers."

Morg eyed his twin. "When did *you* get to be so wise?"

"When I was born first, of course! Eldest is often wisest, as the old saying goes." Smirking, Kor pulled himself up onto the driving bench of the wagon he had used to come down the hillside. Releasing the brake, he shifted the direction lever to put the cart in reverse, and stepped on the movement lever. The cart lurched . . . and then stopped. A couple of experimental taps did nothing. Rolling his hazel eyes, Koranen glanced at his brother. "Mind refreshing the spell?"

"If you think a clueless idiot like me can *manage* it," Morg retorted.

"Hey, I never once thought you were an idiot," Kor reassured him.

Stooping to reach the locomotion runes carved on the axel hub, Morg paused, looking up at his twin. Who was smirking. "And the clueless part?"

Koranen grinned.

"I should make you *walk* home," Morganen muttered, though he reached for the carved and painted runes anyway, readying himself to infuse them with fresh magical energy.

"Not when I have to pick up Danau for supper," his twin countered.

"How are the containment crystals coming along?" Morg asked; only part of his attention was needed for the familiar task of cart enchantment.

"They're almost done growing. We managed to get three seeded in the solution last night. Rydan was reluctant to start the process, but I convinced him that the crystals would still be useful to have on hand, even if he never agreed to the extraction ceremony." Koranen waited while his brother chanted under his breath, then gingerly tested the lever as soon as Morganen pulled free of the undercarriage. The cart rolled backward smoothly. "Nice work, Brother. I guess you're not so clueless after all."

Raspberrying his twin might have been immature, but it was very satisfying for Morg.

"And when the remains weren't identified or claimed after three years, I convinced the morgue to let me bury them, on the grounds that 'it could have been me' . . . which it should have been, and which it was, if only in a weird, roundabout sort of way," Hope said. She switched her gaze from the enchanted clouds drifting across the ceiling to her freckled friend. "I *had* to give her a decent burial, even if it was only as a Jane Doe."

"Of course," Kelly agreed. She had dropped by within the first fifteen minutes or so of Hope's arrival in these crowded quarters, calling Hope's name from the corridor until she popped her head through one of the many doors lining the second-floor hall.

Lying on the broad bed in Hope's suite, surrounded by dressers and recliners, suitcases, framed photographs, and various other paraphernalia of another life on another world . . . Kelly acknowledged it was too difficult to refute that *this* woman—Haupanea—was the same woman she had known in the other universe.

"Let me ask you this," Kelly offered. "If you're from this universe—and I'm not doubting that—but if you're from this universe, and you worshipped Kata and Jinga . . . *and* you are a Seer, a mouthpiece for the Gods of *this* realm . . . how did you reconcile your faith and your beliefs with the need to blend in with your—or rather, the original Hope's—Catholic relatives?"

"As a Seer, I was a mouthpiece not only for Nauvea, but for all the Gods, should They have chosen to act through me," Hope said. "So, to *my* way of thinking, the fact that I was born to be the potential instrument of *all* the Gods extended to the deities of the other universe."

"So, what, you kept yourself open to God? Just in case?" Kelly asked, glancing at her friend.

Hope shrugged. "Why not? I'd studied enough of the various major religions in your world to know that a good deed performed in one Divine Name was the same as a good deed performed in another Name, over there. Which is exactly how it works *here*. I had no qualms about remaining open-minded."

"I can understand that." Kelly sighed, then stretched. "I *missed* talking with you. And I haven't stopped to rest like this in the middle of my day for a *long* time—not even to pounce on my husband. Which has grown a bit frustrating. I mean, we've been having unprotected sex since the night we married, but . . ."

"I think that question will resolve itself shortly," Hope said. "There has to be a certain balance maintained between the universes. Matter for matter, life for life . . . like all that wheat Morg shipped over for me. There's enough mass and potential life in all those bags to balance out quite a lot of the stuff I had shipped back across."

"Yes, but shipping wheat isn't the same as getting pregnant," Kelly pointed out. Then she sighed. "Though I'll agree that being pregnant while I'm still trying to jump-start this kingdom wouldn't be easy. However did *you* manage it?" Kelly asked her. Then laughed ruefully at her words. "I meant, being a *ruler*.

"The duchy was already established, I'll agree, but you were, what, sixteen years old when you had to take over? Even Saber was older than that when his parents died, and he's told me plenty of times how hard it was for him to take over County Corvis and manage it successfully."

"It *wasn't* easy," Hope confessed. "But I had been trained by my parents and tutors in how to make good decisions, and I had Lord Niktor. He'd been my parents' seneschal. Keeping him on as my advisor reassured those who weren't so sure that a duchess so young was capable of making good decisions. They trusted *him*, so when he agreed with *me*, it made them think *my* policies and commands were wise enough to be heeded. You would have liked him. He was sort of like Baron Gregor, from the Middle Ages Society? Only less balding."

Kelly laughed at the reminder. "Almost *anyone* would've been less balding than him—if he'd only given in gracefully and trimmed his hair or shaved his head, and stopped trying to *hide* it . . . !"

"Ah, yes, the Baron of Bad Comb-Overs," Hope agreed, chuckling. "It's bad when they don't know *how* to hide it, but worse when they refuse to learn."

"Even Lady Danielle had more dignity with her hair loss," Kelly said. "But if this Niktor was like Baron Gregor, then he must've been a true marvel at organization."

"Oh, he was. Intelligent, well-mannered, with a force of personality just strong enough to exhort our people into doing what needed to be done, yet self-effacing enough to leave me looking strong in the eyes of others. I miss him. And Giolana, and . . . Everyone in the duchy, really." Hope sighed, briefly closing her eyes. "It's like I've lost them twice now."

"Um, speaking of the duchy . . . do you want it back?" Kelly inquired lightly. "Because if you do, that's a little awkward, what with the whole floating crown thing and all . . ."

Freeing a hand from behind her head, Hope patted Kelly on the arm. "Relax. I've found my calling, and it *isn't* leadership. Mind you, I wasn't bad at it . . . but I'd *much* rather spend my days playing with the Food of the Gods."

"Are you still on about that?" Kelly asked, twisting onto her side and propping up her freckled head with one palm. "I've been here for roughly a year, and I actually don't miss chocolate anymore. At first, I did, but *cinnin* is a spice that's close enough to cinnamon to please my taste buds, and I've always enjoyed honey and nuts. And the fruits on this island are tangy-sweet enough for a treat. I really don't miss it."

Rolling off the bed, Hope righted herself and crossed to the dressing chamber. It didn't take her long to find what she wanted. Poking her head back into the bedroom, she eyed her friend speculatively. "So . . . if I were to offer you, say, a dark chocolate almond cluster . . . you wouldn't be interested?"

One of Kelly's brows quirked upward. She pushed up onto her elbows, eyeing the other woman. "Do you really think a mere almond cluster would be enough to change my mind?"

"Maybe . . . and maybe it's something *better*," Hope offered, sauntering back into the room with her hands tucked behind her back. "*Maybe* I've brought across a box of those little cinnamon-chocolate pastilles, which I know you love, but which are so *very* hard to find, even in the other universe."

Sitting up, Kelly held out her hand. "Prove it. *Prove* you have cinnamon-chocolate pastilles."

"But I thought you didn't *miss* chocolate," Hope teased, sashaying closer to the bed.

"If this isn't *your* duchy anymore, then this is *my* island, and *all* imports will be taxed by the Crown, whether they arrive by sea, by air, or by mirror-Gate. Fork 'em over, sister!" Kelly ordered sternly.

Laughing, Hope pressed the box into Kelly's wriggling, demanding fingers. "You are *so* easy to bribe!"

"Ha! Do you know how few chocolatiers *put* cinnamon and chocolate together?" Kelly scoffed, opening the box. She paused to examine the lid, and more specifically, the image framed by the gilded rectangle centered on the lid. "A silhouette of a castle at sunset? Did you come up with this design idea before or after I left the other world?"

"After, of course. Morg told me about the flags you had made, so I adopted that as my logo. Hellaciously expensive to print, and it doesn't change color, but it looks good. Go on, taste one," Hope encouraged her.

Plucking one of the thin, dark brown discs from the box that was embossed with a five-pointed, fluted star, Kelly sniffed cautiously. Her eyes narrowed, and she took a small bite. Within moments, her breath sighed out of her as the chocolate melted on her tongue, sweet, bitter, rich—and then sucked back in as the heat of the cinnamon hit. Kelly moaned and popped the rest of the chocolate past her lips. "Oh . . . oh, *Gods* . . . thith ith *delicious*! Mmm, I'd f'gotten wha' chocolate *felt* like . . ."

"It's not just a taste, is it?" Hope agreed, settling onto the edge of the bed. "It's a whole-body sensation. The scent, the glossy darkness, the smoothness on the tongue . . . the bitter and the sweet of it . . ."

"An' in my fav'rite, the fire," Kelly added, mumbling a little as she rolled the melting flavors of the pastille around her tongue.

"The only sense that chocolate doesn't have intrinsic to itself is sound . . . unless you count the moans of a well-satisfied customer," Hope said, mouth quirking up on one side in amusement.

"Mm-*hmm*!" Kelly agreed. She selected another pastille, mouth working visibly as she devoured the last of the one in her mouth. Swallowing, she popped the next one in and savored it, too. "Mm, Gods, if you made this, you're a *genius*."

"As I said, I *think* I've found my calling," Hope confessed dryly.

"Oh, that was so good—you know, Saber *loves* spicy-hot foods," Kelly stated, quickly fitting the lid back onto the box. "If you'll excuse me, I'm feeling, um . . . well, let's just call it the urge to share a few pastilles with my husband."

"Chocolate *is* an aphrodisiac." Hope chuckled, rising along with her friend. "You go pounce on him and enjoy introducing him to it. I need to figure out how to seduce Morganen into trying some— he's insisting that I court him until he forgives me for lying to him. However good my reasons may have been at the time."

"If that young man has even *one* functioning taste bud, he'll be eating out of your hand within a week," Kelly agreed. Then paused. "I just remembered—I don't know if Morg told you, but we'll be restarting the Desalinator in six days, and that means three days' worth of salt water will be flushed nonstop through the pipes. Water pressure is being diverted to the reservoir tanks to ensure fresh drinking water, so go easy on any activity that requires taking frequent baths. Additionally, it means that all qualified, able-bodied persons age fifteen on up will be expected to pull a couple of shifts of block-hauling duty down at the processing plant. This includes you, me, and everyone else old enough to work in the warehouse.

"Sorry to have to welcome you home, only to make you work like a mule within the first week," Kelly apologized, "but even I'll be hauling salt and algae blocks during the restart days. We're in the middle of importing a bunch of newcomers to help ease the workload, but Danau says the lowest setting post-restart will be twelve times what we're currently producing . . . and for three days, we'll have to run it at the fullest capacity. So things are going to be a little crazy."

"Believe me, it's not been so long ago that I can't remember just how *much* water, salt, and fertilizer blocks that Desalinator can process, even at the usual half-strength," Hope reassured her. "If you need access to the control chamber, just let me know; unless things have been deliberately changed, the doors should still be magically keyed to open for me."

"You'll have to consult with Danau and Koranen for that—apparently, the two of them together have enough power to restart the whole system." Kelly glanced at the box in her hand. Prying open the lid, she popped another thin disc past her lips and smirked. Heading for the door, she fluttered her fingers at her friend, mumbling around her mouthful. " 'M off to a royal conferenfe . . . oh, God, thith ith *good* thtuff . . ."

"Have even more fun than I would," Hope encouraged her. "And *don't* talk with your mouth full! You're *supposed* to be a queen."

Another flutter of her freckled hand was Kelly's only acknowledgment.

THREE

Morganen arrived at her door just as the sun was setting. Not that Hope could see the sun, as her windows were on the southeast side of the wing, but she had opened the curtains, earlier. The golden glow had almost faded from the uppermost stones of the ramparts when he knocked, interrupting her efforts at sorting through all the belongings she had shipped across the Veil.

She hadn't realized how deep the shadows had grown in the front chamber, until she banged her shin on a low table still laden with photo albums. The albums, she had expected to be shipped across, but not the table. There had been tons of wheat exchanged for all of these mementos of the other world in addition to her precious cacao plants—things for Kelly as well as for herself—but as she grunted and hobbled the rest of the way to the door, Hope wondered if it was really worth it.

Opening the door, she straightened in time to meet Morganen's worried aqua gaze.

"Are you alright?" he asked.

"Just banged my shin, that's all. Is dinner ready?" she asked.

"It will be, soon. And you'll be put on the chores roster, since we haven't hired a lot of servants, yet," he added. Craning his neck, he looked over her head, into the sitting room. "Why didn't you have any lights on? I should have told you how to . . . um, that is, you *do* remember how to use a lightglobe, right?" Morg amended, blushing.

"It hasn't been *that* long, Morg—and they did have certain light sources that were similar to our lightglobes," Hope told him. "No, the light from the windows was adequate for a while, and then I just got used to the growing darkness. Until I hit my shin."

Bells rang out, interrupting her. Morg smiled and waited for the brief tune to end before speaking again. "*Now* dinner is ready." Offering his elbow, he smiled when she tucked her hands around it. "I think I'm getting used to you being . . . you know . . ."

"Short, but complicated?" Hope quipped, joining him in walking up the corridor.

Morganen snorted at that. "You're not nearly as short as Danau is." He glanced at her as they headed for the heart of the palace. "You also have a fuller figure than her."

Blushing, Hope wrinkled her nose. "I hope you don't mind. What with the chocolate and all, I've gained a few pounds since the last time I was here."

"Why should I mind?" Morg asked her, visibly puzzled.

"In the other universe . . . let's just say they have some strange notions of what a woman's weight should be. Strict, in some ways, when it comes to the dictates of fashion. If you're not thin, you're not beautiful, and all that," she dismissed. "Kelly was closer to the ideal over there than I ever was."

"As thin as Kelly was? She was starving because she was being driven out of business. What has starving oneself to do with how beautiful a woman can be?" he asked. "Starving yourself isn't healthy!"

"Try to tell *them* that," she said. "My philosophy has always been, so long as I'm active and healthy, I'll be fine. But over there . . .

like I said, they have some very strange notions about physical appeal. And I've sort of grown used to their perspective."

"Wait," Morg said, stopping them near the junction of the three easternmost corridors. "Are you fishing for *compliments* from me?"

Hope grinned and struck a coquettish pose against his arm. "No, just seeing if you'll come to my rescue . . . and giving you the opportunity to do so. After all, you *like* playing 'the hero.' "

"Do I?" he challenged lightly.

"Oh, yes. I figured it out from our conversations. You *like* being able to swoop in and save the day. You may be modest about it, but you're as much of a champion of others as your eldest brother is . . . or am I wrong, and you're not the least bit heroic, deep down inside?" Hope inquired politely.

"I suppose I could admit that I am, deep, *deep* down inside. Well hidden. You'd hardly know it," Morg mock-confessed. He enjoyed the sound of her laughter, light yet husky. The same laugh from before she had stepped through his mirror. They started walking again. "So . . . having me come to your rescue is your ploy for seducing me?"

"Well, heroes usually get to be rewarded. And you have rescued me from the mild worry that I'm not attractive enough for you," she pointed out. "It's a small thing, so it probably only deserves an equally small reward."

"I suppose that's fair. But what would a 'small reward' be like?" he asked her.

"Like . . . this." Tugging him to a stop, Hope rose up onto her toes—he was about five inches taller than she—and kissed him on one smooth-shaved cheek. Pulling back, she smiled. "How's that?"

Morganen pretended to mull it over. "A *small* reward. I presume these opportunities will grow increasingly heroic, with equally increasing rewards?"

"Hopefully, yes, but that's just *one* of the ways I plan on seducing you," Hope offered, shrugging her shoulders. "There's also the flirtatious glances to explore, the delicate yet publically acceptable touches, the little in-jokes that close couples share but which the rest of the world don't quite get . . . And of course, if *you* have any ideas on how you'd like to be courted, do let me know."

They resumed walking up the main corridor toward the donjon, the octagonal hall at the heart of the palace. "My own version of courtship? Let's see . . . Kelly and Saber courted by first yelling at each other, then getting bitten by watersnakes and having to share a bathtub while the poison worked its way out of their systems. I have no intention of being bitten by anything but you, so that one's out. Wolfer and Alys . . . well, their courtship started as a friendship. Like ours has. But they were separated for several years, and I don't intend to be separated that long from you."

"Agreed. How about Dominor, and Evanor?" Hope asked.

"I prefer equality in a relationship, so I'd rather not put either of us up on a slave-block, like Dominor. Not even if Kelly were to lose her wits and make slavery legal on Nightfall," he added, wrinkling his nose in distaste. "And neither of us are like Serina, brilliant and focused on her work, but hopelessly absentminded about mundane details. Evanor and Mariel . . . well, I'm not about to lose my power, and you're not a Healer who could restore it, but . . . Mariel *has* mentioned how musicians have perfect hands for massages, and Ev countered that Healers do know how to touch their patients."

"So you think you'd like a little massage?" Hope asked, catching his meaning.

"Yes. Trevan and Amara, um . . . I sincerely hope you're not going to be nearly as high-strung as her. And I'd really rather not have to chase you around like he had to chase after her," Morg added.

"But wouldn't that make your being heroic a bit difficult, if you're not having to dash off and rescue me?" she pointed out.

"Maybe, but not constantly. Small heroics like compliments and kisses are fine for everyday use, but not the big ones," he stated.

"Which would be just as exhausting for the rescuee as for the rescuer," Hope agreed. "What about Rydan and his lady?"

"You know, I have no idea how those two actually got together?"

Morg confessed. "I mean, I know she snuck into his sanctum, and that she uncovered how he's sensitive to emotions as well as magic, but the rest of it's a mystery to me. Whatever spell or ability she used on him to get him to allow her into his life and his heart, it's nothing I recognize. Then again . . . they mostly did it in the middle of the night. Even *I* have to sleep sometimes."

Hope smiled. "In other words, they did their courting in secret, whereas I plan on courting you openly."

"Exactly. As for Koranen and Danau," Morg concluded, naming his twin as the next on the list, "they literally complement each other magically: She's ice, and he's fire. They're also learning to complement the other areas of their lives together, as well. Since you and I aren't in need of a neutralizing force for our unique abilities, we shouldn't have to court like my twin and his bride-to-be did. Which is to say, awkwardly."

Remembering one of his most recent whiteboard confessions, Hope grinned. "Did you really smack him upside his head for not asking her out? Literally whacked him one?"

"Absolutely. But *don't* tell Danau I had to encourage him. She's sensitive enough about her worth as a woman. She'd take it the wrong way," Morganen cautioned her. "As an insult to her worth, rather than an indictment of his idiocy."

"My lips are sealed," Hope promised. "So, where is the dining hall these days?"

"North wing, first room on the east from the donjon, second floor. It's just for family, though. We haven't picked out a grand feast hall for entertaining guests, yet. Why? Where was it originally?" Morg asked her.

"The chamber used for private meals, usually breakfast and lunch, was the first one in the north wing, but it was on the *west* side, second floor," Hope informed him. "East side was for supper with small numbers of guests and duchy officials. We used either the ballroom or the donjon for banquets, though they were more often buffets than formal meals. Sometimes, we would ring the balconies with narrow trestles and riser seats and have performances—plays and minstrels—on the main floor, with courses of food served between each act. Other times, we'd have a banquet with concentric rings of tables on the main floor, though those feasts were usually the ones served on holy days.

"My favorites were the plays, though it wasn't always easy to see over the railing when I was too young to sit with the adults on the ground floor," she added, nodding at the stone balustrade as the donjon came into view.

Releasing his elbow at the archway, she crossed to the balcony and braced her hands on the stone rail, looking out over the broad, eight-sided hall. Even in here, the walls and columns were painted with the image-shifting paint, though the carved stone banisters had been left bare. The current painted image complemented the chamber, being an illusion of rose brambles twining their way up lattice-strewn walls. Long, scroll-like banners hung down the fronts of the eight main pillars that helped support the broad, domed roof, each banner painted with a color-shifting sunset above the black silhouette of an island. Down on the floor, an awkward sort of asterisk had been formed by red strips of carpeting.

A glowing object hovered over one of the carpets that angled off almost directly across from her. It floated above a gilded, aquamarine loveseat. Hope didn't have to ask what it was; she already knew Kelly had successfully summoned a Gods-blessed Crown. If anything, the sight of the hovering diadem reminded her even more strongly than the painted walls and dangling banners that this was no longer *her* Nightfall. Her instincts twitched at that thought.

"I *should* do something about that, shouldn't I?" she muttered, thinking aloud.

"Do something about what?" Morg asked, joining her at the railing.

"The question of the duchy," Hope said, shaking her head lightly. "I'm not about to stand in the way of Nightfall becoming a kingdom, nor Kelly's claim to lead it, but I do need to figure out *how* to relinquish my claim to it. I'm sure I'll come up with something," she added, giving Morg a brief smile. "I usually do, when it's important."

"Is there really a need for you to relinquish the duchy?" Morganen asked, curious. "I'd think that, once Kelly performed the Ringing of the Bell, there'd be no going back for anyone on Nightfall."

"Well, I don't *know* that I have to formally relinquish it"—she shrugged—"but it never hurts to cover all the bases."

"Cover all the what?" Morg asked.

"Otherworld reference," Hope dismissed. Spotting movement partway around the octagonal balcony, she nodded at the next level down. "Looks like the others are gathering for dinner, too."

"Then we'll join them." Offering her his elbow once again, Morganen escorted her the rest of the way to the dining hall. Just before they reached the door, he asked softly, "You do remember my descriptions of everyone? We didn't exactly do a round of introductions, earlier."

Slanting him an amused look, Hope lifted her dark brows. "Why, is there a test?"

"Dazzle me with your mnemonic skills, my lady . . . and I'll tell you how well you passed, afterward," he offered lightly.

"Will there be a reward for getting all of them correct?" she teased back, smirking. "Particularly a kiss on *my* cheek?"

"Yes . . . depending on your success," Morg promised. Pulling his attention away from the humor in her brown eyes, he opened the door for her.

Entering, Hope quickly counted the dozen or so bodies in the room. Heads turned her way, making her tally of faces with identities easier. Some looked curious, some thoughtful. Mustering a warm smile, she started at the head of the table with her strawberry blonde friend and the golden blond man she had met in person a few times before. "Hello, Kelly, Saber."

They nodded back politely. Kelly smiled and patted her husband on the thigh. "Saber loved the chocolates, too. Thoroughly. Thank you."

Saber flushed and slanted a brief, quelling look at Kelly. "Yes, thank you. A most interesting treat."

"You're welcome. And . . . you're Wolfer, and you're Alys," she said next, nodding to the most muscular of the men gathered at the table and to the woman with curly, honey blonde hair.

"I hope you remember where the original plantations were, Your Grace," Wolfer stated, his voice deep yet quiet. "With the death of Baroness Teretha, we're at a loss to tell where the most fruitful farmlands used to be."

"I'll see what I can remember. Call me Hope, please—I'm not really the Duchess of Nightfall anymore, and I'm certainly not the girl I used to be," she demurred. Glancing around the table, she shook her head. "I don't see Dominor or his lady, Serina, but they're overseas still, aren't they? Along with Mariel, the Healer? That would be your wife, right, Evanor?" Hope asked the light blond male seated at the table.

"Yes, she's overseeing the last stages of Serina's pregnancy," he agreed, his tenor as smooth as Wolfer's was deep. He gestured to the youth at his side, a boy with curly brown hair and green eyes. "This is my next-son—"

"—No, let me try," she interjected. "Morganen's told me so much about all of you, I want to make sure I get all of you correctly named. You're Mikor," she said. "Son of Mariel and Milon the Seer, and next-son of Evanor."

Mikor nodded. "Ev says you're a Seer, too, like Father was. Is that true?"

Hope blinked. Her first impulse was to say *yes*, but she technically hadn't felt the touch of anyone, God or Goddess, since leaving for the other world. Including after her return. "Well, I *was* a vessel of the Gods for a while. But then I had to go far away, beyond Their reach. Until the Gods touch me again . . . well, I'm not sure if I still am. All I know is, I'm happy to be back home, however much things may have changed in my absence."

The boy nodded again. "I know what that's like. I miss the Retreat, sometimes. But I like being among other kids. It's more fun, out here. Do you do sword fighting, or are you like Aunt Kelly and do the non-sword stuff?"

"Non-sword stuff, but I'm not nearly as good at it as she is," Hope confessed, smiling. She turned her attention to the man next to him, his reddish blond hair pulled back from his face by a leather thong. Next to him sat a woman with long black hair and piercing gold eyes. "And *you* are Trevan, the Master Artificer in the family, and your lady is the lovely Amara. Mayor of the new city."

"Lovely, high-strung, and opinionated," Amara amended wryly. "If you've the time, I've several questions to ask you about the layout of the old Harbor City, down in the western cove. We've redone the layout, but your input is welcome."

"I'd be delighted to answer what I can, but it's been over five years from my own perspective, and two centuries from yours. Now . . . the other redhead is Koranen, Morganen's twin," Hope continued. "And the lady next to you is Danau . . . and in between you and Trevan in birth order is the missing sixth brother, Rydan. And . . . um . . . don't tell me—Rora!" she remembered. "That's his lady's name. Rora is Amara's sister, and Serina and Mariel are *like* sisters, but it's an honorary thing, not a birthright or a blood-right . . . right?"

"Very good!" Morganen praised her. He leaned in, pressing a soft kiss to her temple, then slid his hand down her back to her waist, guiding her toward one of the empty seats.

No sooner had he pulled out the selected chair than the door opened and two more people entered. One was a woman with light brown hair about the same shade as Morganen's, the other a man with locks almost as long and dark as Amara's. They nodded at the others and headed for the far end of the table from Kelly. Ignoring the chair held for her, Hope shifted to intercept the new couple.

"You must be Rora. I'm Hope." She held out her hand in impulsive greeting.

The other woman dropped her green eyes to the outstretched palm, and her welcoming smile faltered. The man at Rora's side frowned and touched her elbow. Retracting her hand, Hope cleared her throat. "Sorry. I forgot. And you're Rydan."

"Forgot what?" Rydan asked sharply, narrowing his dark eyes warily.

Hope glanced around the room, making sure the only ones in there were family before she answered. "I forgot that she isn't supposed to be touched, given what she still carries. I wanted to thank—"

"You *told* her about that?" Rydan demanded, glaring at his youngest brother.

Instinct prompted Hope to step between them, hands going to her denim-clad hips. "No, he *didn't*. Or rather, he didn't *have* to. I *already* knew about it two hundred years ago."

The tall, black-clad brother frowned down at her. "What?"

"Ah, Rydan, this is Hope," Morganen interjected, making the introduction. "We forgot to tell you about her."

"I've already seen her before, through your mirror?" Rydan retorted.

"What he's trying to tell you is that I'm *more* than just Hope O'Niell," Hope said, recapturing his attention. "I also used to be Madam Mist."

"*You're* Madam Mist?" he repeated, flicking his hand at her. "But . . . you're from another universe! How can you be the voice of the last Guardian of Nightfall?"

"I am, or rather was, Duchess Haupanea, Guardian of Nightfall. I was displaced when the destruction of the last Convocation also shattered the Portalways. Of course, I didn't *know* I was going to be displaced, but I did know I had to prepare the Fountain for your own Guardianship. That's why I had Lady Abeyda lay all those spells. As I said, I wanted to thank you for taking care of the Fountain of Nightfall," Hope told him. "I'd, um, also like a tour of the Underhalls at some point soon, to see how much more work has to be done to turn it into a suitable temple for the Convocation. We have to have a suitable home for the Gods as part of the overall preparations."

"Wait—you *knew* Nightfall was going to be the new home of the Convocation?" Kelly demanded, rising from her seat at the far end of the long, food-laden table. "Why didn't you tell *me* all of this?"

"Because I *couldn't*?" Hope reminded her friend pertly. "It just wasn't ever the right time or the right place. Not to mention I didn't know if you'd even succeed or not until Morg told me about *her* existence last week, when we discussed *his* little temper fit over what it will take to create the Gateway of Heaven." She poked her thumb at Rora first, then at Rydan.

"Not that! I meant, how did you know there has to be 'a suitable home for the Gods'?" Kelly asked her. "We only found out about the ceremony when Danau brought us a copy of the Scroll of Living Glory from Menomon."

"From Menomon?—Didn't you read the one in my scroll-cupboard?" Hope asked, eyeing her friend.

Kelly frowned. "What scroll-cupboard?"

"The one up in my old quarters, the ducal chamber above the donjon hall? The place where Morg says you and Saber are now sleeping? It looked like a wardrobe, only it had racks of scrolls stuffed into it," Hope told her. "Surely you noticed it?"

Kelly gave her a blank look.

Evanor shook his head. "It might have been one of the 'unnecessary' bits of furniture we moved out of there, back when we cleaned up the chamber for your use, Kelly. If I remember right, we only glanced briefly through the chests and wardrobes to look for possible clothes you could wear, before shifting most of it down to the attics for storage. I'd say most of your things ended up in the attics," he told Hope. "Either that, or they were tossed out by the previous exilees that might have lived here."

"I think I remember a cabinet with scrolls," Wolfer offered. "But I don't remember which attic it went into."

"You don't *remember*?" Hope groaned. "Do you know how many attics and crawlspaces this place *has*? Kelly, all of my dream-scrolls were in that cupboard! My scryings, my Prophecies—the indemnity clause for paying all those damages! How could you have missed the significance of all that?"

"Because I'm *not* from this planet?" Kelly shot back.

"Hope, don't worry. If it's still in the palace, we will find it," Morganen reassured the woman at his side as she groaned again, covering her face with her hands. "Eventually . . ."

"What I'd like to know is the answer to Kelly's earlier question," Saber stated. "How did you know that the Convocation would be reinstated on Nightfall?"

"And don't tell us *you* foresaw it in some Seer's vision," Rydan added. "There are too many chambers down there, from too many *decades* that someone spent carving them out of solid granite, for it to have been started in *your* lifetime."

"It *wasn't* me. The work started with Seer Telandro," Hope explained, lowering her hands to her sides. "My, um . . . sixteenth-great-grandfather . . . seventeenth—the third Duke of Nightfall. Nauvea visited him in a dream-sending, foretelling how Nightfall would be a future home to the Convocation of the Gods.

"That was about four hundred . . . sorry, *six* hundred years ago." She felt her cheeks flush as she corrected herself, and tucked her hands into her back pockets, shrugging. "Anyway, after that visitation, gifted masons and stone carvers on the Isle would find themselves visited by Nauvea. Not like a Seer in direct touch with the Gods, mind you, but . . . they would find themselves impelled to come work in the caverns that eventually were hollowed into the Underhalls."

"Nauvea is a Goddess?" Rydan asked her, frowning. "I've never heard of her."

"The Goddess of Dreaming—an old God, mostly forgotten

even by my day, but She was the former Patron of Nightfall, and the Patron of my family," Hope explained.

"All this time, I've been impelled by a . . . a half-dead Goddess?" Rydan asked, confusing Hope. At her puzzled look, he explained. "Ever since I found those halls under the northern mountains, I've been *compelled* to carve these images, some horrible, some sublime, and very few of them scenes from anything I've ever personally seen."

"From the sound of it, I'd certainly say so," Hope agreed, giving him a shrug. She couldn't stop the smile that spread her lips, not when a single refrain kept echoing back and forth between her heart and her head. *He's been compelled by my Goddess—been visited by Nauvea—which means She's still alive . . . !*

"This is all very fascinating, but Danau and I have spent a very long day trying to get the city ready for the Desalinator's revival. And while we stand here chatting, our food is getting cold," Amara pointed out. "Not that it's a bad thing in the summer, but the flavors are best when they're fresh."

Morganen held one of the chairs again for Hope before settling down in the one next to her. Rydan held a chair for his lady as well, though his gaze remained on Hope's face. "So . . . you really are Madam Mist? I must thank you in turn."

"Thank me?" Hope asked him, curious.

"By setting things up as you did, instructing me on what to do with the island's Fountain, you gave me a sanctuary, a place to hide from the rest of the world when I needed it most. Even if you had to do it through temporally preserved spells. I am . . . very grateful for it. I'll have to find some way to repay the favor," Rydan added dryly.

"Keep your favors for your own wife," Morg ordered his brother. "She's the one who figured out *why* you needed a sanctuary."

"Jealousy? From you?" Rydan arched a brow. His query was brief, but it was pointed enough to make both Morg and Hope blush. Smirking at his youngest brother, Rydan accepted the bowl of fresh-picked greens Amara passed his way.

Morg glared at his sibling. Hope touched his wrist, giving him a reassuring smile. Pausing long enough to serve herself from the bowls and platters being passed around the table, she picked up her fork with her right hand and shifted her left one down to Morganen's white-clad thigh. That distracted him from his irritation.

"Speaking of your wife, Rydan, you really do need to let the extraction ceremony happen," Hope said, changing the subject.

Rydan lost his smile faster than the glow of a lightglobe could be double-rapped off. "I will *not* endanger my wife!"

His cold, hard assertion didn't intimidate her. "You will, because she will *not* be endangered—don't argue with me! I know the others have been trying to get you to agree; Morg told me all about it. Your concerns are valid, but I Prophesied her survival, and I have never once been wrong."

"When did you Prophesy that?" Rydan challenged her. "Show me the letter—recite me the verse!"

"I *would*, if someone hadn't packed all my Prophecies into the *attics*," she retorted, slanting a glance in Kelly's direction. "Giolana wrote it down on a scroll about two years before I vanished. It went something along the lines of . . . *the joining of dusk with the joining of dawn*, something, something about *waiting long* . . ." Rubbing at her forehead, Hope struggled to recall what her younger self had recited, gripped by a visit from her Patron. "Um . . . *Freed from brief death at the hands of the wise* . . . *Brought forth in triumph, the Gods shall return; with burden abated, and* . . . something, something, I can't remember . . . um, *the offering accepted, new age shall arise* . . . or something like that."

Rydan rolled his dark eyes.

"What? I can't help it if Nauvea fancied Herself a poet! Look, the important thing is, most of it spoke fairly clearly of the Convocation shifting from Aiar to Nightfall," Hope argued. "Morg told me that your bride's nickname from Seer Draganna's Prophecy was the 'Dawn', and that you're associated with the onset of night. So it makes sense that, if Rora's a Living Host and she has to go through the extraction process, that she's the one 'freed from brief death' at the hands of someone knowledgeable about such things," Hope explained. "Morg *also* mentioned there's a Witch on the island.

"Everyone knows the Witches of Darkhana are the wisest in all matters pertaining to the shifting balance of life and death. You truly have no cause for concern, what with all these signs and portents coming together to ensure her survival," she told Rydan.

"Up until a few weeks ago, none of us had heard anything about Darkhana, other than that it was somewhere west of Fortuna," Kor stated. "You're asking us to place our faith in something we don't understand."

"You forgot that the Portals collapsed after you left," Morg added. "Without a quick and easy means of cross-continental travel, Katan has grown rather isolated over the last two hundred years."

"I wasn't exactly in a position to notice that," Hope returned dryly. "Suffice to say, in my day, we knew what a Witch could do. Considering their kingdom is at least half as old as Fate's Empire, I seriously doubt they've forgotten all those abilities in a mere two hundred years."

Rydan sulked. There was no other way to describe the almost pouting glower he gave the food on his plate. Rora touched his arm, drawing his attention to her. His expression softened a little, then hardened as he pinned Hope with a hard stare. "Can you *promise* she will survive?"

Hope gestured with her free hand, the one holding her fork, since the other was trapped nicely between Morg's palm and thigh. "I am just a mouthpiece of the Gods, Rydan. A mouthpiece half a decade out of practice. But from what I learned of Prophesying while I Saw . . . I'd say, yes. All the signs are coming together. If you take the appropriate precautions, she *will* survive."

Again, he sulked, though this time it was more thoughtful than petulant. A heavy exhalation was followed by a terse nod. "*Fine.*

We'll go through with it. Tomorrow, after breakfast. But I'm holding *you* personally responsible, should anything go wrong. And *only*
if Rora agrees to go through with it."

His wife touched his arm again. Meeting his dark, worried gaze,
she nodded. "I know I have to do this, Rydan. I can't live with this
thing inside of me forever. It's too dangerous to keep within me,
and too useful if we extract it. Since it must be done, I'll put my
trust in the Gods that I'll survive."

"If anything does go wrong, Rydan, I'll pass along my own complaints to the Gods as well as yours—*Gods*," Hope exclaimed softly,
but from her heart. "It feels so *good* to be able to *talk* about these
things!"

"What things?" Morganen asked her.

"*These* things. I used to sit at the dinner table in the room across
from this one, discussing Prophecies with Mother and Father, with
Niktor, Abeyda—even my scribes chimed in whenever they thought
they saw a possible interpretation of my Foreseeings. But if I'd tried
doing that in the other world . . ." Digging into her salad, Hope
shook her head and sighed. "Suffice to say, I am *very* glad to be home
again, back where everything is logical instead of *techno*logical—
and where no one will look at me strangely just because I hear
voices in my head!"

One of the other women chuckled faintly at that, but Hope
didn't know which one. It wasn't Kelly; she knew her friend's voice
too well, and that wasn't it. Morg squeezed her hand in gentle comfort, making her smile at him. It didn't matter whose sense of humor she had tickled, so long as she had amused the man at her side.

"So . . . did your brothers take over the other towers for their
own workrooms?" Hope asked him, glancing briefly over her shoulder as she strolled around the chamber.

Cabinets and shelves lined half of the walls, some stuffed with
books, most cluttered with pots, jars, caskets, and sacks of spell

components. Cabinets filled part of the remaining space, with who knew what behind their wooden doors. Three tables occupied part of the floor space, while the rest was broad and smooth, painted a flat gray suitable for scribbling runes with chalk.

Magic usually worked better with some sort of focus material, something to imbue with the life force of the mage and contain it. Runes could shape the spells, but they were usually temporary, marked in chalk or ink on a surface. The rare permanent ones were either carved in specially prepared materials, or carved by specially prepared blades. Ointments and salves could be applied or infused, and there were hundreds of ways to make amulets, sigils, talismans, Artifacts . . . thousands of ways, she knew.

"Saber thought it best if we didn't set ourselves up to accidentally destroy the palace. Koranen came the closest to it," Morg added, mouth quirking in a fond smile for his Pyromancer twin. "Both he and Saber have forges attached to their bases, as does Rydan, though Rydan's tower is almost completely empty. Most of what he does, he's done in secret down in the . . . what did you call them?"

"The Underhalls," she said, idly picking up a book.

Morg watched her fingers caress the carved wooden panels of the cover, admiring her gentle curiosity. She set it down, only to pick up the top one of a second stack. He dragged his attention back to the topic at hand. "Trevan's workrooms are even more cluttered than mine, but then, he focuses a lot of his attention on Artifact construction. Dominor does a lot of rune-work and spell designing. Kor and Rydan both forge sigils—you'll probably be receiving sleep-wards and fire-wards for your bedchamber from them, soon. But Koranen does a variety of fire-based spell-work, while Saber makes a lot of weapons and armor.

"Rydan works predominantly in stone. Lately, that's meant raising a lot of the frames for all the new buildings down in the city. Wolfer . . . he has a tannery set up in his tower. He's the weakest of the eight of us, magic-wise, though he's as strong as the average mage. Serina is weaker than Dominor, Mariel comes after her, somewhere around Evanor's level, and Alys is the weakest of the three women who can cast magic—I don't count Rora, as all of her magic is spent in containing her Fountain.

"Evanor does instrument-crafting and other sonic magics—a lot of it those *ray-dee-oh* music boxes you and Kelly told me about. They're a luxury item, but they're selling madly on the mainland," Morg added. "In fact, we just had a series of performances in the new concert hall over the last few nights, and Evanor managed to record some of it for sale. Sound-based spells take well to brass, though it's not always easy to get the metals for the alloy. The mainland is still being a pain about permitting certain kinds of trade with us."

"Centuries may come and go, empires may rise and fall, but bureaucracies will always be a pain," Hope commiserated. "And your own kind of magic?" she asked, moving over to one of the shroud-draped mirrors. "What do you specialize in?"

"Well, I can do most everything that my brothers can do—we had the same teachers—but I also do a lot more potions work than them. Though not nearly as many as Mariel does, as a Healer."

Hope inhaled and smiled. "Mm, yes. This room has a nice herby scent to it." Moving to a short, blank stretch of wall next to the covered mirrors, she lifted her hand, palm gliding an inch or two from the age-worn stones. "What's behind here?"

He hadn't expected that. "You can sense that?"

"Yes. I never knew just how sensitive I could be to magic, until I was exiled for four years. And then you opened that doorway to the other world, and I could sense every time you opened the Veil, and let all that magic leak through." Rubbing her fingers together, she lowered her hand. "It was like being locked out in the cold for far too long. Eventually, you get used to the numbing ache of it . . . but the first time the sun kisses you with its rays, or you run across a bit of fire-heated metal . . . it stands out to you.

"I expect my sensitivity will go away in a few weeks. But you didn't answer my question," she reminded him, turning to face the mage. "What's behind this wall?"

For anyone else, Morganen wouldn't have answered with the truth. But every sign pointed to Hope . . . Haupanea . . . as his Destined bride. Even he knew a husband shouldn't keep important secrets from his impending wife. "I built a short-Portal to a set of caverns I've excavated under the southern mountain range."

Her dark brown brows rose at that. "A short-Portal? I thought that, after the Shattering, Portals couldn't exist anymore. That the aether was too disturbed, and that the knowledge of how to create and maintain them had atrophied from Katani mage-lore."

"It wasn't a widely known art in Katan to begin with," Morganen admitted. "But it's still actively practiced and taught all the way up in Fortuna . . . so I 'borrowed' a few tomes on the subject from certain well-stocked libraries shortly after we arrived here. I needed to, in order to create my personal library. I knew there wasn't enough room in the palace to store all the books I wanted, or enough room for crafting the blank tomes I would need. Not without my brothers noticing."

"Ah. So . . . how many books *do* you have?" Hope asked him, tilting her head.

The coquettish tilt made her curls brush against her cheek, making Morg wish he could do the same with his fingers. *Wait . . . why can't I? Just because she's supposed to seduce me to make up for lying to me, that doesn't mean I can't court her right back . . .*

He shrugged, strolling closer to her. "Probably close to ten thousand books, if not more. I read six or seven a day, on average." Lifting his hand, Morg gently tucked her locks behind her ear. "Possibly around two thousand scrolls, too, maybe a little less. It's harder to get my hands on enough good leather for scroll parchment than it is wood pulp for book paper. I've had to adapt quite a few copying spells to be able to transfer text from scroll sheets to bound pages."

Hope chuckled. "You sound even worse than me. I would have brought more books across if I could have, but I didn't want to steal away all of your wheat. Or send across too much living matter versus nonliving."

"If you want more books, we can always send across bags of sand," Morg offered, shrugging. "That's innocuous enough."

"Maybe we can do that, sometime." Her hand lifted to his hair, brushing back the lighter brown strands. The feel of her fingers against his skin, gentle and warm, made him shiver. She smiled, her brown eyes gleaming. "I kept wondering what you looked like. I knew you'd be something like your eldest brother, and you did describe your hair and your eyes . . . but what I see now is even better than what I'd imagined."

Morg blushed. He wasn't strong and confident-looking like Saber, or muscular like Wolfer; he didn't have the commanding presence of Dominor, or the smooth, eloquent voice of Evanor. He lacked Trevan's red hair and charm, certainly didn't have the brooding air of mystery that Rydan projected, and even his own twin had a cheerful, youthful appeal that was hard to duplicate. Hearing that she found *him* attractive made Morg blush with pleasure.

The fingers caressing his jaw slid below his ear, delving into the hair at the nape of his neck. Hope tugged him close, tilting her face up to his. Willing, Morganen obliged her by tipping his own head. But she stopped before their lips came within a finger width, withdrawing slightly.

"This isn't too forward of me, is it? By modern standards?" she hesitantly asked him.

"No, not at—" Before he could finish "all," she captured his mouth with a warm, slow kiss.

This was what he missed. With the arrival of Kelly and the others, he had finally been able to enjoy the delights of female companionship again—the way a woman thought in intricate little twists and turns, the way they cared for others with gentle strength, their attention to details, and their little comforts and touches that made a home out of a mere shelter. But this, the physical side of courtship, he hadn't had in a very long time.

Arms slipping around her back, Morganen cradled her curves against his body. Soft and scented, warm and womanly. A hint of the honey-*cinnin* pastry they'd eaten at dessert. Her faint moan as she opened her mouth, tongue flicking and gliding against his as she tasted him in return. Even the way she pressed her hips and thighs against his, unafraid to touch him as fully as possible, all of it thrilled and pleased him.

Losing himself in the kiss, Morganen slid his hands down her back, pulling their loins closer together. His fingers slipped over the rough waistband of her trousers, then bumped into the pockets stitched in back. For a moment, he was disconcerted, unable to move them any lower, until he realized his hands were perfectly placed to keep her against him. It proved useful when she ended the kiss, pulling back slightly.

Feeling his hands in her jeans pockets, Hope quirked one of her brows in amusement. "I take it you've found my pockets?"

He wriggled his fingers, adopting a thoughtful look. "Yes, I think I have. They're much nicer than a belt-pouch, for certain things."

"Good." She smiled at him, then wrinkled her nose and lifted a hand, covering a yawn. "Pardon me. Your company isn't boring in the least. But it's been a very long day—a couple of hours' difference between here and there on top of everything—and I'm afraid I'm kind of tired."

"Then I shall escort you safely back to your room," Morg promised. The physical ache she had stirred was bearable; part of his heart was equally disappointed, but it was soothed when she bobbed up on her toes and kissed him quickly.

"Thank you. We will continue *this* conversation another time, yes?" she asked, giving him a hopeful, teasing look.

Morg didn't need to be coaxed. Kissing her back, he released his hands from her pockets, turning to guide her back out of his tower. "Most definitely."

Forewarned through a note Kelly had sent down into the city the previous night, Priestess Ora joined the Nightfall family for breakfast. The Darkhanan Witch looked much like she always did, her blonde hair plaited into a coronet on her head and the hooded, black, deep-sleeved robe draped over her shoulders that she always wore, regardless of the weather.

In concession to the clearing skies and rising temperature outside, the robe hung open, revealing a light green, knee-length tunic and beige trousers. With her feet wrapped in leather sandals and no signs or symbols of her holy order about her, she didn't look like she had prepared herself for a major ceremony. In fact, she had dressed remarkably like Morganen had, save for that black overrobe thing.

Rydan eyed her warily, his eyes rimmed red, but said nothing during the meal. He ate with his left hand, the right one entwined with Rora's. Morganen watched Rydan just as carefully. If the sixthborn of his brothers was going to protest against the coming extraction, it would happen within the next half hour. But Rydan didn't say anything; his wife ate in similar silence, focusing her right-handed attention on her food.

Kelly wiped at her mouth with her napkin and set it down. "If it's alright with you, I'd like to be on hand for this extraction thing. Any objections?"

"I want Morg there, as well." Rydan slanted his youngest brother a look that let Morg know he was wanted for "containment" reasons, just in case the priestess had some personal agenda.

"I'd like Hope to be there. She might Foresee any complications that might arise," Rora added.

Hope, prying the meat from the tough, leathery shell of a *cidine* fruit, blushed. She didn't contradict the other woman, but didn't think she would See much. Not when she hadn't heard any Gods whispering to her since her return to this world.

"Saber, are you interested in coming?" Kelly asked her husband.

He shook his head. "I would, but water rationing started last night. I have to make the rounds with the city constables, making sure people are saving water instead of wasting it."

"I'm torn between coming with you to oversee my sister's safety and doing my duty to the city along with Saber," Amara admitted. The black-haired woman nibbled on her lower lip a moment, then shook her head slowly. "I have to trust you fully at some point in time . . . and the city needs me. Unless you need me, Sister?"

Rora shook her head. "I'll be fine. Rydan and Morg can keep me safe enough. And you are needed down at the harbor, particularly with water rationing in effect."

"If it gets as hot as it did a few days ago, it's going to be hard to keep people from turning on the cold-water pipes in their houses. Someone has to go door-to-door, offering to cast cooling charms," Koranen added, glancing at the short, slender woman at his side. "I can cast some of those myself. I know you have to oversee the scrubbing and refurbishing of the latticeways, Danau, but if it does get hot . . ."

"Let me guess. I'll be the most popular girl in town," she muttered, rolling her blue eyes.

"So, where are we going to do the extraction?" Kelly asked the others.

"Not in the Fountain Hall," Rydan stated. "But . . . somewhere underground. Somewhere secure."

"Somewhere comfortable, for Rora's sake," Ora added, speaking for the first time since her arrival. "Somewhere with room to maneuver, as well."

"The amphitheater would be a good place," Hope offered. "It's that tiered, circular room not far from the Fountain Hall. It has benches to lie upon, though no one in the family wanted to go to the expense of bringing down cushions without knowing when Nightfall would actually host the Convocation."

"I can always bring the lounging couch from my workroom," Trevan offered.

Rydan eyed his twin skeptically. "Considering what I know about you and that couch, you can keep it up there. I'll fetch something of my own. You, Priestess, do you need any herbs or holy symbols for this . . . soul-saving ability of yours? Any chants or ceremonies?"

"Everything I'll need, I already carry with me," Ora reassured him.

Rydan hesitated a long moment. Morganen could almost feel his taciturn sibling's struggle, then the sixthborn brother nodded.

"Let's get this over with . . . but if you cannot do as you say you can, I *will* blame you for her death," he told the northerner.

"Understood," Ora agreed calmly.

Evanor frowned at the others as they started to rise from the table. "Saber, Kelly, need I remind you that it's *your* turn to clear the table? Prophecy or not, we are *not* going back to living like pigs."

The boy, Mikor, snickered, though he carefully didn't look at any of the adults.

Giving his nephew an annoyed look, the eldest of the brothers started gathering up the breakfast dishes. "We need to hire more servants."

Morganen waited impatiently for Rydan to finish murmuring to Rora. Not that he cared to rush the extraction of the Fountain she carried inside of her, not when the only way to relinquish the singularity from her unconscious control was to kill the poor woman. It was just that, the longer they waited amid the heavily carved, gray white splendor of the amphitheater, the more chance there was for Rydan to change his mind.

The only way Morg's family could assert their independence as a fully fledged kingdom was to have Divine Patronage. With the independent, egalitarian-minded Kelly as their incipient queen, that meant requesting Patronage of all the Gods and Goddesses in this universe, since the outworld-raised woman refused to demand that anyone on Nightfall worship a specific deity.

But to get the Patronage of Heaven itself, they had to open the Gateway to Heaven. That required combining two Fountains. Normally, Fountains anchored themselves into a particular place shortly after their Living Hosts died, but if the correct spells were performed, a portable Fountain could be created. The trick was to extract the Fountain from within Rora without permanently killing her.

The first phase of the extraction process had already been completed. Rydan was Rora's Guardian, attuned to the powerful magics of the singularity born into her body. That singularity came with natural, inborn protections, but that meant either they waited for Rora to die of natural causes, or her Guardian used his attunement to circumvent those protections.

Morg didn't blame his brother for his reluctance, not when extracting the Fountain required Rydan to kill his own wife.

Unfortunately, if they didn't succeed in attaining Patronage within the next handful of months, the mainland would be legally free to quell the Nightfall "rebellion" by violent means, threatening everyone else's lives. If they didn't extract Rora's singularity, separating the Fountain from its Host, she would continue to be the target of every power-hungry mage who had ever heard a whisper of her existence. It had only been a few days since the last such attack, in fact.

Nor had the mage Yarrin been the only threat. Right after Morg, Kor, and Danau had conquered that problem, one of the Counselors of Katan, Lord Consus, had contacted Morganen to warn him of an expedition from the distant land of Mendhi, birthplace of the written word. The Councilor of Sea Commerce wasn't supposed to help Nightfall in any way . . . but not to tell them of the Mendhites' plot to steal away the Living Host and hopefully murder Queen Kelly in the process had been too much for the middle-aged mage's conscience.

The longer Rydan delayed in going through with this extraction, the longer all of them would be in danger. It was with relief that Morg saw his elder brother tenderly kiss Rora's fingers, then her lips, before straightening away from the padded bench he had found for her to rest upon. His voice, deep and dark with tightly controlled emotion, echoed slightly off the walls.

"Are you ready, priestess?"

Ora lowered the scroll in her hands, a carefully made copy of the Scroll of Living Glory, brought all the way from the archives of the Guardian of the underwater city of Menomon. Supposedly there was another copy of the Scroll somewhere on Nightfall, but Morg couldn't fault the chain of events that had brought this particular piece of parchment to the island. Not when Danau had turned out to be the perfect woman for his power-plagued twin.

"Before I begin," she stated, "there is something, or rather, someone I must show you." Rolling up the scroll in her hands, she passed it to Kelly to hold. Ora took the time to fully close the black robe she wore. When the front edges were fully overlapped, she lifted her hands to the deep hood draped down her back and spoke. "The power to preserve a soul is granted not to the Host half of a Darkhanan Witch, but to the Guide half.

"It is the Guide who is dead, and thus it is the Guide who holds most of the knowledge of and control over the realm of the Dark, the place that all souls must cross before they can reach the Afterlife. To ensure that your wife will not be alarmed by his presence, I would like to introduce my Guide to all of you, before we begin."

"*His* presence?" Rydan asked her.

She flicked the hood over her head, hiding her face, and tucked her hands up the deep, long sleeves of the robe. A slight stoop of her body hid even her feet from view, then she straightened again and lifted the cowl from her . . . or rather, *his* face. The slender, blonde-haired, green-eyed mage-priestess had somehow transformed herself into a taller, broad-shouldered, black-haired, blue-eyed man.

Bowing slightly in greeting, the man in the robe addressed them. "Greetings. I am Niel—no need to bother with introductions," he added as Kelly drew in a breath to speak. "Whatever Ora sees, I have seen; whatever she hears, I have also heard."

"Okay, we can skip the introductions," Kelly allowed, eyeing him askance. "But . . . *how* did she just . . . er, you . . . You're not even the same size!" the redheaded woman complained. "And aren't you, well, dead?"

Niel chuckled. His grin made him seem wholly alive and very human. "Technically, this is still my wife's body. It is merely shape-shifted by holy magics to appear as my own."

"Ora is your *wife?*" Rora asked, giving voice to the confusion in the others' faces. "How is that even possible?"

"To shorten a very long story, we went through a marriage ceremony so that Ora could claim one of my inheritances shortly after we were joined . . . and grew to love each other very much over the years—that is a reassurance to *you*," he added, nodding to Rydan. "Given how protective I have seen you be toward your wife, I would not want you to suffer any troublesome thoughts, knowing that I must take her soul into my arms. She will be as safe with me as if she were my blood sister."

"Oh!"

The soft exclamation came from Hope, so softly that Morg didn't think anyone else heard it. He slanted her a curious look, but she shook her head, dismissing his silent question. Resolving to ask her later, Morg watched as the man Niel covered his head and hands again, stooping to include his feet. A moment later, he—or rather, she—straightened and revealed her coronet-braided hair again.

"Once I have physically embraced your wife, I will nod when Niel has also embraced her soul. At that point, you will use the first spell to put her to sleep and the second spell to slow and stop her heart. According to the Scroll, the singularity will then manifest, rising from her chest. At that point, you must cast the third spell to transfer it into the special power crystal, as outlined in the text. You did bring the crystal?"

Rydan winced. "No. But it's not far from here."

"I'll introduce Rora to the sensation of her soul being touched by my Guide while we wait," Ora offered. "It can be unnerving if you aren't expecting it."

"Do not start the extraction without me," Rydan ordered, striding for one of the archways leading up out of the tiered hall.

"As if we could," Ora muttered dryly. Crossing to the padded bench, she nodded to Rora. "The sensation of being soul-touched can vary. You might experience a ticklish feeling underneath your skin, or a kind of pressure in your lungs. You might see things behind your eyelids, even with your eyes wide-open. But most of all, you'll be able to hear Niel's thoughts as though he were speaking deep inside your ears."

Morg choked.

"Impossible!" he rasped, coughing. "That's against the Laws of God and Man! No one can hear another's thoughts. Only the Gods can do that!"

"The Laws of God and Man state that no *living mortal* may hear the thoughts of another *living mortal*," Ora corrected him. "Niel is quite dead, for all that he may have seemed very much alive a moment ago. I myself cannot hear the thoughts of another living being, though I can and do share my thoughts with *him*, whenever both of us will it—I assure you, this ability is not one he treats casually, nor will he exploit it. Whatever thoughts you may have during this experience, Rora, Niel will hold them in the strictest of confidence."

Doubt creased Rora's forehead. She mulled over the priestess' words for several long seconds before finally sighing. "It's not as if I have a feasible choice. This thing I carry, if it stays inside of me, it threatens everyone around me, far more than it would threaten us if I do allow it to be extracted. Just . . . don't tell Rydan."

"I'm not that stupid," Kelly snorted. "None of us are."

Nodding agreement, the Darkhanan priestess offered her hand to Rora. The former Shifterai woman clasped it—and power *arced* between the two of them. Morg stared, wide-eyed with shock, as bright light seared out of Rora, thrusting itself into Ora. Fine, golden strands frizzed out around her head, ruining the sleek, circular plait of her braid.

She wrenched her fingers free after a moment, ending the connection. Lifting a shaking palm to her head, she smoothed down the hairs as best she could, though they resisted her efforts. "I . . . uh . . . That's never happened before . . . *Why* were you trying to give me all that power? I didn't ask for it."

"She wasn't," Morganen answered for the dazed woman seated on the bench. "It was an accident. One that's happened before. I don't know why, but the one time *I* touched her, by accident, her power shoved itself into me—your hair's not going to go down on its own," he added as the priestess tried using both hands to quell the static.

"I *definitely* wasn't expecting that," Ora confessed, her light alto voice shaking slightly. Even her hands trembled when she stared at them. "Is this going to keep happening if I touch her again?"

"Quite possibly." Lifting the wrist encircled by his cryslet, Morganen flipped open the hinged lid of the communications bracelet. Tapping the numbers for Rydan's cryslet, he waited for his brother to open the connection. As soon as he saw Rydan's dark eyes, he spoke. "Bring all of the crystals you and Koranen seeded. We're going to need them."

The view of Rydan's face jiggled a little as he adjusted his end of the small, hinged scrying mirrors. "All three? Why?"

"Remember what happened to Rora and me, when we accidentally touched? The priestess, here, suffers from the same problem. We may need the spare crystals for containment."

Rydan grunted something and snapped the lid shut on his end. Morganen closed his own cryslet.

"You say you have the same problem?" Ora asked him, still absently smoothing down the hairs on her head. She frowned thoughtfully at him, then held out one of her hands. "Touch me."

"I'm not like Rora," Morganen warned her, crossing the dais. "I won't thrust my power into you."

"But if you react like me, then you're like me. You're a powerful mage, aren't you?" she asked.

"Very," he agreed, taking her hand in his. The moment he did so, Morganen could *feel* the energies buzzing under her skin, too much power to contain comfortably for long. He also felt her pushing some of that energy at him. Aware of how she felt, he accepted the influx of magic, until the pressure leveled out between them. It didn't take long for the hairs at the back of his neck to start prickling, but his hair didn't fluff out. Her own straggling strands sagged, turning limp and lifeless once again.

"As I thought," Ora said, freeing her hand. "Because of the way you and I access magic, we are capable of becoming conduits for great power. But we cannot do so for more than a few seconds at most. We're not Seers. Unfortunately, this poses a problem." She turned her attention back to Rora. "In order to enact the extraction ceremony, I must touch you physically for several minutes. But if I cannot touch you safely for more than a few seconds at a time . . ."

"What if both of you were to touch her?" Hope asked, joining the conversation. "Wouldn't that halve the power being thrust into each of you? I may not be a mage, but I *was* a Fountain Guardian for a while. The strength of magic and the ability to withstand it follow an exponential curve. Maybe, if the two of you shared the burden, you could last for more than a minute?"

"Actually . . . if we touch Rora, *and* touch you," Morganen offered as inspiration struck, "then maybe *you* could siphon off some of that excess energy. Seers are born with the ability to harbor the power of the Gods Themselves. By comparison, surely a single Fountain isn't too much trouble?"

"A single Fountain *isn't* a trouble; I just cannot *do* anything with the magic I'd hold," Hope reminded him. "It has to be pre-purposed. Which begs the question, what *could* I do with it, if I were to be the repository of all that power?"

"Hold one of the crystals and channel the excess energies into it," Morg told her. "Ora has to concentrate on helping Niel hold Rora's soul. My job would be to try and bleed off more of the energies than she does, so that the two of them aren't too badly distracted. Your task would be to take all of that energy from both of us and stuff it into one of the crystals Rydan is bringing—if the two of us each holds one of your arms, Rora would be free to recline on the bench, and you would be free to hold the spare crystal in your hands. And then, um . . . Kelly could hold ready the crystal designated for the singularity, I suppose."

"Hello, I'm *not* a mage, remember? The last time I played around with magical powers, I blasted poor Rydan with a spell-reflective mirror, if you'll recall," Kelly chided him, touching the pouch slung at her waist.

"You don't have to be a mage to hold a power crystal," Ora reassured her. "You just have to make sure your hands are wrapped in enough layers of silk for insulation. The crystals should be handled solely by silk anyway, in order for them to remain untainted and unpurposed."

"Well . . . fine. But if I lose another finger because of this, I'm reserving the right to bitch about it," Kelly warned all of them. "Just because Morg successfully reattached the last one doesn't mean I'm interested in going through the experience a second time."

"Here, let us practice the theory," Ora offered, holding out her palm to Hope. "First we touch you, then we touch her. A short touch only, just enough to tell whether or not it will work."

Hope eyed the hand offered to her, then shrugged and clasped it. "Why not? But if I lose *my* finger, I reserve the right to yell. A lot. I've never lost a finger before, and I really don't want to."

Ora smiled. "Understood. Morganen? For a count of three?"

Taking Hope's other hand, Morg twined their fingers together, then held out his other hand to Rora, leaving the final step up to her. Ora offered her own as well. Bracing herself visibly, the woman on the bench gingerly touched their proffered palms. She gasped, power arcing out of her fingers and her forearms . . . but it was reduced on both sides. A crackle of writhing lightning, not the blinding brightness of before.

Three heartbeats after it began, Morg and Ora pulled their hands away from the Living Host. They both glanced reflexively at the Seer, still joined to them. Hope blinked a couple of times, then released their hands. Lifting her fingers to her curls, she patted them experimentally, then smiled wryly. "Well. That was a lot more tolerable than either of you made it look. I don't think I'd want to spend more than a minute or two doing that, not without some kind of outlet for all that energy . . . but it seems I'm still enough of a Seer to channel raw power."

"Good!" Ora praised. "Rora, did you hear Niel speaking to you, just now?"

"Yes . . . I could both hear and feel him. It was a little unnerving," Rora confessed, touching her chest with one hand. "Like a tickle around my lungs and a whisper right behind my head. But . . . not unbearable. Just unusual."

"The sensation will magnify once he actually embraces your soul," the priestess warned her. "But now that you're prepared for it, we can proceed as soon as your Guardian returns. Which brings us to the last part of the ceremony. Once the Fountain is extracted and embedded in the crystal, it will need to be moved. According to the Scroll of Living Glory, it should not be allowed to rest in one place for more than a few minutes at most for the first full turning of Brother Moon, and *never* be allowed to stay still for more than half an hour, ever."

"So I gathered," Kelly agreed, lifting the rolled-up scroll in her hands. "If it anchors itself in one place, we'll never be able to budge it again, and never be able to reopen the Gateway to Heaven. Without the Gateway, we cannot invoke the Convocation of the Gods.

On the plus side, keeping it moving around will make it difficult to track and steal. On the minus side . . . it does say that both the Guardian and the former Living Host will be able to access its powers, but does that mean only the two of them will ever be able to move it?"

"Unfortunately, no," Ora warned them. *"Anyone* will be able to pick up and move the crystal, provided it's carried in enough silk, or by a levitation spell. That's one of the reasons why the Convocation has moved from kingdom to kingdom over the millennia. The other is that the crystals do eventually age and shatter."

Morg narrowed his eyes. "What do you mean, shatter? Is that how the last Convocation was destroyed, by the crystal literally shattering and destroying the heart of the old Aian Empire?"

Ora blushed. It was a very odd sight, for the woman was normally very self-composed. "Um, no. That's *not* why the Empire Shattered. No, this is just a disintegration of the crystal itself. After about eight hundred years, it will crack, collapse into pieces, and release the singularity. The singularity becomes impossible to move without reinstalling it in a new crystal . . . but since it takes a full day to grow one, and only half an hour to anchor the singularity in one place, it usually just means a second permanent Fountain is formed."

"So, what? We need to come up with an 'official crystal mover' or something?" Kelly asked. "Or rather, a handful of people to take turns moving the crystal for a few hours each, to keep it from anchoring itself?"

Ora nodded. "That's what they had back in Aiar, a special, oath-bound priesthood dedicated to walking the last crystal through the labyrinthine corridors beneath the High Palace."

Rora frowned. "Wait . . . how could you know about that? I was *in* those old corridors and vaults, searching through the ruins beneath the Shifting City, and I never saw or read anything like that. How could you know all this?"

"As I told Her Majesty when I arrived, I am geased to appear before the Convocation of the Gods and tender an apology for something I did," Ora explained patiently. "I have studied all the records of the old Convocations that I could find, in anticipation of the day a new Convocation would arise. There are records of such things, if one knows where to look . . . and I have done a lot of looking, over the years."

Movement off to the side notified them of Rydan's return to the amphitheater. A large stone chest floated in his wake, a scrap of age-mottled, pink silk visible where it had been caught in the edge of the lid. Ora stepped back.

"Suffice to say, I know more about the old Convocations than most people now alive. I suggest, Your Majesty, that whoever you choose to 'walk the crystal,' you pick mages who can be oathbound by their own powers to simply move the crystal, and neither to abuse nor to abscond with it."

"I noticed there's a line in the Scroll, something about an oath the crystal-movers should take," Kelly agreed. "But there's a limited number of mages on the Isle, and only a dozen at most whom I'd trust, even with an oath."

Ora snorted. "Who said a mage had to move it? Wrap it in silk!"

"We'd have to completely trust whoever handled it," Morg pointed out. "Even I'd give one, to prove I was trustworthy."

"Well, whoever you choose, do it soon. Neither the Guardian nor the Living Host will be able to do it entirely on their own," Ora reminded them.

"What about you?" Kelly asked her. Morg eyed his sister-in-law askance. She explained herself. "You're here to ensure the Convocation is renewed. You are already compelled to be here, and compelled to protect the Fountain-imbued crystal from misuse. Would you take an oath to be one of the crystal-movers?"

Rydan reached the dais. The conversation, encountered past its midpoint, earned them a bemused look from the black-haired mage, but he quietly set the floating chest on the ground and waited for them to finish talking.

"I would not accept a *permanent* placement as a stone-walker," Ora demurred. "I do have a life elsewhere, one which I intend to return to once my business before the Gods is completed. But I could and would swear upon my very powers to do my share of safely walking it around until I have completed my business at the Convocation, and I will swear an additional oath to take no steps toward removing this particular Fountain-crystal from Nightfall's control, either before, during, or afterward."

"Then we'll start with Morg, Hope, Rydan, Rora . . . and you, for as long as you are here. And then Saber, Wolfer, Alys, Trevan . . . plus Dominor and Serina when they return from Natallia. Evanor, too," Kelly decided. "I'm not sure about Mariel, though. She's a Healer and could be called to tend to a patient at any time. We don't have enough Healers on the island to spare her for something as simple as 'dog walking', as it were. I don't think Amara can be oath-bound, as her magic doesn't work like a mage's. She's also too visible to be absent, as Mayor of Harbor City. The same with me."

"No one here doubts your trustworthiness, Kelly," Hope told her. "You're the very reason why we're trying to resurrect the Convocation. But you are right in that you couldn't be oathbound, whether or not it's necessary. You just don't have the magic for it. For myself, I can't be oathbound, either, because I don't have any magic of my own. I'm merely a conduit for it."

"Ah. Well, then you'd be exempt. Except I'd trust you to guard it with your life . . . so you're back on Fountain-walking duty. Sorry," Kelly apologized. "I can't be absent for too long without raising questions, but you can be. With . . ." Kelly paused long enough to flick out her fingers, counting, "twelve people, that's two hours of walking a day. That should be enough for the job, at least until we can figure out who else we'd trust enough for the job. It's a pity Baroness Teretha was murdered by that idiot Yarrin," she muttered, mouth twisting downward at the memory. "She would've been on the list, too."

"All of that presumes it is safe for *this* woman to touch my wife,"

Rydan reminded her. "If she reacts like Morganen did, that isn't safe."

"Don't worry, Rydan. We've figured out a way around it," Rora reassured him, patting his arm. She glanced at the others, hands knotting together in her lap. "Well . . . are we ready?"

Kelly unrolled the scroll still in her hands. "Let's just read through what passes for the instructions one last time, to be absolutely sure we know what we'll be doing."

free hand on the wall next to her shoulder. He leaned in close enough that he could feel her breath on his chin and throat and held her gaze. Somehow, he had to express what he felt in words. Normally he was eloquent, even glib with words, but it was hard to think when he was this close to her. When he could smell her, warm and slightly musky, somewhat flowery, and entirely *here*. Still, he tried.

"You *are* my best friend. You are also my predestined bride. The Gods may have sent you away, but *I* brought you back," he reminded her. At the skeptical quirk of her brow, Morg realized how possessive that sounded. Her culture—Kelly's culture, the one Hope had just spent five years fully immersed in—asserted equality for all people in all things. Acknowledging that, he said, "You *do* have a choice in the matter. You could walk away . . . and you *might* even convince me to not follow you. But I think you'd have to argue for a year and a day to get me to stop caring about you. Or at least, to stop pestering you. Maybe."

He smiled slightly to let her know he was teasing, at least in part. Having grown up with so many brothers, he had found females to be fascinating by contrast. But, of all the young girls he had befriended as a boy and the women he had known in his short adulthood before being exiled to Nightfall, it was this one who filled the corners of his life. He had occasionally sought the company of others, but only because he had thought of them at the time. Hope was always in his thoughts.

But how to let her know that? Probably by just telling her so, I guess. He licked his lips and inhaled, ready to try. The touch of her hand on his cheek, warm and light, stopped him. Her gaze had slid down to his mouth. Now her thumb grazed his lips, tracing their curves before dragging down his lower lip just a little. Distracted, he smiled. *So she wants my lips open, does she? Well, how about her own?*

One moment, she was examining his face, lit by the glow of the suncrystals embedded in the tunnel ceiling. The next, his head blotted out the light, and his mouth brushed against hers. It was an ambivalent kiss: On the one hand, it felt right and natural that he

Guide until today, let alone that they were married . . . But enough about her." Slipping behind him, Hope caught his free hand as she came up on his other side, twining their fingers together. "So. If Rydan and Rora are best friends, and Wolfer and Alys, and so on and so forth . . . would you say that you and I are best friends?"

Morg lifted a brow, giving her a questioning look. Not for lack of an answer, but to probe at her line of inquiry.

"I mean, do you think *we* could ever love each other that deeply, someday? As both best friends and lovers?" Hope clarified.

She knew her revelations about her past had changed things between them, but Morg had communicated with her for almost ten months in the other realm, and had done so almost every single day. Even if it was just a short note scrawled by one or the other of them on the whiteboard in her kitchen, trading a few lines back and forth, they had communicated. They had shared thoughts and dreams and found they had quite a lot in common, regarding how they viewed life. Though she wasn't going to ask for his forgiveness outright, she wanted to know if he was ready to head in that direction, or was still resentful of her deception.

Drawing in a breath to reply, it took Morganen a moment to realize why he was so ready to dismiss her concerns: Her past truly did not matter to him. This was the same woman he had talked with, laughed with, shared secrets with, even been scolded by . . . as a good friend should have rightfully scolded, particularly over his initial interference in Rydan and Rora's relationship.

Hope—Haupanea, Nea, whatever she chose—was still *his* Hope. His friend, and more. Shifting closer, he backed her up against one of the tunnel walls. It was carved in a long, single panel, depicting a rock-strewn desert, and Morg couldn't think of a less apt place for his revelation. Not when this woman had brought a richness into his life greater than even the greenest, leafiest ravine on the Isle. She was more than a mere friend to him. More than his Destiny, even.

"Morg?" Hope asked, looking concerned.

Mindful of the crystal slung over his shoulder, Morg braced his

FOUR

◦✤◦

"Sweet Nauvea—that *kiss*! For a moment, I thought he was about to jump her, right then and there!" Hope swore. She ran her palms over her scalp yet again, trying to smooth down the static-filled mess of dark brown curls, but it refused to deflate. "Not that I could blame him, what with her finally breathing again and all. I don't think *I* breathed until she did again."

"Same here," Morganen agreed. His own hair still crackled a bit from the extraction, but experience with the phenomenon suggested that only a solid bit of magery would get rid of the excess energy thrumming through his veins. All he could do was drag his hair back into a ponytail—a very fluffy one—with a bit of thong. Of course, the contents of the makeshift sack he carried didn't help.

The crystals had been filled with immense energy, though only one had been seeded with Rora's singularity. Enough magic had bled off through Morganen and the priestess for Hope to fill the two spares, making all three faceted spheres glow brightly, plus the extra that Hope herself still carried.

"And the way Rydan both cried and laughed with relief as he held her—he's really very much in love with her, isn't he?" she asked. "I mean, deeply in love with her."

"She's his best friend as well as his wife," Morg pointed out. "She understands him. None of my family really understood Rydan. And because we wanted to respect his privacy . . . and not deal with his moodiness . . . we just let him withdraw from us. Rora didn't let him withdraw from her. Whatever it is that they do at night, they've deepened their relationship through working together . . . although, now that I think of it, all my brothers and their wives are like that."

"Like?" Hope asked. Snippets of this information had come to her during their months of awkward talking-and-writing, but she wanted to know more.

"You wouldn't notice it in Evanor, since Mariel's not right there, but the two of them fit together like a perfectly sung duet," Morganen said. "Kelly and Saber are like the two halves of a roof, determined to shelter everyone around them while providing unwavering support to each other. Wolfer and Alys have been friends since childhood, but it's become so much more, now that they're adults. Even Amara and Trevan are each other's best advocate, encouraging each other in everything they do."

"So I've noticed. The only couple I haven't actually seen in action are your thirdborn brother and his wife. I'm looking forward to meeting both of them," Hope added. "And their baby once he or she arrives."

"I think they'll enjoy meeting you," Morg agreed, smiling. "I wonder if Serina knows anything about Darkhana? Guchere, Sundara, and Aiar were the limits of how far away I could successfully scry—which reminds me, I'll have to have a chat with Priestess Ora about how similar our powers might be. I've never encountered another mage so similar to me."

"My instincts are saying she might actually tell you a few things," Hope admitted, "but I also think she'll be closed-mouthed about all her other secrets. I mean, we didn't even know the name of her should kiss her, with no hesitation on his part and no doubt on hers. On the other hand, it thrilled and unnerved her that *he* was kissing her of his own volition, that *he* was the one making her feel weak with an intoxicating lust.

Fingers slipping to the back of his head, Hope swayed into Morganen's kiss, shifting away from the wall as she returned it. A moment later, she bumped back into its carved edges again, pressed there by his body. Lifting her other hand to his chest, Hope smoothed her palm over his flexing muscles. In his sleeveless, summer-weight tunic, there wasn't much that the age-softened linen could hide from her touch.

He was definitely taller than she, but not overly muscled like his elder brothers. Not weak by any means; there was enough strength in his lean frame to make her feel warm and weak in a good way. She wasn't a weak-bodied woman herself, and didn't like it when a male was so slender, she felt like she could break him in two during an embrace. She had no fear she'd break this particular man, however, not when he pressed her to the wall, kissing her with a thoroughness that said he wasn't going to let her go until he felt good—very good—and ready.

It had been too long since her last lover; Hope had almost forgotten how good it felt to be pressed to a wall by a man intent on kissing her thoroughly. She cupped his nape and slid her hand to the small of his back, pulling their bodies even closer together. Angling her head, she devoured his mouth with lips, teeth, and tongue.

Groaning his appreciation for her enthusiasm, Morg kissed his way across her cheek to her earlobe. She gasped and giggled, clutching at him when he licked her ear, then squirmed to get away when he nipped at her neck, where she was most ticklish. His other hand came up to hold her in place . . . and something *clunked*.

Both of them stilled, then pulled apart, staring at the silk-swathed crystal dangling from his hand.

Upset that he had forgotten their task, Morganen groaned and pulled back from her. "Jinga's Tits."

Hope stared at him, aghast. "Jinga's *what*?"

Morg froze, reminded abruptly that while she was originally from his universe, she wasn't from his *time*. Something which was a commonplace oath in his era could easily have been the height of blasphemy in hers . . . and she *was* a Seer. Mouthpiece of the Gods. He blushed in embarrassment. "Uh . . ."

"Morg, Jinga is a *God*," she stressed, lifting her hands. They bobbled graphically as she gestured sharply between them. "He doesn't *have* tits!"

Worry gave way to relief and amusement. Chuckling, Morg shook his head. "It's just a common, mild oath. The *really* bad one is to mention Kata's endowments. I, um, didn't upset or offend you by swearing in front of you, did I?"

Hope snorted, hands going to her hips since their moment of passion seemed to be over. "You should hear how Kelly's people go about it. Bodily functions used crudely and repetitively to the point of boredom. Excessively, and with very little variety. And no, I'm not offended—more like amused! *'Jinga's Tits'* . . . ha!"

Relieved by her snickering, he nodded. Lifting his other wrist, he eyed the tiny glowing dots on the oval lid of his cryslet. "We still have another hour and a half of walking to do, before it'll be Trevan's turn." Shifting his gaze to the corridor, he glanced back the way they had come, then up the tunnel in the direction they were headed. "Speaking of which . . . where are we?"

She peered both ways, then shrugged. "Somewhere near the western ravine, I think. Your brother did a lot of carving in this section, and even opened up a few new passages. If we keep walking . . . that way, I think I might spot something that's still familiar."

"You *think*?" he challenged her dryly, entwining his free hand with hers. The Fountain-crystal hadn't stayed in one place long enough to lodge itself permanently, but neither could they stop to make love. Hope didn't protest when he started walking again.

"Well, it *has* been five years since I was last down here, from my viewpoint," she reminded him. She swung their clasped hands as they strolled. "I take it I'm forgiven?"

"Only if you promise you'll still try to seduce me," Morg bartered, slanting her a teasing look.

"Only after we're done 'walking the dog' here," she quipped, nodding at his pink-wrapped prize. "So . . . what shall we talk about, to get our minds off of groping and snogging and other intriguing activities we can't stay put for?"

Morg affected a thoughtful look. "Actually . . . I believe Trevan said that, with the application of a certain mass-lightening spell, it *is* possible to walk and make love at the same time. Care to try?"

She gasped in mock-affront, then grinned. The soft sound she made reminded Morg of a similar noise she had released earlier. He glanced at her as they emerged from the tunnel, strolling onto a bridge that spanned a chasm-like cavern. Their footfalls, while quiet, still managed to echo off the uneven arc of the ceiling over their heads.

"Hope . . . before the extraction, you gasped at one point. What was that about?" he asked her.

Frowning in thought, Hope cast her mind back to the moment he mentioned. So much had happened, she couldn't quite remember for a minute or two. Only after she strained her memory back to the beginning of the whole post-breakfast ritual did she remember. "Oh! I remember now. I simply had a thought on the whole duchy-versus-kingdom thing. You know, how to clarify my birthright regarding the island, versus Kelly's claim on it as the incipient queen. There might actually be a way around it."

Morg shook his head. "I'm afraid I'm not that familiar with inheritance laws. But if there *is* a way to circumvent Kelly's claim, I'm sure the Council will be looking for it. I should mirror-call Lord Consus about this, when we get back." He glanced around them and gave her a wry look. "*If* we get back. Does this chasm look familiar to you?"

"We're in the west ravine, third level," she said, confident of her surroundings. "I know where we are, now."

"Good. I've only been down here once before, when we helped stave off the Fountain infiltration by that Xenos fellow down in Menomon. And that was only as far as the Fountain Hall." Morganen eyed the walls as they reached the far side of the broad span. "So . . . anything interesting down here that we could go see?"

"Well, you've seen the amphitheater, and the Fountain Hall," she said. "There are guest quarters and servant quarters, guard barracks, the kitchens, the storerooms, the laundry pools, the stables, the—"

"*Stables?*" he repeated dubiously, interrupting her litany. "In *this* place?"

"Yes, they're near the Great Doors. It's a grand entrance in the middle of one of the cliffs northeast of the Desalinator, not far from the harbor," she explained. "It's for all the steeds and harness teams the many visitors would be riding or driving when they attended the Convocations. The castle was built in a size suitable for ruling over a duchy—we had lost our independence by the time it was rebuilt," she explained, catching his puzzled look, "but it's too small to host something of such grand and far-reaching importance as the Convocation of the Gods.

"That's why my family started expanding the few natural caverns down here into this vast complex." She gestured at the stairwell splitting off from the corridor they were following. It spiraled down into a chamber they could see ahead, for the corridor curved to follow the cavern wall, hosting a balcony on one side and several empty doorways awaiting the installation of their doors on the other.

"Hope, there *isn't* any grand entrance northeast of the Desalinator," he reminded her. "Trust me, my brothers and I have been over every inch of this island. At least, on the surface. Only Rydan knows what lies beneath it. We would have noticed huge doors in a cliff-face at some point—and I certainly would have noticed a spell to hide them. I knew about the Fountain Rydan's been protecting all this time, and of the various entrances into this maze, but I've kept my mouth shut and myself elsewhere out of deference to his need for privacy."

"Well, they're not actually *at* the face of the cliff," she hedged, shrugging. "There's a thin curtain of stone still waiting to be broken through. We couldn't go around *announcing* that we were preparing to be the next home of the Convocation," Hope said, exasperation rolling her eyes. "Aiar was a mighty Empire, far bigger than Katan. If the Great Doors had been excavated fully, *someone* would have noticed and reported it, and quite possibly blamed the mainland for our personal, Prophecy-driven ambition.

"If that had happened, the Emperor of Aiar could have threatened to leave out the Names of Kata and Jinga at the next Convocation, weakening Katan's political power. Which would have diminished the faith of its people, which would have lessened the Gods' power," Hope told him. "My family may have preferred Nauvea to a pair of foreign Patrons, but She hadn't much power left, and our people had accepted the Patronage of Jinga and Kata. We certainly weren't about to travel overseas for an attempted theft of the Gateway of Heaven, and we definitely weren't interested in drawing attention to ourselves by making anyone *think* we were thinking of doing so. It was just too dangerous."

"You have a point," he conceded, gently squeezing the fingers still laced with his. "But now we're in the position of resurrecting the Convocation, and we do have a powerful neighbor to beware of . . . which is yet another reason why I should contact my favorite Councilor. I need to see if he can dredge up anything on inheritance rights that might affect our bid for independence. Katan may not be as powerful as Aiar once was, but it is powerful in its own right, and most of its Councilors hold a grudge or two about us. You can pursue your idea if you want, but I'd like to know what the current inheritance laws are."

Hope let it pass. What she had in mind would definitely fix any problem, if she could pull it off. Instead, she changed the subject, asking him for details about Kelly's first few months on the Isle, a subject unmentioned in any real depth before now. That lasted them until Trevan called Morg on his cryslet, letting them know it was time to return and pass along the Fountain-infused crystal.

Once they returned to the palace, Morg parted from her, lingering just long enough to give her a thorough kiss. He left to go make a mirror-call, and Hope headed for the ducal council chamber, which Kelly had mentioned was the place where she met with her islanders. It was easy to find the right room, despite the painted illusion of a deep, green forest lining the corridor walls on the ground floor, because the walls were lined with patiently waiting men and women, too.

This is why we always used the audience hall. I wonder why Kelly isn't using it? Bemused, Hope headed toward the door, only to receive frowns from the men and women waiting in line.

One of them, a deeply tanned figure who looked like he came from the old port city of Salia, waved her off, poking his thumb behind him. "Hey—get in line, and wait your turn!"

"Relax. I'm not here for a petition," Hope demurred. She wasn't quite sure what her role in the new government would be, other than that she didn't want the responsibility of ruling over anything bigger than a confectioner's kitchen, but she supposed she could qualify as an advisor of sorts. Before she could say as much, though, one of the women behind the dark-skinned man nudged him.

"Don't you know who that is?" she hissed.

"A woman who's cutting in line?" the man retorted.

"No! My neighbor said that his coworker over at the tiling house said that the Gods brought back the old Duchess of Nightfall! That's her!"

The man glanced at Hope, his dark brown eyes skimming over her foreign clothes. "She doesn't look *that* old to me!"

"I'm telling you, it's *her*! My neighbor's worker said that Lord Morganen said so himself. Milady, are you, or are you not, Nea of

Nightfall, the Duchess who disappeared back when Aiar Shattered?" the woman asked boldly.

Hope hid her grimace in an awkward smile, not quite sure how to answer that question. "Excuse me, but I'm needed by Her Majesty . . ."

Escaping into the room, she found Kelly dealing with a pair of men clad in color-stained aprons over equally mottled clothes.

"No! I'm sorry, but you *cannot* go dumping your dyes into the sewers!" Kelly argued. "Those sewers feed back into the Desalinator, where the contents are filtered out for compost-blocks, and the water is purified again for drinking, yes, but there are too many dangerous chemicals in the dyeing process to assume that the Desalinator can safely filter out all of them. You will have to find an environmentally responsible manner of disposing your chemicals."

From the bewildered looks on the two men's faces, Hope knew Kelly's terminology had lost them. She cleared her throat, catching her redheaded friend's attention. "Perhaps if I translated that?"

Kelly gestured at one of the seats on the outside of the V-shaped table she occupied. "By all means. Good luck."

Nodding in acknowledgment, Hope moved up to join Kelly at the flat-ended point of the table. Pulling out one of the chairs, she seated herself, laced her fingers in front of her, and addressed the men. "Listen. Before you can dump your dye-water down the drains, you will either have to use the correct combination of plants and minerals to neutralize the dyes so that they are rendered nontoxic, boil down and concentrate your dyes for reuse, or find and pay a mage to extract the undrinkable, unhealthy parts of the dyes you use."

"Begging pardon, milady, but half the dyes *can't* be reused," the darker-haired of the two petitioners argued. "Once they're used up, they're used up. And we don't *have* the plants and minerals necessary for cleansing the water. They're not native to this island."

"Then either you pay a mage to clean the impurities out of the water before it goes down the drain," Kelly asserted, making the lighter-haired man scoff in protest at the expense, "*or* you take the time to boil out the water by nonmagical means, being mindful of any fumes generated, and store the residue for decontamination for the day when you can afford to pay a mage, or can import the necessary neutralizing agents.

"And don't even think of secretly burying it in some refuse pit—you'll face a thousand-goldweight fine per pound of waste material if you do," she warned the two dyers. "We have only one island to live on, and we are *not* going to poison the land, the water, the animals, the fish, or especially ourselves." Rummaging through the papers on the table in front of her, Kelly found a blank scrap and a pen. "Now . . . we'll impose a fifty-silver fine per gallon that you were caught dumping down the drains. That's twelve gilders, to be kind and round it down, since you had the good sense to admit what you did wrong when confronted.

"If you do not have the cash on hand, this amount will be doubled and added to your yearly tax tally, Seldic, Grallen." Kelly nodded at each man as she named him, setting the paper aside. "Remember, you are *required* by your citizenship to work for six hours each day during the desalination restart at the end of the week . . . but if you put in extra hours, you will get a tax credit, ten copperas for each hour worked, but only up to twelve hours per day—I *won't* have you overworking yourselves, either. Overwork leads to careless mistakes and injuries."

Hope pulled the sheet closer, examining it and the others on the table, while Kelly asked if the men had the money to pay her on the spot. They mumbled something about having half the fine down in the city, and Kelly dismissed them to fetch it, with a gentle but pointed reminder that if they didn't return to her with the money within a day, they would be dismissed from the island in punishment. Once they were gone, Kelly held up her hand to keep the dark-skinned man from entering, rolled her shoulders, and sighed.

"I don't know *how* you managed to do all of this, Hope, back when you were in charge," she muttered under her breath. "I know I can do it, but it's more annoying than satisfying, most of the time."

"Why do you think I'm happy to let you keep the responsibility of it?" Hope quipped back, amused. "Interesting taxation system you have."

"Serina set it up. I'll be glad when she's back among us. I don't suppose you'd act as my court scribe?" Kelly asked her. "Technically, that's Koranen's job, but he's turning into more of a Lord Ambassador than a Lord Secretary. Rora would be willing to do it, and she does have the experience for it, but until she and Rydan start living a daylight schedule—fat chance—it's too impractical to ask her."

"I suppose I can help out a little," Hope agreed. "I really do want to set up a chocolate shop, though."

Kelly grinned. "I don't blame you—do you have any more of those chocolate-cinnamon pastilles? Saber *loved* them. And if you could, you know, make a sauce out of it . . . ?"

Grinning, Hope eyed her friend. "You, the perennial virgin?"

"Hey! *You* were the one who showed me my first porn movie," the freckled outworlder hissed back.

"Only because I got saddled with hosting Sara's bachelorette party." Hope started to say more, but the man lurking in the doorway at the far end of the room cleared his throat. "Right. Um—why are you holding audiences in here, anyway? There's a perfectly good audience hall in the south wing."

"Because this one has a desk?" Kelly pointed out, gesturing at the V-shaped table. "Or at least a table big enough for my mess. Saber would be here to help me organize it, but he's overseeing the city militia down at the training hall this morning."

"Kelly, it's your castle. You can put a *bed* in here, if you wanted to. Just move in whatever furniture you need," Hope told her. "The important thing is, the audience hall has *seats* for all those poor people out in the hall to rest on. Or it should."

"Well . . . that may be," Kelly allowed, "but with you back, it doesn't entirely *feel* like my castle. And . . . and, well, I wasn't *thinking*, alright? I've been trying to get this island organized ever since our first two citizens arrived, and my days just keep getting busier."

Hope patted her on the arm. "We'll set you up with a decent audience hall by tomorrow." Beckoning the waiting man to step up between the two arms of the long table, she asked, "What is your name, and the nature of your petition?"

He glanced between her and Kelly, and settled on Hope as the more important topic. "Are you *really* the old duchess of this place? That lady seemed awfully sure . . ."

Kelly sighed and rooted through the papers. Digging out a flat white stone, she passed the disc to Hope. "Here. Once the rumor gets out, they'll just keep asking and asking, and possibly get the story utterly wrong in the process—all the rest of you out in the corridor, come on inside!" she called out, raising her voice. "Come on, file inside—all of you get to be witnesses to an old piece of island history. Come on in, don't be shy!"

Turning the Truth Stone over in her hands, Hope thought about what, exactly, she wanted to say. When the petitioners, young and old, had gathered in the council room, she gripped the stone. "My name is Aitomas, the last Emperor of Aiar."

She paused to display the blackened handprint on the stone, raising it high over her head so those in the back could see it before the coloring faded. Gripping the stone firmly, she kept her arm over her head and switched to the truth, pausing only to display its unblemished surface now and again.

"My name is Haupanea, and yes, I was the former Duchess of Nightfall, two hundred years ago. The Gods spared Nightfall from the devastating energies trying to collapse the Nightfall Portal by using me as a channel for those energies. I was cast beyond the Veils into another world . . . and now I am back. I did *not* come back to reclaim the Duchy of Nightfall.

"I am happy that Nightfall is becoming its own kingdom again, and I am very happy that Kelly—whom I first met in that other world—is going to be in charge of it. She does so with my blessing." One last display of the unblemished Stone, and she was free to lower her arm before it could grow tired. Turning to Kelly, she leaned in close enough to whisper in her friend's ear. "Speaking of which, there's something I want to do, to settle any further questions of who should be in charge of the Isle. With your permission and participation, of course."

"Name it," Kelly said.

Hope whispered her idea into her friend's ear. Kelly wrinkled her freckled nose, grimacing as Hope continued, outlining the procedure. She pulled back as soon as the dark-haired woman finished.

"Ugh . . . Between Uncle Broger and the Council of Katan, I was hoping to avoid anything of the sort ever again," Kelly complained.

"It *would* solve the problem for all time," Hope pointed out.

"Maybe, but I'm not a mage," Kelly reminded her friend. "Will it even work?"

Hope shrugged. "That's the beauty of it. You don't *have* to be a mage. *I'm* certainly not. Nor is the average citizen. The only requirement is that both of us put every ounce of meaning and feeling into the ceremony that we can. The only question is, can you do that?"

That made Kelly snort. "Of course I can! I couldn't think of anything I'd like better." Pushing back her chair, she rose to her feet, then paused. "Um . . . right, we'll need a knife. Son of Sting!"

Hope quickly rose as a dagger *popped* into Kelly's hand. "*I* go first," she told her friend, holding out her hand for the blade. "Not you. It doesn't work if you're the one instigating this particular rite."

"You're the one who knows what we're doing," Kelly agreed, handing over the blade. "Um—the rest of you are invited to stand witness to the, uh, following ancient rite of . . . ah . . ."

"Blood-Bound Kinship," Hope supplied, switching the dagger

to her left. "Remember to do this on your right hand, since you're right-handed."

Kelly flinched a little as Hope positioned the blade over her own palm. "You're not going to cut off anything, are you? I have a thing against losing any more fingers, thank you."

"Oh, please, it's just a little blood," Hope dismissed. "Now, what we do is that I cut myself and make the offer in a vow, and then you cut yourself and accept it in a vow, and we press the cuts together and proclaim our new kinship in front of all these witnesses. Straightforward, yes? Remember, you have to put your *will* into the words you say. That's what invokes the oath and makes it binding."

Nodding, Kelly squared her shoulders. "Right. Ready."

Laying the edge of the blade against her palm, Hope drew in a breath, braced herself, and began cutting her skin. "I, Hope, being also Haupanea, Duchess of Nightfall, bind unto my blood this vow: I swear before all the Gods that I take Kelly of the family Doyle into my blood and into my line as my eldest sister, granting and ceding unto her all of the rights, responsibilities, privileges, and powers of the eldest-born member of the blood and the line of the duchy of Nightfall."

Crimson welled up from the sharp-stinging cut and trickled, warm and wet, to the edge of her palm. Hope handed Kelly the knife hilt-first, and watched in silence as her friend gripped the knife awkwardly in her left hand. Drawing in a deep breath, Kelly grimaced, set the blade to her palm, and cut herself.

"I, Kelly Doyle, being the incipient queen of Nightfall . . . bind unto my blood this vow . . ." Wrinkling her nose, Kelly paused to watch the blood well up from the cut. "I swear before all the Gods that I take Hope, also called Haupanea, as my el . . . uh, as my *younger* sister, accepting all of the rights, responsibilities, powers, and privileges she grants and cedes unto me . . . and in turn acknowledging her full lineage rights as my younger sister, as members of the blood and the line of the duchy of Nightfall."

She started to say more, but Hope quickly shook her head, silencing her friend. Clasping Kelly's crimson-smeared hand with her own, she gripped it firmly. That made the cut sting and ache, but she ignored it. "Blood calls to blood, for you *are* of my blood. So swear I, Hope of Nightfall, being also Haupanea of Nightfall."

"Blood calls to blood, for I *am* of your blood. So swear I, Kelly Doyle of Nightfall—*ouch!*" Kelly hissed through bared teeth.

Wincing herself at the sudden surge in pain, Hope gripped Kelly's hand firmly, holding their burning palms tightly together. Kelly grunted, squeezing back just as hard until the pain faded. Once her hand felt better, Hope nodded and relaxed her fingers. Kelly released her own, gingerly examining her palm as soon as their hands parted.

Hope didn't need to look for confirmation; the burning sensation, tingling with power, had been enough to tell her the Gods had accepted and approved their blood-bound oaths to each other. But she did lift her hand toward their audience of curious citizens and nudged Kelly into displaying her own.

Both of their palms were a little dirty from smeared, drying blood. The darkening stains couldn't hide the cleanly healed scars that had taken the place of the bleeding cuts, however. Nor their distinctive blue white hue.

The man whose petition turn it was lifted his hands and cheered. "Witnessed!"

"Witnessed!" the others shouted, making Hope wince as their voices rang off the stout walls of the modest council room.

"Thank the Gods," the woman, the one who had identified Hope, stated firmly. "My three-greats grandmother was born on the Isle, all those years ago, and hearing that the old duchess had come back gave me a bother! Rightfully, this island belongs to your bloodline, milady . . . but if the Gods accept *her* as your sister, then I can follow *her* with a clear conscience . . . and I do want to follow her. She's far more sensible about the common person's wants and needs than that Council ever was!"

Amused, Hope reseated herself. "Well, I've discovered since

living Elsewhere that I don't *want* to be the duchess anymore. So I'm quite happy sticking Kelly with the job of ruling you all."

Digging a kerchief out of the pouch belted to her waist, Kelly gave her newly made sister an amused, sidelong look. "Don't think you're getting out of administration chores all *that* easily, Sister. You'll still have to earn your keep, same as everyone else on the Isle. That includes sitting at my side and advising me . . . particularly when I accidentally start spouting outworlder concepts and terminology, like with those two dyers.

"Speaking of which . . . everyone else, back out into the hall," Kelly sighed. "Except you, sir. You're up next. By tomorrow, we should have a far better venue for all of this . . . right, Sister?"

Hope grinned and rose from her seat. "I'll get started on it right away."

Kelly choked. "*Excuse* me? Did I not just say you were to sit your butt down beside me and *help* me manage all of these concerns? Am I, or am I not, your big sister? Get your butt back in that chair, woman!"

Dropping back into her seat, Hope mock-pouted. "Come on— you can't blame me for *trying* to escape?"

"Yes, I can. Here, take the notes on names and stuff," Kelly ordered, passing her the nib pen and inkwell, as well as some unmarked sheets.

Eyeing the Katani-style implements, Hope sighed and muttered under her breath. "Remind me to introduce Morg to the idea of ballpoint pens, sometime . . .

"Alright, milord, let's take it from the top, again," she stated aloud, readying herself to be as good a scribe for Kelly as Giolana had once been for her. "Your name, and your reason for seeing Her Majesty?"

*H*ome *at last.* Tired from a long day piled with papers and scrolls, political maneuverings, and a few odd looks from some of the people he had passed in the corridors of the palace, Lord Consus of Kairides dropped the satchel of paperwork on the desk in his study and dropped his lanky, middle-aged body into the padded chair behind it. For a long moment, he let himself relax into the embrace of the soft brown leather, then ran his hands up his face and over his thinning, graying, reddish brown hair.

His stomach needed something soothing. Flicking his fingers, he muttered a spell meant to ring a bell down in the kitchens. While he waited for a servant to answer the summons, the Councilor of Sea Commerce made a face at his satchel. Opening it with some reluctance, he pulled out a scroll sent to his office only a short time before he had left, the first on his to-read list.

The scroll looked innocuous enough; it was formed from that new, thick-fibered paper with the fresh, stiff, creamy color that was easy on his tired eyes. Consus untied the ribbons holding the rods together and unrolled the long sheet, skimming through the neatly inked laws copied onto it. *Ah, that's what this is . . . and what I remember them being*, he acknowledged, reaching the end. *Simple, straightforward, and clear-cut.*

Though why the Nightfall brothers are interested in Katani inheritance laws and their impact on any possible claims for independence is beyond me. There are no direct descendants of the duchy of Nightfall in existence.

The door to his study opened, and Carolos stepped inside. Consus glanced up, hands shifting to reroll the scroll. The manservant bowed to him, but did not meet his eyes, an oddity. Consus wasn't one of those mage-lords who demanded subservience from his servants, just good service. Naturally, the man had appeared promptly.

"You summoned me, milord?" Carolos asked.

"Yes. I need one of my stomach-possets. And something light for supper," he directed the younger man, retying the scroll shut. "Soup, or salad—prepared the usual way."

"Nothing greasy or spicy," Carolos agreed, bowing again. The whole staff knew that Consus' gut disagreed with him these days, due to the stresses he had suffered over the Nightfall debacle. Hesitating, Carolos glanced around the room, then nodded at the scrying mirror hung behind the desk. "Milord . . . will you be making a mirror-call?"

That was an odd thing for the younger man to ask. Setting the scroll on his desk, Consus narrowed his brown eyes. "Why do you want to know that?"

"Um . . . I was hoping to beg your indulgence to call the magescribe near my father's home. His health hasn't been well, and I would like to talk with him before he . . . Forgive my impertinence for asking," Carolos added, again not quite meeting Consus' gaze.

"I will assist you with your mirror-call after I have eaten. Your father lives west of here, if I remember correctly, so there will be time before nightfall for him to be summoned to a local mirror," Consus stated. "Now, leave me until my supper is ready. I have business to attend to."

"Yes, milord." Bowing again, the servant left the room, shutting the door quietly as he went.

Satisfied that he would be alone for a while, Consus turned to the mirror on the wall behind his desk. Unlike the mirror over the fireplace, which was covered in a drape-cloth for privacy—though a cloth would not stop it from activating, if it chose to do so—the one behind his desk was uncovered, standing ready for cross-continental communication. A glance at his aethometer, a silver-and-brass dial in a wooden stand on the shelf below the mirror, showed that it was a calm-aether day. A propitious sign for reaching all the way to Nightfall Isle.

This was not a conversation he wanted to have to relay through one of his sub-offices. Standing, he faced the mirror. A few muttered, mnemonic words, a stroke of the frame, and the reflection of his study and himself rippled and pulsed with a wash of blue light, then with yellow, tinting his study. A moment later, Morganen of Nightfall appeared in the mirror, his light blue green eyes warm with carefully constrained mirth. The younger mage spoke.

"Greetings. You have reached the mirror for Nightfall Isle, home of the Corvis brothers. Unfortunately, my siblings and I are busy at the moment . . ."

Rolling his eyes, Consus waited patiently for the pre-enchanted message to end, and the mirror to pick up a pulsing peach color. Familiar with the bizarre spell, Consus sighed. "Answer the mirror, Lord Morganen. If you still want to discuss our business, that is."

The enchantment ended with the standard closing statement. Grimacing, stomach knotting with stress, Consus turned away from the mirror. Whenever the other mage answered was when he would answer. In the meantime, Consus had a stack of import/export summaries of various port city activities to read.

When he was halfway through the third one, his mirror chimed. Abandoning his work, Consus stood up again and tapped the rune-carved, wooden frame, activating the mirror for communication. Morganen—the real one, clad in a light blue, sleeveless tunic—appeared.

"Good afternoon, Councilor. Sorry it took so long to reply; I've been instructing some of our magically gifted citizens each afternoon, and couldn't interrupt my class."

Consus winced. "Don't call me that. As far as I'm concerned, this is simply between two private citizens. Speaking of which, your part of the deal . . . ?"

"Salt-block production is about to go exponential," Morganen told him. "We're reviving the desalination plant within a week."

"Tell me something my agents *haven't* already uncovered," Consus countered, waving off the offer. "Everyone on the eastern wharfs within a week's sail of your island knows you're demanding settlers who can to haul blocks of salt and algae for several days in a row. If you want that scroll, you'll have to provide me with something a lot better than old news."

"Fine. As you may know, we've been looking into resurrecting the Convocation of the Gods," Morganen offered, only to be cut off by Consus' hand again.

Stomach churning, Consus said irritably, "Yes, yes—something I *do not* know?"

Morganen's mouth twisted, but more like a grimace. "I'm getting to that part. If everything goes well, the Convocation will happen within a full turn of Brother Moon. Nightfall will be thoroughly Patroned and fully independent well within our year-and-a-day. *Now* can I have the scroll?"

That was sooner than Consus had expected. Twisting, he picked up the scroll. "Since you're supposed to be the more powerful mage, *you* can open the mirror-Gate and fetch . . . it . . ."

The door to his study had opened, cutting him off in midsentence. Eyes widening, he watched as Carolos stepped all the way inside and out of the way . . . leaving room for Duke Finneg, Councilor of Conflict Resolution, and four mage-soldiers of the Katani Guard to march into his study. All five men wore armor, Finneg clad in red-dyed, rune-carved leather, the Guard in teal tabards over plain brown but still rune-carved leather.

The dark-skinned Councilor sneered at the stunned, older mage. "Lord Consus, you are hereby charged with high treason for aiding and abetting the land of Nightfall, an act expressly forbidden to you by King Taurin himself. Submit to our custody quietly, admit to all of the charges that will be laid against you, confess *all* of your crimes, both this one and any others you may have made . . . and the courts *may* be lenient with you.

"Resist"—and here, Duke Finneg bared his white teeth in an unpleasant approximation of a smile—"and it will be my pleasure to personally throw you in the Oubliette."

Jinga's Tits! Snapping his fingers, Morganen froze his image in the mirror that hung on his workroom wall. As soon as he was sure his absence wouldn't be noted, he snatched up a piece of chalk and scribed a one-way silencing spell on the mirror, one that would let him hear the men in Consus' home, but prevent them from hearing him.

It was necessary, too; whirling away from the mirror on the wall, Morg snatched up a pot from his shelves—then cursed aloud and tossed that jar back onto the planks, grabbed the *other* pot, put it on one of his worktables, and fumbled off the lid. He didn't need to make an opening in the Veils to an entirely different universe; what he *needed* was the powder that would turn a mirror into a Gate onto another part of *this* world. Hurrying to his cheval-mirror, he quickly activated it with a pulse of ambient energy drawn from the very air.

Adjusting the view with quick touches along the wooden edges framing the looking glass, he rolled the stand away from the wall, toward the middle of his workroom floor. A sharp-spoken spell, a gesture slashed between the two mirrors, and magic rippled in a wash of red across the glass in the cheval stand. Within two heartbeats, it resolved into a view of Consus' study, as seen from just in front of the first mirror. Both surfaces showed Consus being pulled out from behind his desk by two of the guardsmen, and anti-magic manacles being brought out of a silk bag by a third.

He *could* have left Consus to his fate; the Councilor of Sea Commerce had been unpleasant, arrogant, and stubborn over the years that Morganen had know him. He was *also* the very same mage who had refused to lend the aid of the Katani Empire to his brothers back when the misogynistic Mandarites had attempted to invade and claim Nightfall Isle for their own.

That very same refusal had helped to fulfill the first verse of the Curse of Eight Prophecy. In the months that followed, Consus had eventually helped Morganen and his brothers, warning them of the Council's invasive visit over half a year ago. That visit had led directly to Ringing the Bell, claiming independence for Nightfall.

Adjusting the mirror, Morg scooped up a handful of powder, summoned his magical reserves, and shouted the words of the

Opening spell. They didn't thunder quite as loudly as the ones he used for opening the Veils between universes, but then, he didn't have to push his magics literally through the fabric of existence itself, just enough to open a regular mirror-Gate. As soon as he did so, he quickly stroked and tapped the edges of the cheval mirror, tilting it on its pivot-arms.

The last time he had pulled this particular trick, he'd had to move bedcovers and bits of burning ceiling out of his way. This time, he had to be careful not to catch the Katani Imperial Guard getting ready to shackle Consus' wrists. A swift stroke, a swoop of the angled viewpoint, and the mirror-Gate swallowed Consus from his thinning scalp downward. Yelping in startlement as the intersection plane swept down over his torso, Consus of Kairides fell through the downward-tilted mirror. The middle-aged mage hit the floor with a grunting *thump*, his legs clearing the mirror as Morganen hastily shoved it back.

A stroke, a flick, a muttered spell to protect the opening, and the intersection plane shifted, rising up toward the ceiling of the study. Morg righted the mirror in its frame, watching from above as the dark-skinned duke rushed to the side of his startled guardsman. Both men peered all around, Finneg scowling and muttering a spell to try to locate the mirror's intersection point, but he only aimed it outward in a circle. Not up.

Abandoning the mirror, Morganen squatted, helping to right the stunned mage. "Sorry about the awkward arrival."

"What . . . ? You . . ." Blinking, Consus twisted his neck, peering at the room, then at the mirror in its cheval stand.

"I know you didn't ask for it, but I've taken the liberty of granting you political amnesty and asylum here on Nightfall," Morg explained, helping pull the older mage to his feet. "Of course, I haven't actually *asked* Her Majesty if she'll grant it, but I'm sure she will once I've explained your situation to her."

Finneg's voice reached them through the other mirror.

"What was that? Political asylum?" Duke Finneg scowled and

turned around, facing the mirror on the wall. "Consus is a Katani citizen and must face Katani law for his crimes! You bring that traitor back *now*!"

Moving back to the smaller mirror, leaving the shaken Councilor on his own for the moment, Morganen wiped off the chalk marks and ended the illusion of himself standing still.

"I think you need to calm down, first," he told the Councilor of Conflict Resolution. "For your information, Councilor Consus has been a loyal citizen of the Empire . . . and it isn't *treason* to share information that is supposed to be publically available to all, regardless of their nation."

Snatching up the scroll Consus had dropped when the guards had apprehended him, Finneg shook it over his head. "*This* is aiding and abetting you Nightfallers, an act which His Majesty *expressly* forbids! If you don't hand Consus back this minute, as soon as your Gods-be-damned year and a day are finished, I'll throw *both* of you into the Oubliette! You won't succeed with your little rebellion!"

Rolling his eyes, Morganen grabbed the chalk and marked a slightly different rune on the edge of the mirror. This one cut off the sound coming into the mirror from both sides of the connection. Finneg's voice could still be heard ranting from the cheval mirror, unfortunately. Crossing to it, Morganen scraped the same symbol on the wooden frame, then shook his head. "I feel *truly* sorry for you, for having to put up with that armored *ass* all this time."

"You have no idea—Gods, the mirror!" Consus gasped, confusing Morganen.

"What about the mirror?" Morg asked, checking both scrying views reflexively. The duke was still ranting, his lips twisting and snapping with each unheard word, but he was striding away from the looking glass on Consus' study wall. "He's still too busy ranting to try to attack through it."

"Not *that* mirror! The one over the mantel!" Consus snapped, reaching up and rubbing away the mark Morganen had made on the

cheval mirror's frame. Sound came back to them mid-sentence as
the other Councilor beckoned Consus' manservant forward. Consus quickly adjusted the viewpoint with a few taps of the frame, tipping it to follow the two men to the fireplace.

"—one you were talking about? The scrying mirror that activated on its own?"

"Yes, milord," Carolos stated, stepping into view. "I came in to
clean—I was told not to clean this chamber while Milord was out of
the house, but it had been too long, and, well . . . shortly after I came
in to work, I heard voices, Milord's and another's. I peeked under the
cloth, and, well . . ."

Carolos reached up and tugged down the linen drape, revealing
a strange mirror composed of two oval looking glasses encased in a
metal frame bent into a sideways figure eight. Grimacing, Consus
flicked his hand at the tableau. *"Get the mirror!"* he hissed at Morganen, mindful of any noise that might alert the other mage to the
cheval mirror's intersection plane. *"Get it, before he does!"*

Nonplussed at the command, Morganen shrugged and twisted
the viewpoint of the mirror-Gate, tilting the mirror back in its
stand. A flick of his hand, a whispered command, and the double-
glazed mirror flung itself off the wall, twisting as it flew through
the air. The edge of it smacked into Finneg's hand, flipping the
scroll free; by pure chance, it landed on the passing mirror, skittered and rolled as the looking glass soared through the intersection
plane . . . and rolled free as it passed into the workroom, clattering
on the floor. Consus shouted in alarm, but Morg had both mirrors
under control.

One hand flung out, halting the incoming mirror before it could
smash against the high ceiling of his workroom. The other flicked
and slid the intersection plane around and down, getting it out of
immediate view of the duke, who had flung his head up to watch the
mirror flying abruptly out of sight. No fool, Finneg spun on his
heel, dark brown eyes narrowing as he sought the path of the intersection plane with his mage-sight.

Leaving the double mirror floating near the ceiling and the scroll on the floor, Morganen grabbed a handful of powder and cast it on the cheval mirror, closing the Gate. Another chalk mark secured any sound from getting through. Morganen glanced at his companion, tucking his hair behind his ears. "There. Your mirror is saved. Now, what's so special about it?"

"None of your business! It's mine, and I'll take it with me when I . . . *dammit*," Consus swore, grimacing again. "I have nowhere to go, and no more than a few coins in my pouch—this mess is all *your* fault!"

Morganen lifted one of his brows in silent challenge. The older mage had the grace to flush.

"Fine. It is *both* our faults. But while I didn't want to be charged with treason—let alone threatened with the Oubliette! I'm *not* happy to be cast on your shores with hardly a silvara to my name," he snapped. "Are you prepared to feed and clothe and house me, as well as shelter me from Duke Finneg's fury? Or the Council's? And what am I to do with myself, now that I am here? Compound my disgrace by turning full traitor and working for you?"

Reminding himself that the older man had a right to be distraught, Morganen crossed to the mirror on the wall. Casting a levitation spell on it, he lifted it from the wall and floated it over to the other mirror. "First we take care of His Unpleasantness. Then we secure your belongings. After that, we take the scroll that started this mess to Her Majesty, and introduce you. I suggest you calm yourself while I work, and prepare a pretty speech for Her Majesty to convince her to let you claim the asylum I've offered—you're not the only one who has gone out on a political limb, you know. Nor are you the first on this island to be threatened with the Oubliette. That was one of our 'choices' when we were ordered into exile."

"*That* was not my decision; that was the fault of the previous Councilor of Conflict Resolution. Speaking of the current one, how are you going to deal with him?" Consus asked, frowning in suspicion. "You're not going to *kill* him, are you? He's a duchy-sized ass, but I won't have his murder on my conscience. Or the murder of those guards."

"It's simple: I double-Gate him. He'll fall through this mirror, once I swoop it down over him, and then he'll fall through that mirror, which I'll position under the cheval glass, ready to catch his fall," Morganen explained, double-checking the pot on the nearby table to make sure it would have enough powder. It looked like it was getting low, so he crossed to the shelves to fetch another filled with the same kind of enchanted, finely ground herbs. "I'll be kind and make sure he and his guards don't fall too far, out of deference to the fact that they're just trying to do their jobs. However zealously.

"I might even pick out a nice, soft landing for them. Something like a midden heap in some back alley. Once they're through, I'll secure your house with a warding spell, then use the mirrors to transfer as many of your belongings as I can."

Consus let out a scoffing noise. "Double-Gating him onto a midden heap may be a clever idea, but do you really expect me to believe you can ward my house from nearly half a continent plus a full day's sail away? *And* expect it to hold against the might of the Department of Conflict Resolution?"

"Of course I do. Just don't expect my wards to hold for more than an hour or two," Morganen warned him, finding the right pot and bringing it back to join the other. "Start thinking of your most valuable possessions and where they can be found, and we'll pull them through in that order."

"My most valuable possession is floating over our heads. The rest of my belongings are easy enough to choose, but I didn't have much in the way of coin in my house," Consus stated, watching the younger mage carefully repositioning his mirrors. "Unless you wish to compound our problem by committing a bank robbery?"

"Sorry. I can bend the law to a point, but *that* would utterly break it," Morg demurred. "That much authority, I do not have. Nor would Kelly grant it. You'll just have to make do with your things from your house. Now, if you'll excuse me for a few moments, I need to find the biggest midden heap in the capital . . ."

"Royal Farms, east of the city," Consus directed him, stooping to pick up the scroll. "They usually have a mountain of manure outside the barns being saved up for winter composting. It's also far enough to travel, by cart or by foot, that we'll have extra time to empty my house."

Morg grinned. "I like the way you think, milord. Royal Farms, it is."

"It's been very disheartening for us," Kelly told Hope as they crossed the drawbridge closest to the eastern tower. "The sex is great; Saber is usually a wonderful, attentive lover, but . . . well, it's become increasingly depressing, because I just . . . I can't seem to get pregnant."

"Have you seen a Healer about this?" Hope asked.

Kelly grimaced, folding her arms defensively across her chest. "Mariel says I'm perfectly healthy. She also says that while I have just enough magic within me—or rather, the otherworld equivalent—to make something like Ultra Tongue function for me, it's possible I don't have enough to keep that going *and* get pregnant. Since life force is magic, and magic is life force, in this universe.

"Unfortunately, I don't know of any way to stop Ultra Tongue from working." She sighed. "Even if it did stop . . . I wouldn't understand *anyone* unless I was standing really close to them and they were actively willing me to understand, or they chose to speak in my language, since I'm told it's a radiant effect as well as a translative one."

"Kelly . . . have you considered that it might be your diet?" Hope asked her friend. Kelly stopped on the ramparts, staring at her. Hope gestured at the forested slopes of the hills receding to the east. "Magic is a cycle, on this world. We eat the plants that give us the strength to live; we generate magical energies that radiate outward and which the plants absorb like sunlight, making them stronger and healthier, and in turn more nutritious for us.

"But *your* world isn't built quite the same. Your nutritional needs are different. It could very well be that there's something in your diet that you're just not getting—some extra *oomphf* that Katani food, for all that it's filled with magical life force, doesn't completely supply for your own particular needs," Hope said.

The freckled outworlder stared at her for several seconds, then shrugged, flopping her arms out. "Why not? That makes as much sense as anything else does! So, what, I import a few fruit trees? Maybe buy some *nice* chickens?"

"Eat chocolate," Hope stated firmly, joining Kelly as she moved toward the door into Morganen's tower. The sun, slanting low and golden from the west, was still hot; the evening wind had sprung up, however, tempering the day's heat with cool gusts that ruffled her dark curls. "Hey, don't laugh; look what it's done for your libido, already!"

"Hope, women have been getting pregnant on my world for millennia *without* chocolate in their diet," Kelly retorted, opening the door to the tower. "Admittedly that was back in the Dark Ages, before exploration and advances in travel opened up the world's food markets, but it only goes to show that chocolate isn't linked to pregnancy where I come from."

"But it *is* a food from your world," Hope reminded her, following her down the curving stairs inside the tower. "Morg told me about the posset he and Evanor came up with, to cure your cramps. How you'd mentioned they were worse, far from your own world. I had that same problem after I was tossed through the Veil; they got worse for me, too. Not intolerably, but noticeably all the same.

"One of the first things I asked Morganen for was for some of the local fruit to eat," she said. "I told him I wanted to give something new a try, but I was secretly very homesick. It was that time of the month, I was having one of those period-induced cravings . . . and shortly after eating a *cinetrine*, my cramps eased. *I* think, if you combine an outworlder diet with a local one, it could satiate your body's nutritional needs long enough to generate enough life-energy to procreate."

"Okay, I can see your point. Even if it's about *chocolate*," Kelly agreed, teasing her friend. "White chocolate has been known to reduce the pain of cramps, above and beyond the placebo effect. And I will admit it has increased my sex drive. But that doesn't guarantee that I can get pregnant in this world!"

Hope shook her head. "Look. Eat your chocolate, pounce all over your husband, and give it a shot. If the chocolate doesn't do the trick . . . we can always pop you across for a visit to a fertility clinic. I happen to know there's a perfectly good one just outside of Oklahoma City, discreet and effective."

"Why would *you* know about a perfectly good fertility clinic?" Kelly asked her, pushing open the door to Morganen's basement-level workroom.

"My cousins—Hope's cousins, Anita and Carlos"—she corrected, following Kelly inside—"had to make use of one this last year. I personally know they're discreet and reliable because—oh! It's you! But . . . that's . . ."

All the thoughts in her head scattered at the sight of the man in Morganen's workroom. He was visibly older, his hair thinner and longer, but he . . . *No, this isn't that pompous idiot who caused the delay shutting down the Portal. His hair is too red as well as too gray, and his eyes are too brown.*

The man turned to face her, his dark red tunic and matching trousers elegantly stitched with whorls of ribbon at shoulders, wrists, and ankles. Yet his clothes looked visibly loose, as if he had lost weight recently. This wasn't the dandy who had meddled with the closing of the Portal, for all that their facial features were quite similar.

"I'm sorry. I don't think we've met . . . but I do know *you*," he added, turning his attention to the redheaded woman. A pause, and he bowed politely. "Your Majesty."

"Um . . . yeah. Hello. Morg . . . what is this gentleman doing on my island?" Kelly asked, turning her attention to the other occupant of the chamber. "If he has business to discuss with me, why did you call me down here? Couldn't it have been done by mirror?"

"Just a moment . . . there! Nice to know my wards have held longer than anticipated," Morg added under his breath. "Alright, milord. Unless you want the biggest pieces of furniture moved across, that seems to be everything small and portable."

"Moved *across*?" Kelly repeated, hands going to her hips. "Morg, what's going on?"

Turning away from the two mirrors at his side, one floating nearly face-to-face with the other where it rested in its stand, Morg sighed. "It's simple. Consus and I have been trading information. Most of it hasn't been overly important, just the sort of things one would want to know in advance, mostly for damage control."

"Unfortunately, today I was caught 'aiding' you. Or rather, him," the older man said, gesturing at Morganen. "I was charged with high treason because His Majesty refuses to let you succeed even in the face of several Prophecies suggesting otherwise. We cannot deliberately go against you, by ancient law . . . but neither are we supposed to lend you any assistance whatsoever."

"Oh. So . . . Morganen plucked you off the mainland and brought you here, is that it?" Kelly asked.

"I took the liberty of offering him political asylum. He *has* helped us," Morganen reminded her. "He helped keep the situation with the Council's visit from boiling over and made sure Mikor wasn't harmed during his questioning."

Kelly's mouth quirked up on one side. "A far cry from not wanting anything to do with us, isn't it? Lord . . . uh . . . Constance, right?"

"Lord Consus of Kairides . . . though I'm in exile, now," the middle-aged mage added grimly.

"What was it you were caught handing over to Morg?" Hope asked, curious about this descendant of the Count of Kairides. With a title like Lord, he was probably just a younger brother, or perhaps a cousin one generation removed, but he even sounded like his progenitor. *A grimmer, glummer version*, she acknowledged. *I wonder how many generations have passed . . .*

"A copy of the laws pertaining to lines of inheritance, including the laws of inheritance versus the establishment of a new kingdom." He gestured at a scroll resting on one of the nearest tables. "I have done nothing wrong, morally. The laws are available to all who wish to read them. But His Majesty . . . and especially His Grace . . . refuse to see it that way. They will automatically assume that I am colluding with you, regardless of where I go. So the question is, do you have the power to protect me from the Empire? And, just as importantly, Your Majesty . . . do you have the inclination?"

"That's a good question. And I'll answer the second one first," Kelly told him. "Yes. I do have the inclination to offer you our protection. Your initial reaction to my presence on the Isle may have been rude and dismissive . . . but your actions set everything that followed into motion. I will not throw an agent of Destiny to the wolves. As for the other question . . ." She looked at Morganen. "Well, Lord Mage? Do we have the power to protect him?"

He glanced at his mirrors and smiled. "I believe so, Your Majesty. I've settled all of his things into two of the suites on the third floor, east northeast wing. If it weren't for the influx of settlers coming to help with the Desalinator, I would have put him somewhere down in the city, but housing is still a bit tight. I will keep an eye on him while he's staying in the palace, though."

FIVE

❦

"Good. Speaking of which, milord," Kelly added, nodding at Consus, "there is a mandatory requirement of all adult residents of the Isle who are strong of mind and body to give six hours of service each day during the three or so days that the Desalinator will be processing seawater into freshwater. That means a lot of salt and plankton blocks to move around. Since you're a Councilor, and thus a mage, your magical efforts would be deeply appreciated during those three days.

"If you choose to stay on Nightfall, you'll get a tax credit in proportion to your effort. If you prefer to leave, you'll have to pay to travel anywhere other than the mainland," she warned him. "We do have a reliable means of transporting people as far away as Natallia, should you choose to go elsewhere. But as I said, your help would be appreciated.

"The Desalinator will be restarted within the week; do make up your mind before then as to whether you'll stay and help, or not."

Consus slanted Morganen a dry look. "So I've been warned."

Righting the mirrors, Morganen floated the smaller one away from the larger and sealed both with fistfuls of powder. As soon as the smaller one rippled and resumed its normal reflection of his workroom, it chimed and flared blue. Sighing, Morg looked over at his sister-in-law. "I suspect this might be the Council, calling about our newest guest. Care to stick around?"

"Why not?" Kelly asked rhetorically.

Nodding, Morganen adjusted the floating mirror so that it faced a wall, then interrupted the prerecorded greeting. Sure enough, an image of Councilor Finneg appeared in the mirror. He was, Morg noted with amusement, wearing fresh clothes, with not a trace of his reddish brown armor in sight. "Sorry about that. I was busy with another call. How can I help you, Councilor?"

"Don't even pretend this is a social call," the Councilor of Conflict Resolution growled. "I know you took Consus of Kairides from his home—and dumped me and my men outside of town in a—a—!" Breaking off, he breathed through his nose for a moment, then ordered, "You are harboring an Imperial criminal on that Godsforsaken island, and you *will* return him immediately!"

Kelly stepped into the mirror's view. "Excuse me, but if I remember correctly, I Rang the Bell half a year ago, severing all ties of allegiance with the Empire of Katan for a full year and a day. Given that you are forbidden by your Gods to interfere in any way with the operation of this incipient kingdom . . . by what right do you make such a demand?"

"Consus is a *traitor*!" Finneg snapped. "He acted specifically against the wishes of his king by aiding you!"

"Councilor Consus did nothing wrong," Morganen countered. "Anyone can ask to see any of the laws of the Empire at any time, thus it was not against the law for him to assist us with our request for copies of those laws."

"Either your king violated Imperial law with his little assertion to the contrary . . . in which case, *he* is the lawbreaker, violating his oaths as sovereign to uphold the laws of his own land . . . or there wasn't any actual lawbreaking going on, in which case, Consus isn't a traitor. Think carefully," Kelly cautioned Finneg. "Which one is it?"

Her politely voiced inquiry made the dark-skinned duke fume, to the point that Morganen could see his skin darkening further from the blood rushing through his face. His arm snapped up, finger jabbing into the surface of the silvered glass separating them. "Death is *too good* for you! *You*, I will have bound and gagged and thrown in the Oubliette! *And* you," he added, jabbing his fingertip at another spot on the glass, indicating Morganen. "And *all* the rest of you! I will find a spell to make you immortal and confine you to a thousand years of the darkest mortal *hell*! I will—"

"—You know, I don't think he's capable of being rational right now," Kelly observed, speaking loudly enough to be heard as she turned to face Morganen. "I think we should just shut off the mirror and let him rant in private. Sort of a time-out until he shows he's capable of good behavior."

"*Good behavior?!*"

Morganen closed the scrying link with a single muttered word and a tap on the mirror frame.

"You, Your Majesty, have more guts than a *jonja*," Consus said in the quiet that followed. "Very few members of the Council would dare turn their back on Duke Finneg . . . and by all reports, you have no magic to protect yourself from him. Yet you do not fear him."

"Bullies are bullies, whether they wield weapons of magic or might," she dismissed. "I've never backed down from a bully before, and I have no intention of starting now—I'm smart enough to go get help, but I don't back down. Unfortunately . . . this means that you, Lord Consus, are going to be a political headache. But I won't throw you out to fend for yourself," Kelly reassured him. "We're in this mess together. I do, however, suggest that you come up with some means of contributing to Nightfall, and perhaps adding to its protection.

"In the meantime, you'll be welcome to join us at supper, which will be at sunset. It's not fancy, but it is civilized," Kelly said. Consus gave her a small bow in acknowledgment. She glanced at Morganen. "If that's all you needed me for, I'll go make sure an extra place is set at the table. Oh, and I'll warn Mikor you're coming. You may remember him as the boy you questioned at the start of your last visit?"

"We were very careful not to harm him," Consus asserted. "It left a bad taste in all our mouths to have to interrogate a mere boy for information, even for the duke. In truth, I admired the boy for his quick wit."

Kelly nodded. "Your restraint was noted at the time, and appreciated. I'll make sure he understands you're not here because of him—it might help reassure him if you reinforced that statement by being polite but distant around him."

"Of course, Your Majesty." He bowed again, agreeing with her request.

Nodding to everyone, Kelly picked up the scroll of Katani laws and left.

Hope remained behind, wanting to stay with Morg. She waited while he rehung the mirror and draped it with a privacy cloth, then repositioned the cheval mirror in the alcove it occupied between a section of cabinets and a span of shelves. When he reached for her hand, she laced her fingers with his willingly enough, and let him lead her and Consus out of his workroom.

"Sunset will be very soon. I'll show you where your things are stored, then escort you to the dining hall," Morganen told the exiled Councilor as they reached the top of the stairs, emerging on the ramparts into golden sunlight cast by the orb burning low on the western horizon. "I have faith you'll be a polite guest while you're here, but until everyone is reassured you won't go wandering off into the private areas of the palace, you should be careful not to stray too far from the public areas."

"I've spent more years navigating the shoals and reefs of politics than you've probably been alive," Consus returned dryly. "I'm well aware that you could consider my sudden presence among you a carefully contrived ruse, a method to secretly spy on you from up close. As soon as feasible, I think I should be removed from the palace and placed in a less politically delicate location. And the sooner you can get the Convocation restored, the better. The longer you delay that, the worse everything will become."

"At least you're smarter than your predecessor," Hope observed. That earned her a puzzled look. She glanced at Morg, who shrugged, leaving the choice of revealing the truth up to her. "I'm the reason Lord Morganen wanted that scroll. A long time ago, before the Gods tossed me through the Veils into another time and place . . . I was Duchess Nea of Nightfall. The one who vanished when the last Portal collapsed.

"That's why I was so startled when I first saw you," she added. "Your hair is redder, and you're a decade or so older, but you look very much like him—Lord Kaidannen of Kairides, *the* Councilor of Portal Management."

The current scion of Kairides gave her an odd look, but then, he didn't know she was mocking his ancestor's pompous introduction. Consus surveyed her outworlder clothes and lifted his brows. "Are you claiming you're two hundred years old?"

"No, just twenty-four," she said. "Two hundred years may have passed here, but I spent only five years Elsewhere. In the same universe Her Majesty comes from, no less."

"All of these things were confirmed yesterday via Truth Stone," Morganen told the other mage, watching him carefully. "One can only imagine the kind of havoc this information would cause in the Council, if they knew the last, lost duchess had returned."

"They'd try to reclaim the island through you," Consus told Hope. "I didn't read the laws on the scroll that closely, but I did read enough to know that they *could* have a legitimate claim, through you. If you really are the rightful duchess. But that begs the question of why you're telling *me* this. To test me? To see if I'll slip this information to my colleagues?"

Hope shook her head. "The news is already spreading across the island. In a day or two, it will hit the ports on the mainland. Everyone will know I'm back. Besides, it was one of my own Prophecies that successfully predicted everything that has already happened. Since I know from firsthand experience that at least some of the Gods have a sense of humor . . . well, why not enjoy the ride, rather than try to hide who and what I am?"

"You wouldn't 'enjoy the ride' nearly so much if *you* were the one threatened with being tossed in the Oubliette," Consus warned her as they entered the nearest wing of the palace. The walls of the fourth floor were painted in a beach scene, with waves lapping lazily at the pebble-and-sand beach.

"Oubliette?" Hope asked, looking to Morg for an explanation. Consus replied first.

"You claim to be a duchess of Katan, and you haven't heard of the Oubliette?" the older mage quipped. He glanced at Morg. "Are you sure that was a fully functional Truth Stone?"

"You forget what era she comes from," Morganen reminded the Councilor. "An age of great peace and prosperity, very stable and with very few politically ambiguous incidents. She took over from her parents, who were well-respected and well-behaved members of Katani society. She herself managed to rule capably after their passing, with no incidents other than the collapse of the Portal to cause King and Council any headaches. There would have been no need to threaten *her* family with the Oubliette . . . and likely she would have been too busy keeping her duchy together following their deaths to have paid much attention to outdated gossip. It's reasonable under those conditions for her to not know what the Oubliette is."

"I do know what *an* oubliette is, a place to put people when you want to forget about them," Hope admitted. "But you make it sound like this one's more than just a mere dungeon cell."

"The Oubliette is a place of absolute darkness, save for one room, a bland, featureless chamber where the mirror-Gate resides," Consus said. "All of the workers, from servants to guards, are blind from birth, or blinded before they go to work there. Its exact location is one of the most closely guarded secrets in the Empire. These precautions are taken so that no one may mount a rescue via any sort of scrying . . . because if a mage is so dangerous that they cannot roam free, yet so politically inconvenient that they cannot be executed or locked up for only a short length of time, they are bound in anti-magic chains and sent to the Oubliette.

"Without their magic, they cannot rescue themselves. Without light to see anything by, their location cannot be scried by anyone on the outside. The only way in or out is the Oubliette Gate . . . which is controlled by the Department of Conflict Resolution. The duke's temperament after his defeat at the hands of your incipient queen," the councilor added, "has caused him to cast two people into the Oubliette in the past five months. Normally, the number is less than two people consigned every five years."

"When we were confronted by the Council, they gave us two choices," Morg told her. "Submit to captivity quietly, or die in a very nasty mage-fight. What they *wanted* to do to the eight of us was bind us in mage-chains and throw us into the Oubliette. None of us would put up with that, and Saber was going to give the order to fight.

"*I* negotiated for us to be exiled here, instead. Isolated as it is, this island has become an alternative to the Oubliette in the last two centuries, particularly for those with large families, or popular followings. My family has both." He slanted a look at Consus, who had been there at that confrontation. "I did so at the prompting of another Seer. There are at least *three* sets of Prophecies converging on this island, if not more."

"I was not aware of any connections other than the Seers Draganna and Haupanea with your family," Consus said, frowning at the younger mage. "Those Prophecies have been under heavy discussion of late, in the Council; it *would* have come up. Who claimed to make this other Prophecy?"

"A man named Milon. He was a Natallian Seer—the late father of the boy you captured and questioned," Morg told Consus. "I made his acquaintance a few years before our exile took place, long before I learned his widow would be coming here."

Consus closed his eyes for a moment, muttering, "*All* I ever wanted was a peaceful, prosperous, *useful* political career. Not a lot of excitement, not a lot of drudgery, just a good, *quiet* life . . ."

"Kelly's world has a saying, one of the most powerful curses I have ever heard," Hope offered. She smiled ruefully at the wary yet curious looks the two mages gave her. "It's quite simple, and quite insidious. 'May you live in interesting times.' Appropriate, isn't it?"

From the oath that escaped the ex-Councilor's lips, it was obvious he agreed.

ᗰorganen stopped outside Hope's door. After dinner, they had escorted Consus to his quarters on the third floor and sketched a small tracing rune on the man's door once it had shut to watch for the door being opened. He didn't think the ex-Councilor would go wandering without permission—no career bureaucrat would be that stupid—but it wouldn't hurt to keep a spell or two attuned in his direction.

But all thoughts of others needed to be set aside. Here he was, at the entrance to her suite, at the end of their first full day together. With their hands still entwined, he gazed at Hope's beautiful tanned face and wondered if he could get away with kissing her again.

She smiled and opened the door, reaching inside just enough with her free hand to gently tap the lightglobe by the door into dimly lit life. Disappointed, Morg offered her a polite smile, prepared to have her leave. To his surprise, she tugged him in after her. Pleased, he shut the door in his wake, only to hear her curse and feel her hand jerk in his as she stumbled.

"God—! Stupid *coffee* table . . . Remind me to find a better place for it, in the morning," Hope groused. She glared at the table for a moment, then shoved it back with her foot, nodded sharply, and limped toward her bedroom. Still towing Morganen by his fingers, she added, "Remind me also to find some office space and a set of rooms I can convert into a confectioner's shop. I have too much stuff in here—half my house's worth—to be able to move."

"It was my idea to bring the table across," Morganen reminded her. "So I should take some of the blame for your poor shin."

"I'll extract penance later." Opening the door, she rapped the light bright enough to make him blink and led him all the way to the bed. "Finally! Alone, at last. No sisters, no brothers, no ex-Councilors, no interruptions . . . nothing to bother us anymore . . . well, except it's rather warm and stuffy in here, isn't it?" Hope commented, wrinkling her nose. "I forgot to open the windows to the night air, thinking only to shut out the heat of the day."

"Would you like a cooling charm on your rooms?" Morg asked her.

"Yes, please," she agreed. "I did live in the heartland of a vast continent and endured overly hot summers galore, but I also lived with air-conditioning—that's a technological version of air-cooling charms."

"Yes, I remember from the books, something about the compression and expansion of some weird gas," Morg agreed, pulling a piece of chalk from his pouch. He gestured with it at the inner wall and its painted illusion of a goat herd. "How about one on the wall?"

"Go for it," Hope agreed, seating herself on the edge of the broad bed.

A few strokes with the chalk, a bit of focused will, and a muttered word shaped the spell. Heat slowly started flowing into the mark, cooling the air by the door. Crossing to the outer wall, he pushed back the drapes that hung over one of the two windows and un-latched the panes. The night air outside was still warm, but cooler and fresher than the air inside her bedchamber. Between the two, a convection current would further lower the temperature within a short period of time. It wasn't always necessary to use great amounts of power to cause a desired effect.

Turning back to face her, Morg wondered what his presence in her bedroom meant. He knew what he wanted to do, which was kiss her again, but there were other things they could do, like talk. And there was the whole fact that not only was she most recently from another universe, with its own unique twists on cultural behavior, she originally came from an older time frame in his own world, with an unknown set of social rules regarding how men and women should behave together when they were alone. It left him feeling rather adrift and unsure of himself.

"Um . . . well. Here we are. Now what?" he asked her.

"Come here," she directed him. She patted the edge of the bed next to her, and when he approached, scrambled up onto her hands and knees and scooted herself back, across the width of the bed.

Morg, eyeing the rumpled covers, warily asked, "Were you rolling around on your bed, earlier?"

"Actually, Kelly was. I gave her some cinnamon-chocolates, and she went wild for them, then raced off to pounce on your eldest brother." Patting the bed again, Hope coaxed him into climbing onto it and stretching out. He propped himself up on his side, his cheek braced in his palm, and she squirmed into a similar posture, mirroring him. Reaching for his free hand, she entwined their fingers. "Now it's your turn. I'm going to seduce you, as promised. And I'm going to introduce you to what the other realm calls the Food of the Gods: *chocolate.*"

"The brown lumpy stuff?" he confirmed, still somewhat skeptical.

Hope rolled her eyes. "*Yes,* the brown lumpy stuff. The main ingredient comes from the seeds of the cacao tree, which are harvested when the seed pods are green. The seeds, which are also called beans, are removed from the pod, allowed to ferment in a pile of their own pulp for several days to leech out excessive bitterness, then spread out, sun-dried, and prepared for roasting. A long time ago," she added, giving him the history of her favorite food, "the beans themselves were used like coins—so many beans could buy you a meal, so many more could buy you a bushel of grain or a sack of vegetables, and so on.

"Anyway, once they've been roasted, the bean shells are cracked open and winnowed out, and the nibs, the seed meat, are then ground into a paste." She shifted closer as her enthusiasm for the subject mounted. "The paste is compressed, extracting the cocoa butter from the cocoa solids. Then they're recombined with various sweeteners, extra cocoa butter, and other ingredients to form chocolate, a delicious, smooth, melt-in-your-mouth treat.

"There are several health benefits associated with good-quality chocolate, and there are several nutrients in the chocolate itself that can alternately have a calming effect, an arousing one, or a stimulating one, or some combination of those three. The taste"—and she deliberately dropped her gaze to his lips, swaying even closer as she leaned on her elbows—"depends on the roasting, the quality of the nibs, and the proportion of cacao solids to sweetener, ranging from sweet to bitter, smoky to fruity. Other flavors can be blended into each batch, combined in various different ways.

"My personal favorite has enough bitter to stimulate and wake up the taste buds, with just enough sweet to temper it into a pleasant experience." For a moment, she was almost close enough to kiss him, and he seemed to expect it. Squeezing his hand, she released it and rolled off the bed, leaving him wanting more. "So. We'll start with the all-important question: Do you prefer very sweet desserts, or modestly sweet, or do you like a mix of different flavors? Fruits, nuts . . . ?"

Morg considered her words. "Nothing too cloyingly sweet, but nothing too bitter, either. And I think I should just try straight chocolate the first time around."

"Good point. I'll pick a mid-grade dark."

Ducking into the bathroom—she would have to get used to calling them refreshing rooms again—Hope found the cup she had placed there that morning and filled it from the cork-stuffed tap. She came back out and set it by the bed, then disappeared into the dressing room. Opening a few wardrobe doors, she found the box she wanted and brought it into the bedroom as well. Stretching out on the bed next to him, she set the box between them and removed the lid.

"These are *pastilles*—basically a fancy word for round, flat discs. Each one makes a very nice mouthful, but I don't want you to eat the whole thing." Balancing herself on her elbow, she plucked one from the box, broke it in half, and offered him one of the halves. "Nip off just a tiny piece of this, and roll the piece all over the tip of your tongue—just the tip."

Leaning forward, Morg did as requested, snapping off a small chunk. Spell-chilled sweetness warred immediately with bitterness, hinting at something slightly fruity and yet slightly smoky. He worked the piece across the tip of his tongue as requested until it melted, then swallowed. The moment it hit the back of his tongue, the flavor changed, intriguing him. "That was . . . tolerable."

Hope smirked, amused at his grudging response. She offered him the rest of the bitten half. "Now take another bite, and this time, roll it along the sides of your tongue, particularly at the back, and also underneath."

Bemused, he nipped off another piece and started rolling it around his mouth. The flavor changed again, becoming more mellow as the chocolate melted. Oddly enough, he could even taste it when he rolled it under his tongue. Involuntarily, little surprised sounds escaped his throat. Something . . . something seemed to ripple through his nerves, filling his senses as it spread from his mouth outward to the rest of his body.

Catching her hand, he brought the remaining bit of chocolate to his mouth, wanting to explore more of the flavor. His skin prickled, nipples tightening, loins stirring—more than they had stirred just from her proximity. There was something *stimulating* about this odd-colored, bittersweet substance . . . something that made him groan with pleasure as the last of it coated his senses.

Chuckling, Hope popped the other half of the pastille into her mouth. Pausing just long enough to drop the lid back onto the box, she leaned over it and kissed him, flicking her tongue around the piece in her mouth so that she could tease his lips with hints of chocolate. Morg responded willingly, his own tongue sweeping in for another taste of the confection. It pleased her when he hooked his hand around her nape and pulled her deeper into their kiss, though that meant the nearer corners of the box pressed into her stomach.

The combination of warm, willing woman and bittersweet candy filled Morganen's senses. He scooted closer, wanting to feel more of her soft body while tasting such an interesting treat. Somehow, it had engaged all of his senses; he could smell the chocolate on their breath, mingling with the faint flowery fragrance she had bathed with, earlier. He could see her eyes, half-closed and almost as brown as the *puh-steel* thing—he felt the crispness of her dark curls, thick and lovely as they draped over fingers he used to hold her in place. And the sound of her, soft moans from her throat, succulent noises from their lips, combining with the bitter and the sweet melting on their tongues.

All of it was quite heady in combination. The box was uncomfortable, though. Persisting until the chocolate faded, Morganen licked at the edges of her lips, then pulled back and let out a reluctant sigh. "Fine. I concede your point. Chocolate *is* good."

"Mm-hmm!" Smug, Hope shifted back so that she could open the box again. "There is nothing in this world—or that one—that is better than a chocolate-flavored kiss!"

Something in her assertion annoyed Morganen. It wasn't until she lifted a new brown disc to her lips that he realized why. "No."

Hope paused, the pastille half an inch from being eaten. That wasn't an agreement-sounding *no*. It was a denial *no*. Which bemused her. "What do you mean, no?"

Plucking the uneaten candy from her fingers, Morg tossed it back into its dark blue box. He picked up the container and twisted onto his back so that he could drop the whole thing on her bedside table. Rolling to face her again, Morg speared his fingers into her dark brown locks. "You sound like you're addicted to that stuff. *My* kisses are better, pure and unornamented. You will grow addicted to *me*."

Nauvea . . . I think he's jealous of my chocolates! Hope didn't have time to explore that amusing thought, for he pulled her back into another kiss. One which unfortunately didn't last very long. As soon as he tried to get close to her again, this time his pouch got in the way. It wasn't as lumpy as the box of chocolates, but it was uncomfortable all the same.

Letting go with a soft sound of disgust, Morganen sat up and released the leather wrapped around his waist, dropping belt and pouch on the floor. He drew up his knees and unlaced his brown sandals as well, intent on tossing them over the side of the bed. A glance at his side showed Hope unlacing her own outworlder footwear.

A twist rolled him onto his knees. As soon as she turned to face him again, Morganen urged her into kneeling as well. Their bodies bumped and met, thigh to thigh, stomach to stomach, breasts to chest, followed quickly by their mouths. The chocolate flavor had faded somewhat, leaving him with more and more of *her* taste. It was more subtle, less sweet, yet just as compelling. She wasn't just a scent, a mere flavor; she was the whole experience. Not just a warm, willing woman, but *his* woman; his best friend, manifested as his Destiny.

Hope found herself quickly overwhelmed. Morganen didn't just kiss her as a man who wanted a woman; he kissed her as if she could give a drowning man his breath, a starving man his food. Somehow they went from kneeling upright together, to her on her back, him pressing her into the soft, feather-stuffed bedding. The air in the room was finally beginning to feel cool, but her skin felt hot wherever he touched her through their clothes, body to body, hands to shoulders and breasts and hips, whatever he could caress.

Her own fingers were busy, clutching at his hair, his shoulders, kneading the lean muscles beneath his tunic. Now that the chocolate had faded, he didn't taste particularly special, but he *was* every bit as enjoyable. With his belt off, she was free to tug up the back hem of his tunic and slide her palms over the curve of his backside, into the dip at the small of his back. Between the velvet of his tongue and the satin of his skin, the half-braced weight of his muscles and the thoroughness of his kisses, Hope was in tactile heaven.

Only when both of them were struggling for air, his legs half tangled in the folds of her skirt, did Morganen ease back his kisses. Resting his forehead against hers, he spent a couple of moments just breathing, panting, before he asked, "Well, am I as good as chocolate? Or am I even better?"

His lighthearted arrogance made her smile. Wriggling her fingers against his back, Hope pretended to consider the question for a moment, then gave her reply. "I don't know . . . I think I'll need a sample of at least a dozen more kisses, possibly two dozen, before I'll know for sure."

Caught off guard by her quip, Morg laughed. That was the quirky sense of humor he had come to love during all their awkward, cross-Veil conversations. He grinned at her. "I'll see if I come up with a dozen really fresh ones, just for you."

"One thing," Hope interjected as he leaned down to kiss her again. That earned her an inquiring look. She gave him a reassuring, if slightly salacious grin. "Would you take off your tunic, first?"

Pleased, Morganen leaned in close enough for a brief kiss. On the end of her nose, since he didn't trust himself to confine it to a short kiss if he touched her lips. Levering himself off of her, he straddled both of her thighs, rucking up the hem of his tunic. "Your desire is my desire—just state whatever you wish of me," he added as he pulled the material over his head, tossing it to the floor, "and I shall gladly comply."

"Remind me to take advantage of that," Hope muttered, admiring the tight stomach and lean chest he had bared.

It was very clear to her that, unlike a lot of the men in the other realm, Morganen exercised frequently. Part of it she knew came from his sword lessons with his brothers. Part of it came from the healthier lifestyle of this world—healthier in the sense of more exercise and fresher foods. There were many ways in which the health care of the other realm was superior—better dental care, better optical, and certain medical procedures that Healing spells had yet to emulate, but Morg was the product of a lifestyle that had never heard of double cheeseburgers and fries.

Just as she reached for his stomach, wanting to feel those tight muscles for herself and see if they were just as satiny-smooth as his back . . . his cryslet chimed.

Breeee-dee-deep! Breeee-dee-deep!

Morganen twitched, startled. Disappointed by the interruption, he gave Hope an apologetic look. "I *have* to answer. It could be an emergency."

Nodding in understanding, Hope watched as he cut off the second ringing midway by flipping up the crystal-and-metal lid of the bracelet.

Quickly angling the oval mirror inside so that it caught him from the neck up, Morganen found himself staring at a visibly excited Evanor.

"There you are! Come to the dining room, quick—and bring Hope!"

His fourthborn brother looked almost giddy with happiness. "Ev? What's up?"

"Serina's given birth—to *twins*! A boy and a girl! Come and meet them in the dining hall—Dom's going to show them in the mirror in just a few minutes!"

The mirror gleamed and resumed a reflection of his face. Morg thought he looked a bit stunned. Closing the lid, he looked down at Hope, who had pushed herself up onto her elbows. His desire to keep kissing her warred with his interest in seeing his newest niece and nephew, leaving him momentarily unsure how to respond. "Uh . . . wow. Twins."

Hope twitched her thighs when he didn't move. "Well? Go on," she ordered him. "Grab your shirt, and let's go!"

Morg flushed, feeling the urge to stay in here with her trump the urge to see his newest kin. "Well, it's not exactly an *emergency* . . ."

The flattery buried in his words made her chuckle. "I'll still be available for ravishing after we've oohed and ahhed over the babies, Morg. Promise."

Relieved, he climbed off of her and sat on the edge of the bed, stooping for his discarded clothes. A thought crossed his mind as he started shrugging back into his sleeveless, summer-weight tunic. "Hope . . . *have* you given that any thought?"

"Mm?" she asked, fishing for her sneakers on the other side of the bed. "About what?"

"Babies. Children, contraception . . . and marriage. To me." He glanced over his shoulder, waiting for her reply.

"I've given babies and children a good deal of thought. The same with contraception. *And* marriage to you," she admitted, tugging on her outworlder shoes. "Not necessarily in that order, nor always connected together. But if you mean contraception in regard to us, before marriage . . . no, that sort of slipped my mind, just now. I did have an anti-conception amulet before, but after being dumped in a world without magic, and, well . . . whenever I chose to play the local courting games, I just used the local methods. Among other things."

A glance over her shoulder showed his brow creasing in a soft frown. Hope guessed the reason readily enough. If he was mildly jealous of her love affair with chocolate, then he would be even less thrilled by thoughts of her past lovers.

"You have to remember that I *didn't know* I'd ever be able to return, Morg. Let alone that my return would coincide with someone else's Prophecy about marriage and mates and the Gods know what else. As far as I knew, I was stuck in that other realm permanently.

So, rather than choosing to be upset and depressed and angry, I chose to accept it, live with it, deal with it, and be as happy as I could about my circumstances," Hope told him, tugging on her other shoe. "We always have two choices about our circumstances, whatever they are. Either we can act in a positive way, or we can react negatively."

"Hope . . . you lost *everything*. Your original home, your livelihood, every single person you ever knew, all of it vanished two hundred years ago, and you didn't know you'd ever get it back," Morg said, lacing his sandals in place. "You certainly didn't get more than a fraction of it back, and at that, this palace isn't fully yours anymore. How can you be positive about all that?"

"It's one of the lessons you learn as a Seer," she told him, adjusting her socks before standing. "Either you embrace the events that unfold in your life—whether or not they're prodded by the Gods—or you cause yourself even more grief by resisting and denying them. It hurt to lose my parents to that storm. But a lot of other people lost their brothers and sisters, their husbands and wives, their sons and daughters, when the rest of the crew sank with the ship. I had to be strong for the sake of all the others who were grieving.

"I had to be positive, to remind them that there was still so much to be thankful for, despite their losses." Looking around the room, with its walls crowded with dressers and bureaus, she shrugged. "Yes, I lost my parents. I also lost my honorary aunt, my wisest advisor, my best friend and companion. But I gained a new best friend in Kelly, and another best friend in you. I even gained an entire family of future brothers- and sisters-in-law, through your family. I regained my home, and more importantly, my world, however greatly they may have changed over the years."

Meeting his gaze over the width of the bed between them, she gave him a wry smile.

"You also have to remember, I lost the person I used to be and gained a whole new me. I've grown and changed, thanks to all the strange outworlder experiences I've had. And if Nauvea hadn't tossed me through the Veils . . . I wouldn't have gained *you*, either," she reminded him. "Should I waste my energy in regretting that? Or embrace it happily?"

She had him there. Morg picked up his belt and stood, slinging it around his hips. "I *don't* want you to regret knowing me. Or loving me, hopefully. But it doesn't negate all of your suffering, nor the fact that I am truly sorry you had to suffer . . . because if you *hadn't* been put into a position to meet me, you wouldn't have suffered."

"I'll accept any sympathy you care to pass my way," Hope promised him, moving around the foot of the bed to join him. "Particularly if it comes wrapped in a hug and a kiss."

Catching her hand, Morganen tugged her close enough to wrap his arms around her. He pressed a kiss to her forehead before tucking her head under his chin. "As I said, whatever you desire, I'll do my best to procure."

Snuggling into his embrace, she returned the hug. "What I desire . . . hmm. Well, I'd like to see my future niece and nephew. And then . . ."

"And then?" Morg repeated, anticipation rising within him.

"And then we should probably get to know each other a little more, before going much farther than just this." She sighed. Feeling him stiffen with disappointment, Hope pulled back enough to give him a wry look. "Hey, *you're* the one who brought up the very practical questions of children, marriage, and contraception. I'm just agreeing with you that they're very wise questions that have to be considered . . . and I haven't been using contraceptives for about a year, now."

Part of him stiffened from something other than disappointment. The thought of her being unprotected right now, ripe and fertile, had a remarkably primitive effect on his flesh. For a brief moment, Morg gave serious thought to ignoring Evanor's summons in favor of giving in to those primitive urges. The urge to strip away their clothes, entwine their bodies together, and start making their own babies. Destiny wouldn't stand in their way, not when their presence in this room had more or less been Foreseen . . .

Two things stopped him: respect for her wishes and familial duty. Honoring her wishes was easy; Morganen cared for the woman in his arms, enough to tell his urges to wait. Honoring his family was also important. Though Evanor was technically the first to be a father, having taken Mikor as his next-son when he had married the boy's mother, Dominor was the first of the brothers to create both a son and a daughter.

Hugging her, Morganen released all but her hand. A tug led her toward the door. "Come on, then. Dom will be eager to gloat over how adorable his children are."

"All newborns are red, wrinkly, and unhappy to be removed from their nice, warm womb, regardless of what their parents may think," Hope told him, remembering her—the original Hope's—cousins and their gloating over their own infants, not so long ago.

Infants I'll never see again, since Hope O'Niell is now officially, permanently missing. She pushed aside thoughts of that particular situation, though Hope knew she would have to discuss it with Morg and the rest, eventually.

"You know, I got an earful this afternoon from Kelly on all the idiocies of the Natallian-Mandarite gender war, and it's not at all the Natallia I remember. They used to be one of our biggest customers, too," she added as they left her suite, "since their warm climate requires a lot of salt for preserving food."

"We've regained them as customers," Morganen reassured her. "We have the mirror-link to the Nuns of Koral-tai, augmented by the Fountainway between their Fountain and ours."

"Good," she praised. "I'm happy that Nightfall's on its way back to prosperity."

Once the link for the mirror hung in the dining hall had ended, most of Morganen's family remained in the chamber, talking and laughing and exclaiming over the two tiny human beings the third-born brother and his wife had produced. Rydan and Rora took off again, for it was their turn to "walk the dog," as the transplanted Fountain was being called, but the rest remained: Kelly and Saber, Wolfer and Alys, Evanor, Mikor, Trevan and Amara, Koranen and Danau, and Morg and Hope. Koranen and Danau had brought up a bottle of wine and a fruit pie from the kitchen along with stacks of tableware and glasses, turning the gathering into an impromptu party.

Rather, most of the gathered family talked and laughed, sitting in their seats around the long dining table. Two of them didn't laugh, and didn't talk all that much. It was Evanor who addressed their quietness when a break in the multiple conversations came along. "Kelly? Saber? Are you feeling alright?"

Kelly had seated herself on Saber's lap, rather than take a separate chair; he was rubbing her back as she leaned against him, comforting her, but he looked like he could have used a bit of comforting himself. Hope guessed the reason within moments, based on the conversation she'd had with her friend earlier in the day.

"It's your own fertility, isn't it?" she asked, deciding now was the time to bring certain secrets into the open. Saber narrowed his gray eyes at her, not happy at having such a private matter brought into the open, but Hope wasn't deterred. "You're worried you'll never be able to have children, because Kelly isn't from this world."

Both of them nodded, visibly reluctant over the topic. Kelly sighed roughly. "We've tried, and tried, and *tried*. And yes, we've both been poked and prodded by Mariel. She says we're both healthy, as far as she can tell."

"Nothing *seems* to be wrong with our bodies . . . but nothing has been happening, either," Saber admitted quietly. He gestured with his free hand at the quiescent scrying-glass on the wall. "Seeing Dom happy . . . It's frustrating."

"Well, I really do think it's the food you *haven't* been eating, Kelly," Hope told her friend.

Kelly rolled her aquamarine eyes. "This isn't about *chocolate*, Hope! Chocolate doesn't fix everything!"

"In this case, I honestly think it will," Hope asserted. "It did for me, when Morg shipped me some of the local Nightfall fruits all those months ago."

"But you said that was for your cramps, not fertility," Kelly reminded her.

"Cramps were only part of it," Hope revealed carefully. She glanced at Morg, then looked back at her outworlder friend. "Right after I found the trace of the door Morganen had made through the Veils, I received a call from my—from Hope's cousin Anita. She was having fertility problems. The normal kind of fertility problems. Anita wanted to know if I—Hope—would be willing to donate some of my eggs, because she and her husband, Carlos, really wanted to have children. And since she and I look very similar, she wanted to ask for my eggs to be paired with his seed, rather than some anonymous donor."

Morg closed his eyes. This was even worse in some ways than Hope being the last, lost Duchess of Nightfall. The woman he loved had created *children* with another man. He opened his eyes in the next moment, frowning in confusion. *How* could she have had children, when she'd been relatively flat-stomached the entire year he'd known her? She continued, forcing him to pay attention.

"I'd just found out that there *was* a way back to my world, or at least to another world, one with magic enough to open the Veils. But . . . I'd basically borrowed the original Hope's life, and I thought the original Hope would've probably agreed, based on all that I'd learned about her. I wanted to honor her life, to sort of make up for usurping her identity," she explained, looking around to gauge their reactions.

The explanation was probably over Mikor's head, not to mention the boy looked sleepy, since it was past his normal bedtime, but the woman Alys was listening intently, and the others seemed to be watching with mixtures of curiosity, confusion, and attentiveness.

The most important witness to her confession, Morg, was frowning softly, but he did seem to be listening with an open mind.

Taking a deep breath, she continued. "So, I agreed to help out her cousin, in the original Hope's stead. I went to the fertility clinic that Anita and Carlos were using, where they have Healers who specialize in such things. They examined me, made sure everything seemed to be in working order, and when the timing was right, dosed me with potions, extracted the eggs my body produced . . . and when they tried to mix them with Carlos' seed in the special container in their workrooms, the eggs they extracted were not viable."

"I'm confused," Mikor stated sleepily, interrupting her tale. Chin propped up in his hand, he furrowed his brow. "Humans have eggs? Like chickens and doves do?"

Hope wasn't the only one who had to stifle a laugh into a cough. She held up her hand, pinching her thumb and forefinger very close together. "Extremely *tiny* ones, and they don't have shells like bird eggs do . . . but yes. All creatures that have both males and females, the females have eggs and the males have seed. The Healers at this clinic extracted my eggs via their strange outworlder abilities and tried to mix my eggs with some of Carlos' seed in a special container— this didn't take place in my body, so I never actually got pregnant. But . . . the eggs didn't start to grow, like they should have.

"The Healers didn't think anything was particularly wrong with that," she continued, using terminology Morganen's family would understand, "since sometimes it takes a couple of tries for the special potions to take effect properly. But the second round they tried, that also failed. Then Kelly came back for that brief visit that one weekend, and I met Morganen . . . sort of . . . and that's when he started contacting and communicating with me.

"I knew by that point that Kelly had gone to *my* homeworld, and that I could get the foods I'd been craving and missing for all the years of my exile. I asked Morg to send some over for me to try, and he was willing to indulge my 'curiosity.' I didn't know eating the fruit would have any particular effect, but my next visit to the clinic, which was to have been the third and final try . . . the eggs they extracted accepted the seed and started to grow," Hope said. "They put them into Anita's womb, where three of them took root . . . and roughly two months ago, she gave birth to triplets.

"They were born early, so they had to stay with the Healers for a while, but they came home a couple weeks ago . . . and I got to hold their baby girl and two baby boys." Hope shrugged, trying not to think too much about never holding them again. "If you go strictly by pure bloodline, they're my sons and daughter. I am their mother, just as Carlos is their father . . . but Anita was the one who gave birth to them, and who will love and raise them as their actual mother. I merely donated the eggs."

"And you think it was the *fruit* that made you fertile?" Saber asked skeptically, arching one honey gold brow.

Morg was glad his eldest brother had asked that question. He wasn't entirely sure of her logic, either.

"Not just any fruit," Hope corrected him. "Both realms have things like apples and pears. They look the same, they grow the same, they taste the same. But we have *toska*, and they have *bananas*. We have *jilbi* berries, and they have *rasp*berries. Chocolate— *cocoa*—is unique to their world. Whatever nutrients Kelly isn't getting in her diet, I think it's in the chocolate I brought across— she's already said it's affected her libido in a positive way! I felt the same way, after eating that Nightfall fruit. I didn't *know* it would have that effect . . . but it makes sense that it would. We do get our life-energy from the foods we eat, and I wasn't eating the foods unique to this world, my birth-world, until Morg sent across a basketful at my request."

Ev coughed and tilted his pale blond head at his dark-haired next-son, who was frowning in confusion again. Too late, for Mikor asked in the uncomfortable silence, "What's a li-bee-doh?"

"Something you hopefully won't have to deal with for several more years," Evanor muttered, blushing. Wolfer coughed behind his hand, as did Trevan. Alys giggled.

"Actually, what she says makes sense to me," Amara offered. The black-haired woman drew the attention of the others with her statement. Under their gaze, she elaborated. "But it's not just because it's some lack of nutrients. After Morganen stole those sacks of wheat from the city stores, I was upset with him, until Trevan told me there has to be an equitable exchange of both matter and energy—life-energy—between the two universes, to keep them in balance.

"*Think* about it," she added. "If Kelly wants to have children in *this* universe, those children will grow up and affect the impact of *this* world . . . when normally her children would have grown up and impacted the course of *that* world. The same for Hope . . . for Haupanea. Normally she would have affected this world. I say she couldn't have gotten pregnant, fruit or no fruit, until after Kelly came across here. And now that she has had children in that world, Kelly is free to have children in this one."

"But Hope came back across," Morg pointed out. "Kelly isn't going back. Not if any of us can help it."

"—Yes, but remember how you *found* her?" Koranen interjected quickly. "She would have died in that house fire, if you hadn't rescued her, Brother. Any impact she should have had on her world would have been negated by that. Removing her from her universe was the same as her dying in the house fire."

"But that doesn't explain her crossing," Kelly said, gesturing at Hope. "Unless . . . well, I suppose the original Hope's life was supposed to have ended five years ago. Hope—Haupanea—carried that life forward, and had an impact out of proportion, because the original shouldn't have had any impact at all, after that first tornado swept through the town."

Saber frowned at that. His arms encircled his wife. "I am *not* giving up Kelly after four more years."

Hope shook her head, lifting a hand in reassurance. "Relax; the

Gods clearly want Kelly here. Morg sent across plenty of wheat, enough that someone who otherwise might have died of hunger in the other world will surely survive and go on to have an impact comparable to Kelly's own actions in this universe. That particular life-debt balance has been addressed.

"As for her continued presence in this world . . . *I* should have lived out the rest of my life. Instead, I missed out on two centuries— two full lifetimes. That imbalance has to be addressed. I think that those two hundred years will be given back and divided, energy-wise, between Kelly and I, so she *should* be able to live out a long and full life."

"Barring mekhadakaks, evil uncles, outraged Councilors, and who knows whatever else might plague me," Kelly muttered. She mustered a smile. "So we come around to having children again, and the karmic balance of it all. If you had three kids, who will grow up to impact the other world in who knows what ways, then I should be able to have three, as well. But . . . where does that leave you? I mean, regarding kids in this world?"

"I'm not sure, but really, I think I'm just resuming my rightful place in this universe, however many decades it's been delayed," Hope stated, shrugging. "By rights, I should have lived long enough to find a husband, have some kids, and live out my life on a happy, prosperous island. Just like you, had you stayed back in that other world, *shouldn't* have lived long enough to go on and have kids. In this world, you *can* have a future. It's quite clear our Gods want you to have one here."

"Well, if nothing else, I suppose Saber and I can always nip across to that fertility clinic you used," Kelly agreed, sighing. She shot Hope a thoughtful look. "I suppose you have a good reason why this never came up until now?"

"Maybe because it just wasn't a good enough moment for that particular subject, until now?" Hope offered. Kelly gave her a skeptical look, and Hope returned it with a sardonic one. "Oh, come on! It was bad enough I had to confess who I really was, right after

I came across. 'Gee, no, I'm not the real Hope O'Niell; I'm actually the duchess who used to own this whole island—oh, and by the way, I left behind a clutch of kids for someone else to raise, back in the other world.' *That* would've been tactful!"

"If you ladies are going to argue semantics for half the night, I'm taking Mikor to bed," Evanor interrupted, scooping the ten-year-old onto his lap. The youth was just sleepy enough that he cuddled into his next-father's chest.

"Okay, okay—all arguments are over. And I'll eat more chocolate. It's not like it's a hardship," Kelly added, slanting her husband an amused, clearly private look. She turned back to Hope, sighing. "Just tell me something: Are there any *more* secrets you've been hiding from us?"

Hope shook her head. "Not that I'm aware of. Or that I can think of, off the top of my head. Of course, I'd like to set up a confectioner's kitchen somewhere in the palace, so I *can* keep you well supplied in chocolate. Just in case it *does* work, and you want to try it a second time," she teased lightly. "Other than that, the only thing that's still unsettled in my life is my status as a Seer. I'd like to find my Prophecies cabinet and reread them, maybe try to figure out which ones have come true in the interim, but other than what the wardrobe contains . . . all I can do is wait for one of the Gods to speak to me."

Morganen touched her back, gently rubbing it with his palm in a way reminiscent of Saber and Kelly at the start of the conversation. She leaned into him, grateful he was still willing to comfort her, despite her latest revelation. *Then again, he knows what being a Seer means, simply by virtue of being from this world. And from having worked with that other Seer, the one who was the boy's father . . .*

"If you still want to be a mouthpiece of the Gods now that you're back, I certainly won't stop you. Or envy you," Kelly told Hope. "I've already been the victim of two or three Prophecies myself. I'd hate to be the one handing them out. As for a little chocolate shop of your own . . . I think we can find you something useful. But only after we finish fixing up the audience hall. Which we'll do after breakfast tomorrow. Tonight . . . you owe me another box of chocolates. If we're going to give your food theory a try, we might as well get started right away."

"Goodnight, everybody," Evanor asserted, hoisting Mikor into a cradled position. He carefully rose from his seat, only to have Wolfer rise as well, taking the nearly asleep boy from him.

"I'll carry him," the secondborn brother offered. "It's a long way to the southwest wing."

"I'll get the door," Alys offered, hurrying forward to open the panel. The two brothers vanished into the corridor, one slender and blond, the other muscular and brown. Alys lingered in the doorway for a moment more, peering at Hope. "Um . . . I don't suppose I could try some of this chocolate stuff myself? Not that I expect it to affect *me* one way or another, since I'm very much from this world, but . . . well, it sounds interesting."

Hope smiled wryly, rising from her chair. "I'll get you a box, too. Anyone else want to try some tonight . . . ?"

Again, Morg stopped outside Hope's door, guided by the dim glow of the lightglobes spaced at intervals along the hall. He had held his tongue until this moment, choosing to support her in the eyes of his family. Now, however, he had to ask, "So . . . was that the reason you didn't want to go any further than cuddling with me?"

"That's part of the reason I wasn't taking outworlder contraceptives," Hope corrected. He had looked concerned about something on the walk back to their wing of the palace. "And . . . well, yes, I didn't want us to become intimate before you knew about Anita's kids. And they *are* hers. She and Carlos wanted them, struggled to have them, and will raise them with love and caring. I'm happy for all of them."

Morg rubbed at the back of his neck, feeling awkward at her words. He had always pictured himself and his future wife with at least a few children, siblings who could play with each other, and play with the cousins his brothers would eventually have. But that was an awkward assertion. "Does that mean you, ah . . . don't want children yourself?"

So that's what he's worried about. She smiled in relief. "Actually, it's the fact that they're *Carlos'* kids that put me off the idea of being in their lives. I like kids, in general, and I wouldn't mind having some, someday. But not with Carlos. I'm glad we only got 'intimate' in a petri dish, after both of us had gone home for the day.

"He's not a bad man, don't get me wrong. In fact, he's perfect for Anita, since they have so much in common . . . but he's definitely not the man I'd have picked out to marry for myself. He's very much into the other world's sports, and I'm not. I'm very much into reading, and he isn't; he likes horror movies, and I don't do that sort of thing." She wrinkled her nose. "Not to mention he has a mustache . . ."

Shifting his fingers from his nape to his face, Morg tested the rasp of his stubble. There wasn't much of it, since his beard didn't grow very fast, but relief at her confession gave him the courage to tease her. "I guess I'll have to shave twice a day, then, just to be sure you'll continue kissing me."

Some of her tension relaxed, at that. Still, she had to be sure, and tentatively asked, "So . . . you're not too upset?"

"Only on your behalf, that you'll only ever be able to watch them from the other side of a looking glass, if 'Hope O'Niell' is to remain the victim of a tornado attack," he told her, dropping his hand so that he could take both of hers in his. "But if you want to have three of your own . . . I could place myself at your disposal for that. Preferably in the bounds of marriage."

"Yes, preferably," she joked. "You, at least, have several hobbies and habits in common with me . . . and I can definitely picture kissing you."

"I, um, thought about what you said," Morg told her. "I thought, what if our roles had been reversed: What if *I* had been the one cast into another world, if I'd been forced to hide my true identity, and so forth. And I decided I probably would have made all the same decisions that you did. Or at least similar ones, given the same choices. So . . . I guess I'm saying I understand all the choices you've made, and I accept them. If that doesn't sound pompous?"

"No," she reassured him, smiling in relief. "It sounds generous. And considerate, and thoughtful, and kindhearted, and a *huge* relief. The fertility thing really was my last big secret."

"That's not entirely true," Morganen hedged, making her frown in confusion. He smirked at her. "I still don't know what you look like without your clothes."

Hope gave him a skeptical look. "You mean to tell me that you, a red-blooded male, really *didn't* try to spy on me when I was changing, or in the shower, or whatever?"

"Oh, I tried," he admitted freely, shrugging. "My mirror wouldn't let me. Mother and Father commissioned it the year before they died. I was only thirteen, and they didn't think a mirror that could scry on someone's naughty bits was appropriate for someone of my tender age, for all that it was apparent even that early that I'd be powerful when fully grown. Afterward . . . well, it's such a finely crafted, flawless mirror, I just never bothered trying to undo the privacy spell. Not that I think I could," he added wryly. "Not when it was embedded into the mirror at its forging.

"As it was, shortly before Mother and Father died . . . Kor was caught literally red-handed with a girl. We were only just fourteen at the time, and Father made a comment about sitting on *both* of us until we were *eighteen* before letting us have any 'adult' fun." Morg shrugged. "I just never bothered with trying to forge an uncensored mirror, after that. Sort of in honor to Father's memory, even though I'd thought it highly unfair at the time."

"I wish I'd known him," Hope told Morg, smiling softly. "He reminds me of my own father. I got caught trying to get a kiss from a boy who was fifteen, back when I was thirteen, and got a very long lecture on 'proper ducal propriety' and horrible chores for a turning of Brother Moon. I realized later that he loved me, because he *did* care about my good behavior."

"What about Hope's parents?" he asked, curious. "What were they like?"

"I never knew them directly. They died in the same tornado that took her," she reminded him. "But from everything I learned from the others, they weren't too far off from my own parents in temperament and parenting skills. The family members I did meet were good people, for the most part."

"For the most part?" Morg inquired, lifting a brow.

She wrinkled her nose wryly. "Well, there's always that one relative who, after having drunk too much, says and does things that are embarrassing at family gatherings. And the cranky oldster who swears nothing is ever as good as it used to be, and the snotty, rebellious teenager who refuses to be respectful of others . . . but for the most part, they were very nice.

"I do know I could have been dropped into a far worse situation, with a far worse family." Hope smiled down at their joined hands, then peered past his shoulder at the door to his suite. "So. You've seen my rooms. Do I get to see yours?"

Morg almost agreed. He wanted to show her his quarters, his books . . . his bed. But he remembered why that wasn't a good idea, and shook his head. "Normally, I'd say yes, with definite enthusiasm . . . but I'd want to hold you all night long. You're scheduled to walk the dog for the two hours before breakfast, so that Rora and Rydan can cook. And I have sword practice right before breakfast, too. Both of us will need our sleep."

She pouted, then stepped close enough to bring their bodies together. "Then could you at least give me a goodnight kiss? Otherwise, I'm going to have to go in there and satisfy my craving for you by substituting chocolate, you realize."

Suspecting he was being prodded, Morganen took the bait anyway. Lowering his head, he rested his forehead against hers. "I am far better than chocolate. Admit it."

That, she couldn't let go unchallenged. "Prove it."

Angling his head, Morg kissed her in slow, succulent nibbles and rolling, tangling tongue-tips, until her brown eyes closed in surrender. Just their lips and tongues touched, but it wasn't enough. Their hands parted, arms sliding around ribs and encircling shoulders, bringing their bodies into alignment. She was delightfully soft in all the right places, with full hips he could grasp and pull against his own, breasts that cushioned themselves against his chest, and a sweetness about her that had more to do with personality than with taste.

Morg shifted one of his hands from her shoulder to her nape, turning her head so that he could press his lips along her cheekbone. He meant to end their embrace and let her go; he really did. Hope had other plans, for she twisted her head and nipped at his throat, latching onto a tender spot with a soft suckle of her lips and a circling swirl of her tongue. That traced an unexpected fire through his veins and dislocated the strength in his knees.

Buckling, he caught himself by the arm still wrapped around her shoulders. She did it again, dislocating his half-formed thoughts of stopping. "Hope . . . I . . . uhhh . . ."

"My rooms," she growled against his throat, before tugging him backward by a hand wrapped through his belt. The other opened the door to her suite. "Now."

I suppose we can set the alarm on my cryslet, he thought distractedly, letting her pull him proprietarily into her sitting room. Eyes on her, he didn't see the low table until his right shin banged painfully into the corner. Grunting, Morg stumbled, twisting his left ankle as his weight came down awkwardly on that leg. He hopped, catching his balance and grunting again, just as Hope whirled to face him. Lust momentarily forgotten, he found himself looking into her concerned eyes.

"Morg! Are you all right?" she asked, worried. "Are you, um . . . Do you want to . . . ?"

He knew in that moment that she'd send him to his own bed to recuperate if he said he was no longer in the mood; his health and well-being were clearly that important to her, more important than her own pleasure. It was also true that his shin felt like the table had gouged a hole in it, and his ankle felt halfway dislocated, it throbbed that much. But rather than putting him off their hastily made plans, her blatant concern soothed the pain into a mere inconvenience. Morg quickly shook his head.

"No. Take me to your bed. Kiss me until it feels better," he ordered. "Or at least until my ankle stops feeling like it's broken."

Her smile came back, sly and feminine. Hope started to lead him back into her bedroom, until she realized he was limping. Quickly slipping her shoulder under his, she helped him half hop his way to her bed. Settling him on the edge of the bed, she crouched and probed gently at his left foot around the straps of his sandal. He hissed a little, but stooped to untie the lacings. It didn't even look swollen, yet.

"Do you know any chilling charms?" she asked, looking up at him. "Or something to create some ice?"

He gave her a wry look. "I get beaten up by my brothers on a regular basis, every other morning. Trust me, I know my chilling charms. *Frilluleo*," Morg muttered, curling up his leg on the edge of the bed so that he could trace his fingers along his skin. "*Frillulenjo akhal*. There, that'll ease any swelling.

"We've all learned the basic charms for bashes, bruises, sprains, and fractures, as well as a few of the more advanced spells. Saber's always been rather insistent about ensuring each of us practices swordplay as well as spell-work. I may be the best of my brothers at magery . . . but I'm the absolute worst of us when it comes to the melee arts," he admitted ruefully. "I've grown rather good at patching myself up, as a result."

"You banged your other shin, didn't you?" Hope asked, shifting to unlace his other knee-high sandal. "How bad is it?"

He nodded. "It hurts, but shin bruises are always painful. It'll heal."

"Well, then, let's get your pants off, so I can kiss it better. And everything else you're wearing, just in case anything else starts aching and needs a kiss," Hope added, daring to tease him.

Morganen thought that was a very good idea. He got as far as unbuckling his belt and dropping it once more onto her floor, before he had an even better idea. "Why don't you take off your own clothes? I'm sure the sight of all the things I haven't been able to see before will be sufficiently . . . yes, distracting . . ."

He trailed off as she stood, pulling her outworlder blouse over her head. She wore a silky white contraption very much like an abbreviated vest, one that barely circled her ribs below her breasts. Given the material was solid, he had seen this much of her flesh before. Hope toed off her outworlder shoes, then tugged the skirt down her legs. That brought her torso forward and down, making her breasts sway and his pulse skip a beat.

This, he hadn't seen in his mirror. Not the cleft of her full breasts, nor the slight gap that was just wide enough for his hand to have slid between. Some of the blood which had been headed to his throbbing leg and foot detoured right back up to his loins. Morg wanted to bury his mouth in that shadowed haven, but he didn't have the chance; stepping out of her skirt and peeling off her socks, she straightened again, clad now only in the shortened vest-thing, and a matching scrap of satiny white fabric clinging to her pelvis.

Now he had a breath-stalling view. Her shoulders were square, her hips rounded, her stomach softly curved and her waist tapered. There were hints of muscles flexing beneath her skin, but the overall impression was of tanned, womanly softness. She wasn't as plump as Mariel was—her hair certainly wasn't as curly—but she did have some of the Healer's lushness about her, and her soft, full curves deeply appealed to him.

She removed her upper undergarment. For the first time in all the months that he had been watching her through his cheval mirror, Morg could finally see her breasts. Their lush curves were clearly delineated, bared in all their beauty. Not just from a lack of blurring, but because they were outlined in a pale silhouette of her vest-thing, as if she had spent time in the sun in just her undergarments. He could see her broad, rose pink nipples, and a little mole on one plump, inner curve. The sight of it made his mouth water, for it looked like a speck of chocolate. It would probably taste of musk and salt from her skin, rather than the bitter and sweet of her outworlder treat, but he had to find out for himself.

Just as he leaned forward to try, she did, too, thumbs hooked into the sides of her final undergarment. Their heads almost collided. Morg flinched back protectively, not wanting any more bruises.

SIX

◦❄◦

Hope shifted back as well. The sway of her breasts seemed to mesmerize him. Leaning forward again, she pressed her lips to his temple, recapturing his attention with the tender kiss. Mouth quirking in a smile that was part amusement, part reassurance, she tugged her panties down her legs, stepping out of them. His gaze flicked downward, following the motion of her breasts, but when she straightened, she saw he was now staring at her dark pubic hairs.

Morg couldn't quite process what he was seeing. Not the lighter, untanned triangle of flesh centered over her groin, but the shape of the dark hairs framed by that triangle of golden flesh. *This* particular revelation had definitely been blurred beyond all recognition by the charms forged into his mirror. Licking his lips, he managed to make his voice work. "You, uh . . . *trimmed* . . . down there?"

"It's called a 'bikini wax,' an absurdly painful piece of outworlder body-fashion, but still practical in a way," Hope stated, amused by his blatant bemusement.

"Practical?" Morg repeated, pulling his gaze away from her loins, up past her breasts, and back to her face. "What . . . ?"

"If you can ever recover the full use of your tongue, you can always find out firsthand what I mean," she teased. He stared at her until she deliberately licked her upper lip, then blushed.

Jinga, Morg thought, struggling to think through the effects of *that* particular line of thought. *She's every bit as forward about lovemaking as Saber claimed Kelly was!*

For a moment, he worried that he wouldn't be adequate for her outworlder-altered expectations, given how lascivious that one, telling action seemed. Trevan might have been the better choice . . . but he discarded that idea firmly. *My Destiny, my bride, my lover.*

Catching her hands, Morg pulled Hope up to the edge of the bed. She sighed happily when he leaned forward again, this time successfully burying his face between her breasts. Inhaling deeply, Morganen filled his senses with the smell and the feel and, yes, the taste of her. That little mole didn't taste like chocolate, but it did make him groan from the salty sweetness of her skin. Mirrors could only show so much, even unblurred ones, but this—she—was real. Real, and here, and *his*.

Arms sliding around her waist, hands smoothing down over the curves of her backside, Morg urged her up onto the bed. She straddled his thigh, putting herself in the perfect place for him to capture one of her tightening nipples with his mouth. Fingers kneading her rump, lips suckling her breast, he groaned again, wondering if he had the strength to stop tasting her long enough to tear off his clothes.

Chocolate was stimulating; he didn't deny that. Even delicious. Hope, however, was pure intoxication. Finer than wine, more magical than a mere spell.

Hope felt powerful, for all that he was still clothed and she was the naked one. He clutched her like he didn't want to let go, groaning as if caught somewhere between bliss and pain. The sound was muffled, hungry, as he gently nipped and licked his way from one breast to the other. Plucking at the thong holding back his long, light brown locks, Hope tossed it aside and stroked her fingers through his hair. It was softer than hers, a sensual delight meant for reveling.

His hunger reminded her of her own desires. She wanted to do everything back to him, and then some, but she wanted to be sure that it would please him. Tugging lightly on the strands entwined in her fingers, she lifted his gaze from her breasts. "Morg . . . make sure you tell me what you like most. I want to know everything you like, in the bedroom."

Releasing her areola with a lap of his tongue, Morg considered her request. It was reasonable, when he thought about it. If he didn't tell her what he liked most, she wouldn't know. He wanted her to know.

"I like this," he told her, nuzzling the soft cleft between her breasts. "Seeing you naked, without obstructions. Smelling the sweat and the softsoap and the perfume of your skin. *Feeling* you in my arms, all of you against me, when all I had for months was your palm pressed against mine. I like *this*."

His desire-filled words, his clutching arms, the craving in his tenor voice made her shiver. It also made her mouth curve in a smile. "Then why don't we get you out of your clothes, so that you can feel all of me against all of you, too?"

She hadn't even finished making the suggestion before he released her, grabbing his tunic. Tugging at it herself, she helped him pull the rumpled light green linen over his head and toss it on the floor. He swayed forward again as soon as his head and arms were clear, kissing and caressing her flesh. He touched her gently, alternating soothing strokes with the lightest teasings, before leaning even closer to lick and suckle her curves.

Amused, Hope enjoyed the feel of his muscles even as she pressed him back. Pushing until he fell onto his elbows, brow quirked in

question, she squirmed off the edge of the bed and bent over, plucking at the lacings straining over the front of his trousers.

Morg groaned again when her fingers brushed against him, confessing his thoughts as he lifted his hips a little. "I love the sight of
your breasts. Like fruit waiting to be plucked and devoured. And
your fingers—Jinga!"

He clenched his teeth, fingers fisting at his sides when she shifted
from tugging on the lacings to cupping him outright. The sight of
her golden palm curving over his groin, the feel of her kneading
gently, it was painfully pleasurable. She took pity on him, or maybe
it was just mercy, sliding her fingers under the waistband so that she
could pull down the fabric. Breathing hard through his nose, Morg
struggled to lift his hips. His ankle didn't like the awkward pressure
being put on it, since it would be a little while more before his healing charm finished tending the sprain, but she pulled off his pants,
letting him drop back onto the bedding with relief, while she discarded the garment on the floor.

Short-lived relief. She climbed back over him. He quickly shifted
so that both of his feet dangled off the bed, making it easier for her
to straddle his thighs. Straddling them meant parting her own,
drawing his gaze back down to that odd yet compelling strip of dark
nether-hair. With her dark brown hair and her golden-tanned skin,
her pelvis framed the paler skin of his manhood, rising up from the
untrimmed tangle of his own brown nether-curls.

"Let me get more comfortable," he managed to say as she leaned
forward, tempting him with the view of her breasts. He wanted to
cup them, but with his elbows holding up his torso, he couldn't really manage it. Stretching out an arm, he pulled down the coverlet
and snagged one of her pillows.

Tucking it under his head, Morganen sucked in a shaky breath.
She had sunk back onto his thighs, but leaned forward just enough
to glide her palms from his hips to his ribs. Letting her press him
back into the bedding, Morg covered her hands with his own.

"Yesss . . . I've dreamed of your hands on my skin," he admitted huskily, guiding her into caressing his ribs. "Every single time I pressed my palm to yours, I wanted the rest of me to feel the touch of your hand . . ."

Hope hadn't expected Morg to take her request to speak his erotic thoughts so literally, but it was giving her ideas. Gently shaking off his touch, she positioned her hands over his ribs and pressed down. "Touching you, like this?" she asked, shifting and pressing, shifting and pressing. He laughed at the odd treatment, and she grinned. "Or like this?"

Her fingers rippled out and in, undulating across his ribs in gentle muscle kneads. Morg groaned beneath her touch.

"Or like this?" Lifting her wrists, she trailed the pads of her fingers from his shoulders to his hips, pausing briefly to circle his nipples.

"All of it!" Catching her hands, Morg dragged them up to his lips. He kissed her fingers, lapping his tongue between each knuckle, then tugged sideways on her hands, urging her into crawling off of him. "On the bed—lie on the bed."

A moment of awkwardness ensued as their bodies bumped and tangled briefly, but he managed to get the pillow tossed back into place, and her lush figure aligned properly on the bed. A snap of his fingers brightened both of the lightglobes in the room, the modestly lit one by the door and the formerly unlit one in its bedpost bracket. The sudden influx of light made her wince and lift a forearm over her eyes.

Morg leaned over her, tossing his hair over one shoulder so that he could kiss her arm without impediment. She shifted her arm out of his way, catching his gaze.

"I want to see all of you," he told her. He slid his focus down the length of Hope's body. "There's so much of you to see . . . long legs, gorgeous arms, breasts, and belly, and thighs . . . and *none* of it blurred from my sight."

Drifting his gaze down her body, he shifted onto his hip, bracing himself on one elbow. That left his other hand free to caress her curves.

"*This* is what I want, to worship you in bed like you're my own personal Goddess . . . blasphemous though that may be," he acknowledged, twisting his lips into a wry smile. "Hopefully, the Gods will forgive me. It's said They can see into men's hearts," Morg added, sliding his palm from her ribs down to the curve of her mound. "If They do, They'll see that mine is filled with thoughts of you."

His finger slipped between the half-shaved folds of her netherlips. Morg sucked in a sharp breath, feeling not only how warm her flesh was, but how undeniably slick. His own flesh twitched and hardened further in response.

"All *sorts* of thoughts . . ."

His last chance to enjoy a woman had been all too long ago. Morg was perfectly normal, indulging in the same solitary ministrations as any other healthy male, but it just wasn't the same as making love with a partner. Now he had the chance to fulfill his daydreams, though actually being with her carried the danger of acting, and reacting, too precipitously. He knew they had to rise early tomorrow, and needed their rest. But he couldn't have removed his fingers from her loins any more readily than he could have removed his arm from his shoulder.

Still, he had told her some of what he wanted in bed. It was her turn. "What do *you* want?" Morg asked Hope, flexing his fingers just a little. "What would you like, here in my bed?"

She laughed. "Actually, it's *my* bed. We're in my chambers, remember?"

"Everything in this branch of the wing was given to me, when we moved in here," he stated, shifting so that his upper leg curled over hers. His foot slotted between her calves, nudging them apart. "That means you're in *my* bed . . . right where you belong."

"But this is *my* ancestral home," she countered, slipping her hand between them. Her fingers caught and clasped his flesh, laying claim to it as surely as his had claimed her own. "I used to own or control everything important on this island . . . and you have become the most important thing in my life."

Her fingers pulled, stroking upward along his flesh.

"I say, I still have the right to own *you*," she murmured, meeting his gaze steadily despite how his pale blue green eyes wavered in and out of focus, thanks to her hand. "What do you say to that?"

His gaze sharpened, despite the distraction of her touch. Morg moved his index finger, delving a little farther into her folds. His circling touch gave her own eyes a dazed look. Keeping his fingertips moving slowly, steadily, he offered, "I say, either we are at an impasse . . . or we agree to share our territory. I will own you, and you will own me."

"Last I heard, that was . . . mmm . . . called 'marriage'. Are you proposing?" Hope asked him, squeezing his shaft in little rhythmic pulses. Her hips moved in time with the stroking of his fingers. "We've talked about it in passing, and you told me long ago you thought I was the Hope in your verse of Draganna's Song, but you haven't actually *asked* me, yet."

She squeezed him a little harder on the word *asked*. Morg liked that very much. Hips twitching, he tried to thrust against her palm, but she had already drawn his foreskin back and her fingers were dry, without much give. Withdrawing his touch from her folds, Morg sucked the moisture from his flesh; Hope tightened her grip a second time, watching him enjoy the flavor.

As soon as his hand was relatively clean, he caught her wrist and gently pulled her hand free of his shaft. As soon as their hands were over their chests, he pressed his palm to hers, almost exactly as they had done over the last ten or so months. The biggest difference was that they weren't separated by the Veils and his mirror anymore, but were lying side by side, naked. Eye to eye, with nothing between them anymore but the truth.

"Hope . . . Haupanea," Morg added, letting her know that he accepted her past despite his initial shock. "You are my best friend. I have told you things I haven't even told my own twin. You've forgiven all of my mistakes and accepted all of my triumphs . . . and you seem to still find me worthy of loving. Now that I know all of *your* secrets," he teased lightly, "I admire you all the more, for your strength, your courage, and your constant joy in life.

"*Nothing* would please me more, than to have the honor of calling you my wife. Will you marry me, and grant me that pleasure?"

Lacing their fingers together, Hope gripped his palm. "I will *gladly* walk the eight . . ." Breaking off, Hope laughed, wrinkling her nose. "Sorry, I forgot for a moment that you came up with a different marriage ceremony than the eight altars of Jinga and Kata. But I'd walk them with you. And I'll recite the vows of the new Nightfall gladly. And, if need be, I'll marry you by Natallian customs, and Moonlands ones, and the leaping-of-the-fire that Amara and Rora's people do. Because I *do* want to marry you."

Morg chuckled at her offer. "I suppose we could ask Priestess Ora to ask her fellow Darkhanan Witches to look up all the wedding customs of all those lands they've been researching, in preparation for the Convocation . . . but I don't want to wait that long, or go through that many rituals."

"Then we'll wed as soon as we can. I *know* you, Morg, for all I've only seen your face for the last two days," Hope told him, freeing her hand so that she could cup his jaw. "To know you any more than I already do, I'd have to live right at your side. As your wife."

Morg nodded. "Kor and Danau plan to be wed this week, before the Desalinator is restarted. Destiny dictates that when *I* am wed, all of us will be wed . . . so we'll have to wait for my twin and his bride to marry, first," he reminded her, cupping her hand long enough to press a kiss to it. Re-lacing their fingers, palm to palm, he shrugged, head still propped on his hand. "Once they're properly married, Danau and Kor can return to her home city after the Desalinator is fixed and tell their Council to stuff their nonsense about women having to take on more than one husband down the nearest refreshing room drain."

Hope nodded, twisting onto her side so that she faced him more fully. "I don't think I'd be able to stand marrying anyone else myself. Some women might fantasize about two or three husbands at their beck and call, but not me. The only man I want is you . . . and I had to lose my family, my world, and too many years of my life to get you." She paused and grinned, showing him she was teasing. "Going through all of that just for you was bad enough; I'm not about to go through all of that again for anyone else."

Her movement had caused a couple of her curls to fall from her shoulder over her chest, redrawing his attention to her breasts. Morg dragged his mind back to the topic at hand reluctantly. "I don't want you to suffer ever again, either. I also don't want to detract from my brother's celebration . . . but waiting a couple of days more means running into the desalination project."

She shrugged, smiling. "So we'll wait until afterward!"

"After the Desalinator, but before the Convocation?" Morg offered.

Meaning to say, *Sounds good to me,* Hope found herself saying instead, "If we can."

That puzzled her into blinking and thinking, *Nauvea? Are You there?* She didn't hear anything in her head, and forced herself to shrug it off. *Maybe it's just my pragmatism showing through.*

"That is, given that rumors of my existence will be hitting the mainland soon," Hope said, "the Council will try to verify it and maybe try to use me against you, and it'll be safer if Nightfall is firmly established as an independent kingdom, rather than an old duchy still under the thumb of Katani rule.

"There's the whole worry over the need for Patronage and the Convocation being the best way to get it . . . and the wedding of a Seer is usually a huge occasion for celebration, within a nation." *Yes, that makes sense,* she thought, reasoning it out. "Perhaps we should wait until after we have that Patronage. The Convocation does seem to be a part of Prophecy, however indirectly, and the last line of your verse is about when we're wed, 'you will be all.' It could be interpreted as 'you are all that you are Destined to be.' Or something like that."

Morg considered her words, and smiled. "We'll be the very first marriage, post-Convocation. I've always been last in my family to do things, not counting magical things. Or at least, not the first. And though we'll be the last to wed . . . I'd like ours to be the first official Nightfall wedding."

"And you *claim* you don't have any of Dominor's competitiveness," she chuckled.

That made him smirk. "I never claimed to have his *level* of competitiveness," Morg corrected her. "But I *have* competed in certain areas against him. And against Trevan."

"If Trevan was involved, I'm sure it has something to do with *lust*," Hope teased, leaning close enough to brush her breasts against his chest. That also brushed his shaft, still somewhat firm and jutting, against her hip.

"*Passion*," Morg corrected, freeing his hand so that he could roll partway over her, coaxing her onto her back for a kiss. "Love, as well as lust."

It started slow, but warmed quickly as their naked bodies brushed and pressed . . . and ended in a tortured groan. Burying his face in her neck, Morganen muttered against her flesh. Hope, distracted by the feel of him, cleared her throat. "What?"

"*Contraception*," he repeated, speaking louder against her skin. She smelled wonderful, felt glorious . . . and he didn't dare go any farther than this. "We cannot make love without it."

Hope snorted. "Nonsense!" That lifted his head. She met his bemused look with an amused one. "It merely means we run the risk of getting me pregnant. And while I'd shudder in horror at having to do anything more intimate with Carlos than donate my eggs into a dish while he's not even there . . . I can definitely see you making love with me, as often as possible." Shifting beneath him, she wrapped her leg around his thigh. "Now, you *can* back off, go to your own bed, and wait a day or two while I talk to a Healer about getting me a contraceptive amulet—assuming one has already been made in advance, it shouldn't take long—or you can stay here, risk loving me . . . and I'll just go and get an amulet later."

"Amulet later," he decided, not needing any further encouragement. A shift of his weight put her fully on her back and placed him between her thighs. That let him rub against her intimately. Morg groaned, flexing his hips. "Gods, I love the feel of you. Warm, soft . . . *wet* . . . Gods, so very *wet!*"

A giggle escaped her. He stilled, lifting a brow in query. "You don't *have* to tell me everything you're feeling," she said. "Not that I *mind* hearing how you feel—I love it—but you don't have to go out of your way to be vocal, or anything. I mean, I'd settle for just an occasional 'nice breasts,' or something . . ."

Lifting up onto his elbows, Morg craned his neck, peering at her chest. "But they're not nice breasts. They're *very* nice breasts. As is everything else about you. You're beautiful. Perfect for me—how can I *not* tell you everything, now that I can actually *tell* you, instead of write it in little chunks and pieces on that damned awkward board?"

"It *was* awkward, wasn't it?" Hope agreed, wrinkling her nose. He kissed it, startling her into a laugh. "Morg!"

"Hope," he teased back, copying her scolding tone. "Even your nose is beautiful!" They grinned at each other, then his smile faded. His hips shifted, rubbing his erection against her folds. "I haven't even seen this part of you, yet . . . but I *am* finally touching it . . ."

He flexed his hips again, eyes rolling shut from the pleasure. He could *feel* how slick she was, how ready to be possessed by him. By *him*. Just that fast, his passion was back. Biting his lip, Morg restrained the instinct to press into her, instead levering himself away from her body, forcing himself onto hands and knees. Opening his eyes, he studied her fiercely even as he crawled backward.

"I need to see *all* of you. *Now.*"

His intensity startled her, coming so soon after their playfulness, but it didn't alarm her. It thrilled Hope, knowing she had driven him into gripping her thighs, pushing them apart for an unobstructed view. An up-close-and-personal view; so close, she could feel each soft puff of his breath against her flesh.

"*Pink*," Morg sighed, finding enough voice to tell her what he saw. "Slick, and pink, all folds and curls . . . the most beautiful thing . . . and the smell . . . Keep your chocolate," he told her. "I'd rather eat *this*."

Startled into laughing, Hope twitched at the feel of his mouth against her, tongue delving into her nether-flesh. She groaned as he pulled open her folds with his thumbs, giving him fuller access to everything, then it was his turn to groan. To suckle. To probe. Every few strokes, he pulled back far enough to stare at her, to breathe on her, before diving back in again.

Clutching at his locks, Hope arched into his fervent, decadent kisses. It had been too long since her last lover. For all the last one had been talented enough, he hadn't been nearly this impassioned. Nor this hungry. Morganen's need was *her* need; she panted with him, strained into him, groaned because of him. Unlike him, she couldn't form a coherent word, though he did pause every now and then to mutter a fervent description of her flavor, her scent, her feel, until she tensed and arched, crying out a strangled attempt at his name. That was good—that was better than good, but it wasn't enough. Oral pleasure was great, but it didn't fill the emptiness inside of her. Only he could do that.

Tugging on his hair, she pulled him up, away from her flesh. "Up here, now! *Take* me."

Hurrying to crawl up over her, he dropped into position between her widespread thighs. His manhood slotted into place, prodding her depths with very little need for adjustment. Everything about him was hot, hard, male, perfect—and yet he stopped, teeth bared in a grimace, his aqua eyes scrunched almost shut, his body so tight, she could see the veins on his arms beginning to pop.

"Morg?" Concerned, Hope reached for his face. "Are you alright?"

He twisted his head, rubbing his cheeks into her palms. Breathing unsteadily for a few moments, he finally relaxed enough to groan, "I feel like . . . like I'm going to lose *control*."

She smirked. "I'll take that as a compliment."

That opened his eyes, his brow furrowing in a frown. "I don't mean *sexually*; I meant, my *magic*. I'll remind you, I'm a powerful mage. That's *not* a good thing!"

"And I'll remind *you* I'm a Seer. I'm *built* for such things," Hope told him, nudging him with a dual touch from the inner sides of her thighs. Tangling her fingers in his hair, she tugged on his locks, trying to coax him down onto her. "Make love to me, Morganen. Lose yourself in me. I will catch you," she promised. "Just love me, and you won't hurt me."

Nodding, he lowered his body until it rested against hers. Not heavily; Morg carefully braced some of his weight on his elbows as well as his knees, she noticed. As soon as he settled, he pressed forward into her. He felt warm and firm, filling her literally and figuratively with increasing satisfaction. Sliding her hands from his face to his shoulders, Hope clung to him. It was her turn to be vocal, though her voice never rose above a low growl.

"Yesss . . . yessss! So hard . . . so *full*," she hissed as he sank all the way in, then slowly pulled back again. "Goddess, I love the feel of you on me, the feel of you in me . . . I love you—I *love* you!"

"Hope—!" He was *trying* to maintain control, but her fervent words in his ear ruined it. Groaning, Morg thrust back in, snapping his hips into her wetness. Some of his magic seeped through his control as he did so, spilling into her. Her fingernails scratched down his back, her face a mask of shining, straining, feminine bliss. Wary, Morg deliberately focused a trickle of power into her, and felt her nails clench again.

"Ohhhh, *Gods!*"

Loving her, trusting her, he released his self-control with a shudder. He pounded himself into her, ground himself into her, growled into her ear. Base, lust-filled words escaped his lips, incoherently strung in rough, bed-creaking grunts.

Her own voice filled his ears, rising and breaking with each of his thrusts, driving him into her faster, harder, wilder, until she yelled with each stroke, until her breath broke and her body shuddered. Spasms wracked her flesh, emerging as breathless, hearty laughter.

Laughter? Morg fumbled a stroke, one of his knees slipping out from under him. She stopped laughing long enough to moan loudly, then gasped right back into laughing again. The sound was very disconcerting; he'd never had a woman laugh at him in the middle of lovemaking. But she didn't seemed to be laughing *at* him, just . . . laughing. Inexplicably laughing.

The only thing that kept him from being offended was the way she clutched at him, pulling him back into her, back into the frantic rhythm he had lost. The feel of her flesh convulsing around his shaft, squeezing him with each breathless guffaw, felt too good to be offended for long. In fact, as he slowly stroked into her again, picking up speed, her humor infected him. He didn't see why she should be so *amused* . . . but she was, completely and thoroughly, and it made him grin.

She gasped and clutched at him, bucking up onto his body, head thrashing across the pillow in clear pleasure . . . and still, she kept laughing, helpless in her mirth. Morganen lost himself in the heat and the scent and the sound of her. Shuddering in his own climax, he clung to her, muffling his yell in the soft skin of her neck. Quakes rippled through his flesh, some from his orgasm, others from her continuing amusement, though she was finally winding down into gasping chuckles, then into breathless giggles.

When she was reduced to snickering, he gathered enough courage to lift his head from the shelter of her fragrant, thick hair and confront her odd behavior. Her face arrested him, the moment he saw it: She was radiant with happiness, her lips stretched as wide as she could smile, and all but physically glowing. Morg felt his own mouth spread and curl, it was such an infectious expression.

Hesitantly, he asked. "Um . . . why were you laughing? My lovemaking isn't *that* bad, is it?"

"What?" She stopped laughing long enough to blink at him, then snorted. "Hardly! Try the exact *opposite*." Hope chuckled again, then smiled and stretched out her arms. "Gods, you're so *good*. I haven't laughed this hard or this long in a *very* long time!"

Morg wasn't sure if he understood her right. "You're laughing . . . *because* I'm such a good lover? That's it?"

Looping her arms around his neck, Hope grinned at her lover. "Morg, when it's *really* good . . . I just laugh! I don't know why, other than that when it's really, really good, I'm really, really happy . . . and when I'm happy, I laugh." Her smile faltered, her brown eyes narrowing slightly in worry. "You're not going to make fun of that, are you?"

"No. I thought you were making . . . *No*," Morg repeated more firmly, dismissing his concerns. "I'm very, very glad I could make you laugh."

Her smile came back. "You made me laugh a *lot*. I like that. Most guys, either it takes a lot of getting to know what I like in bed, or . . . well, I haven't laughed more than a dozen times, before. But I love how *you* can make me do it."

Resting half on her and half on his elbows and knees, muscles lax with repletion, Morg contemplated her claim. He managed a shrug after a moment. "It might have just been a fluke, a random chance . . ."

"No, no; you definitely made me very happy," Hope asserted. "I'm quite positive about that."

"But it *could* have been a one-shot spell," Morg argued. He made a show of shaking his head slowly, sadly. "No, I'm afraid we're just going to have to do this all over again. A brand-new spell isn't trustworthy if it cannot be successfully repeated. Again, and again, to be absolutely sure it's being cast right."

She chuckled at that, amused by his assertion. Morg grinned back, delighted that he could make her laugh again so quickly, though not quite from the same context. He grinned at her, until he realized he was still buried inside of her, embracing her, smelling her, seeing her right here in his arms, where he had daydreamed of her so many times before. His smile gentled.

"Remind me to worship your Goddess of Dreaming."

"Nauvea?" she asked. "Why?"

"Because She's just fulfilled all of my daydreams about having you here in my bed," he confessed.

"*Your* bed, is it?" Hope challenged again, raising her brows. "This is my room, therefore this is *my* bed. Where I've daydreamed about having *you* in my arms."

"*My* bed," Morg repeated.

She opened her mouth to challenge him, but he moved quickly, surprising her by climbing off the bed, muttering something that made her skin tingle and feel warm. Scooping her off the bedding, he lifted her easily in his arms, making her gasp and clutch at his neck. "Morg?"

"*My* woman, *my* bed—you have a knack for making me feel rather possessive," he added, heading for the door. Thanks to the levitation charm he had just cast, it was relatively easy for him to juggle both her and the door lever, opening the door to her bed-chamber. "I'm not sure if I like it, yet."

"You're not?" Hope asked, confused.

"I mean, I've always prided myself on being a reasonable, civilized gentleman," he added, checking briefly for the position of the low table that had tripped him earlier, before striding for the sitting room door. "I like being polite and well mannered. It's more fun, overall. But there is something about you—will you get the door? No?—Something about you," he continued, reaching that latch as well, "that makes me feel very primal and uncivilized."

"Um, Morg . . . you're not really taking us outside, are you?" Hope asked, her words coming quicker as he managed to open the door. "Because we're both stark-staring *naked*, here!"

"Anyone wandering around *my* corridors at this hour of the night will just have to suffer," he told her. "Because I am carrying *my* woman to *my* bed, where I plan on making her laugh long and hard all over again. Do you have a problem with that?"

He paused in front of the door to his suite, deliberately waiting for her to answer. The lightglobes spaced along the hall were dimly lit, but she could tell by craning her neck that they were alone. The fact that he didn't *care* if they were caught like this was kind of flattering, and a bit thrilling. Twisting back to face the door, Hope freed a hand from his neck, grasping the handle. She gave him a smile as soon as the panel swung open.

"I guess I don't, do I?" she offered, smiling at her lover.

Feeling happy enough to have laughed long and hard himself, Morganen carried Hope all the way to *his* bed.

"*Someone* is going to pay for this," Trevan grumbled. He slanted a dark, green-eyed glare at his next-eldest brother. Evanor ignored him, buckling on his protective armor. The fifthborn brother tried again. "We haven't even had breakfast, yet! *How* can we fight on an empty stomach?"

Morg barely heard the exchange. He was terribly tired—entirely by his own fault—and it was almost too much of a bother to put on all of this cumbersome armor. He wanted to be back in his bed, with his Hope, instead of preparing to be bruised and battered in the name of self-defense. Bruised and battered further; lovemaking exercised muscles that sword practice certainly didn't.

"Do you expect our many enemies to wait until you've finished your meal before they attack?" Saber returned calmly. The firstborn of the brothers had already shrugged into his armor and was inspecting the racks of practice weapons in the corner of the salle.

"I suppose *you're* at fault for scheduling us this early, and not Ev?" Trev accused, facing Saber but poking his thumb over his shoulder at the palest-haired of the brothers.

"It was necessary, Trev," Evanor finally admitted, adjusting the fit of his elbow guards. "The schedule had to be changed around so that someone would always be 'walking the dog,' as Kelly has so amusingly named it. Not to mention Koranen's impending wedding."

"At least Priestess Ora was willing to bind her powers in an oath to 'walk the dog' while we're watching Kor and Danau wed," Saber agreed. "She's a strange woman, but trustworthy enough."

Morg remembered the kiss he and Hope had shared, before leaving her to enter that hidden passage on the ground floor of the palace so she could go 'walk the dog.' Only the fact that the Fountain *had* to be moved frequently kept them from prolonging their embrace, or even returning to his bed for more of the passion that had delayed their sleep and left him too tired to pay much attention to his brothers.

Not receiving enough sympathy, Trevan turned to look at the fourth member of their sparring team. "What are *you* grinning about?"

Morg blinked, coming out of his reverie. He struggled to smother a yawn and focused his attention on the redhead. "What? I wasn't paying attention."

"Why are *you* grinning at this ungodly . . ." Trevan trailed off, eyeing his youngest brother in suspicion. A smile curled his lips, splitting them apart in a big grin. Of all of them, the self-professed lover of the family would have to be the one to catch on that quickly. "*Congratulations*, Little Brother! I trust the lady is equally happy this morning?"

"Trevan, what are you babbling about?" Saber asked, moving closer. "Morg, finish getting into your armor. You're sparring with Evanor this morning, not me, so stop dawdling."

"I'm talking about Morg," Trevan stated, gesturing at their youngest sibling with an air of importance, "and *Hope*. You know, last night?"

Another smile spread across Morganen's face as he remembered more of last night.

Saber grunted, shifting to help Morg finish buckling on his breastplate. "Stop daydreaming, and start armoring."

"And be responsible, when you tumble with her. She is from this universe, and liable to get pregnant," Evanor added.

Color tinged Morg's face. He ducked his head, fussing over the armor straps.

Trevan eyed him speculatively. "She *did* enjoy herself, at the very least?"

Morg grinned. As the last of the brothers, his previous tumblings hadn't been very noteworthy. Everyone else had done it all before—excepting Koranen, of course, for obvious reasons. But this, *this* was something Trevan hadn't ever claimed to have done.

Leaning forward, he confessed, "I made her laugh."

Trevan quirked one coppery-blond brow. "You made her . . . laugh?"

"Twice! The second one took a bit more to pull off than the first," he admitted, "but I just remembered everything you and Dom used to boast about, and applied it as best I could. And I made her laugh again! It *wasn't* a fluke!"

Green eyes met aquamarine warily. Trevan nodded slowly, carefully, as if Morg were some sort of unknown, mage-wrought beast. "That's . . . good. I think."

Morg grinned and explained. "I made Hope so happy, she *laughed.*"

"Ah. *Euphoria* laughter," Trevan acknowledged, nodding in understanding. "I've heard of it, but I haven't actually managed it." A speculative look crossed his face. "I wonder, if I could get Amara to relax enough . . ."

Saber's hand smacked lightly into the back of Trevan's head. "Get your head out of the bedroom and into your helmet, Brother. You spar with me today."

Trevan waited until the firstborn brother retreated again to the weapons rack before sticking out his tongue. Keeping his voice low, he muttered, "I do wish he wouldn't be so serious all the time. Lovemaking is a joyous thing, but he's acting like he's never heard of it this morning!"

"I think he's still embarrassed, regarding last night's frank discussion of his and Kelly's fertility problems. Mention 'chocolate,' however, and I'm sure you could get his mind to wander in a more pleasant direction," Morg stated. He clapped his fifthborn brother companionably on the back. Or maybe it was in commiseration. "But if I were you . . . I'd wait until *after* he puts down his blades."

Trevan snorted. "Trust me, I'm not suicidal."

A knock on the salle door startled all four men. Evanor, as the closest, crossed to the panel. Opening it, he frowned and stepped back, glancing over his shoulder at the others. As he did so, they could see their newest arrival: Lord Consus of Kairides.

"I am looking for Lord Morganen," the ex-Councilor said. He eyed the mirror-lined room warily, clearly more of a spell mage than a combat mage.

"Over here," Morg responded, quickly knotting a loose strap around his thigh as his tassets threatened to flop. Crossing to the door, he looked at Evanor and tipped his head, until his fourthborn brother got the hint and moved elsewhere. Focusing his attention on the middle-aged mage, Morg asked, "Well? You wanted something?"

Consus eyed the others, then stepped backward, beckoning Morg into the hall. The illusion-paint lining the wall showed a dark, gloomy swamp, the kind filled with mud and vines and gnarled tree trunks. The lightglobes lining the corridor did their best to dispel the gloom, but their cheerful, steady glow could only counteract the dark browns and greens by so much. In the distance, near the archway into the donjon, Morg could just make out a rounded mud-hut, lit from within by the flickering glow of firelight. Other than that illusion of the swamp-hut, they were alone in the west hall.

"What did you want?" he repeated, letting the door to the salle swing shut.

Clearing his throat, Consus spoke in a murmur. "Do you remember the warning I gave you, of the Mendhites that were coming to your island?"

"Yes, you said that they were coming to Nightfall to stop us from successfully restarting the Convocation. I haven't forgotten them," Morganen promised.

"And that they were hired to assassinate your queen," Consus reminded him. "I did not tell you at the time, but . . . the person who hired them was Duke Finneg. Or rather, the person who promised to reward them if they should 'accidentally' kill her was His Grace. It . . . would not have been politically astute of me to have revealed that particular detail before now."

Morg nodded, understanding the older man. "Yes—you were in an awkward position before, balanced partially on a fence between the Council's side and ours. Now you've slipped off the fence almost entirely, and not onto your original side."

"Nor comfortably," Consus agreed, wincing a little. "But . . . honor compels me to warn you that His Grace has contacted the Mendhites again. He has decided to 'change the rules,' though I'm afraid he did not specify how or why. Only that he has called the lead ship from Mendhi to dock at Orovalis City and wait for his arrival. Orovalis is only a day's sail away. Based on the Dakim's reply—that's their ship's captain, I believe—they'll reach port within three or so days. Which means they could conceivably be here within four. I thought you should know."

"Thank you," Morg said, dipping his head in acknowledgment. "That man, when I rescued you . . . he said something about that mirror I brought across for you. Is that how you found out?"

The older mage flushed. He hesitated a long moment, lips parting, compressing, parting again, then finally spoke. "That mirror is a dangerous Artifact. Dangerous in the wrong hands," the ex-Councilor clarified. "You may have saved me from the destruction of my career, but that does not mean you are worthy of being entrusted with it. The Council is even less worthy; they are a committee, a collection of self-focused ambition. The *only* person I trust right now not to abuse that mirror is myself . . . so I'll thank you not to seek it out."

"So long as the secrets of your special mirror do not compromise the safety of Nightfall Isle and its inhabitants, they can remain your secrets," Morganen allowed. "But be advised that, in staying here, you may have to reveal the secrets of your mirror at some point, in order to protect Nightfall's best interests."

"That is why I have given you this news. My safety is now linked to Nightfall's." Consus hesitated again, then added with diffident honesty, "You and I have worked well enough together. Or at least, both lands are still currently standing, our peoples unharmed. Which could be construed a success in some measure."

"Some measure, yes," Morganen agreed, folding his arms across his chest as best he could, given that his arms and chest were clad in pieces of protective, wax-boiled leather. "Given that we do have a workable relationship of at least partial, established trust . . . I trust you'll consider me for your confidences, when the time comes?"

That quirked one of Consus' reddish brown eyebrows. "Do you think you can handle the sort of secrets revealed by the mirror?"

"Do you think you can?" Morg countered, and received a nod at the telling question. "I thank you for the warning, milord. Please do what you can to keep an eye on this situation in your . . . secretive scryings. Somehow, I don't trust His Grace to remain completely stable."

"Somehow, I agree with you," the older mage quipped. A bow, and he turned to stride away.

"One moment," Morg called out. "How did you know where to find me?"

"When I was awakened this morning by . . . the duke's machinations . . . I found a maidservant sweeping the hall, and asked her where you'd be. She referred me to the chalkboard chart on the wall outside the dining hall, then told me where to find the salle."

A bow, and he left.

The older mage was canny enough to have undoubtedly read the whole chore roster. Morg returned to the salle. He was scheduled to spar with Evanor, the official Lord Chamberlain of Nightfall Castle, so there would be time to discuss their need for better secrecy.

"Yes . . . oh, yes!"

Morg slowed his footsteps. This morning, he had seen Hope briefly at breakfast before having to go down to the cove and assist the various construction projects in Harbor City, casting mass-lightening spells so the non-mage laborers could maneuver heavy rafters and other such items safely into place. He had checked all the horseless carts in use by both his family and the desalination plant workers, refreshing their transportation spells. It was a good thing he was only physically tired; magically, he'd been in top form today, not breaking a sweat even once.

"Yes, yes, just like that! That's *perfect!*"

He slowed even more, hesitating outside the door. Seeing her at lunch had extended into the early afternoon, with Morganen floating yet more objects, this time all of the strange equipment she had brought across from the other world. At some point in the morning, after fixing up the old audience chamber and helping Kelly handle the problems brought before her by the populace, Hope had surveyed these three interconnected salons, double-checked to make sure no one else needed them for anything, and declared them perfect for her own needs. But then the *tiffen*, the light afternoon meal they had adopted for the warmest months of the year, had parted them again.

"Oh, Trevan, this is so *wonderful!* I didn't even know if you could manage it, but you did!"

Morg wasn't sure what to make of her exclamation, or the odd humming sound impinging on his awareness. He'd been forced to go off and teach his late-afternoon classes in magic. Two of his sisters-in-law, Alys and Rora, hadn't been formally educated in spellcraft and magery before coming here, and there were five others on the island, four young students and one oldster identified over the last handful of months as mild to moderate in their magical abilities but lacking in training.

Someone had to teach them, and of all his brothers, Morganen had the widest base of knowledge, and the most free time on his hands. Trevan usually spent most of his time working with the construction crews down in the city these days; Dominor was currently overseas with his wife and new children, and the others all had their various tasks, ones which used up most of their time, their attention, and their energies. Only Morg had both the knowledge and the power to spare to teach magery to their handful of pupils. Mornings were out, as the younger four were still enrolled in the normal sort of classes, the standard education that all children were due—at least, that was the standard back on the mainland, and Kelly had decreed it would be the standard for the island.

The priestess Ora had offered her services as an instructor of foreign magics, but Morg hadn't accepted; these were his students, and her magics were not only an unknown quantity, they were holy magics. He didn't think it would be appropriate to teach such things before the Convocation had begun and the petition for the Gods' protection and Patronage of Nightfall had been accepted. Undaunted, she had asked to be a student, and he had reluctantly agreed. Thankfully, she had been nondisruptive, quiet, and studious.

Unlike Hope's next comment, which scattered Morg's wits for a moment.

"Oh, Trevan—I could *kiss* you!" he heard Hope exclaim through partially open door. "Except your wife probably wouldn't like me doing that, of course."

"My *wife*? From the foolish way my little brother was grinning his head off this morning, if I even looked cross-eyed at you, he'd probably fry me into a little smear on the floor," Trevan joked back. "Oh, don't give me that look. Morg isn't one to carry tales. He just looked excessively smug and claimed he made you very, very happy last night. And *I* couldn't be happier for both of you!"

Smiling at the memory, Morg slipped into the first of the rooms that were slated to become Hope's chocolate shop. He caught sight of Trevan first; the redhead had his back to the door, hands on his green-clad hips as the fifthborn brother stared at whatever was on the table beyond.

"Alright . . . I've got all my notes for this *electromagizmo*, as you call it. I'll tidy them up tonight and work on creating a second one tomorrow morning. It should go faster, now that I know what I'm doing. It'll have to be before lunch, though, since I'm due to work with the new buildings on the south side of the bay between lunch and *tiffen*. Will you be available for more testing?" Trevan asked Hope.

She stood on the far side of the table, Morg noticed, clad in a sleeveless, light blue tunic-thing from her world, the kind that buttoned down the front . . . and she was looking at him. Morg, not Trev. Her brown eyes gleamed warmly as she smiled at him.

Turning to see what had riveted her attention, Trevan groaned. "Oh, for the love of . . . ! The two of you can be lovesick all you want after supper and before breakfast, but right now, I need you *here*, with me, still fully capable of thought."

"Oh, I *am* thinking, Trev," Hope drawled. "And I'm quite sure it's nothing you haven't thought of before, regarding your own beloved . . . but I'll give you a few more moments of my attention before I wander off in a lust-filled daze." She winked at Trev, then beckoned Morg closer. "Come and see what your brother made for me, Morg."

Moving up beside his brother, Morganen looked at the table. Several lumpy objects had been arranged on the surface along with stacks of paper and writing implements. Some were part metal, part something that looked vaguely like uniformly dyed, highly polished leather but which wasn't—*plastic*, that was it. A series of wires and cables led from the objects to one of the two spare power crystals from the previous morning. It had been wrapped in a web-work of metal wires twisted into runes and mathemagical symbols and suspended in a cube-shaped frame.

Or rather, it was the other way around; Morg realized it the moment he reflexively checked the apparatus with his mage-sight, and Saw the energies flowing from the crystal to a strange contraption with two heavy stone rollers rolling and spinning over a stone disc set in some sort of tub. That was the source of most of the humming noise he had heard. Another had a sort of odd-shaped cylinder which rocked back and forth.

"This is the *melangeur,* or cocoa-nib grinder," Hope told him, touching the rim of the roller-and-disc's tub. "It's a very small one, barely four hundred pounds for the rollers, but it'll work for my initial needs. Once the beans are roasted and shelled, this is where the nutmeat is turned into a paste and blended with other ingredients to make the chocolate. I also have other machines, including a cocoa press, but these two are the most important. This one is the *conch,*" she added, touching the rocking top of the cylinder-thing, "which refines and blends the various ingredients together at a very specific temperature, giving chocolate its characteristic snap when broken, and its ability to melt so deliciously on the tongue.

"Your brother—genius that he is—has managed to cobble together a system wherein the magic in a power crystal is converted into the *electrical* energy these machines need to run. I wanted to get solar-power panels," Hope added, wrinkling her nose, "but they're awfully expensive, and it would've been very hard to explain why I needed them, nor would there have been any guarantee that they'd work in this universe, since the rules on power generation are just a little bit different. But anyway . . . we think from Trev's calculations that one of these crystals that Rora empowered will be sufficient to power all the machines I'll be using for up to half a year. Maybe even more, if everything goes well.

"That's provided you'd let me have this one, of course, and provided I can hire employees to help out, since some of the chocolate-making process can take up to two days straight," she finished ruefully. "And I do need sleep . . . especially after last night."

"Unless Rora or Rydan had need of it, since it's her energy . . . I don't see why not," Morg admitted, trying not to think of why he was so tired, either. "You'd have to recharge them from one of the Fountains on the Isle, of course, but that's not the difficult part. That's getting the replacement parts for when these Artifacts wear down," he warned her. "The masses and energies exchanged between the two worlds have been balanced, and we no longer have someone in the other world acting as our purchasing agent."

"*That* might not be necessary," Trevan said. He touched a stack of books lying half-buried under the papers scattered on his side of the table. "Hope's given me a manual of machine specifications and some textbooks explaining the terminology and measurement systems. Once the Convocation is over and things have settled down construction-wise on the island, I'll be looking into re-creating these devices as magic-driven Artifacts.

"Speaking of which, I'll need to borrow this *amp-gauge* thing for tomorrow, to refine the resulting runes that control the conversion of magic into the right kind of electrical energy," he told Hope, unclamping the little pincher-things on the ends of the wires attached to one of the plastic boxes. "But with luck, I can have two or three conversion boxes made, and then it'll just be a matter of seeding more power crystals, force-growing them with Kor's and Rydan's help, and then empowering them from the Fountains."

"Good! I brought across a *deevee dee* player and several of my favorite *movies*," Hope agreed. She smiled slyly at Morg. "I know *you* liked watching movies with me, even if it was only through the intersection plane of your mirror. I felt it hovering at my side on more than a few occasions."

Morg shrugged, smiling back. "What can I say? Your illusion-box plays were the closest we've come to watching a troupe of actors perform since we left Corvis County. And . . . you were there."

"If you're done with *me* for the day," Trevan interjected dryly, though not without a touch of humor, "I'll just take the gauge thingy and my notes and leave you to your courting."

"Thank you for all your help, Trevan," Hope told him, smiling.

"You're helping me turn my dream of my very own chocolate shop into a reality. I'll have to figure out how to repay you."

"You're family," Trevan demurred, smiling back. Then he grinned and elbowed his youngest sibling. "I'll just beat it out of Morg, whenever I want recompense."

Morg gave his brother a dirty look, but let the copper-haired mage leave without protest or retaliation. Returning his attention to Hope, he moved around to her side. She flicked little levers on the sides of the machines, stopping them, then disconnected the wires attaching them to the rune-caged power crystal. He stopped next to her, leaning in close enough to smell the faint combination of flower and female in her hair.

"I missed you," he murmured. "I kept looking at my sisters-in-law all through their lessons and thinking how much I wished you were there instead." She smiled at that and leaned into him, prompting Morg to wrap his arm around her shoulders for a sideways hug. "It's just as well, of course. I wouldn't have been able to focus on today's 'exciting' lesson of Artifact power gauging through the use of mage-sight and pendant dowsing."

Hope smiled at his dry recitation. "Your afternoon sounds about as exciting as mine, since Trev and I were talking *voltage* and *amplitude* for the last two hours. But it was more interesting than helping my sister adjudicate petty quarrels over whose dog ate whose ducks, and who was responsible for the loss, since the ducks weren't being tended in their fowl-yard, but had instead been allowed to wander into a third party's field." She chuckled at the memory. "You should've heard Kelly when she said, 'You *will* learn to get along as neighbors,' and the looks on the petitioner's faces when she outlined her version of a fix to the problem."

"She's an interesting woman. I'm glad to have her as a sister-in-law . . . wait. Kelly is going to be your *sister-in-law*, once removed, not your sister," Morg pointed out, frowning at the top of Hope's dark brown head. "And technically, we haven't married *yet*."

Lifting her hand, Hope showed Morg the scar on her palm. It was bluish white, clean, and straight, a perfect mirror image of the one Kelly now bore on her own skin. "I told you I came up with a way to resolve the whole duchy-or-kingdom problem. It's quite simple: I took her as my blood-bound older sister, yesterday."

"I can't believe I missed seeing that," Morg muttered, gently touching her scar with his free hand. "But it makes sense. As the elder sibling, she automatically inherits everything, including the right to claim the rulership of the duchy."

"Katani inheritance law is that the eldest living child is the first and foremost heir to the parents' property. Particularly any inheritable claims, such as noble titles and estates," Hope agreed. "I was fairly sure that wouldn't have changed in the last two hundred years, considering it's been the law for almost two thousand."

"That was very clever of you," he praised. "Of course, it happened before Consus came across . . . which means I wish in a way that you had told me. If I'd known, I wouldn't have asked him for a copy of the inheritance laws, which is what put his career and his life in jeopardy."

"I *was* going off of what I knew of inheritance laws from two hundred years ago. It wasn't likely, but the laws *could* have changed," she offered. "Of course, Kelly had a chance to read the scroll last night, and she told me this morning that everything's in order. She's officially the eldest of my immediate bloodline, so for all intents and purposes, she *is* the Duchess of Nightfall."

"And are you both happy with that?" Morg asked.

Twisting into his arms, Hope looped her own around his waist and smiled up at him. "Couldn't be any happier. Kelly is happiest when she's managing a dozen different projects and making a positive difference in others' lives. And I'm happiest right where I am. A woman with both a wonderful man and a burgeoning career I love."

Her declaration warmed his blood. Morganen debated lifting her onto the table to make love to her, but it was still filled with odd machines. Not to mention the door was still open, and he didn't want to get caught, like Ev said he'd nearly caught Wolfer and Alys together down in the kitchens, back before his fourthborn brother had regained his voice. Pulling back from her, he caught her hand, intending to lead her up to their rooms; they had half an hour before sunset, which meant just enough time . . . to . . .

He stopped and stared at her knees. Her bare knees, above equally bare shins and ankles. She wore loose-cuffed shorts in the same light blue material as her sleeveless blouse. Last he'd seen her, she had been clad in ankle-length pants. "Hope . . . you wore *that* in front of my brother?"

"What, my shorts? Of course. It's rather warm in here, if you hadn't noticed," she returned, free hand resting on her hip. "Unlike *some* people, most of us don't have the ability to cast cooling charms . . . which is why I was snuggling up to you, just now. You cast one on your clothes earlier, didn't you?"

"Well, yes, but . . ." Giving up, Morg let her win the argument. He *had* cast cooling charms on himself, earlier, while *she* was only a Seer, a conduit for magical power. She couldn't generate it herself, let alone shape it. "Alright. You've worn those things all over the other world, in the summer. I suppose you can wear them here. But you do realize that Saber's going to complain about Kelly showing off *her* legs to all and sundry the moment she starts wearing them? And that he's going to come complaining to *me*, since I'm your betrothed and supposedly have some say in the clothes you wear?"

"That 'supposedly' just saved you from sleeping alone tonight," Hope quipped. "I don't dictate what you wear, after all. Though if you *wanted* to wear shorts, I wouldn't object. In fact, I think your legs are quite gorgeous," she told him. "If you wore shorts, all the other women might want to stare at them, but I'd be very smug about it, because they're *my* legs to touch, at the end of the day."

Morg blushed at the compliment. "Just so long as no one else touches them . . . Come," he said, tugging lightly on her hand. "We have just enough time before supper for you to *touch* my legs all you want. If you want?"

She grinned. "Oh, *yeah.*"

Grinning back, Morg hurried both of them out of the converted salon. Sunset and supper weren't that far away.

SEVEN

❖❖❖

Augur frowned at the rain dripping beyond the open windows of the Harbormaster's hall. The temperature was still warm outside, but the sunny days had given way to a persistent, dripping rain, turning everything muggy and humid. That meant the latest influx of visitors and would-be settlers had crowded into the pipe-cooled building. The windows had to stay open to ensure that the air stayed fresh, but they did little to dissipate the dampness of both the air and the mood of the people being processed by him and his agents.

Stamping the papers of the latest family to migrate to Nightfall, a two-husband family with two adopted sons, Augur sighed. "That's the last of the paperwork, then. Please keep these registry papers close at hand for the next ten days, until your citizenship is approved and your neighbors get to know you. Don't forget your temporary warehouse voucher. We're currently reduced to housing people in tents along the south edge of the cove," he apologized, "but your

less-immediate belongings can be safely stored in one of our ware-
houses until you can rent a more permanent home. Any questions?"

The shorter of the two men shook his auburn head, and the
taller collected the papers and voucher. Both smiled in visible relief
at being welcomed. Nightfall welcomed all sorts of married couples,
whether traditional or otherwise. If they hadn't been accepted, he
wouldn't have put up with being nominated for this job. Augur
sighed again, missing his own mate, but Marcas had sailed off with
last night's tide to haul in yet another batch of immigrants for him
to process.

"Welcome to Nightfall, and I hope you will be able to lead
happy, productive lives . . . Next?" he called out, reaching for the
latest in the stacks of spell-copied papers Her Majesty wanted filled
out on each entrant to the Isle.

Four men approached. Three were rather tall, with the same
light brown cast to their skin that Augur had, but with much rounder
faces. Foreign sailors, from the looks of them. The last one was average in height, heavily muscled, dark-skinned, and had the oval
face of a Katani. Not a foreigner, but rather someone from the
northernmost shores of the mainland. All four men were clad in
long, brown cotton pants, long-sleeved gray tunics, and brown knee-
high boots, and all four had matching rings on their littlest fingers.
Other than that, there was nothing to pair the fourth man with
the other three.

The Harbormaster nodded at the stack of white discs on his
desk, the same as the stacks on the other four desks in the processing
hall. "Each of you take up a Truth Stone and state your names in
turn."

The three tall foreigners hesitated; the dark-skinned man picked
up one of the white marble discs. He curled his fingers and thumb
around the edge of the Truth Stone and stated, "I am called Thetteris, from Port Staldis." Uncurling his fingers, he showed the clean
white surface, proving the truth of his words. "Why do you need to

know our true names? Are you planning on casting some sort of name-based magic on us?"

"Hardly. The Stones are merely to verify the truth of your reasons for coming to Nightfall," Augur explained, as he had explained to about a quarter of all the people he had seen in the last handful of days. "There have been rumors of an unspecified threat from agents either from within or without the mainland, and in her desire to see her people safe, Her Majesty requests that all visitors to the Isle, temporary or permanent, be asked their intentions on a Truth Stone. It's not like we don't have the Stones to spare," he added, attempting to lighten the moment. "We have plenty of pure white marble, and the mages to make them.

"Now, what are your intentions while you are here on Nightfall, Thetteris of Port Staldis? And do you intend to cause harm to any of the people here on Nightfall during your stay with us?" Augur asked. "For that matter, aren't you from the north coast, not the south?"

"I've lived in several places, and travel extensively. I'm here to arrange the purchase of several tons of salt for the coming autumn. The city Aquamancers say the herring run will be outstanding. These are some of the crew that will be coming here in a week to pick up the shipment," Thetteris added, gesturing at the men with him. "Damin, Edmin, and Faramin, of the family Rau Fan. Their vessel is being repaired back on the mainland, since it was said your shipyards aren't fully functional, yet. I didn't want to wait for the repairs to be finished, not when rumor has it you'll be doing a full production run very soon . . . and not when the rumors say every salt-hungry sailor is headed your way. I want the order for Port Staldis put first on the buyer's list."

"Sorry, but you'll have to take your turn. There's a good twenty buyers booked into the Green Block Inn that I personally know of, and who knows how many more," Augur warned him, making notes on the paperwork. "But there should be plenty of salt for all, and at a very decent bulk price. You also haven't stated that you have no

intentions of harming anyone while you're here on Nightfall. I'm
afraid you'll have to swear it on the Truth Stone before you'll be allowed off the docks."

Thetteris gripped the stone firmly in his hand, the ring clacking
softly against the stone. "I have no intention of causing harm to anyone on Nightfall, save only in self-defense, if I absolutely have to."

Relaxing his fingers, he displayed the clean, unblemished marble.

"Alright . . . Damin, you're next. Pick up a stone, state your name,
and your intentions for being here."

"He has already stated our intentions for us," the tall foreign
sailor said. "Why should we say it as well?"

"Because there's a very slim chance that what you've told Thetteris, here, isn't the full truth. You probably are telling the truth,"
Augur added smoothly, "but Her Majesty, Queen Kelly, has insisted
that all visitors be asked these questions, so as to ensure the safety
of her people. Rumors of danger may only be rumors, but they may
also be the truth. It's better to ask and confirm that you mean no
harm, than to risk otherwise."

Damin hesitated.

"You can always refuse, but you'll be deported off the island on
the very next outbound ship," the Harbormaster pointed out. "At
your own expense."

The tall sailor picked up one of the discs, wrapped his fingers
firmly around its edges, and stated his name. "I am Damin, I am
here for a shipment of salt, and I have no intention of harming anyone on this island, provided they do not try to harm me first. I also
do not like having my honor questioned."

Uncurling his fingers, he displayed the all-white Stone. Augur
nodded. "It wouldn't be, if it weren't for the rumors, as I have said.
Edmin?"

Damin passed the stone to the tallest of the three, who gripped it
carefully and confirmed his identity. As did the one named Faramin.
Augur filled out the paperwork in two sets, one for the visitors to
keep, and one for his office's records.

"If you wish to earn a further discount on the purchase price of the salt blocks, you can volunteer to spend a few hours shifting blocks over the next three days, while the Desalinator is being restarted. If you want to have a fresh bath, tonight is the night to have it, though you'll have to pay extra for the luxury; all water run through the island's pipes is being rationed at the moment so that the people and the animals will have drinking water. Starting at sunrise, the entire system will be flooded with salt water, which means anything coming out of a tap for the next two-plus days will be undrinkable."

"Why is it being flooded with salt water?" Thetteris asked, frowning.

"It has something to do with how the Desalinator is energized for separating the incoming ocean water into freshwater and blocks of salt and algae—don't ask me anything more than that." Augur shook his head. "I'm a Harbormaster, not an Aquamancer. All I know is, it'll take about three days for the water to go from salty to fresh, and then we'll have plenty for drinking, bathing, and producing the goods which you've come here to buy.

"These are your registry papers." He stamped their papers and handed over one half of the copies. "Please keep these documents close at hand during your stay; you've been authorized to stay on the island for half a turning of Brother Moon. The Green Block Inn is located to the northeast; follow the street signs up to the Desalinator on the first set of hills, and you'll be able to see the distinctive greenish roof tiles along the way. If the Green Block is full, there are two more inns in that neighborhood, and people who can tell you where to find them. Welcome to Nightfall, and I hope your stay and your prospective business turn out to be worth your time. Next?"

A woman and three children approached, as did another woman from the side. The second woman held up her hand, holding off the mother. "Apologies, milady, this will only take a moment . . ."

Augur belatedly recognized her as one of the servants from

Nightfall castle and beckoned her forward. "Dellen, isn't it? If you're quick about it, you can have a moment. What did you need?"

"Milord, the palace is asking for a couple of registry forms for newborns. Lady Serina and Lord Dominor have returned with their children, but there aren't any blank forms up there," Dellen said.

"We're going to run out of blank forms down here, at this rate," he returned, separating out the preprinted sheets she needed. "And see if those mages can come up with a copy-wand of some sort, to make all this paperwork go faster. The Empire's scribes like to use them, and they'd be nice for *us* to have."

The servant rolled her eyes. "Like everything else, it'll probably be put on hold until after the Desalinator is up and running. But I'll write down your suggestion and put it in the 'to be dealt with soon' pile. Or rather, piles," Dellen corrected. "Thank you—and thank *you* for your patience, milady."

"Um . . . is it true, what they're saying? The old duchess has really returned to the Isle? My family used to live here, way back on my father's mother's side," the mother asked.

"Yes, it's true," Augur confirmed. "Haupanea of Nightfall has been returned to the Isle by the grace of the Gods, after having been misplaced through time as well as space. But she isn't going to be the duchess anymore; we have an incipient queen with a brand-new kingdom that we're going to establish firmly, which we'll do very soon," Augur reminded her, idly wondering why he had agreed to take on this repetitive job. "Now, if you could pick up this Truth Stone and state your name and the names of your young children to verify your identities, since we do have other people waiting beyond you . . ."

"Mmm . . ." Inhaling deeply, Hope cuddled little Timoran. From his near-bald head, with its fine fuzz of colorless hair, to his tiny little toes, scrunching and relaxing as they poked out of the soft cotton blanket wrapped around him, he was adorable. "Even the way they smell is beautiful! Newborn babies are the most precious thing in the world, aren't they?"

"They're stinky, they're messy, they're noisy, you'll never have a worry-free moment ever again . . . and I really hope you're right," Kelly returned, cradling Timoran's sister, Galea. The baby's peach-fuzz hair was sparse yet dark enough to be seen, sort of like Dominor's. She yawned a huge yawn, and Kelly smiled wistfully. "I really do hope you're right about me being able to conceive. This world has so much potential in it, I wouldn't fear bringing a child into it nearly as much as the other one."

"Pollution, crime, environmental disasters, overpopulation, the ever-present threat of nuclear holocausts . . . I can see your point," Hope agreed, carefully adjusting her grip when the newborn squirmed and tried stuffing his fist in his mouth. Like Kelly, she had seated herself on the edge of Dominor and Serina's bed, twisted sideways enough that she could converse with her newly made sister, as well as Timoran's father, who was shifting belongings from bags to chests. "But on the other hand, this world has its own flaws: mages who try to steal what's not theirs, thinking that might equals right, spells that go wrong, dangerous creatures formed from warped experiments, individuals who are as powerful as nuclear bombs in their own way . . ."

Galea made a *mehh* sound, lips pouting in a suckling motion. Her little face scrunched up. Kelly gently rocked the newborn, soothing her. Serina was in the refreshing room of Dominor's suite, enjoying one last bath all to herself before the Desalinator started up again. "I sincerely doubt a single person is capable of creating the same kind of massive devastation a nuclear warhead can."

"What about the Shattering of Aiar?" Dominor asked her. He was still unpacking the belongings he and his wife had used while at the Retreat in Natallia. "Amara says the hole that used to be their capital is big enough to hold tens of thousands of her people each winter, with only a few tribal Families forced to take shelter in the buildings up on the crater's rim."

"We don't know if that was something caused by a mortal, or something caused by a God, or even by the shattering of the power crystal that was supposed to have been holding the Gateway to Heaven open," Kelly pointed out. "Aside from Morganen shoving a ship faster than the speed of sound, I haven't seen anything truly spectacular out of a mage. Not on the nuclear holocaust level, at least."

Hope frowned, trying to recall an instance to support her words. "Well . . . there *was* that one woman. It happened just a couple of years before I left here—some woman accused the Empress of Fortuna of some gross injustice, and in her fury at the Empress' denials despite all the evidence otherwise, she opened a rift in the courtroom floor."

"Please, Rydan could probably do that by sneezing," Dom scoffed.

"Maybe, but can he open a rift all the way to the molten magma?" Hope countered. "The person who told me this tale said his brother had *seen* the lava rock lining the courtroom floor, brought up from the earth's depths as a reminder that the 'impartial justice of Fortuna' wasn't completely impartial or just."

"A mage managed to open a rift all the way to the magma of this planet?" Kelly repeated skeptically. Galea grunted again, and her lips pursed against her tiny fist, though she couldn't yet suckle it. Her tiny face scrunched unhappily. Glancing at Timoran, who was also pursing his mouth, she sighed and looked at their father. "You might want to go check on your wife, Dom. Make sure she hasn't drowned, or whatever. I have a feeling these two will be ready for their next snack very soon."

"Considering I tucked her into the tub without either her babies or her blackboards, she's probably ready to come out," Dominor quipped, heading for the door to the refreshing room.

"It's true, Kelly," Hope insisted. "There were a couple of different reports of the matter, though the man whose brother had visited the courtroom had more details to share. I just wish I could remember her name." Her mouth curled up wryly. "Of course, it was over two hundred years ago, but I'm sure some records survived. We could always ask the Guardians to relay a query to Fortuna, if you wanted confirmation."

"No . . . I've seen enough weirdness. I suppose it's possible that someone could have that much power in their little pinky," Kelly allowed. She rocked Galea as the infant grunted again, shifting her arms so that she could offer her own littlest finger for the newborn to taste. "But *my* little pinky just has yummy, gummy, sweet auntie goodness, doesn't it? Doesn't . . . ?

"Oh, *great*," Kelly muttered, losing her smile as she glanced down. Hope had brought across jeans, blouses, shorts, and so forth for Kelly to wear. A darker patch had appeared on the green T-shirt she was wearing, just below the white-painted words, *Official Mistletoe Tester, Ready And Willing*. "I think Galea just sprung a leak— Dominor, don't you people have any anti-leaking spells?"

Galea *meh-mehhed* a little louder when Kelly raised her voice, but otherwise didn't stop gumming Kelly's finger. A giggle could be heard through the mostly closed door to the refreshing room, light and feminine. It was followed by what sounded like Dominor trying to hush his wife.

"I *heard* that!" Kelly called out. "Don't make me invent a tax against piddling on the queen!"

Hope choked on a laugh, quickly focusing on her own armful of newborn.

"You smell like a baby . . . and like a woman," Morg murmured in her ear. "A beautiful combination. I wouldn't mind smelling more of it."

"Sorry," Hope muttered back, lifting her head so she could kiss the edge of his jaw. "I've just been certified pregnancy-free, and I'm not taking off my contraceptive amulet until after we're wed."

Morg sighed. Conceiving a child before they married wouldn't be too shameful, but it would be better to wait until afterward. He contented himself with just holding her. With the rain turning into a full-blown summer storm outside, the evening had turned cold . . . but he couldn't hold her forever. Supper was about to be served. Sighing with regret, he squeezed her one last time and stepped back. "Time to go to the dining hall."

Hope bit her lower lip, uncertain she wanted to go. Her instincts were warring with his statement. At Morg's questioning look, she explained her thoughts. "With Serina and Dominor back, everyone's going to be focused on one of two things: either the work on the Desalinator tomorrow, or the babies. All you and I have to do for the desalination project is stand in line and haul blocks around. Or float them. And the babies . . . they're sweet, but they'll still be there tomorrow, and the next night, and . . . well . . ."

"And?" Morg prompted.

"And, well, can we just get some plates of food and bring them back here?" Hope asked. "We're going to be very busy the next few days, and I just want more time with you right now, while we can spare it."

He considered her request. Almost every meal that Morg had ever had since being exiled had been shared with his brothers. It felt strange, contemplating a quiet evening with Hope, but not unwelcome. His brother had done something similar when courting the Aquamancers. "Did you want to go to one of the restaurants down in the city?"

Shaking her head, she snuggled against him. "I want some quiet time with you, before everything starts happening."

Unsure what to make of her statement, but mindful of the threats lurking in wait for his family, Morg asked, "Is that a wish, or is that the Seer in you talking?"

"Just a wish. Nauvea still hasn't spoken to me," Hope admitted quietly.

When he hugged her in sympathy, she sagged against him,

accepting his comfort and the strength that lay underneath it. But she was hungry, and their afternoon meal had been hours ago. Sighing, Hope pulled back, managing a smile.

"If you'll go get the food—since you can float the plates and such—I'll fix up a table for us."

Morg cupped her cheek, noting how she was trying to be cheerful, rather than just being naturally cheerful. "The Gods *will* touch you again. Once a mage, always a mage. So, once a Seer, always a Seer. I'll be back shortly."

Hope surveyed the room absently as he left. *He's right. I've never heard a case of a Seer—a true one—being abandoned by the Gods. Plenty of stories of false prophets being exposed for frauds, but I* know *Nauvea spoke through me.*

I just have to be patient, dedicate my dreams and daydreams to Her, and . . . we'll be alone while we're eating, she thought, distracted by the idea that was taking shape. *Daydreams* are *Her specialty, and I* have *had this one particular daydream in mind for a while, now . . .*

Hurrying to set the stage, she rooted through the linen shelves in his dressing chamber, searching for the oldest bedsheet she could find. Once she had her quarry, she moved around some of the smaller pieces of furniture in his bedroom, the chest at the foot of his bed, the chair by his dresser, and spread out the aging linen. There wasn't a way to start a blaze in the fireplace, though there was some wood in the wood box next to the hearth. Hope searched fruitlessly for a tinderbox until she remembered that Morg was a mage.

Feeling a little silly, she retreated to the refreshing room to use the facilities and wash her hands. Rain rattled against the windowpanes, and thunder rumbled in the distance. *If the rain sticks around, they'll have to cast dryness spells on the blocks of salt and algae tomorrow . . . Oh, stop obsessing about work, just for one night. You'll all be far too busy for three whole days, so just enjoy what you can tonight.*

Returning to the bedroom, she adjusted the glow of the light-globes with raps from her knuckles until the ambiance was suitable for a bedroom picnic. Then she crossed to one of the windows and

opened the glass panes, though she left the shutters closed. That let
in the sound of the rain without the threat of actual droplets, and
enough of a cool breeze that a fire in the hearth would be pleasant.

With the storm providing their mood music, she moved into the
sitting room, gathering up all the cushions she could find. Plump-
ing them, she scattered them into a sort of nest, re-draped the sheet
over them for protection, then hurried out of Morganen's chambers, entering her own. Somewhere in the supplies she had sent
across, she had a jar of ganache waiting to be opened. If she set it on
the edge of the hearth, it should warm up and melt while they ate
supper, providing them with the perfect dessert.

Another thought struck her. Jar in hand, she dug through her
dresser, making a mental note to move it into his quarters, or maybe
find them a slightly bigger suite to occupy. Once she had what she
wanted, she hurried back into his suite and set the jar on the low
stone shelf in front of the fireplace. Stripping and tossing her jeans
and T-shirt into the laundry basket, Hope shrugged into the scrap
of silk. She hurried to adjust the garment before he returned, then
remembered her hair.

Dashing into the bathroom, she found his hairbrush and stroked
it through her curls. A check of her reflection in the mirror showed
too much perfection when she was done, so she set down the
brush and raked her fingers through her dark locks, ruffling them
until she looked like she had just come from his bed. Posing in
the mirror, she imagined his reaction. He'd be startled, but hopefully appreciative. He might even stop in his tracks, if she were
lucky . . . and possibly drop his magically lofted burdens, she realized belatedly.

*Which wouldn't be so lucky. Better wait for him in here, until he's set
them down.*

She heard his voice calling to her from the other end of the
suite, and poked her head out the bathroom door. "We're eating in
the bedroom, Morg! I've arranged for a picnic in here. Would you
set everything down on the sheets, and then light the fire for me?"

Ducking back inside before he could see her, she checked her appearance in the mirror one last time, adjusting the fit of the brown, lace-edged silk. She heard the faint clatter of silverware, then his voice speaking an incantation, no doubt lighting the fire. Pulling open the door, she draped one forearm against the post, positioning her body as artistically as she could.

Hearing the door open, Morg straightened from lighting the wood she had readied. He turned to face her, to compliment her on the idea of an indoor picnic and to question her about the old sheet she had draped over the cushions . . . and lost the strength in his legs. Collapsing onto his knees, he gaped at the vision she made.

Hope was wearing . . . something . . . thin and brown and scanty. It lifted her breasts just enough to show how full and ripe they were, and arrowed down between her thighs with such a narrow scrap of fabric, it was just as well she had done that bizarre otherworld shaving-thing with her nether-hairs. From the tumble of dark brown locks spilling over her shoulders to the light golden hue of her garment-bared hips—he didn't know leg openings *could* be cut that high without compromising the integrity of a garment—she was . . . she was . . .

She was *stunning*, he supposed. Absolutely stunning. That was the only possible description, because she had absolutely stunned him. If he could trust his arms not to give out as well, he would have crawled to her. Assuming the painful, sudden state of his arousal would let him move, of course. Morganen wasn't sure he was even breathing, he was just so . . . stunned.

He watched her leave the doorway where she had so artfully, devastatingly posed and stroll toward him. He had to meet her, even if he could barely remember how to move. Dropping onto his hands, Morg crawled toward her, ignoring the soft lumps of fabric in his way and the warm squish of—

"Oh, Morg." Hope giggled. She hurried to cross the last few feet between them as he paused and looked down at his hand. His knuckles had landed in what looked like a mound of mashed sweetroots, and his nose wrinkled in embarrassed disgust.

Dropping to her knees on one of the cushions, she caught his wrist, gently drawing his fingers to her mouth. Someone had added butter and *cinnin* to the mash, enough to give it an enticing flavor. Combined with the taste of Morg, it was delicious. Perfect for the kind of picnic she had in mind.

A glance at his face showed him still mesmerized by her, his bright blue green gaze roving from hand to breasts to hips to face and back. Hope smiled. "You know, if you were a little more naked, this kind of picnic would work a lot better."

"What?" Dragging his eyes back to her face, Morg blinked at her.

"You've already got a head start," she explained, nodding first at his messy fingers, then at the two plates he had brought, with their strips of chicken in sauce, sweetroot mash, steamed vegetables, and buttered rolls. "Why don't you take off a few more layers of clothes . . ." she added, pausing to lick more sweetroot from his fingers, ". . . and I'll show you what kind of picnic I mean?"

Comprehension sank through the lust stunning him. The fog in his brain was a bit too strong for him to think clearly, however. Tugging his hand free, Morganen closed his eyes, concentrated, and cast his power. "*Sartorlagen.*"

Air *bampfed* as his clothes leaped a body length to one side before dropping to the floor. Opening his eyes, he noted that her garment had transported free as well. But he wasn't satisfied. Not yet. He shifted to move over her, intending to press her down onto the floor and find his satisfaction, but she moved as well, crawling and twisting and landing on her back amid the sheet-covered pillows.

Reaching for the plate he had touched, Hope scooped up more of the mashed root with two of her fingers, and smeared it on the inner curve of one soft, plump breast. Then held out her fingers, offering him the lingering bits of paste. The silly, messy, sensual offering distracted him from the urge for instant gratification. Now the old sheet made sense, to protect the cushions she had gathered. She was offering herself to him as well as the mash, Morganen realized, and had intended both of them to be part and parcel of their meal all along.

The thought was both arousing and tempering. *It wouldn't be right to rush the moment*, he decided, silently telling his aching body to wait for its fullest satisfaction. Capturing her fingers with his lips, he suckled the food from her flesh. *And I am hungry in more than one way.*

She knew she had ensnared his cooperation when he snagged a strip of meat in his fingertips and dragged it over her other breast a few times, painting her nipple with gravy. Placing half the strip in his teeth, Morg leaned over her, offering her a bite of the other half. The move smeared some of the mashed sweetroot and gravy across his own skin . . . but then, that was the point of this feast.

Lifting her head from the sheet-draped cushions, Hope nibbled at the chicken until their lips met in a half-eaten, messy kiss. Morg dropped part of the chicken on her cheek, making her wrinkle her nose and laugh. He grinned and chased it down with mock-growls, licking and nipping until she squirmed up onto one elbow, grabbed a handful of warm, mashed root, and smeared it across his jaw, quickly following the trail of her fingers with a broad lap of her tongue. Morg groaned and pushed her back down, sucking at the food smeared on her breasts.

The rain hissed outside the open window, and the fire crackled softly on the hearth; the sounds were broken by suckling noises, soft groans, and the occasional laugh. When most of the food was either gone or smeared irretrievably on the sheet, Morg coaxed her onto her back, lifting and parting her knees. He smirked at her, unaware that he still had a smear of sauce on the side of his nose. Hope grinned back.

"And now, for dessert . . ."

He started to lower his head between her thighs. Hope stopped him with a hand on his forehead. "Dessert," she said, "is on the hearth, in that jar."

Shifting his gaze from his goal to the fireplace, Morg spotted the jar. All of his attention had been focused on her until now. Spotting the sunset-and-blue label, he rolled his eyes. "*More* chocolate? Haven't I taught you that *I* am better than chocolate, woman?"

"Oh, you're definitely superior to chocolate in many ways," Hope agreed.

Morg was surprised by her ready admission. "I am? You admit it freely?"

She laughed. "Even I'll admit that chocolate is only *food*. I do know I need other things in my life. Conversation, laughter, and a whole range of touches, from tender to passionate. *But*," she stressed, lifting a finger to the side of his nose and scraping off the last of the sauce, "I see nothing wrong in combining the two great loves in my life. Cake is sweet and satisfying, filling in a way that frosting can never quite manage on its own, but the cake is so much sweeter when it's been decorated . . . Wouldn't you agree?"

Licking the gravy from the side of her finger and trailing the tip of her digit over her bottom lip, Hope smiled at him. Giving in to her encouragement, Morg stretched out, snagged the jar, and brought it between them. A twist of the metal lid popped the seal, revealing the dark, half-melted contents.

Thoughtful, Morg contemplated the bittersweet liquid for a moment, then squirmed down the length of Hope's saliva-dampened body. Nudging one thigh out of his way, he positioned himself in front of her femininity, making sure the jar was within reach. Hope lifted herself onto her elbows and made an inquiring noise.

"You said that cake is filling on its own, but is also better with frosting. You are the cake. This is the frosting," he said, meaning the jar of half-melted sauce. "Lie back and relax while I experiment."

Chuckling, she eased back down onto the cushion-strewn floor. "Morg, I was trying to imply that *you* are the cake, and how I wanted to frost *you* with the ganache. I—ohhh!"

He had started sampling his "dessert" plain and undecorated, interrupting her train of thought. Eyes fluttering shut, Hope felt him lapping a second time, savoring the moisture that had seeped free during their sensual supper. Conscious thought slipped away with each swipe of his tongue, each nibble of his lips, until he pulled back, leaving her bereft.

Before she could protest, he daubed something cool and smooth on her nether-lips. Then the heat of his tongue came back. Grabbing at the sheet, she clutched the stained cotton, enduring the pleasure his touch roused in her flesh. Moans escaped her throat, accompanied by little whimpers mixed with unsteady pants.

She had never denied the existence of her hedonistic side—she was *alive*, which was more than she had expected to be after the Portal had collapsed, and that meant gratefully reveling in life itself— but until tonight, it hadn't been so thoroughly explored. Chocolate was one of her passions, with good food being another, and she could firmly add lovemaking with Morganen to the top of that list. Combining all three in one night was a heady, head-spinning experience.

Morg was very thorough. He licked and suckled until the last traces of chocolate were gone, until all he could taste was pure, salty-sweet Hope. Her moans had evolved into needy cries over the course of his taste-testing. He knew why, of course; he had licked to *taste* her, not to satisfy her.

The sound of her unfulfilled whimpers was too stimulating to deny any longer. Moving the jar up beside her shoulder, he sighed in satisfaction when she shifted from clinging to the sheet to wrapping her arms and legs around him, pulling him down on top of her. Food was good, chocolate was fine, but this was what was necessary in his life: pure Hope.

A moment of probing, a helpful twitch of her hips, and he sank deep inside of her with two sure thrusts. His breath escaped in a moan. Lowering his mouth to her cheek, he nuzzled aside her curls and breathed into the curve of her ear. "*This* is the finest thing in life. Becoming one with you.

"Body . . . mind . . . more body," he added as he pulled out a little, then pushed back in. She moaned in his ear and clutched him tighter. Lifting his head, he flicked his hair out of the path of the firelight and smiled at the sight of her, illuminated by the dancing, golden glow. With her neck arched, her lower lip caught in her teeth, she was a living portrait of passion straining toward ecstasy, eyelids fluttering shut. Morg never wanted that look to end. "You are so beautiful. A gift from the Gods Themselves . . . a gift I will always treasure."

Chocolate brown eyes opened and focused on him, then turned dazed again with each of his slow, steady thrusts. Shifting his weight, he paused long enough to free his arm. Hope groaned in protest, heels bumping on the backs of his thighs in the effort to make him move again.

Satisfied she wanted him, Morg dipped his fingers into the jar, swirled them around, then stuck them in his mouth, sucking the gooey liquid from his skin. Rich, bittersweet pleasure rolled over his tongue. It wasn't the bulk source of his pleasure by any means, but Morg was forced to admit it did fill in the empty cracks and forgotten corners rather nicely. *Frosting on the cake, indeed.*

Dipping his head, he claimed her lips for a kiss, sharing the fast-melting sauce. At the same time, he drove himself deep into her body, grinding his hips in that circular way she particularly liked, the way he had learned to pleasure her over the last few nights. She groaned loudly, tongue sweeping in to claim the taste of him and the ganache mixed together.

Fingers twining in his hair, she pulled on the long strands, then raked her nails down his back, finally digging them into his buttocks. Morg spasmed into her in just the right way to tip Hope over the edge of her pleasure. Which was a good thing, because with another shuddering thrust and a kiss-muffled moan, he climaxed, too.

Through the haze of her own bliss, she could feel the little pulses that said he was spilling himself in her, and felt the laughter bubbling up within her. Tipping her head back, she let her amusement escape, hugging him in her joy. He kissed her bared throat, soft salutes of his lips that both tickled and wordlessly told her how much he cherished her.

A happy sigh hummed from her throat; Morg felt it against his lips and allowed himself an equally pleased smile. Sweat prickled along his spine; his skin felt sticky, particularly wherever it had been smeared with food, and he wasn't entirely sure he had the strength to roll off of her, never mind head into the refreshing room for one last bath before the freshwater in the pipes turned to salt water, but he didn't particularly care. Nothing could have wrung greater satisfaction from his flesh than feeling his wife-to-be shuddering—and more important, laughing—with the pleasure he had given her. Chocolate and all.

That thought curved his lips, making it hard for him to continue kissing her. Summoning his strength with a deep, inhaled breath, he rolled off of her. Unfortunately, that bumped his arm into the jar, toppling it and sending a puddle of chocolate sauce leaking onto the sheet . . . and into the loose strands of his hair.

Groaning, Morg righted the jar with an awkward, chocolate-smeared fumble. He drew in a breath to cast a cleaning cantrip, but Hope stopped him. Encircling his wrist with her fingers, Hope drew his hand to her lips. Just like that, they were back at the beginning of this literal mess, only it wasn't mashed sweetroot she licked from his flesh this time.

His manhood twitched. The softness of repletion was being replaced by the hardening of renewed interest in such things. Sighing, Morg relaxed into the sheet-covered lumps of the cushions, ignoring the ganache coating his locks. "You do realize we're going to need a long, thorough bath, after this?"

"Duh," Hope muttered, lapping between his fingers. She paused long enough to add, "I *did* consider the fact that we wouldn't be able to bathe for the next few days when planning this little picnic. Better to enjoy it tonight, than merely want to do it tomorrow."

He chuckled and pulled her close with his free arm, hugging her.

Then reached for the puddle of sauce and deliberately smeared some of it on his chest. "I do believe it's my turn to play the cake for your frosting, correct?"

The speed with which she abandoned his fingers for his chest proved it wasn't a rhetorical question.

Dellen eyed the green-clad stranger in curiosity, slowing her sweeps of the broom in her hands. Almost everyone was down in the city, working on the Desalination project. Petitions had been put on hold for the next few days, so there was no reason for him to be there. *So why is he all the way up here? And what is he carrying?* "Excuse me, milord. Can I help you?"

The dark-skinned man turned, balancing a large, thin, paper-wrapped package against his linen-clad hip. He offered Dellen a smile. "A delivery for the duchess. I was told to take it to her quarters. Could you show me where to go?"

"I can take that," she said, leaning the broom against the nearest painted wall so she could hold out her hands. "What is it?"

"Some sort of old heirloom from the mainland, that's all I know. Probably a wall sculpture. It's very heavy," he warned her, offering her the package.

Dellen grasped it and *oofed* at the weight. It was very bulky and felt sort of like several paintings tied together, only heavier than that. He quickly took it back, giving her an apologetic smile.

"Why don't I just keep carrying it, and you lead the way for me?" he offered.

"I suppose that'll have to do," she agreed reluctantly. "This way. What's your name?"

"I'm Thetteris. I work down on the loading docks," he added. "You are . . . ?"

"Dellen, first-floor maid and general errand runner. So, um . . . when did you move to the Isle?" she asked, glancing at his muscles. "Have you always been a dockworker?"

"More or less. How much farther?" Thetteris asked her, hefting the package.

"We have to go almost all the way to the far end of the east wing, and up a floor—unless this is supposed to be delivered to her workrooms?" Dellen asked the dockworker. "Her suite is rather crowded with things from the other world. Why don't we just go to her workrooms? That's on the ground floor, and not quite as far."

"Her workrooms will be fine, just so long as she gets it," Thetteris agreed, hefting the package again. "Um . . . what do you mean, the 'other world'? How can that be, if she's the real Duchess Haupanea?"

"The Gods tossed her out of our world, through time and the Veils, and dropped her into the other, back when Aiar Shattered and the Portal systems collapsed," Dellen told him. "That's where she met Queen Kelly, but she didn't tell Kelly that she was from this world until she came back through the Veils—if you ask me, I wouldn't take on the life of a Seer for all the money on the mainland. Or have anything to do with magic. Seers and mages lead very strange lives."

"A practical woman," Thetteris praised her as they entered the huge octagonal hall of the donjon. "What made you move from the mainland?"

"I moved because I heard their sovereign-to-be isn't a mage," Dellen confessed. "I grew up in the County of Darglis, and that family abused their powers and their position, coveting freeholdings and demanding rights from families that had been free of manorial obligations for generations. They used their magics illegally against the people they were supposed to be protecting, and they didn't care about the rights of non-mages.

"I was very glad when the Department of Conflict Resolution finally put an end to their wickedness, but the cousin they made the next Countess wasn't that much better. She didn't abuse her powers, but she did abuse her credit with all the merchants and craftsmen in the area."

"And you really think some outworlder is going to be vastly different?" he asked, his tone skeptical. "Power corrupts, and the strong will always prey on the weak."

"Maybe . . . but I've listened to her when she's settled disputes. She really does have a different viewpoint," Dellen insisted. "She digs down for the truth, lays it bare, and then makes the parties involved clean up the mess they've made. In fact, she insists on personal responsibility, regardless of what that person's station is—there's only a handful of us maids and footmen to take care of this huge, sprawling place so far, but she's taken out the trash and swept the floors and scrubbed the dishes, just like I do. She *expects* to have to do it, and does it without magic, with no complaints. And she pays her way, either in hard work or solid coin. She's very admirable."

"You sound almost enamored of her," he said, giving her a sidelong look.

Dellen blushed. "That's the other reason why I moved here. I, um, you know . . . like women as much as I like men. Not that I'd ever . . . She's happily married, but she's also kind of pretty, so I like the view. But that's all. I'm not courting anyone at the moment. And there's always something to be said for a strong, handsome, muscular man," she added, shifting her gaze down over his green-clad body. It was very apparent he worked on the docks for a living; there weren't many other jobs that would keep a man so strong. "Do you, um . . . have someone special in your life?"

"No one. You're not unattractive yourself," Thetteris added, smiling slightly. "But as soon as I've delivered this, I'll have to get back down to the docks and finish up my work there, then hurry out to the Desalinator for my shift. We could always meet this evening, around sunset?"

Dellen wrinkled her nose. "I'm scheduled for the late shift, sorry. Down this hall," she directed him. "And then we take the left-hand corridor, and you can put the package in one of the rooms she's taken over for her *chock-lit* shop. She brought lots of very strange equipment from the other world, and a lot of plants to make the outworlder treat. I've had a taste of it already; it's quite good. I think I know where she keeps the sample-boxes in there, if you'd like to try some."

"You'll have to forgive me if I don't try any. I'm not so sure outworlder food would be very safe," he demurred. "Who knows what they put in their food?"

That made her laugh. "I've talked with Hope about what goes into it. We can get sugar from the cane fields on the northern coast, and maybe even imported from the south edge of Aiar. Cream and milk from our dairy cattle. Eggs for a thickener, and she thinks *vanna* from Darkhana will make a good substitute for something called *vanilla*. She says they have a spice called *cinnamon* that's like our world's *cinnin*. Isn't that funny? She says they have chickens and cattle and cats and dogs, only they don't call them by the same names . . . but for two entirely separate universes to have similar foods that do share similar-sounding names?"

"Is it much farther to this workroom place?" Thetteris grunted, hefting the package onto his other hip.

"Not far," Dellen reassured him. "That door, up ahead. That's one of the rooms she's claimed. Not like they don't have enough of them in this place; it takes me a full day just to dust and sweep and tidy the first-floor rooms. Thankfully, I don't have to clean them every single day. Here, let me get the door for you," she offered, moving ahead of him to open it. "Just set your package on one of the tables, there. If she wants it elsewhere, there'll be plenty of hands up here to move it for her."

Nodding, the dockworker eased the package onto the indicated table. She turned to lead him back out again, and heard him mutter something behind her. It sounded . . .

Dellen blinked and stared at the wall of the corridor. Last she remembered, it had depicted a wheat field. Now it showed fluffy white gray clouds drifting across a light blue sky.

Great. I'm wool-gathering. She shook her head and picked up the broom leaning against the painted atmosphere. *Just because it's a*

*warm day with almost everyone out of the palace is no reason to slack off
your duties, woman. You wouldn't see the Queen slacking off her duties on
a day like today . . .*

"He 'played the cake to your frosting' last night?" Kelly repeated
under her breath, arching a brow in skepticism.

Hope nodded, pausing just long enough to tuck a loose strand of
hair behind one ear before reaching for the next block of compressed sea life. Like Kelly, she had dressed in a sleeveless top, jeans,
and comfortable shoes, with gloves to protect her hands and her
hair pulled back in a practical ponytail. Together, they formed one
pair of a two-sided chain of human bodies, nothing more than two
more sets of hands suitable for lifting and shuffling the blocks from
the conveyor ramps in the freshwater buildings all the way to the
warehouse at the center of the desalination complex.

The rain had ended, thankfully, but the heat had come back,
leaving everything a little muggy this morning. That meant the algae blocks smelled a little more strongly than normal, but it was an
old, familiar smell for Hope. For the others in the line, it caused the
occasional explosive sneeze, including Kelly. The freckled outworlder quickly aimed it into her shoulder, then chuckled in the
next moment. That made Hope glance up in curiosity.

"You sure he wasn't 'beefcake'?" Kelly quipped slyly, sniffing to
clear her nose.

Choking on a laugh, Hope shook her head. "I didn't even think
about it that way . . . but you're right. *All* of these Corvis brothers
are prime examples of beefcake, aren't they?"

The stocky, curly-haired, ex-Gucheran man working next to
Kelly raised his hand between blocks. The supervisor for their
chain caught the gesture, nodded, and turned to look for a replacement. Anyone who needed a drink or a trip to the refreshing room
was allowed to do so, but only if there was someone to take their
place in the line. The theory was, the more hands there were to

shuffle the blocks along, the lighter the overall load for each worker. So far, it seemed to be working smoothly.

Sure enough, a tall, dark-haired fellow volunteered to step into the shorter man's place. He was dressed oddly for the rising heat of the morning, since he wore a long-sleeved tunic as well as trousers; most of the other men had either sleeveless tunics or had opted to strip off their shirts entirely. Kelly wrinkled her nose, making Hope curious as to why. She overheard the reason in the next moment.

"You should've asked to join a taller group," Kelly told the man beside her, helping pass him the next block in tandem with the others lifting its compacted mass. "We're too short; you'll get a crick in your back from having to stoop so much just to match our lifting heights."

The man eyed Kelly askance, brow creasing in a soft frown. Hope felt a strange prickle on the nape of her neck, and wondered if it was her Seer's instincts reviving, or just a trickle of sweat. *Wait . . . he's the one that's sweating*, she realized, seeing the beads dotting his tanned brow. There was something about his rounded face that was vaguely familiar, for all she was fairly certain she'd never seen him before.

"Why should you care?" he asked. "You are the queen. You order, and your subjects obey."

Kelly snorted. "My being a queen doesn't mean you're supposed to ignore your common sense! You're *not* supposed to injure yourself on the job. Everyone in this stretch of the line is short, whereas you're tall.

"You should be waiting for a relief placement over in that line," she added, jerking her chin over her shoulder at the salt block line for their particular pair of processing ramps where the workers were taller on average, though perhaps not quite as tall as this particular man was. "I'll have to remember to have a word with that supervisor about this on my next drink break—bend with your knees, not with your back, or you'll injure it."

The tall man eyed her again, his expression somewhere between bemused and befuddled. But he bent his knees rather than stooped his spine and worked in silence next to her. Something hung up the blocks back by the conveyor ramp, and for a few moments, a section of the human chain had nothing to shift down the line. Hope stretched out her back, hands behind her hips, while Kelly mopped at her brow with the back of her wrist. Grimacing, she dug into the pouch slung at her hip, fumbling out a small hand mirror as well as a handkerchief.

Midway through mopping her face with the fabric, she paused and frowned down at the circle of silvered glass. Hope opened her mouth to ask a question, but her instincts—and it *was* her instincts; there was no mistaking *that* sharp of a prickling along her nerves for mere sweat—made her hold her tongue. A moment later, the blocks started coming down the line again, idle hands forced into swift action to make up for lost time.

Kelly quickly stuffed the cloth and mirror back into her pouch. She worked in silence for a few more moments, then spoke with a level of casualness that didn't fool her best friend. "It won't work, you know."

The tall man frowned softly again, looking as bemused as Hope felt.

"You haven't broken any laws, so far. And you are helping out with the desalination project. For that, I thank you," she added politely. Turning her head, hands working automatically as she shuffled the current block along the line, she added, "But if you *do* try to attack me, or harm anyone else on this island, I'm going to break your butt, and sling it all the way back to the Great Library at Mendham. I trust I have made myself clear?"

"I don't know what you're talking about."

"*Sure* you don't," Kelly drawled. "But just to be on the safe side, you'd better raise your hand and wait for a replacement. Then either take yourself to a taller-bodied line, where you won't risk hurting your back . . . or get yourself and your companions *off* my island, before you *do* break the law. Because we *also* know you didn't come here alone . . . along with your twenty or so ships, strung out from Harbor City to Mendham."

Now Hope recognized him, or rather, his origins. Roughly six years ago—from her perspective—she had seen someone like him, tall, tanned, and moonfaced. Those were the marks of the Mendhite race, like the way most Gucherans had very curly hair, or how Aians had broad foreheads and pointed chins.

"I still don't know what you're referring to . . . but if you think I am here specifically to harm you, why not arrest me?" the tall man asked the woman at his side.

"Because you haven't broken the law, yet. Unless you *choose* to follow through on the petty reasons why you were hired to come here . . . you will remain a guest of Nightfall, the same as anyone else. But I'm not stupid enough to shove temptation in your face. So be a *smart* man, raise your hand, and find something else to do besides work right next to me. Because I guarantee you won't enjoy the experience if you do try anything illegal in my presence—and get a drink of water while you're at it," Kelly added. "You're sweating too much; I don't want you collapsing from dehydration, either."

He stared at her, confusion clear in the crease of his brow, but finally raised his hand, signaling that he needed another break. A Katani woman stepped into his place within a few moments. Hope watched the Mendhite head out of the building, pausing twice to turn and stare thoughtfully at Kelly's back. The second time, he noticed Hope staring back, and hurried out of the building without a third glance.

She shook her head, pausing to re-tuck the same straggling lock that had escaped her ponytail earlier before returning her hands to the mindless, repetitive task of passing blocks down the line. "I don't know if that was wise, or not, letting him know that you knew."

"I planted a seed of doubt in his mind," Kelly returned, speaking under her breath once again. "He had tattoos on his face, hidden by a glamour. I saw them through the mirror. He could have attacked, just now. Of course, it might've been difficult for him to escape with so many citizens standing around, but he could've done it, and I would've been hard-pressed to defend myself. But you'll notice I expressed my concern for his well-being. That puzzled him.

"No doubt he came here expecting to have to take down some redheaded usurper of a would-be tyrant," Kelly added, flashing Hope a quick grin. "I'm not even going to speculate on what the Council may have told him and his companions about me. But it's very much a truism that if you treat people with compassion and kindness, they're far more likely to react in kind, or at least they'll hesitate when it comes time to hurt you."

"In other words, you reap what you sow," Hope murmured. It took her another moment to realize what Kelly meant. "Wait—that's one of the Broger incident mirrors, isn't it? The one you used to reflect lightning onto Rydan a few weeks ago?"

"The one and the same," Kelly admitted. "We'll just call it my one point of vanity, constantly carrying it around. Or maybe my one point of wisdom."

Nodding, Hope returned her attention to her part of their work . . . though she kept a wary eye on the movement of the people laboring around the freshwater hall, looking for another tall, round-headed, tanned figure, visibly tattooed or otherwise. She didn't see one, but that didn't mean they weren't somewhere on the island. Morg had told her about Councilor Consus' warning shortly before her arrival, along with most everything else that had been happening on Nightfall.

Now it would be her turn to tell him about this particular incident. Kelly might place some cautious trust in her "seed of doubt," but Hope wasn't going to rely on it. Instinct said that Morg and his brothers needed to know. *Perhaps at Kelly's next break, I can convince her to use her cryslet to warn the others . . .*

The thought made her wrinkle her nose—and then hastily muffle a sneeze into her bicep as that stirred up the plankton dust infiltrating her sinuses. *A pity I don't have one of my own, yet,* she sighed, sniffling. *But everything's just gone by so quickly, and I haven't really needed one until now. Ah, well. Yet another thing to be placed on the "deal with it after the Desalinator is up and running" list.*

"Thank you for the description, Kelly, Hope. I'll start looking for the others. Make sure you tell Saber, and *stay in public*. They'd be fools to attack you where your citizens would react."

Closing the lid of his cryslet, Morg sat there on the stool positioned next to one of his worktables and frowned in thought. He didn't deny he had been forced by the increased influx of settlers to reduce how much he warded and watched the island for unexpected approaches . . . but the ships that traveled to Harbor City took familiar routes. Only the wards along that stretch of the Isle had been reduced. All other beaches, cliffs, and coves were still covered.

I've only received two ward-alarms in the last week, when ships strayed off course. But they corrected their headings as soon as they figured out where along Nightfall they had approached, and they certainly didn't drop off any unregistered passengers. Everyone has been coming onto the island via the docks. That means Augur and his people should have a record of their arrival . . . and should have used a Truth Stone to discern their true identities and purposes.

That thought made him frown again. *How does one get around the spells embedded in a Truth Stone? Obviously via more magic . . . possibly some hidden amulet, though it would have to touch the Stone to neutralize it . . .*

At least Hope and Kelly's report confirmed that Lord Consus had spoken the truth, days ago. Mendhites *had* traveled a full third of the way around the world, if not farther, all to reach Nightfall and steal away the power of the Living Host, so that they could resurrect the Convocation of the Gods for themselves. *I'll need to check on the "dog" stone, make sure it's safe and secure, but I should also check my library down below, to see what sort of illusions and truth-averting spells could subvert a Truth Stone so easily. Or maybe drain it, in which case they'd have some sort of power crystal via which they could be tracked . . . though I doubt finding these Mendhites will be quite so easy.*

I have . . . half an hour to get the information I need, he decided, checking the glow of the tiny crystals dotting the oval rim of the cryslet lid. *That should be plenty of time to find the dispelling and tracking spells I'll need. And to boost the protective spells around the palace, to make sure the Mendhites can't get in here unnoticed.*

"Ugh. It's too hot. If I never have to lift another block of *anything* in my life again, I'll be quite happy about it," Kelly muttered, sagging onto one of the many wooden benches and stools some thoughtful soul had provided, along with narrow trestle tables suitable for holding pitchers and cups of drinkable water and platters of food. The water was still plentiful, stored in kegs stacked against the walls of the four buildings housing the saltwater tanks, but the food had been reduced to mere scraps.

Someone else had erected crude awnings, providing shade for those laborers taking a break on the benches. Some of the volunteers were still eating a late lunch from the communal buffet; others were taking advantage of their allotted ten minutes per hour. Yesterday's rain clouds had given way to oppressive, muggy heat, and the freckled outworlder was sweating because of it. She pulled out the kerchief from her pouch again and wiped at her face and neck.

Kelly sighed and continued. "Not that rain would've been good for the blocks, but I'm glad the Healers are keeping an eye on everybody. The last thing we need is people collapsing from heat exhaustion during all of this."

Hope inhaled deeply, enjoying the moist air. The heat and humidity weren't exactly comfortable, but it was *her* island's heat and humidity. Of course, that didn't mean working hard in such weather was enjoyable, but resting wasn't bad. She sighed and looked at her blood sister. "You do realize you'll have to do all this work over again tomorrow? And probably some of the next day as well?"

"*Joy*. More hours of backbreaking labor. I'm tempted to tell Saber to get me somewhere semipublic long enough so I can be ambushed, just so we'll get that part over and done with," Kelly added under her breath. Her husband was busy consulting with his twin, trying to figure out the best way to get them all safely back up to the palace again. "If we stay down here, I'll have to keep working, just to put on a good show of civic duty."

"You're the one who declared herself a queen," Hope reminded her. "You made your coronation robes, now sweat in 'em."

That made Kelly laugh. "Actually, I forgot to make some. I guess my aqua silks will have to suffice." The redhead sighed wistfully, glancing at her darker-haired friend. "You know, I used to wonder, why *me*, out of the five women Morg said he was keeping an eye on? What made me different from all the rest? Now I know what it was. You."

Reaching up—though her arm muscles protested at the movement—Hope smacked Kelly on the back of the head, just above her ponytail. "Don't be an idiot! He picked *you* because you were perfect for Saber, and you needed rescuing. He didn't even *know* about me, at the time. Nauvea sent me to a place where I'd meet up with *you*."

Kelly gave her a mock-dirty look, rubbing at the back of her head. "You're going to give me a swelled head if you aren't careful—*one* way or another. Oh, hello, Wolfer!"

The secondborn of the brothers had approached while she spoke. His hair, fluffier and thicker than the rest of his brothers', looked positively frizzy in the humidity. Combined with his golden hazel eyes, he looked more like a lion than a wolf to Hope. But she wouldn't have known about the pun in his name, if she hadn't first learned Kelly's native tongue.

"Kelly, Hope. Saber's found a way to get up to the palace, presuming Hope can open the door for us," he told them, his deep voice soft-spoken. "Kor and Danau are hard at work at the moment."

"Ah, the warehouse," Hope agreed, grasping the idea. She pushed to her feet, feeling tired muscles creak. Another day's hard labor lay in wait for *her* tomorrow, too. "A pity those two haven't had a chance to really enjoy their honeymoon, but the Desalinator couldn't wait. Particularly if the Mendhites are indeed here. There's a mirror downstairs, in the office refreshing room. It's not connected to anything, but with a bit of translocation powder from the office cupboard, it'll connect to one of the mirrors up at the palace. Probably one of the ones in Morg's workroom."

"Exactly. Come." Wolfer waited patiently while Kelly stood and stretched, then paced beside them, keeping an eye on the men and women taking their leisure at the seats and tables placed under the awnings.

Hope didn't see any sign of a Mendhite, but then, she didn't think assassins would be stupid enough to attack in public. *Which makes the man's appearance in the line puzzling, now that I think about it. Why would he risk exposure? Morg said that Consus mentioned Mendhite Painted Warriors would be coming to assassinate Kelly and steal Rora's Fountain. It's clear they came with glamour-spells to disguise their tattoos, but their sheer foreignness could have given them away all the same.*

They had to dodge around blocks being lifted in a long, living chain up to the second floor of the vast, multistoried warehouse in order to get to the old distribution offices. At least here, Hope felt very much on familiar ground. Unlike the palace, with its spell-painted walls, the warehouse looked pretty much the same as she remembered it.

Of course, they couldn't have known that she'd have a magic-reflecting mirror on her, but they could've prepared for other means of magical discovery . . . and probably did, hence the long-sleeved shirt. If it isn't covered up by magic, it cannot be uncovered by a counterspell. They also didn't disguise their general appearances. Then again, Hope allowed, *with the loss of quick, cross-oceanic travel thanks to the loss of the Portals, the odds of anyone knowing what a Mendhite looks like in this corner of the world is very low. Even I had to take a few minutes to realize what nationality I was looking at, when I sort of recognized that man.*

The distribution offices were empty, disconcerting her. She had half expected them to be filled with clerks' desks and filing cabinets. Shaking off the strangeness of walking into empty rooms, she led the way to the back chamber and laid her hand confidently on the spot on the wall where the door was hidden.

Nothing happened.

Blinking, Hope shifted her hand, gauging the presence of the door by the way it felt. It was definitely the right section, cool and a little clammy feeling, though the stones themselves were completely dry. It still *felt* like Aquamancy to her Seer's senses . . . but the door didn't open. Frowning, she lifted her hand from the surface, absently rubbing the faint grit from her fingers. The straight, faint lump of the scar on her palm caught her thumb, which caught her attention. Hope chuckled ruefully, remembering *why* she was scarred.

"Well?" Wolfer asked. "Can't you open it?"

"*I* cannot," she stated. She smiled as she turned to Kelly. "I can't, because the door is set to open for an Aquamancer of sufficient power, *or* for the rightful ruler of Nightfall. Since I'm not an Aquamancer, door-opening duty falls to *you*, Sister. The default for inheritance is always the eldest sibling."

Her graceful bow and sweeping arm made Kelly blink. Hesitantly, the other woman lifted her freckled hand and pressed it in the same spot Hope had touched. The wall vanished, making Kelly gasp and jerk her hand back. She blinked, aqua eyes wide, as the wall returned after a few seconds, then she grinned fiercely and touched the wall again.

Again, the wall disappeared. Kelly lifted her hands over her head in triumph. "Look, I can do magic. *I* can do *magic*—and not just summoning my dagger! Hah!"

Hope chuckled, amused by her friend's delight. Then laughed heartily when she caught Wolfer rolling his eyes. "Oh, give her a break, Wolfer! The only time I've ever been able to do magic, it's always been something pre-purposed like this doorway, but that doesn't mean it's not fun to do, anyway."

"Play with it later," Wolfer ordered Kelly. "Saber wants you and Hope safely up at the palace, while he and Morg hunt for the Mendhites. I need to get back to Alys. I don't want her stressing herself with too much salt block floating on her own."

"Fine . . . spoilsport." Laying her hand on the reformed stones of the wall a third time, Kelly dissolved it completely.

Someone had set lightglobes in brackets on the walls of the stairwell, illuminating their way into the hidden depths of the desalination plant. *Probably Koranen,* Hope guessed. The seventhborn brother was a Pyromancer, after all; lightglobes were easy for him to make. *How odd, that he can combine his powers with an Aquamancer well enough to double her own strength. Your fellow Gods certainly work in mysterious ways sometimes, Nauvea. Do They share Your sense of humor?*

There was no reply, of course. She didn't expect one so soon after her resumption of worship, either. But it would have been nice to know her chosen deity was listening. Doubts over Nauvea's continued existence were not something she could afford to feel for very long.

Consus checked the wards sealing his chamber door, making sure his quarters hadn't been disturbed. It cost him energy to do so, most of which he had already spent working the midnight-to-morning shift down at the desalination plant. It was beneath his skill and his power as a mage to work as a mere laborer, but these Nightfallers had given him sanctuary, and he owed them repayment for the cost of his food and lodging.

Still intact. Good. Of course, the servants won't have dusted or tidied while I was gone overnight . . . but I've grown used to doing that myself, ever since I acquired that mirror, he acknowledged, dissolving the seals on the door. Entering the sitting room, he reapplied the wards, then turned to look at the double ovals of silvered glass. And blinked at the image that flickered through first the left side, then the right.

It didn't last long. In fact, he wasn't sure he had actually seen anything, if it weren't for the gray mist that was still clearing after he blinked and squinted his tired eyes. *Someone with the dark skin of a northerner approaching one mirror . . . and walking away from the other?*

No, exiting *the other mirror,* he realized. *But . . . I've never seen the Barol mirror show a mirror being used as a Gate before! I didn't even know you* could *scry on a mirror being used as a Gate! One would think the opening of the Gate would interfere with the reflective properties of the glass, rendering it unsuitable for copying to another mirror's perspective!*

Frowning, he headed for the refreshing room. Long hours of tedious, repetitive casting of levitation and dust-suppressing charms had left him tired and ready for sleep. The ex-Councilor almost dismissed the event, except for the sight of the smaller mirror over the sink, marked along its frame with anti-scrying runes, reminded him that the Barol mirror *never* activated without some reason compelling it. A reason connected to the person observing its activation.

The mirror activated when Carolos was alone with it. That much was made clear, he thought, using the facilities. *It showed him a scene of me talking with Morganen, agreeing to give the Nightfallers information— aiding them against King Taurin's expressed wishes. Something that he obviously felt was wrong, to betray the trust of his employment with me by reporting what he'd seen to Finneg's Department.*

So what is so personally important to me about seeing what was probably Finneg traveling by mirror-Gate? The mirror shows what is *happening, not what did or will happen . . . so it could only show me a very brief snippet of what the duke was doing,* Consus reasoned. He washed his hands at the sink. *Just that he went traveling somewhere important to me. Except there's nothing on the mainland that's important to me.*

I've no close family, no close friends—a few who enjoyed a well-aged

bottle of frostwine and a game of cards from time to time, but no one inti-
mate enough to worry over. And now that I am exiled from my home, with
most of my belongings in tow, I've no possessions to fret about, either. Ev-
erything I care about is . . .

Here. The middle-aged mage narrowed his eyes, squinting once
at the anti-scrying runes on the mirror over the sink. *This isn't the*
only mirror in the place. I've seen them in other refreshing rooms—this
was once a duchy of great and ready wealth, to have so many mirrors ev-
erywhere.

The only mirrors that would concern me would be the mirrors here, *on*
Nightfall Isle. And he did remark that it would take a link with a mirror
inside *the palace to be able to invade this place—Gods! Is he here to cap-*
ture me? Or the Queen?

Not bothering to wipe his hands on the towel provided, Consus
hurried out of his quarters. He kept a wary eye on the shadows cast
by the intermittent lightglobes, for the shifting paint on the walls
showed the dark boles of trees and underbrush in a dense forest,
here on the third floor. The walls of the stairwell showed slow-
fluttering birds in a flock against light gray clouds, and the walls of
the second-floor corridor were a cheerful, bright, dusty-dry view of
rolling sand dunes beneath a deep blue sky.

Unfortunately, when the youngest Corvis brother had gestured
in the direction of his quarters, the walls had looked entirely different. The undulating swells of near-featureless sand disoriented the
older mage. *Last time, there had been a pond, with deer and meadow*
flowers, and a large oak . . . there-ish, by that lightglobe? Or was it far-
ther down the hall, at that other one . . . ?

Jinga's Balls, I don't have time to play guesswork! Summoning up
some of his remaining energy, Consus concentrated, shaping his
will. A snap of his fingers helped release the spell. *"Dorminia Mor-*
ganen lacariat!"

A will-o'-the-wisp appeared, floating in front of his fingers.
Normally the spell was useful for finding hidden holds on ships
with suspected caches of smuggled goods. Altered, the wisp of light

paused only a few seconds, then zipped toward the second of the two choices down the hall. Consus hurried after it, checking behind him to make sure the Councilor of Conflict Resolution wasn't lurking in the early morning shadows.

Just as he reached the door, it flung open. Energy crackled; Consus ducked reflexively, raising a protective ward. Thankfully, nothing struck his magical barrier. Instead, Morganen of Nightfall lowered one glowing fist, muscles visibly relaxing. The young man had apparently donned his trousers hastily, for the front wasn't even fully laced. Instead, he held them up by his other hand, giving Consus a view of the pale skin at Morganen's hip.

Magic fading from his fingers, Morg rubbed his face with his free hand and sighed roughly. "Milord Consus . . . Is there a particular reason why you're casting magic outside my bedchamber? At this hour?"

"I needed to locate you. I have reason to believe that Councilor Finneg may have entered either the city or the palace through an unwarded mirror. I do not know if he has only just arrived, or has just departed. My . . . source of information was extremely brief, and thus limited."

Aquamarine eyes sharpened. Morg lowered his hand. The older mage's revelation looked like it was fully awakening the younger man. "Of course. That odd, double mirror of yours. One of these days, you and I *will* have to have a talk about its capabilities. Particularly if it has anything to do with this island and its safety. But we have a bigger problem. Are you *certain* you saw the duke mirror-Gating to or from the palace?"

Consus hesitated, then shrugged. "The glimpse was very brief. The scryings appear only as the events happen. I could not be certain of the location, nor entirely of the identity . . . but the only northern Katani male whose movements I would have a vested interest in viewing would be the Councilor of Conflict Resolution, and the only mirrors that would be important for me to see him traversing would be a set that linked somewhere to or from this island."

"A vested interest . . . ?" Morganen prompted.

"The mirror shows only whatever is of interest to the viewer, or something the viewer can affect or act upon. But it also only shows what *is* happening, at that moment. Had I arrived a few moments earlier, I would have seen more." Glancing up and down the hall, Consus folded his arms across his chest, uncomfortable with any conversation regarding the Barol mirror's secrets. He owed the younger mage some information, but not all of it. Certainly not the ultimate secret, that the mirror technically belonged to the Lady Alys of Devries. "We need to act on what information I do have. The longer we stand here, debating what I saw, the more time His Grace may have to infiltrate the secrets of your home. Or carry them back to the Council."

"Fine. I'll make some calls, wake up the others. If he's in the castle—if any of them are, or have been—we should be able to either find them or traces of their auras. I'd cast a blood-mirror to scry the immediate past," Morg added, mouth twisting wryly, "but I did that just a few days ago, and it's never a good idea to do so twice in the same turning of Brother Moon."

"I have had recent experience with a more ritualistic version of past-scrying. It takes almost a full day to set up, but once arranged, it can be reactivated repeatedly for up to a week, if necessary. I still have some of the components for it," Consus found himself offering. "If you can provide some molly-leaf and tincture of mandrake, I could attempt to re-create the spell. Presuming you're willing to wait several hours for the results."

"I'll get you the components as soon as I've contacted my family," Morg said. "We'll need to do a sweep of the palace first, which might resolve the problem . . . but if nothing else, a decently brewed scrying-salve can be useful to have on hand in the near future."

Consus nodded, then hesitated. "The, ah, duchess . . . She's a Seer, not a mage. She should not be left unguarded. Finneg can be ruthless when performing his duties."

"She's in a safe place, attending to an early morning chore,"

Morganen dismissed. "If Finneg or the Mendhites can even find her right now, they're far more resourceful than can be credited . . . and if they *could* breach the defenses protecting her, my brothers and I would already know. Let me get my cryslet, then I'll walk with you. Try to recall if there was anything familiar about the locations the duke seemed to be Gating through."

EIGHT

✦━⟨⟩━✦

"There you are. You missed quite a bit of excitement," Kelly told Hope, catching up to her as they approached the doors to the dining hall.

"Oh?" Hope asked. Turning to glance at her friend, she twisted her knee, making her grimace and favor it quickly. Yet another morning of walking around the granite-carved corridors of the Underhalls had left her legs aching. They joined the twinges left over from yesterday's efforts down at the Desalinator. Wincing, she faced forward again. "Remind me to ask one of the Healers for a painkiller potion. So, what happened?"

"Morg woke up all the brothers to do a full magical sweep of the grounds. If you'd been up above, you'd have seen them pacing inward through the halls and courtyards, like they did way back when I first arrived," Kelly told her. "But instead of searching for a mekhadadak infestation, they were looking for traces of unwanted guests."

"Did they find any?" Hope asked, distracted from her aches.

"I don't know, yet. I think they just finished the sweep a little while ago. Maybe we'll find out at breakfast," Kelly added, shrugging. "I mean, it's obviously safe enough, since Saber called to let me know I could come down out of our room."

"That reminds me, when do I get a cryslet?" Hope gave Kelly a wry, pointed look. "After all, I *did* explain the basics of cell phone technology well enough that the boys could grasp it and replicate it as an Artifact."

Kelly blinked. "That's right, you don't have one, yet. I suppose we could get you one this afternoon, after we're done with our shift at the plant—don't give me that look!" she chided Hope. "Evanor's scheduled to work down there this morning, too, while Mikor is in school. He's the one in control of the cryslets, since he's the communications expert in the family. He could get you one immediately, but having to do the sweep has put him and his son behind schedule."

"What, is Mikor being a slug-in-bed?" Dominor asked, approaching the door from the donjon side of the corridor. He had his daughter cradled gently against his chest with one arm, the other escorting his tall, pale-haired wife, who was cradling their son in one arm and a chalkboard in the other.

"He's always been like that when he's gone to bed after a warm summer's night," Serina dismissed. "It didn't happen often in the mountains around the Retreat, but when it did, Mikor would stay half-asleep until he could take a cool rain-shower."

"I was always much more reluctant to get out of bed on cold mornings, not warm ones," Hope admitted. She changed the subject back to the morning's events. "So the Palace *is* safe, right?"

"As safe as we can determine, though Rydan claims the aether was disturbed in the east and south wings by people with 'disagreeable emotions' being aimed toward us," Dominor told them. He freed his right hand from Serina's waist, opening the door to the dining chamber for them. "I'd hate to have his ability, but other than his claim, we've no evidence anyone unauthorized entered the compound."

"Rora can't even use her 'Seeing' ability, now that the Fountain's been extracted," Serina added, following Hope and Kelly into the longish room. "She used to be able to question the universe in simple yes-no ways, but all of that vanished, following the extraction. According to my research over the last few months, it's because the Fountain tied her to the *knowing* of the Dark. These Darkhanan Witches, like Priestess Ora, can ask questions of the place between Life and the Afterlife, and receive simple yes-no responses. It's fascinating, really."

"No wandering off on side-paths," Dominor instructed his wife, holding out a chair for her at the table, still balancing the cream-wrapped bundle of their daughter against his chest. "Your current task is to eat and replenish all the nutrients you just gave our children."

"Good morning, my love," Morganen murmured, rising so that he could hold Hope's chair for her.

"*Good morning,*" she whispered back, since Serina was speaking again.

"If you didn't take such good care of me, Dom . . . Let's just say I don't think I paid enough for you, after all," Serina teased her husband. The pale blonde Arithmancer caught sight of Hope's confusion and smiled. "I screamed at him while I was in labor that I'd only paid the equivalent of a sway-backed donkey for him, when I bought him off the slavers in Natallia ten months ago."

"Only by the value of the Moonlands," Dom dismissed, kissing his wife on the temple before taking his seat at her side. Galea fussed a little in his arms, then settled back to sleep. "By Natallian standards, you paid a royal ransom for me. Or rather, ransomed me from a lifetime chained to royal bedsheets—no offense, Kelly, but I'm glad *I'm* not pinned under a queenly thumb."

"I think *someone* has been neglecting his sword practice, given how long he's spent sequestered in a nunnery of late," Saber returned, slanting a mildly irritated look at his thirdborn sibling. "But practice will have to wait. We haven't been able to find the Mendhites since Kelly first saw them, and we haven't been able to find the Councilor of Conflict Resolution. I want each of you—all of the mages in this family—to lay wards and telltales over the doors, windows, halls, and chambers of this place.

"If anyone unauthorized and unrecognized as part of this household comes into the palace, I want to know about it within minutes of it happening," he ordered.

The door opened, admitting a short, blue-haired woman clad in a sleeveless gray leather vest and matching leather trousers. She beamed a smile at everyone, heading for the far end of the table. "Isn't it a *glorious* morning?"

Several sets of puzzled eyes glanced her way, but it was the petite redheaded woman, Danau, who addressed her. "What's put you in such a good mood, Ama-ti?"

The blue-haired woman beamed a smile at her fellow Aquamancer. "I had the most *lovely* date with Cammen Del Or, the tea merchant. The kind that lasted all night. Anyway, I only came back up here to bathe and change clothes, then it's back to overseeing the freshwater distribution for all the households in the city. I suspect Chana is dying for me to replace her, since it's such a long, boring shift at night."

"That's it! We'll have the ladies watch who comes to them for freshwater," Morg told the others. "All they have to do is watch for glamours disguising the Mendhites and the duke, and we'll catch them as they come looking for a drink!"

"I think I have a True-Sight pendant in my workroom somewhere," Trevan offered. "If not, it won't take long to enchant a new one. I know exactly where the book is with the directions to make that Artifact."

"Unless they were smart and brought their own," his wife, Amara, pointed out. "Or stored it, if they arrived before the Desalinator was restarted, since that's what the residents were supposed to do over the last week. It's only the transients and those without enough jars and vases to fill for their familial needs who have to replenish their supplies from the reservoir each day."

"Nothing we can do about it if they have," Kelly said, shrugging. "But the amulet is a good idea all the same. The more ways we use to try and find these people, the more nets we're casting into the river, in hopes of catching at least one little fish."

"*I* intend to catch all of our unwanted fish, and fillet them if they try to harm us," Saber stated. He met the eyes of each adult at the table, sober and serious. "Remember, cast your wards both inside and outside the palace walls . . . and if you get into trouble, sing out Evanor's name, and he'll hear you speaking. He's reinstated his old communication spell as an emergency measure—mostly for young Mikor's sake, but it'll do for our own as well. And use your crys-lets."

Hope glanced at her bare wrists. She still needed to get one for her own needs, but Evanor hadn't come to breakfast, yet. *Ah, well. Not like I'll be alone, since I'm working alongside Kelly for most of today and either beside Morg or in his arms for the rest of it.*

*I*t was the sigh that woke her. Heavy, frustrated, and nearby. Sleepily, Hope inhaled to clear some of the muzziness from her head, snuggled closer to the warm body sharing mattress space with her, and sighed herself. "Sorry," she mumbled. "Was I snoring again?"

"No," Morg dismissed, speaking quietly. "Besides, I've told you, you have a cute snore. I don't mind it."

It was dark in his bedchamber, hard to see anything, but Hope could feel the tension in his muscles. "What's wrong?"

"I can't *find* anything. They're mages. They *should* leave some sort of trackable trace of their energies in the aether. But only Rydan could find hints of emotional residue, and that's not the same thing," Morganen complained. "What good is being the best of my brothers, if I cannot solve this puzzle? The duke and the Mendhites are dangerous, but nowhere does it say in Prophecy that I defeat them, only that I get the chance to marry you. I'd put that off to ensure it, since an attack would threaten everyone, but . . . not forever."

"Mmm." Hope thought about the problem. Nothing had happened all day long to disturb their work. No sign or spark of any unwanted, unauthorized presence on the Isle. "Maybe they're wearing magic-dampening amulets?"

"Some of the wards I've cast should be sensitive enough to detect even those," he said, sighing again.

"Well, maybe the Council of Mages has been working on getting around those sensitivities," she offered. "They do have a subdepartment for Spell Research, under the Department of Conflict Resolution if I remember right . . . which is something Councilor Finneg would have access to, wouldn't he?"

"Maybe, but that's an unpleasant thought. And they're not supposed to directly interfere or oppose our bid for independence for a full year and a day," he reminded her. "The one person I could've asked to investigate his actions back on the mainland is now sleeping on the floor above us. We're operating blind, only able to react and not act."

"Mmm." There wasn't much she could say to comfort him, since she knew it was true. Hope held him a little closer for a while, then lifted her head far enough to peer at the glow from her new cryslet, marking the hour and minute. "Blehh. I have to get up in another ten minutes."

She felt Morg shift, heard the soft rustle as he turned his head. "Don't you mean twenty?"

"Walking around the Underhalls is rather boring on its own. I was thinking I'd swing by my workrooms and pick up a manual to read. I've got more than a dozen different types of machines to manage and maintain once I get my business going, and I'll have to be familiar enough to both explain them to my future employees, and convert them into magical terms for your brother Trevan to try and replicate. What I've got is sufficient for a small production rate, but I also imported enough trees to at least double the amount of chocolate I could make, if not triple."

Morg shifted just far enough to find and press a kiss to her forehead. "Sounds like you have a lot on your mind, too."

"No more than any other budding businesswoman," she agreed. Hope smothered a yawn into his shoulder, then sighed. This time it was happier than the previous one. "I'm looking forward to the challenge, though. I'll be bringing culinary delight to thousands. It's not quite as important as restarting the Desalinator, or saving the island from an unspecified Disaster . . . but I think giving joy to people's taste buds is worthwhile enough."

"*I* still think I'm superior to chocolate . . . but I'll concede that it is special. Which makes *me* extraordinarily special by comparison," Morg boasted. He squirmed and chuckled when she pinched him, catching her hand and lifting it to his lips for a kiss.

"*Yes*, you're special, too," Hope agreed. "But all I'm sharing with the others is the wonderful world of chocolate. I am *not* sharing you."

"Good. I don't want to be shared." Twisting onto his side, Morg kissed her. It was more of a loving kiss, not an arousing one, but that wasn't a bad thing. He pulled back after a few moments, sighing again. "I'd love to continue, but you have dog-walking duty, and a book to find."

In the dark, Hope's kiss landed on the corner of his mouth. "That's a bookmark kiss. It'll hold my place, right there, until I can get back to it tonight."

"I'll look forward to it," Morg agreed, reaching up to brush the dark sphere of the lightglobe sitting in its bedpost bracket.

They both squinted against the sudden soft glow, waiting for their eyes to adjust. When she could see without blinking, Hope slid out of the bed. She smiled to herself as Morg watched her stretch her naked body before padding toward the dressing room and the clothes she had moved into it, confident that he loved her.

Hugging his pillow—an unsatisfactory substitute for what he wanted to hold—Morg awoke from his light doze at the ringing of his cryslet. For a moment, he was disoriented by the noise, then lunged for it, flinging up a hand to smack the lightglobe overhead. Squinting against the abrupt, bright light, he opened the lid. Alys peered up at him through the oval-shaped mirror.

"Morg? Um . . . sorry to interrupt, you know, whatever it is you're doing," his curly-haired sister-in-law offered, blushing in that shy way of hers. "But could you finish up soon, and send Hope down here? I'm getting tired of walking in circles."

Frowning in confusion, Morg tilted the cryslet in his hands, checking the time. His eyes widened sharply, and he quickly looked back into the mirror. "You mean she's *not* down there already?"

Alys' gray eyes widened. "Uh . . . no? She's not still up there with you?"

Fear raced through him, adrenaline chasing away the last of his sleepiness. *It's possible she could've tripped . . . but surely she would've called someone on her cryslet! Mariel, at the very least. I know she took it with her. That means . . .* Aware that Alys was peering at him in concern, Morg quelled his rising panic. Action, not reaction, was what they both needed. "Alys, if she's not down there with you, then she's missing. I'm afraid you're going to have to stay down there and keep walking the crystal until someone comes to relieve you."

Wide-eyed, she quickly nodded. "I'll keep it moving. Just, um, make sure no one gets down here. I don't know how *safe* I can keep it, on my own."

"Call Dominor and Rydan. Make sure they're both aware the Underhalls need protecting. I have to call the others." Pressing the translucent white crystals that served as controls for the cryslet, Morganen ended the link with Alys' cryslet and called Saber's. It took his eldest brother a few moments to answer, nor did Saber's gray eyes look any happier than Alys' had. Thankfully, Saber came straight to the point.

"What's wrong?"

"Hope is missing. She didn't meet up with Alys downstairs. I don't care if she's just fallen down and hit her head; I want this treated like a full-blown emergency," Morg ordered his brother.

Saber snorted. "It *is* a full-blown emergency. Call Evanor and tell him everything. I'll activate the illusion-guards. I want the compound locked down against everything, including any scryings not attached to the crystal towers—she *may* have just fallen and hit her head, hopefully just knocking herself out, but I wouldn't count on it.

"Have Ev wake everyone, even the servants," Saber added. "I want a nose count and a double-check of all wards. If anything so much as sneezes, even a bug out in the gardens, I want it investigated. I also want you to personally ensure Alys is still safe."

"She is. She's the one that contacted me about Hope. I told her to keep walking, and to call Rydan and Dom and tell them what's gone wrong." Relieved his brother was taking Hope's absence seriously, Morg spared a thought for his sister-in-law. "You make sure your own woman is safe."

Saber's gray eyes slanted to one side, and a wry look twisted his face. "She's getting dressed. I sincerely doubt she's going to sit this one out."

"You bet your sweet ass, I'm not!"

Morg managed a wan smile at the sound of his sister-in-law's voice. "Keep her safe all the same. Make her wear Rydan's and Koranen's ward-sigils, or something. I'm going to call Ev."

Stay calm . . . she cannot *have fallen down a stairwell and broken her neck. You haven't married her, yet,* Morg reminded himself, ending the call and punching the rune-numbers for Evanor's cryslet. *She* will *live. Every last one of your brothers has acquired the bride of their heart, and your verse proclaims that "When Mage has wed, you will be* all." *That means all of you get to have happily wedded lives. Yourself included.*

"Come on, Evanor . . . wake up!" he ordered his own reflection, waiting impatiently for the cryslets to connect. If he wasn't concerned about Mariel peering over his brother's shoulder, he would have risen already and started searching for something to wear. Not that a Healer wouldn't have seen any number of naked male bodies, but she *was* his sister-in-law, and Evanor was a slightly better swordsman than him.

Just as the mirror flickered and shifted, showing his brother's sleepy, frowning brown eyes, a thought struck Morg. "Consus . . ."

"What?" Evanor asked. "Did you call this cryslet by mistake?"

"No—Hope is missing. Saber wants everyone awake and searching for her, servants included. Secure your wife and son while you're at it," Morg tersely ordered his fourthborn sibling. He would just have to contact the ex-Councilor next.

"I'll have them join Serina and her twins. She can keep all of them safe," Ev agreed. The view of his face jostled as he moved, then the lid snapped shut, ending the connection.

Morg rose as well, finishing his earlier thought as he headed for his clothes. *Consus didn't have enough time last night to try the past-scrying spell. We don't have much time right now, either, but it's the only lead we have . . .*

"*A*ttackers, *north wing, second floor, tenth room!*"

Morganen sprinted up the hall, Evanor's voice still ringing in his ears, the scene from Consus' past-scrying still playing behind his eyes. Hope entering her workrooms. Bending over to peruse the outworld tomes on one of the bookcases she had appropriated for her needs. A dark-skinned shadow entering the room behind her, flinging up his hand, and casting a bolt of pale green light. Hope collapsing, her dark curls flying out to hit the books she had been studying. Finneg scooping her up, and carrying her toward a section of wall that shimmered briefly into a mirror before vanishing again.

He *needed* to get to that mirror, to try to find it despite whatever spells had hidden it from his and his brothers' search yesterday, to force open its Gate and step through. But his brothers were in trouble right *now*. Whatever the reason the Councilor had stolen his bride-to-be, she wasn't his bride yet. *She* will *survive—both she and Draganna have Foreseen it.*

Finneg won't, *when I get my hands on him*, he promised in a silent snarl, hooking his hand around the edge of the door so that he could use his momentum to fling himself inside. One of the Mendhites was on his knees, whimpering, another was being spell-squeezed by his secondborn brother, and the third, backed up against one of the walls—vanished, the moment Saber glanced behind him. *Oh, no you don't!*

"*Repunum vis!*" Magic washed outward from his out-flung hand, bathing the room. It limned the frame of the tall, spell-shrouded man, revealing how he was sidling out from beneath the threat of Saber's longsword. "*Falla takei!*"

The rippling outline jerked off its feet, flinging bodily past Saber. Morg clenched his fist, halting the body-shaped aura in midair. As he did so, Kelly eased around him, hurrying to the side of a woman on the ground, tucking a familiar, spell-reflective mirror back into the pouch slung next to her knife.

He belatedly recognized the woman on the ground as Dellen, one of the castle maids. She seemed to be rousing under Kelly's touch, meaning she was alive, and therefore not an immediate concern. Lifting his other hand, he swirled it, adding his power to his secondborn brother's. Tightening their combined grip.

"Stop—Gods, stop!" the Mendhite cried out, tanned face contorted in a grimace.

"That's *enough*, Morg," Kelly ordered. "Hold them, don't kill them."

Morg eased his grip a little, but didn't release either man. Behind him, he heard others approaching and turned his head just enough to see Consus making it to the doorway, visibly winded. He came into the room just ahead of the dark-haired figure of his thirdborn brother. Reinforcements had arrived.

"Councilor Finneg stole a woman, this morning," Morg stated, switching his gaze between the three foreigners, one still a horizontal blur in the air. "He stole her through a hidden mirror-Gate. Where did he take her?"

None of them answered. Morg tightened the grips of his spells on the two he controlled. The one held midair gasped, his transparency fading away.

"*Where* did he take her?" he demanded, anger, frustration, and fear roiling up within him. He tightened his spells again when they didn't answer; a sharp gesture included the third man, who cried out in pain as Morg's magic put pressure on his broken arm.

"Morg! *Enough!*" Kelly snapped, rising from the maid's side.

"They know where he took her, Kelly. I want to know!" Morganen growled. He clenched both fists harder, making all three of them cry out.

Kelly stepped around the one on his knees and slapped Morg. It wasn't a bruisingly hard blow, but it did sting, and it did shift his attention to her. "You do *not* torture prisoners! Torturing people is evil, and *we* are *not evil!*"

"Kelly, they *stole* Hope!" he protested. "We have to get her back!"

"Yes, we do, but *we* do not torture people," she repeated. "She may be my sister and my best friend, and I've known her a hell of a lot longer than you have, but no matter how *good* the cause, no matter how good your intentions, if you torture people, it is *still wrong*. You *cannot* justify it, Morganen! I left that madness behind me when I came here, and *we do not torture people on Nightfall*. That is *official* Royal Policy on this matter!"

"But—!"

"Put. Them. *Down*," she enunciated, meeting his gaze fiercely.

"There is a part of me that is *very* tempted to send them to sleep with the chickens, but there are *other* ways to get the information we need! They are lawbreakers, and they will be clapped in spell and chain, but they *will* be given medical treatment, and they *will* be given food, and water, and a place to rest and wait while I decide what their punishment will be."

Morg's teeth ached, his jaw was so tightly clenched, but he eased his spells enough to lower the hovering Mendhite to the floor. He didn't release his anger, though he kept it under control. "Then *how* do we find her?"

"You said Finneg stole her, right?" Kelly asked. Both Morg and Consus nodded. The ex-Councilor answered her query in more detail.

"I had set up the start of a temporal scrying, so when he woke me, I scried the past to watch the woman's actions," Consus told her. "His Grace appeared in the doorway when she reached one of the rooms on the ground floor. She was struck by what looked like a sleep-spell, and carried by him through a hidden mirror. Beyond that was beyond the spell's ability to scry."

"Then Councilor Finneg has acted against the independence of this incipient kingdom, and broken Nightfall law by attacking and kidnapping one of our citizens," Kelly said, squaring her shoulders. "Lord Morganen, you are hereby authorized to go to the Council of Katan and use any *reasonable* means to convince them to cooperate in locating Councilor Finneg and Hope of Nightfall.

"Torture is *not* reasonable, Morg . . . but if necessary," Kelly allowed, "you have my royal permission to kick their butts. Literally or figuratively. But *try* diplomacy first. That's an order."

"Yes, Your Majesty." He held on to the three Mendhites while his brothers consulted among themselves and Dominor left in search of some anti-magic chains to imprison them. The thirdborn of his siblings muttered something about his wife having a set as he left. Glancing at the middle-aged mage among them, Morg addressed

Consus. "Lord Councilor, I would appreciate your cooperation in finding a mirror-link I could turn into a Gate somewhere at the capital. You needn't come along, but the longer I'm delayed in going after her, the worse her situation may become."

Consus held up his hand. "I can get you into the Sea Commerce sub-office in Orovalis. From there, the mirrors on the walls connect directly to my old office, and to the Hall of Mirrors. Just remember, it's still the middle of the night, that far west. We can try to find the hidden mirror in that room in the meantime, and attempt to invoke its last known link. I have some books on mirrors by an Aian mage, Kerric Vo Mos, that might contain some useful spells."

"You read Kerric Vo Mos, too?" Morg asked, briefly distracted. He shook it off. "Fetch the books—and watch your back out there. We've found the three Mendhites you knew about, but for all we know, there could be more."

"When Dom comes back, I'll want him to study the prisoners for the way they managed to elude our wardings," Saber added.

"Majesty," Consus stated, turning back just as he was about to step through the door. "If you *are* going to resurrect the Convocation . . . I suggest that *now* would be a good time to begin, if you can. The Council will undoubtedly try to delay and stall your claim of interference by one of their officials. Once you have the Gods on your side," the middle-aged man told her, "you *can* call upon Jinga and Kata to hold Their people accountable. *If* you can re-create the Convocation."

"I'll resurrect it because I don't know how many more attacks we'll have to face, as more idiots come along to try to get their hands on the Living Host," Kelly told him. "The only way to stop the attacks is to open the Convocation. As for the Gods . . . I'll put my trust in my Lord Mage, here, to smack the Council upside their heads until they agree to play nice with us. Resurrecting the Gods will take more time than Hope has right now. But thank you for your help in this matter. None of us will forget it," she promised.

Bowing, Consus left the room, dodging to avoid one of the red-headed brothers as he came skidding up to the doorway. Trevan poked his head inside as soon as the other man was clear. "Amara's sniffing through all the rooms, looking for others. I'm about to join her—they might be able to hide themselves from our magics, but I doubt they can hide themselves from our noses. Is everything under control in here?"

"Finneg stole Hope, but otherwise, yes," Wolfer told him. "I'll shift shape and join you as soon as these filth are secured."

"Hurry up," Morg ordered the others, once more feeling the urgent press of time. Hope was missing, and every moment of delay meant unimaginable things might be happening to her. Things which he would have to avenge. "I do have a bride to find, remember?"

*N*oise roused Hope from a strange, muggy dream of being blocked in by leafy green bushes coated in dangling strands of moss. The voice continued as she struggled to open eyelids that felt weighted down by giant green fire trucks. Which was an absurd thought, because fire trucks were a rich red or a bright yellow . . .

"*Special* session means a session that is to be assembled *immediately*. Awaken His Majesty now!—*Yes*, I have that authority! I have an Empire-sized *conflict* that needs to be resolved immediately, therefore the Council needs to be called *immediately*. Now stop being an incompetent fool and do your job!"

Inconsiderate asshat . . . Goddess, why does he have to be so loud? Can't he take the phone into another room? she thought with sleepy irritation, and tried to frown. The attempt allowed her eyelids to unglue themselves. Prying them open, Hope blinked against the light coming from the moon-shaped orb suspended in a wrought iron bracket over her head.

Lightglobe.

Oh, Goddess, I'm home again—but I'm not at home! Eyes widening, she quickly looked around, careful to not move her aching head just yet. She was lying on a couch in an unfamiliar room with walls decorated solely in whitewash and ornately framed paintings. Off to her left, across the room, she spotted the source of the voice. All she could see was the red-clad backside of a man with the dark skin of northern Katan, arguing with whoever was on the other side of the gilded mirror he was using.

"Tell His Majesty that Councilor Finneg has found a viable source of resolving the *conflict* with Nightfall Isle, one that will involve no bloodshed . . . and which will put an end to the impudence of the Corvis family once and for all. *Tonne!*"

The image in the mirror shifted, telling Hope that it now reflected the room she was in. Hastily she shut her eyes and breathed slowly, deeply, doing her best to imitate a state of slumber.

"If *that* doesn't wake up His Laziness, he's not worthy of ruling the Empire!"

She heard footfalls and struggled to keep her muscles lax, her expression still. They approached her, and she felt the padded leather dip slightly, felt the warmth of his body as he seated himself next to her. Felt his breath on her face.

"At least you're not as ugly as that freckled foreigner. And you are a duchess. Taking you won't be onerous, nor a stain on my family's status and pride."

She felt heat passing over her face and forced herself to stay calm, to breathe slowly and steadily; her instincts demanded it.

"Do I awaken you now and inform you of your fate? Or would you fight it, since your presence among them makes you seem friendly with those rebels? Do I coax you to my side, or just wait for His Majesty to declare you a ward of the Empire, on grounds of mental incompetence just for siding with them . . . ?"

Breathe . . . just breathe . . .

"Seduce you, I think," he murmured. "It would save all of us a great deal of legal trouble if you could be convinced into joining our side. And, if necessary, I can enchant you into compliance, or at least silence until the Council sanctions my actions." A pause, and she felt his fingertips feathering along her brow, brushing back her curls. "They have very little vision, selfish concerns for their focus, and only the massive weight of bureaucracy to give them a sense of drive . . . which can be an advantage. A good general knows how to manipulate his own side, as well as his foes'."

Hope felt him move away from her and carefully kept herself breathing calmly. She heard a faint *click* through the soft, faint rush of air passing through her nose, and wondered what was going to happen next.

"We'll need this to confirm your identity . . . Time to awaken from your nightmare, Your Grace. I can only hope you're smart enough to be grateful for your rescue . . ."

A *word* exploded in her ears, soft-spoken, but hitting her with all the impact of chugging a quad shot mocha—an otherworldly, caffeinated mistake she had only made once in her life. Gasping, eyes snapping open, Hope struggled to calm the jump-started racing of her heart. Muscles twitched as she flicked her gaze around the room, once again taking in everything she could see. This time, she allowed herself a slight jump as she spotted the man who had kidnapped her, faking startlement.

"Don't worry . . . You're safe, now," he crooned, holding up one hand. "You have nothing to fear from me."

Bullshit, she thought, but kept her derisiveness buried deep under a confused, wide-eyed expression. Pushing up onto her elbows—her arms felt lethargic and rubbery—she stared at him. He lounged against the edge of the couch arm, down by her feet, muscular arms folded across his chest and a crystal-tipped wand in his hand. "Who . . . what . . . what's going on? Where am I? Who are you?"

"I am Duke Finneg of Luichan, Councilor of Conflict Resolution," he stated smoothly, giving her a slight bow of his head. "At the moment, you are a guest at one of my estates. Please relax, remain calm, and you will not be harmed. I need to ask you a few questions first, before I can answer any further of your own."

Licking her lips, Hope nodded cautiously, doing her best to seem wary—as would be natural in her situation—but otherwise ignorant of the things she had overheard. What she really wanted to do was leap away from him, activate her cryslet, and call for help. There were two problems to that plan, however: one, her cryslet was missing; and two, even if she did have it, she suspected she was well beyond the reception range of the crystal-tipped towers that dotted Nightfall Isle. Instead, she scooted backward until the other arm of the couch supported her ribs and spine, and gestured vaguely for him to either take a seat or continue.

"This is a truth-wand . . . in case it has been a while since you last saw one," he added with a slight smile, holding up the short, slim rod. "Their function hasn't changed much, I'm sure. Please answer my questions truthfully—remember, I *am* a Councilor, and as a representative of your government, it is your duty to cooperate with me."

"How do I know you really are a Councilor?" she shot back, lifting her chin.

A quick smile curved his full, dark lips. "Smart woman. Very well." Activating the wand, he held the glowing tip over the back of his other hand. "My name is Maisie." The glow winked out. A moment later, the crystal gleamed brightly again. "My name is Duke Finneg of Luichan, and I am the Councilor of Conflict Resolution for the Empire of Katan."

He smiled again as the glow stayed steady. Hope gave him a slight nod when he glanced her way. "Fine. You speak the truth. Now, why am I here?"

"I haven't asked my questions yet—mind if I sit next to you?" he asked, twisting his hips and sliding onto the couch by her feet, a little closer than felt comfortable to her. "Just hold out your hand, and speak the truth. There . . . now, are you truly the Duchess Haupanea of Nightfall?"

With that wand hovering over her hand, Hope knew she couldn't lie. But she could stretch the truth. "Before I was cast out of the world by the Shattering of Aiar, yes, I was the Duchess Haupanea of Nightfall. But a couple of centuries have passed since I last ruled the duchy, and others have claimed independence for the Isle. It isn't really a duchy anymore." The bright glow didn't wink out. Hope hid her relief, glancing up at the duke. "Why do you need to know my identity?"

Duke Finneg gave her a reassuring, consoling sort of smile. "The Empire will be relieved to have one of our peers back . . . but we are deeply troubled by the circumstances plaguing your home duchy. It isn't right that these interlopers have invaded your home, overtaken your lands, and claimed your ducal rights, privileges, and properties for their own selfish, wasteful uses—they may *seem* friendly," he added quickly, "and I'm sure they've treated you as well as they thought they should . . . but really, when you get down to it, they *have* stolen your birthright.

"That is very much against the law. Nightfall Isle is yours, not theirs, and it is my solemn duty as a Councilor of the Empire and the head of the Department of Conflict Resolution to redress this grave injustice on your behalf," he promised.

"What . . . um, what do you plan to do about it?" Hope asked him as he deactivated the wand. The last thing she could remember was stepping into the chambers reserved for her dream of a small chocolate factory, intending to select a book to read while walking the Fountain-infused crystal so that it would not become lodged in one place, rendering it useless for evoking the Convocation of the Gods.

Surely enough time has passed that Alys has called someone about my not showing up to relieve her? Morg has to be looking for me . . . actually, he might even be frantic about my absence right about now, since I'm clearly no longer on the island. Whoever this idiot thinks he is, I pity him when Morg catches up to him . . .

"The first step, of course, was to remove you from their immediate influence and control. To give you the space to think clearly and rationally about your situation," Finneg told her. "As soon as we heard that the last, lost Duchess of Nightfall had returned, we immediately contacted their so-called government, but they absolutely refused to let anyone speak with you. They didn't want you to reclaim your rights—I'll bet they didn't even mention the four or five mirror-calls I tried to make over the last few days, did they?"

"No, they didn't . . . but how do I know you're telling the truth?" Hope countered. "How do I know you really have my best interests at heart?"

Reactivating the wand, he held it over his hand. "My deepest, most fervent wish, Your Grace, is to restore Nightfall to its rightful place as a duchy of Katan. And I fully intend to do whatever it takes to achieve this goal."

The crystal stayed bright. Forced to pretend ignorance, Hope nodded reluctantly. "It seems you do have the duchy's interests at heart. But they Rang the Bell. I've seen the blessed crown floating in the heart of the donjon with my own eyes—I've felt the touch of the Gods holding it aloft. That kind of feeling cannot be faked."

"We did not stop their attempted claim this last fall because we thought you were dead, Your Grace," Finneg told her, deactivating the wand again. He set it on the table beyond the arm of the couch and gave her a reassuring, rueful smile. "The fact that you are clearly alive, and have just as clearly been returned to us—before these interlopers have achieved a manifestation of Patronage—is an indication from the Gods Themselves that you are *meant* to resume your rightful place as Duchess of Nightfall.

"Surely even you can see the hand of the Gods in the timing of all of this?" he asked her.

With the Councilor waiting expectantly for a reply, Hope was forced to respond. Thinking quickly, she said, "There, um, does seem to be *some* truth in that line of thought. But they *did* Ring the Bell, and did so in the name of all the Gods. Surely Fate wouldn't have allowed it, if I was meant to resume my former place as duchess?"

"Fate works in mysterious ways . . . and Fate doesn't always take the most obvious of paths. But such speculation is a moot point; you have been returned to us and your presence revealed to me before the independence of these upstarts can be finalized. This means it is the responsibility of the Empire, and my office in particular, to ensure that you are restored to your rightful life." Finneg shrugged apologetically. "I'm afraid we cannot send you back in time, nor restore all of the friends and family you have lost, but we can restore all of your legal rights, responsibilities, and properties.

"Now, I've called for a special session of the Council to convene within the hour, to discuss the matter," he told her. "All you have to do is state unto His Majesty—that would be King Taurin, in case those interlopers didn't bother to tell you—and unto his Councilors under truth-spell that you are the Duchess Haupanea of Nightfall, and that you wish to reclaim all that was torn from you, those many years ago. That is all we'd need to be able to take the appropriate steps to legally reclaim your inheritance for you."

His expectant, encouraging look told her she couldn't stall an agreement for very long. Clasping her hands in her lap, Hope composed a way to find out what would happen if she *didn't* agree to his scheme . . . which would be a very logical and quite possibly successful scheme, if it weren't for a certain fatal flaw in his plan.

"Well, that's very, um, considerate of you to go to all this trouble on my behalf. But I'm still not certain it's the right thing to do," Hope told him. "I mean, it has been two centuries by this world's measure, and five years by my own. I know you have gone to a lot of trouble, and I'm very flattered and grateful that the government of Katan still cares about me, though all who actually knew me are long gone . . . but, um . . . Well, what if I chose to not pursue the reclaiming of my duchy?" she asked, looking at him to gauge his reaction. His friendly smile stiffened. "I mean, would that get you into trouble with the Council?"

His face relaxed a little bit, but there was a gleam in his dark brown eyes she didn't quite trust. "It's not quite that simple, Your Grace. When you went missing and were presumed dead, when the island's water supply ran nearly dry, there were no living relatives close enough to attempt the restoration of Nightfall to a functional level, let alone its prime. The duchy was presumed lost, the people evacuated, and the responsibility of what was left of the island fell to the Empire to manage. Without an adequate water supply, we never resettled it even in part, so it became a sort of dumping-ground for troublemakers. Such as the insurrectionists currently laying claim to the land, former scions of County Corvis, far to the south and west.

"But with you alive and well, there *is* a bloodline able to lay claim to the island. With the Desalinator restored to functionality, there will be an adequate supply of freshwater to continue to support a population, plus the income of all the salt blocks and so forth extracted by the desalination system. This means the island must be managed by competent leadership. The Council does not believe the Corvis brothers, or that . . . woman . . . are suitable leaders." His lips twitched into a sneer as he mentioned Kelly, then smoothed into an apologetic smile. "In preceding years, we had not the resources to spare to make the duchy prosper. Now we do have those resources . . . and the Empire *will* reclaim Nightfall."

Hope suppressed a shiver at the determination in his tone. She focused on staying attentive, as if she were honestly considering his words. Not that she was convinced, but his logic was convincing. She just didn't trust the red-clad Councilor seated beside her.

"I can understand that, after five years of not having to shoulder the burdens of leadership, you might be reluctant to resume your place as an active manager of your duchy," he continued, scooting closer to her in a visible attempt to be more persuasive. "You were young and alone the first time around. To suddenly have all of that responsibility thrust back into your lap would indeed be burdensome. But you don't *have* to be alone. Nor do you have to face these interlopers on your own, in case you fear their reactions—or worse, their reprisals."

Here it comes, what was hinted at when I overheard him speaking to himself. Blinking at him, Hope asked with innocent puzzlement, "How do you mean?"

"It's quite simple. All you'd need is a partner, a helpmate. Someone who could take up the burdens of rulership for you," he coaxed her, leaning just a little closer. Hope tried not to shrink away as he continued. "Someone experienced, someone accustomed to the demands of governing a duchy—but of course, it would either have to be a blood relative," he added swiftly, "of which we've established there are none, or it would have to be . . . a husband."

She felt her face burn with a rush of blood, then grow icy and pale. *Oh, Goddess . . . it is as bad as I feared.* "I, ah . . . right. So you're suggesting that if I don't feel, um, adequate to take up the reins of the duchy all over again, I should pass them to a . . . husband."

"Not just any husband," he reassured her. "Someone accustomed to taking charge, someone who cares about the Empire and its citizens. Someone who can firmly pull Nightfall back into the fold. That . . . woman . . . is not one of us," Finneg asserted quietly but firmly, shifting even closer to Hope. "She wasn't born to this world, nor was she born to the responsibilities and privileges that come with a position of leadership. She doesn't even have any magic! To allow her to rule over even a tiny piece of the Empire is a perversion in the eyes of God and Man."

"A perversion . . ." Hope repeated, struggling to hide her dismay behind a blank expression.

"She is unnatural, and unworthy. Above all, she has *no right* to claim your inheritance. If you do not want to re-shoulder the burdens, then let *me* do it," Finneg coaxed, leaning closer.

"You?" she asked, glancing at him.

"Why not? I have experience with my own duchy, I am comfortable wielding authority . . . and I love every *inch* of Katan as if it were my own duchy," he breathed, dropping his gaze first to her mouth, then lower, roaming it over her shoulders, her breasts, and the hands knotting themselves together in her lap. He covered her restless fingers with his own. "Even your inches of it . . ."

Hope stiffened, disliking how much he was crowding her. He stiffened as well, pulling back slightly. Frowning, Finneg shifted his grip, turning her palm up. The move displayed the straight line cutting across the padded flesh of her palm. His frown deepened, and he rubbed his thumb along the bluish white mark.

"Magic . . . There's magic in this scar. Blood magic."

Damn. Ah, well . . . it was too good to last long, Hope silently sighed. Lifting her chin, she said aloud, "There's a little flaw in your plan. It isn't the incipient independence of the island's new inhabitants that is stopping me from resuming my place as the Duchess of Nightfall."

He lifted his gaze from her hands to her face, brown eyes meeting brown in wary suspicion.

"Katani law states very clearly that noble succession falls upon the eldest blood child in a particular family line . . . and I took Kelly as my blood-bound *elder* sister just a few days ago. By law, by magic, by blood, and by the clearly marked will of the Gods Themselves," Hope stated bravely, "my *best friend* is now the rightful Duchess of Nightfall. It is *her* lawful right to reclaim the duchy. *Or* to turn it into an independent kingdom."

The fingers that cradled her scarred palm tightened, bruising her flesh. Hope winced. Duke Finneg tightened his grip, then pressed her hand flat against her thigh. A muscle twitched in his jaw. "*That* can also be worked around. Once she is dead, the line of inheritance falls back upon you—and in case you prove *unwilling* to resume the duchy, your firstborn child can be made the new duke or duchess!" His hand shifted from her fingers to her stomach, pressing in on her belly, while his other arm came around her shoulders, keeping her from squirming away. "All it takes is declaring you mentally incompetent, a marriage to ensure the inheritance is legal, and the planting of a seed in your belly."

Revulsion churned her stomach. Hope wanted to hit him, to shout that she'd *never* let him touch her in that way, but instinct prickled along the nape of her neck. Instinct, and two words. *Firstborn child* . . . They whispered along her nerves, soothing her inner agitation. Lifting her chin again, Hope met his manic gaze calmly.

"Then I'm afraid you'd be thwarted again. *My* first child has already been born."

He narrowed his eyes sharply. "You lie!"

"Bring back your wand," she countered. "I'll *show* you I speak the truth."

Staring at her for a long moment, he finally shifted to snatch the wand off the table. Catching her wrist, he activated the wand, holding its glowing tip over the back of her hand. "Repeat yourself!"

"I made Kelly Doyle my blood-bound *elder sister*, conferring upon her all the rights and so forth of the eldest born of the Duchy of Nightfall," Hope repeated, speaking slowly and clearly so that there would be no doubt of what the wand was reacting to. Under its steady glow, she added, "I have also given life to not one, but *three* children in the other universe, two sons and a daughter. Those children are *beyond* your power to capture and control, because the *only* person who knows the exact location of that universe is Morganen of Nightfall . . . who *will* be looking for me.

"Your best bet for surviving that encounter is to let me go, here and now," Hope warned him. "By Katani Law, there is nothing you can do to me that will give you control of the Duchy of Nightfall. You won't be able to get your hands on my firstborn child without Morganen's cooperation, and he will not cooperate with you.

"You also cannot kill Kelly *or* me, because we're *both* citizens of the incipient kingdom of Nightfall. I didn't just make her the new duchess by making her *my* sister. I made myself *her* sister. As her younger sister, I'm the next in line for the succession of the Nightfall throne . . . and by law, you are *forbidden* to interfere with the government of the new kingdom, *including* its successors. Unless and until my *elder* sister changes the laws of Nightfall governing inheritances, the default is the eldest blood offspring. Which would be her and then me and then my firstborn child . . . in another world."

His dusky brown cheeks darkened further. The hand clenching the truth-wand trembled, then he shoved off the couch with a shout of wordless rage. He almost flung the still-glowing rod across the room, then checked the movement. Spinning, he jabbed his free hand at her. "You haven't won! *None* of you will win!"

"There is nothing you can do to me," Hope repeated calmly. "Nothing, but to return me to Nightfall . . . and accept its Destiny."

"*Never!*" Slashing his hand at her, he zapped her again with a bolt of palest green.

The banging on his outer door only stopped after Morg flung open the panel, sleeveless undertunic dangling off of one arm and the laces of his trousers half-tied. "*What?*"

Lord Consus eyed his half-dressed state, addressing the reason for his interruption. "I went back to my quarters, was in the middle of scrying a good location for you to Gate through, and caught a conversation between the Council Secretary and some servant on one of the duke's estates, via the Baro . . . via the special mirror I have. It seems His Grace has called a special Council session, but hasn't shown up yet. If you hurry, you can catch them while they're all still gathered."

Morg finished shrugging into the light blue silk shirt. "I have to get some Gating powder from my workroom . . . and I think it would be prudent to pick up some empty power crystals along the way. Just in case I do have to 'kick their butts,' as Kelly put it."

That arched the ex-Councilor's brow. "*Empty* power crystals?

Would you not wish to augment your magic with fully empowered ones?"

Smirking, Morg pulled his hair free of his collar and tucked his tunic into his dark blue trousers. "Let's just say I know a few more tricks than the average mage." Tugging on the laces, he fastened them more securely. "I'll need another moment to add a few odds and ends. Armbands and such, some decorative, some protective— would the Council take offense if I wore a sword?"

"Definitely. It's the Council of Mages. Magic is the *only* yardstick by which a person's status is measured . . . and perhaps any political secrets you might hold."

"Of which, I have none," Morg agreed dryly. He left the door open, heading back to the inner chambers of his suite. Behind him, he heard Consus hesitate, then follow.

"I do have one request," the former Councilor of Sea Commerce stated as Morg opened the jewelry casket on top of one of his dressers, sorting through it for more than just his cryslet to wear.

"And that would be . . . ?"

"Queen Samille is likely to be there. She is *not* a mage . . . but she is very levelheaded and compassionate. If you must 'kick butt,' do not harm her," Consus told him.

"I have never once been inclined to harm innocents," Morg returned, slanting the older man a chiding look. A thought crossed his mind, quirking one light brown eyebrow. "Do you have a *special* fondness for Her Majesty?"

"More like a special fondness for avoiding political wrist-slitting," Consus retorted. "Marrying Her Majesty was the smartest thing King Taurin ever did. The lack of magic makes her as close to a commoner as one born into a landed, ennobled bloodline can get. She is loved by our people, and they *will* take offense against Nightfall if she is harmed by one of you."

"Good point. If it becomes necessary to impose my demands on the Council, I will take extra pains to make sure she remains unscathed by any conflict." Morganen tossed back two rings and selected a multiple-jointed armband instead, one inscribed with protective runes. Grabbing a belt and pouch from the rack hung just inside the dressing room door, he asked, "Any other bystanders I should be aware of?"

"Not unless some of the pages are in the Council Chamber. They might be on hand to serve an early breakfast to the Councilors, or they might not be." Consus shrugged.

"Fair enough." Grabbing a second, empty pouch from the shelf below the rack, he threaded that onto the strip of black leather. It was large enough to hold a jar of Gating powder. A third one followed it, meant for the power crystals he might need.

Might . . . more like will need, he thought, shooing the older mage ahead of him, out of his quarters. *Somehow, I doubt the Council will give up Hope's kidnapper willingly. I'd better be ready for a fight . . .*

I'll need lots of chalk. If they truly fling everything they've got at me, I might end up with more power than the crystals can handle . . . and I really shouldn't use it for my own benefit . . . damn, where's that book on transmutations? Should be on the . . . second left set of shelves in my workroom, somewhere near the top . . . assuming I'll have enough time for a quick refresher on what to mark. Eyeing the older man as they strode up the corridor, toward the end of the wing, Morg gave him an assessing look.

"I'm not stupid enough to ask you to follow me to the mainland. I'm also not stupid enough to trust my own powers alone when facing down the Council of Mages," he stated candidly. "If you will not follow me in person, will you at least be willing to follow me by mirror?"

"And stand ready to intervene if things go southward?" Consus asked, not looking all that surprised by the request. "Your family is foolish, sending you to negotiate with the Council without backup."

"That's because my family has an actual inkling of the power I wield. But even I can be hexed unconscious by a lucky shot. Will you watch my back?" Morg asked him.

"Such a request implies a certain trust in me," Consus murmured. He said nothing more as they climbed the spiraling steps at
the end of the corridor, brow pinched in a thoughtful frown.

Morg let him consider the request in silence. Only when they
had emerged in the gray light of early morning, crossing the drawbridge connecting the east-northeast wing to the outer compound
wall, did the older mage nod to himself, then speak again.

"You have dealt fairly and faithfully with me. I'll do it, on one
condition," Consus told him.

"And that is . . . ?" Morg asked him, both wary at the hidden
cost and simultaneously amused that there was one.

"Access to any Kerric Vo Mos writings that I haven't already
acquired, *or* five new tomes of my choice. To read, not to own," he
clarified. "And by 'or' I mean if you only have three Vo Mos tomes
I haven't read, I get to choose two more to peruse from your personal collection."

"You'll have to provide me with a list of books that you already
have and narrow down your choice of other possible tomes by subject and author, as I have a *very* large personal library . . . but you
have a deal," Morganen agreed, holding out his hand.

Clasping it, Consus gave it a shake, sealing their agreement.
"Let us hope I get the better end of this bargain. I won't take on the
Council for you, but I *will* Gate you out of there if things go south-
ward."

"Hopefully, that's all the backup I'll need," Morganen promised.

"Thank you for being ready so quickly," Kelly told the blonde
priestess as Rydan closed the mirror-Gate. Rather than risk traveling all over the place, it had been suggested that Rydan use one of
the mirrors down in the Underhalls to fetch Kelly to safety, and she
in turn had requested one other woman's presence in the amphitheater chamber buried beneath the northern mountain range.

"This is why I'm here, Your Majesty," Ora agreed, shaking out the long, black robe that was her odd priestly vestments. "Niel has gone into the Dark to warn the others. It will take at least an hour to spread the word from Guide to Guide and prepare everyone for transfer—he will tell his assigned contacts, and they will spread out to tell theirs. Once that hour is up, you will need to be ready for an influx of holy representatives."

"Beg pardon?" Kelly asked her. "Holy representatives?"

"In the Scroll of Living Glory, the text says something along the lines of, 'And there shall be a place of contemplation and a voice of expression for each facet of the Divine made manifest in the holiest of halls.' It says it in more than one way, too," Ora added. "I know from my previous visit to these Underhalls that you have the 'places of contemplation,' the carven images of other lands and the symbols of each Patron Deity. That was my main concern regarding the physical location of the Convocation, a concern which has been successfully alleviated, thanks to this place."

She gestured at the intricately carved walls of the amphitheater, and by extension, the rest of the underground complex. Some of those walls had been carved by previous generations; others had been augmented by Rydan himself. Kelly's sixthborn brother-in-law was busy moving the mirror off to one side, storing it where it would be reasonably safe, yet accessible if they needed to Gate something or someone else into the Underhalls. *An apt name for a creation guided by the Goddess that Hope worshipped*, Kelly recalled, looking around at the pale gray-speckled walls. *Considering we're under a mountain range.*

"As for the 'voice of expression' part, I interpreted that to mean that each God and Goddess should have a priest or priestess from Their people's holy orders present at the Convocation," the Darkhanan priestess told her, recalling Kelly's full attention.

"But, gathering up all the necessary clergy would take too long," Rora protested, glancing between the redhead and the blonde. "If we're to protect the Fountain, we need to invoke the Convocation *now*. We don't have months to transport everyone here. We have hours at best, or maybe a day or two."

Ora gave both women a wry look, her green eyes glinting with ironic amusement. "It just so happens that my fellow Witches were sent out not only to gather all the Names being worshipped, but to select true and faithful servants for transport. It is not often discussed with outsiders, as it would be a great and pestering inconvenience for others to know . . . but the dead are not the only ones my fellow Witches can escort through the Dark—you need only ask the Menomonites we arrived with how puzzling it was that I have not a single bag of luggage, yet have been able to access a wide variety of possessions wherever I go, for proof of this ability."

"You can *transport* people through the Dark, the place ghosts cross when they're on their way to the Afterlife?" Kelly repeated. "Living people? Physically move them, like you were some sort of mirror-Gate?"

"More like a Portal . . . and far less pleasant than a Portal," Ora warned her. "The journey is not without its drawbacks. Darkhanans are raised not to fear the Dark, but even for us, to physically move through the Dark is an unpleasant sensation. It is cold and breathless, and not something to be attempted lightly. Nor is it something to be attempted alone by the untrained. If the Portals were still active, if the aether were smooth enough to make such vast, world-spanning connections, it would be worth the immense amount of magic it takes to create a direct, physical doorway for the crossing. But the aether is too perturbed, the Portals cannot be crafted, and mirror-Gates are too short-range."

"But, the Fountains . . . No," Rora sighed, correcting herself, "the Fountains are as bad as mirror-Gates. They're too few in number, they're scattered too randomly around the world, and they're too heavily guarded to be used for casual transport. And it would still take days and weeks and quite possibly months for people to get to them, even if their Guardians willingly revealed their locations and lowered their wardings."

"We can bring the holy voices here, and do so in a matter of hours," Ora agreed. "But sending them home again . . . they may not be willing to make a second living journey through the Dark. And they may expect your help in garnering passage back to their homelands, in exchange for coming here to complete the Convocation.

"These are *good* men and women, selfless and true to their vocations," she told Kelly. "Many are not from the upper ranks of their hierarchies, and most do not have the budget for long-distance travel. My fellow Witches were instructed to select true servants of the local Gods, and specifically to avoid those who were motivated by a thirst for power. You wouldn't want anyone at the invocation ceremony who would attempt to wrest control of the Convocation from your hands, after all."

"I see you've given this a lot of thought," Kelly observed.

"*Years'* worth," Ora agreed dryly. She stiffened slightly, cocking her head as if listening to something, then nodded. "The first of the Guides has been alerted. Niel will contact the rest of his assigned half dozen in a moment. In turn, each of them will go on and alert six more, as will those Witches, and so on. If everything goes well, be ready to receive the first representative within the hour."

"One man can teach ten men how to fight, and each of those men can teach ten more; those hundred can teach another ten, and those thousand ten more, until in just six rounds of instruction, an army of a million can be readied for war," Kelly murmured half to herself. She smiled at the curiosity from the other two women. "It's an old saying from the other world. Hopefully we won't have a million people coming to the island, though. Thanks to Morg's massive trade of our wheat for Hope's cacao trees, we're a little short on emergency food supplies."

"No, there are only three rounds of contacts to be made. There are three hundred sixteen Gods and Goddesses, and two hundred forty-eight priests and priestesses in need of summoning," Ora said. "That was what I meant a couple of weeks ago by at least two days' warning, to get them ready to travel. Since you told me you'd work on the Convocation following the Desalinator, I figured it would be good to have my fellow Witches instruct their targets to have traveling bags packed and readied. You need only supply them with food and lodging during their stay, and assist them in finding their way home again, should they prefer a more conventional means of travel."

Kelly grimaced. "It figures; with every major religious and political power, there's a major price tag attached. Ah, well. A couple of rainbow pearls taxed off of my sister-in-law should be enough to buy sufficient passage home for these clergy. But as for housing and especially feeding them . . . we have the beds, but the food's going to strain our resources the most. At least the Desalinator's almost up to full speed, so we'll have plenty of water for them to drink by the end of the day.

"Are there any *other* surprises buried in that less-than-crystal-clear Scroll of Living Glory I should know about?" Kelly asked the blonde priestess. "Facts, wild guesses, semisolid postulations?"

Ora ticked off the list with her fingers. "A place dedicated solely to the hosting of the Convocation, decorations representing the various lands and Patron Deities, holy representatives of the worshippers of those Patron Deities, a mobile Fountain, a stationary Fountain . . . food to feed a few hundred guests, places for them to rest . . . You might want a few pitchers of water or maybe some fruit juice on hand to keep your throat wet while you're reciting all those Names and associated titles, plus the list of priests' names and selected petitions or boon requests they might be bringing," she offered, "but other than that . . . I think we have everything covered."

"Petitions and boon requests," Kelly repeated flatly, brow creasing in a frown. She rubbed her forehead, sighing roughly. "This is beginning to sound like I'm the organizer of a *convention*. What next, panelists demanding small, chair-filled rooms for holding lectures and roundtable discussions?" Ora, Rora, and Rydan eyed her askance. Kelly sighed again. "I wish Hope was here. *She'd* have gotten the joke, poor though it was."

"Morg will fetch her back," Rydan stated, his voice quiet but as sure as the granite of the mountains enveloping them. "If you will excuse me, Hope showed me the location of the grand entrance the other night, while she was 'walking the dog.' If we are going to resurrect the Convocation, that entrance needs to be exposed to the world. I'll have to take down the veil of stone between the doors and the outer hillside and double-check the last of the protective runes and wardings."

"Go, then. And thank you, Rydan," Kelly told him. "You, above all of your brothers, have done the most to make this possible, carving this place. If . . . *when* we pull this off," she corrected herself, "it'll be thanks to you, most of all."

Nodding curtly, he turned to his wife, cupped her face in his hands, and kissed her soundly. Kelly and Ora watched, amused, as Rora blushed and returned the embrace. They parted after a moment, and Rydan shot his sister-in-law a pointed look. "Rora has the magic, but you have the cunning. Keep her safe for me. And yourself as well."

Kelly patted the two pouches slung at her waist. "I still have the mirror, and I got smart and picked up the courtiers-in-a-marble before coming down here, the ones Saber modified for voice-activation and combat, as well as conversation. Anyone tries attacking us again, they'll get an unpleasant surprise, trust me."

"Good." Striding away, Rydan left the amphitheater hall.

Ora snorted. "He completely ignored my presence, and all the powers I wield. What am I, a slice of cheese? A mere topping, to be added or dispensed with on a whim?"

"You may be powerful, but you're not a part of the family. That's what makes us reliable as well as strong, to his way of thinking," Rora told her, amusement curving her lips. "No offense is meant. You're just not family."

"None taken. I suggest we start getting everything ready for the impending arrivals. You're not the only one who might get thirsty during the opening ceremony. It'll kill time while we wait, if nothing else," Ora offered.

Nodding, Rora led the way out of the hall, being the most familiar with the twists and turns of the sprawling, subterranean complex.

NINE

❦

A *left turn . . . smile at the nice courtier,* Morganen instructed himself, giving the woman in the embroidered linen gown a polite half bow as well, *and hope she's an early riser, not one of the Council already leaving the chamber . . . Ah, there's the T-junction up ahead. Right or left doesn't matter, because those are the nearest doors into the Council Chamber. Replete with guards. I guess the Council is still in session.*

Good. To the right is the Hall of Mirrors, to the left is the way to the Gardens of Discussion, with several paths back to the various bureaucratic offices. He silently recited Consus' advice, steadying his nerves. It didn't help that the aether of this place was rich in natural magic, shed from the constant proximity and high density of so many mages. The prickling of all that energy kept trying to raise the fine hairs along his nape and forearms. *Right. Time to pull a Rydan and open those doors. Act like you have every right to be here . . .*

The teal-clad guards eyed his approach with mild curiosity, until the heavy, ornately carved doors they guarded *clicked* and started swinging open. They gave the doors a startled look, then glanced back at him. Morg gave both teal-clad men a nod, as if confirming the Council had indeed opened the doors in expectation of his arrival. Their uncertainty gave him just enough time to stride between them, slip through the opening, and shut the doors faster than he had opened them.

The *clack* of the latch catching hold wasn't quite loud enough to disrupt the noise of half a dozen Councilors standing at half a dozen mirrors on the lowest level of the rectangular, terraced chamber, each one apparently speaking with some member of Duke Finneg's staff, either personal or bureaucratic. Above that central floor, ranks of carved wooden chairs and small desk-like tables were spaced around the long, broad, vaulted room.

Roughly two-thirds of those seats were filled. Half of the Council present looked rather put out that they were in here at all at this ungodly early hour, while the other half appeared to be more asleep than awake. Morg couldn't blame either half, since he, too, would rather have still been in his bed. Preferably with Hope cuddled at his side. Instead, he had to rescue her somehow.

"*You!* What are *you* doing in here?"

The irritated demand came from King Taurin. Morganen recognized the man from his visit to the island over half a year ago, though his dark hair had been scraped back into a braid and his chin covered with a short, neatly trimmed goatee, altering his appearance. At their sovereign's shout, the other occupants of the room either quieted, straightened up, or turned their unhappy-at-the-hour frowns on Morganen.

"Good morning, Your Majesties, Councilors," Morganen stated politely, descending the shallow tiers of the rectangular hall. He greeted the King of Katan with a polite bow, adding a second one to the woman at his side, Queen Samille, then nodded to either side to include the Councilors. "How I came here is irrelevant, because I am here for the same reason as you: Duke Finneg, the so-called Councilor of Conflict Resolution. I'm afraid he has broken Katani Law . . . and the Laws of God and Man."

Taurin narrowed his brown eyes. "What do you mean, he has broken the law? And who do you think you are, striding in here as if you have the right to be in here, let alone make such accusations?"

Morg gave him a slight smile. "I *think* I am Her Majesty's ambassador, directed by her to find Duke Finneg and extract the whereabouts and safe retrieval of Her Majesty's sister . . . whom the Duke kidnapped less than an hour ago. If you doubt my words, I have a Truth Stone on me and stand ready to use it. I saw with my own eyes in a past-scrying how Councilor Finneg attacked and incapacitated Hope of Nightfall, and how he Gated her off the island. Kidnapping is very much against the laws of both Nightfall and Katan . . . and as a government official, his rash actions have created a very serious dilemma for your government.

"If Hope is returned swiftly, safely, and utterly unharmed, and if Duke Finneg is stripped of his titles, office, and privileges and remanded into Nightfall custody for sentencing and punishment, Queen Kelly will be willing to overlook any repercussions that may otherwise fall on the Empire due to his rash acts," Morganen told King Taurin and his Councilors. "If Hope has been harmed, Her Majesty will be less than lenient with His Grace.

"If the Council refuses to assist in her recovery and his arrest and remanding for Nightfall justice . . . she *will* hold the Empire responsible for the rash actions of one of your Councilors. He *is* a high-ranking official of your government, and everything he does, good or bad, reflects upon all of you."

"I heard a rumor that this 'Hope of Nightfall' is one and the same as the 'lost Duchess of Nightfall,'" one of the Councilors said. "The one who was a Seer. Is this true?"

"The one and the same, Haupanea of Nightfall," Morg confirmed, glancing at the northern Katani male. A quick check of the room showed that all of the bodies gathered, roughly a hundred if not more, looked to be fully adult. *No pages, then. Good. The only non-mage in the room is King Taurin's wife. That'll make this easier, should they try to make things harder for me.*

"Prove it," a woman off to the other side challenged him. Opening the first of his pouches, Morg pulled out the white marble disc he kept in there.

"I am a mekhadadak," he stated flatly, gripping the stone. Pausing to display both sides of the blackened imprint of his palm, Morg waited a couple of heartbeats for the lie-detecting darkness to fade, then gripped the Truth Stone again. "Hope of Nightfall, who was unlawfully kidnapped by Councilor Finneg this morning, was once the former, lost Duchess Haupanea of Nightfall, blessed Seer of the Gods."

He flipped the disc with his fingers, displaying its pristine, unblemished surface.

King Taurin smirked. "So *that's* why he called this session . . . and why he kidnapped her. To reinstate her as Duchess of Nightfall, the *rightful* ruler of the island."

"That would be a little difficult, Your Majesty. Hope *was* the last duchess . . . but she isn't, any longer," Morg told him. At Taurin's frown, he explained, "As I said, Duke Finneg has kidnapped Her Majesty's *sister.* In specific, her blood-bound *younger* sister. Hope ceded all rights of inheritance to Kelly when she made Kelly her *elder* blood-bound sibling.

"It is Kelly who is now the rightful Duchess of Nightfall, should she seek to resurrect that particular title. But that poses a problem. You are bound *not* to interfere in the governance of the incipient kingdom of Nightfall," Morg reminded him, shifting his gaze to include the Councilors silently watching their confrontation. "Hope, being Kelly's closest kin, is next in line to the throne . . . and given how a member of your own government has—"

An exclamation from one of the other Councilors cut him off. "Your Grace! There you are! We've been trying to—"

"Kai, lusai!"

Morganen's frame jerked mid-turn, snapping straight and tall, stiffly postured at Attention. King Taurin smiled grimly as he stood. Beside him, his wife blinked her blue eyes, looking as startled by the abrupt attack as Morg felt.

"Surely you didn't think we didn't learn from our last encounter, did you?" he asked rhetorically, shifting around the edge of the table. "We studied what went wrong with that mess. Researched certain spells. That one *is* rather handy, isn't it?"

Stepping around Morganen, he approached the mirror. Teeth clenched, Morg struggled to break the spell, ears straining to hear what was going on behind him. It was an insidious piece of magic, for a quick probing proved it wasn't a physical attack. That left a mental attack, using his nerves against him, not his muscles.

"Duke Finneg, you have some explaining to do regarding your recent actions," Morg heard the Katani sovereign say. The mirror was placed beyond his current field of view, but he could still hear.

"I apologize for calling the Council session together a bit prematurely, Your Majesty, but my original plan had to change a little bit," the duke returned smoothly. "Speaking of which, I'm tendering my resignation as Councilor of Conflict Resolution. If anyone from Nightfall asks, tell them it was effective as of yesterday morning, which will give the government legal protection from my actions . . . but I do request that you hold off on processing the paperwork and making it official until after I've completed my current task. You can reinstate me after it's all over."

"Current task?" Taurin inquired.

Morganen fought to trace the root of the spell. Muscles, his nerves could prod into flexing free. But an attack on the nerves themselves was insidious. *It has to be an aural command—start with the ears and work your way inward. Trace the path of the spell . . . and* ward *yourself against it being used a second time. Whatever this is, it's a spell easy enough for even Alys to use! Find it!*

"I'd tell you, but then you'd lose plausible deniability, Majesty.

Suffice to say that, as soon as I've completed the second phase of my revised plan and disposed of the evidence, you need only challenge those Corvis fools for leadership of the Isle, and then dispense with this nonsense of independence once and for all."

There! Feeling the magic curdling his nerves, Morganen tore it from his inner self. It resisted. Taurin was the most powerful mage in the Empire . . . but Morg was stronger. Whirling as soon as his muscles were free of the command to *stop, stay*, Morg quickly spotted the mirror. Striding toward the framed view of the dark-skinned mage, he reached for the pouch with his jar of Gating powder. "Where is she, Finneg? *Where—*"

Taurin punched his fist at the mirror's edge, breaking the carved wooden frame. The mirror cracked, glowed, and shattered, making everyone within two body lengths flinch back from the flying shards. Morg stopped, wide-eyed with disbelief.

"You . . ."

"Destroyed it?" Taurin finished for him, his tone mocking. Dusting off his clothes with a cleansing spell, he planted his fists on his hips. "Duke Finneg is *our* citizen. *We* will decide what to do, regarding his actions."

Morg shifted his gaze from the ragged remnants of the frame to the arrogant, dark-haired king. "You will *find* him again, you will contact him by mirror, and you will deal with him for his crimes. You will do these things *now*, and you will ensure Princess Hope's *immediate* safe return."

"No."

Again, Morg stiffened, this time with rage.

"This is *not* your so-called little kingdom," King Taurin told him. "You have no jurisdiction here, and you have no authority to make such demands."

Fingers still clenching the Truth Stone, Morg lifted it. "I speak the truth! Duke Finneg *kidnapped* Hope of Nightfall—he has all but admitted his illegalities himself!"

"Oh, we *will* get around to investigating your claims. In about a week or so. We're very busy right now," Taurin added, his tone condescending.

Morg closed his eyes. Just for a moment, but it was necessary to wrest control of his vision away from the reddish black haze of rage threatening to obscure his sight. *I knew it wouldn't be that easy.* Two deep breaths gave him sufficient control to open his eyes. Seeing Taurin's smirk didn't help his temper. Turning around, Morg crossed back to the king's council table, heading for the woman still seated in the other ornately carved chair.

"Your Majesty," he greeted her, bowing his head. His hand tucked the Truth Stone back into its pouch, then opened the one next to it. "Lord Consus has spoken of how highly regarded you are by the citizens of the Empire. He says the smartest thing King Taurin ever did was to marry you."

"Are you *threatening* my wife?" Taurin demanded behind his back. "Is that a threat?"

"No. I have no cause to harm Her Majesty, whatsoever. She is innocent of any wrongdoing, as far as I know." Pulling out the egg-shaped, fist-sized power crystal, wrapped in fine, twisted wires of silver and gold, Morg gently picked up the blonde woman's hand and deposited the wire-caged stone in it. "Hold on to this tightly, Your Majesty," he told her quietly. "It should protect you from anything that might happen in the next few minutes."

Her blue eyes widened in alarm. Morg didn't give her a chance to recover her composure enough to actually question him. Turning back to her husband, he met Taurin's gaze. Internally, he stretched out his mage-senses, hooking feelers into the aether around him to draw in the power he would need. Externally, he kept himself calm.

"I'll give you a second chance, Your Majesty. *My* sovereign has instructed me to deal diplomatically with you, provided you assist in the recovery of her sister in a *timely* manner. If you fail to do so, I have been authorized to take any and all appropriate measures to convince you that cooperation *is* the better choice," Morg warned the older man. "Choose wisely, but choose *quickly*."

"We'll get to it. In. A. Week," King Taurin repeated, enunciating each word crisply. He smirked at Morganen's scowl, spreading his hands to indicate the men and women in the room. "Do you think you could get me to change my mind? There are over one hundred of us here in this hall! *The* most powerful mages in the Empire gathered into one room . . . at least, the ones who could be bothered to get out of bed this early," he added dryly. "What do *you* think you can do?"

Morganen turned slowly, taking in the faces of the men and women around him. Some were old, some were young, but most were middle-aged. At the height of their powers. A blink allowed him to shift to mage-sight. Every last one of them was warded as trained mages usually were, but the wards he could see were the standard sort, the kind taught by Katani tutors and mage academies. *Nothing to surprise me, then . . . though there's definitely a few more than the seven I've grown used to sparring with, of late.*

Willpower was inextricably tied to belief, however. Morganen did not allow himself a single heartbeat of doubt. A shift in focus switched the intake feelers into tendrils of control. They twined through the aether, wrapping around each bubble-ward. Morg completed his slow circular scan of the Council and faced King Taurin again.

"What can I do? I have asked you, nicely and politely, for your aid in this matter. Nightfall's complaint against the actions of Councilor Finneg is both just and righteous. You cannot call upon Jinga and Kata to aid you in thwarting me, because you are bound by the Laws of God and Man against interfering with Nightfall's bid for independence. And it could be argued that your refusal to help recover a kidnapping victim in a swift and timely manner—when it is quite possible that Duke Finneg intends to *kill* her, because you *don't* know what he has planned for her—is acting against Nightfall's bid for independence, as she *is* Queen Kelly's default heir."

"Perhaps, but you cannot call upon any God or Goddess to aid *you*. Unless you've succeeded in manifesting a Patron Deity?" Taurin asked, visibly skeptical. "Oh, right . . . You're trying to re-create the old Convocation of the Gods. Had any luck with that?"

Taurin's smirk said he didn't think so. Morg stared levelly at him. *A few more seconds to set the tendrils of my control* . . . "I have asked you nicely to assist me. You have been cruel in your replies. I have asked you diplomatically to redress an injustice. You have mocked the spirit of the law, *and* its letter. All I have left is politeness. So I will ask you one more time to aid me. *On bended knee.*"

Power *slammed* through the room. Chairs toppled, and tables skittered, papers fluttering to the tiered levels of the floor. Whether they had been standing or sitting did not matter; every single woman and man, save only for Morganen and Queen Samille, landed painfully on their right or left knee. The King of Katan wasn't the only one to grunt at the impact, but he was the first to struggle back to his feet. Until Morganen ruthlessly jerked him back down again with blunt force of will.

"I am still asking you *politely*. Will you assist me in capturing your renegade Councilor, Duke Finneg, and finding our lost princess, Hope of Nightfall? Or must I ask you *not* so politely?" Morganen inquired, looking pointedly at the kneeling, grimacing king.

"*Baluleth kaleillo!*"

The shout came from behind and to the left. Morganen snapped his gaze—and his tendrils—that way. He didn't know what the spell was, but he didn't have to know its exact nature; it reeked of elemental fire and was easy to tear apart. The orange red bolt slowed and stopped within a body length of his shoulder, dissolving in greenish gold sparks that faded like a heat wave.

The spell's dissolved power arrowed into the dark crystal held by the woman seated beyond his other shoulder, charging it with the faintest of glows. Her husband ceased struggling to stand, switching his efforts instead to the task of throwing a spell of his own at Morganen, something both hot and acidic, forcing Morg to shift from holding him down to disassembling his magic. And his first attacker, now that the tendrils of Morganen's magic were no longer holding her down, struck again with a second, lightning-based attack.

Both spells shredded rapidly into harmless multihued sparks, but it forced Morganen to release Taurin physically, and it gave time for two more to struggle free of the compulsion to kneel, and then three more, and five, and nine—ever since that renegade mage, Xenos, had attempted to infiltrate and overtake not only the Fountain of Menomon, but the Fountain on Nightfall Isle, Morganen had practiced dismantling his brothers' spells. He was good at it, but this was more than seven sets of magical attacks.

Thankfully, his tendrils were doing their job; having targeted each mage's aura, they intercepted the incoming spells, stopping and shredding each bolt and wave and explosion of power. But within half a minute, Morganen couldn't *see* the Council, the dissolving sparks were that thick. Even switching back to normal sight didn't help, for the act of tearing apart each spark released physical energy as real bursts of light.

Dazzled, he closed his eyes and clung to his will. Nothing was getting through to him, a grateful fact that bolstered his faith in himself. As the attacks eased, then slowed to a trickle, Morganen opened his eyes. Squinting, he turned his head to peer through the Technicolor mist at Queen Samille, wanting to make sure she was still safe.

The sight of the shimmering bubble that enveloped her both pleased and relieved him. At some point during the attack, Taurin had moved, and was now scowling at the tangible wardings shielding his wife. "Samille, are you alright? Can you hear me? What did that bastard do to you?"

"I . . . I'm fine! Unharmed, completely unhurt. He said this thing would keep me safe . . ." It wasn't easy to see through the egg-shaped shimmer, but the glow from the power crystal was visible as she lifted it in indication.

"As I said," Morganen stated, startling King Taurin into whipping around to gape through the mist at him, "Her Majesty is innocent of all wrongdoing in this matter. Queen Kelly was quite specific that I take no *unreasonable* measures in persuading you to assist me in recovering our missing lady. But since I guessed *you* might be unreasonable . . ."

The last of the spell-residue faded, allowing the others to confirm with their own eyes that Morg had not been harmed. That he indeed stood among them without a single scorch mark or scratch. Muscle ticking in his jaw, Taurin glared at him.

Morg returned it with a sardonic smile. "Let's just say I brought a few precautions. Now, are you going to be reasonable, perhaps even honorable about helping me to rescue an innocent victim of an unwarranted crime? Or do I have to switch from merely asking to something less pleasant?"

Taurin stared at him for a long moment, then looked around the room at the members of his Council. At the end of his slow turn, he stared at Morganen again. Once more, a muscle twitched in his jaw.

"Kill him."

Morganen winced as the faster Councilors cast their spells at him. They exploded in puffs of multicolored light, followed by a veritable blizzard as the slower-reacting mages caught up. His tendril-spell, developed after the fight with Xenos, successfully intercepted each incoming spell based on the auras Morganen had already identified. Initially fueled by his own power, they now drew their energy from the attacks themselves. So long as no one new attacked, the tendrils would simply shred and absorb all that power.

But that carried a risk. Reaching into the largest of the pouches slung at his waist, Morganen pulled out two more power crystals. Neither was wrapped in wire, but they weren't meant to be makeshift Artifacts. They were just power collectors. Tying them into the hailstorm of shredding energies, as soon as they began to glow, Morganen left them to float in midair. His hands went to the flap of the smallest pouch, ready to loosen it and cast its contents into the air as well, but something lunged at him through the mist.

The shock wave of the protective warding-sphere plowing through the dissolving spells gave him barely enough warning. Morganen flung himself out of the path of the Katani sovereign's blade. The Councilors kept casting their spells; he could see with a blink of mage-sight that they had targeted his aura in order to be certain their spells struck true. None of them had realized yet the tendrils were part and parcel of Morg's aura.

Those tendrils only protected him from a magical attack, not the physical one Taurin aimed his way. There was only so much ducking and dodging a mage could do. Morganen dug into his pouch as he bobbed and twisted away from each swing and lunge. Flinging out handfuls of chalk-sticks, he broke them into thumbnail-sized pieces with a slash of his hand, and sent them flying out across the room with another snap.

Taurin nearly skewered him through the armpit with that maneuver. Gritting his teeth—hating that he, the least skillful of all of his brothers, was being forced into combat—Morganen summoned his sword. *"Markasset!"*

The blade was shorter than Taurin's, but all he needed was to block the incoming blows. Blocking, he could do; he didn't have the reach or the muscles of the taller, broader man. That was just as well; Morg didn't think Kelly would consider killing King Taurin a *reasonable* act.

Mindful of the others in the room—though he could not see them through the dense, bright fog surrounding him—Morganen didn't allow himself to be backed up into someone else's physical attack. He met each blow obliquely, slipping the other blade to his right or his left where he could, confining the bout to a small space on the lowest level of the chamber. Defending himself automatically, Morganen began inscribing runes in midair with his left hand. Unseen through the mist and the shouted spells of the Council, the pieces of chalk obeyed his will.

He almost lost his spellcrafting when something hit the side of his head during a dodging spin. Jerking to face this new threat,

Morganen quickly parried Taurin's next attack, rolling his eyes in both relief and disgust at the sight of one of the hovering, glowing power crystals. *Idiot . . . now get back to your work, and* don't *trip over his queen!*

At least I'm holding my own, he acknowledged silently. Taurin managed to bind their swords together, hilt to hilt. Their wards met and meshed, striking the sparks that steel had not.

"Your brother had a reputation as an excellent swordsman," Taurin taunted Morg, bearing down with his greater muscles. His face was sheened with sweat, his eyes bright with hate. "But if he's been teaching *you* what he knows, then those rumors are blatantly untrue!"

"I came here to rescue the woman I love," Morg retorted. "Killing you in front of the woman *you* love wouldn't be in the spirit of my mission!"

Rather than resisting any further head-on, he twisted, shoving his opponent to the side. Taurin stumbled into something obscured by the mist. From the thump and the feminine yelp, he had found the table where his wife sat. Tempted by that blatant, bent-over target, Morganen refrained from smacking the older mage in the ass with the flat of his blade. Instead, he backed up and resumed scribing runes in the air with his free hand, moving the corresponding pieces of chalk scattered around the room.

There, Your Majesty, he thought, thinking of his sister-in-law, not his target. *My one piece of true diplomacy in this farce . . .*

"Enough . . . *Enough!*" Taurin shouted from somewhere beyond the thick, bright mist shrouding Morganen from the rest of the room.

Morganen shifted, finding the floating power crystals by their brilliance. Squinting, he tossed his sword up in the air with a brief spell to levitate it somewhere over his head where it wouldn't endanger anyone. With both of his hands freed, Morganen marked more of the runes he needed, carving them into the air in glowing trails that became more and more visible as the last of the incoming spells were shredded and distributed between the three crystals in the room.

Aware of just how *much* energy had been socketed into those crystals—multiple spells from most of the Council—Morganen added a small tap line from Queen Samille's crystal to his spellwork. It wouldn't do to have that crystal explode in her face from too much magical pressure, when it was supposed to be protecting her.

"*How* are you still standing?" King Taurin asked Morganen, pacing in his agitation. His sword had been placed on the table before his queen, leaving his hands free to gesture impatiently. "You just had the might of the Empire flung at—*what* are you do-ing?" he demanded, breaking off to stare at the increasing number of glowing runes that *weren't* fading along with the last of the spell-shredded mist.

"Showing you . . . what you could do . . . if you'd put your heads together," Morg told him distractedly. "Instead of up your backsides . . ."

His fingers flicked rapidly as he shifted forward to scribe his marks on fresh, unenchanted air. It wasn't easy, talking and casting at the same time, but the months he had spent teaching the untrained mages on the island had taught him how to lecture and demonstrate simultaneously.

"The walls!" someone shouted. Morganen thought he recognized the voice as the Councilor of Taxation, Lady Thera, but he couldn't spare enough attention to be sure.

"He's marking something on the walls!" another mage called out.

Most of the Council spun to examine the walls and the snippets of chalk scribbling on the painted spans of plaster and stone. Now that they weren't casting spells against him, the soft clicks and scrapes of half a hundred segmented sticks were audible. Again, Morg moved forward; he didn't have Serina's expandable chalkboards to work with, just the very air itself for his work surface, and his own energies for his calligraphy.

"You . . . you *stole* our magic?" Taurin asked, shock widening his eyes. "You *stole* our powers, and put them in those power crystals! Blasphemy! Blood-magic!"

"*Hardly*," Morg snorted. "Aquamancer Tanaka Zhou Fen, creator of the Desalinator of Nightfall, proved it was possible for a mage to borrow the powers of others. *Without* staining one's soul with the taint of evil. So long as I do not benefit *directly* from—"

Samille yelped, startling him. One of the Councilors had crept up to her at her seat, his movements unnoticed until the moment he snatched the wire-wrapped crystal from her hands. The pudgy man charged Morganen with a cry of triumph, free hand glowing with violet fire.

"*Now* I can kill you!"

"*Trennbik!*" One hand scooping toward himself and the other thrusting out, Morganen forcefully separated the Councilor from his stolen prize. The overweight mage flung backward, *thudding* onto the floor with an audible grunt. Morg caught the wire-wrapped crystal, glaring at the other man. "*Traitor*," he growled, startling the others in the hall. "You *knew* I had given this to Her Majesty to protect her from harm, and you *stole it from her*—that's an act of treason by *any* kingdom's standards! You do *not* place a non-mage in danger during a magical duel! *Fazzak, foroudak!*"

The stones of the tier he had landed on bulged up out of the floor and snapped around the Councilor's wrists and ankles, shackling him in place. Striding back to the table, Morganen held out the crystal to Samille once more. Glancing up at her husband, who had folded his arms across his chest but otherwise hadn't moved, she cautiously accepted it. The ward-sphere returned, bubbling her in a protective, pearlescent mist.

"That crystal has been enspelled to protect *only* you, Your Majesty," he told her, raising his voice enough that the others would also hear. "It will *not* save anyone *else* from my wrath."

Scraping his hands through the aether as he backed away from the table, Morganen scribed the last few runes of his chalk-marked spell.

"Do you think to *threaten* us?" Taurin growled, shifting his fists to his hips. "I don't know what foul magic you've bartered out of a Netherhell to protect you, but if you think you can kill us, it is *we* who will kill *you*!"

Morg fixed the other man with a contemptuous look as he carved the last rune in the aether. "*I* don't kill."

Snapping his fingers, he triggered his spell. The walls exploded with light. The Councilors nearest the perimeter flinched and cried out protective spells . . . but nothing happened to them. Dozens of chalk-scraps clattered to the floor, and from the floor up, the walls transformed. Color and opacity drained upward like a roiling, rising cloud of smoke being sucked out of a jar by an aeration charm.

Stone and plaster, paint and wood, all of it altered. Crystal took its place, clean, clear, and flawless. The transformation revealed the guards stationed at the doors, who twisted and stared behind themselves, startled by the alteration. It displayed the backs of the mirrors hung on the walls of the Hall of Mirrors off to one side, and a crosscut of the beams and floorboards of the second story on the other side. Including the porcelain receptacles of a refreshing room . . . and a very startled male dressed in the livery of a palace servant, hastily fastening his trousers.

Embarrassed by his gaff, Morg quickly levitated several pieces of chalk, outlining the section of wall involved. A few wriggles of his hand reversed the spell, restoring the unexpected view to plaster-painted stone. Power drained out of all three stones, until the two hovering in the air were nearly dark, and Samille was once again visible through a watery-looking wall of power. Cheeks burning, Morganen faced the Katani King.

"Power corrupts, and political power is no exception . . . but the eyes of your Empire *are* upon you, Majesty, and your people *do* witness everything you do. Consider these walls as my gift to you. A *reminder* that everything you do reflects upon the people you serve," he told king and Council. Fishing out the Truth Stone once more, he held it over his head, clenching it in his hand. "*None* of my powers come from the Netherhells." Tossing up the unblemished disc, he left it hovering over his head. "You have *not* tried more than a fraction of my power . . . but you *have* tried my patience."

"All I have seen here is some gimmick designed to steal *our* power. I haven't seen you using your own," Taurin shot back. He thrust a finger at Morganen. "I challenge you to use your *own* powers, and nothing *but* your own powers, in a Duel Arcane!"

"Taurin, no!" Samille cried out, rising from her seat in alarm. "If *you* challenge anyone and they win, they'll win the Throne!"

"Oathbind yourself to use only your own power against me, and the challenge will stand, Morganen 'of Nightfall,' " Taurin told Morganen, chin lifted arrogantly.

"Taurin! Have you lost your senses?" the blonde queen demanded, grabbing his arm.

"Yes, have you?" Morganen asked him, wanting to be sure Taurin wasn't merely posturing.

Lifting his hand, Taurin summoned the floating Truth Stone. It smacked into his palm, his fingers curling around the disc's edge. "I swear on this Stone that, if you oathbind yourself to use *only* your own magic, with no outside source for augmentation, I will challenge you to a Duel Arcane . . . winner to take and hold the Throne of Katan."

"Please, I'm not stupid," Morg shot back, eyeing the unblemished disc. "Make the same oath, Your Majesty, and you have a deal. But if anyone else interferes, not only is the deal over, you'll *all* track down Finneg and Hope, and hand *both* of them over to Nightfall . . . or I will tear down this palace with *all* of the power that I can command, until nothing is left standing but the people who live here!"

"You wouldn't dare. And you *couldn't*," Taurin sneered.

Sinking his tendrils into the floor beneath their feet, Morganen let his own sneer rumble literally through the stones in tangible warning. "You try my *patience*!"

"Cheap theatrics!" Taurin scorned. "Speak your oath first, and I will *consider* giving my own."

"*Fine.* I, Morganen of Nightfall, bind unto my powers this vow: that *if* King Taurin of Katan also limits his powers and the conditions of his challenge in the same way, I shall accept his challenge to a Duel Arcane between us, using only my own personal magic and drawing upon no other magical source for the duration of said duel . . . but that any interference from any other individual will negate the limitations on my power, in regards to my retaliation against said interfering individual during the duration of said duel . . . and in no way shall this oath limit my powers outside of said duel. So swear I, Morganen of Nightfall."

"Now swear your own oath," Morg ordered the king as power rippled visibly across his frame. "Or face my *impatience.*"

"You swore well. You could have been a law-sayer, if you hadn't been born into the wrong family." Taurin shifted his gaze to the others. "*Any* interference in this duel will be considered an act of Grand Treason, and the offender will be cast into the Oubliette. So say I, King Taurin of Katan."

Returning his attention to Morganen, he spoke his piece.

"I, King Taurin of Katan, bind unto my powers this vow: in offering challenge to a Duel Arcane with Morganen of Nightfall, and upon his acceptance of said duel, I shall restrict my own powers within the boundaries of the duel to nothing but my own personal magic and draw upon no other magical source for the duration of said duel . . . but any interference from any other individual will negate the limitations upon my own power, in regards to my retaliation against said interfering individual during the duration of said duel . . . and in no way limiting my own powers outside of said duel. So swear I, King Taurin of Katan."

Energy snapped across Taurin's body. Turning away, Morganen swept his hand through the air. Stray papers and the shattered remnants of the mirror Finneg had used skittered across the floor, baring a broad circle on the lowest floor of the Council Chamber. Two of the mirrors skidded back on their wooden stands; the rest had been placed on higher tiers. Beyond the Councilors, some of whom had righted the chairs and desks nearest them, wide-eyed servants and curious courtiers peered through the stout glass, no doubt wondering what was going on inside the altered walls.

Once there were no possible distractions, Morganen crossed the roughly outlined circle to the far side and faced the King of Katan again. Morg dissolved the tendril that had associated itself with Taurin's aura, and detached the rest of those tendrils from himself, sending the lot into the two dimly glowing crystals still floating by the desk. The spell would continue to defend against the others' magic on its own instinctive cognizance, but not against Taurin's, abiding by the letter of his vow.

"Well? It's *your* challenge to give, not mine. You already know what I want out of you, instead of this stupid duel."

Muscle ticking in his jaw, Taurin stepped into the emptied patch of floor and lifted his hands. "I, King Taurin of Katan, challenge you to a Duel Arcane, Morganen of Nightfall. Mage against mage, mind against mind, might against might."

"I, Morganen of Nightfall, accept your challenge to a Duel Arcane, King Taurin of Katan," Morganen replied. It had been a long time since any of his brothers had dared to challenge him, and he hadn't been sure for a moment that he would remember the ritual words. But he did, and lifted his own hands, fingers spread and slightly curved, as if he could clasp palms with the man standing four body lengths away from him. "Wrath against wrath, will against will, word against word."

Power welled up from both men, manifesting as huge, misty-hued arms. Magical hands flexed, met, and clasped in midair—and just that fast, Taurin powered his will into his mist-hands, curling the real ones in echo of the tightening of his magical grip. It was faster and harder than Morganen expected.

His own fingers bent backward for a moment, making him wince and grit his teeth. But the physical reaction to such strong magical pressure wasn't nearly as painful as, say, physically wrestling with Wolfer. His secondborn brother was the strongest in their family physically, but the weakest magically. Morg could have used the magical equivalent of the same sorts of physical tricks he used to escape his brothers' grasp, but that wasn't the point of a Duel Arcane: It was all about raw power and raw will, and that meant stiffening his determination and bending back Taurin's own metaphysical hands.

If he took a certain small pleasure from Taurin's pained gasp and jerking wrists, well, Morg was only human. And he had run out of most of his patience with the other man. Both men tightened their grasp, hardening their determination to win, to not be the one to yield.

Sweat beaded on Taurin's reddening brow. Morganen felt his own skin growing hot and damp. Mist-arms bulged with veins and tendons. The border between their two manifestations began to glow as all that life-energy compressed in a very finite space.

Sparks skittered free as each mage increased his efforts. They escaped the intersection of their powers in silent, minor explosions, but no one spoke. No one wanted to interrupt the duel and be accused of interfering.

At the edge of his awareness, Morganen saw one of the crystalized doors being pulled open, heard the murmur of one of the guards responsible, and the curt reply of the nearest Councilor for them to stay out of the matter and out of the room. Taurin took advantage of his distraction, strengthening the vise of his mental grasp. Morganen flexed his own will, staring into his former sovereign's eyes with unshaken determination.

None of his brothers could best him at this. None of them, not even Rydan, had been able to defeat Morganen's stubborn determination, nor surpass his sheer personal power since his nineteenth year. It was the reason—the only reason—his brothers had listened to their youngest sibling when Morganen had told his brothers they were not going to fight for their rights, back when the Council had tried to throw them into the Oubliette four years ago.

The last time he had fought his brothers in a Duel Arcane, it had been a jokingly offered challenge of two against one, Rydan against his right mage-hand, and Dominor against his left, both striving simultaneously to bring him to his knees. Morg had held his own against both of them, and driven them to their knees.

Wisely, they had both yielded before either was harmed, though both were strong. So was Taurin, at least as strong as Rydan had been back during that last duel, possibly stronger . . . but not as strong as Rydan and Dominor combined.

The King of Katan grimaced, baring his teeth. His limbs trembled with effort. One knee buckled, dropping him to the floor. Behind him, Samille squeaked, muffling her cry of alarm behind a hastily clapped hand. He grunted and shoved back to his feet with visible effort. The silent spatter of sparks became a spraying hiss, scorching the floor where they fell. The scent of overheated stone spread through the room.

His other leg buckled, slamming Taurin to his knees with a grunt. The mage didn't yield, though his own sweat-sheened arms bulged with muscles and veins, echoing the duel-wrought limbs wrestling for dominance between the two men. Morganen increased his power incrementally, breathing deeply but steadily.

Sweat trickled down the bridge of his nose, detouring into one eye. Ignoring the sting of salt, Morganen tightened his will a little more.

Sna-ap!

Taurin screamed, body buckling as his arms and hands bent unnaturally. "*I yield! I yield! I yield!*"

"*Don't kill him!*"

Quickly easing the pressure, Morganen swept his arms through the air, dissolving the power poured into his mist-limbs in favor of recasting it into a cushioning spell. Sleeves of glowing energy cocooned the other mage's arms, straightening and shielding his limbs from further injury.

"Whoever is in the Department of Healing, attend to him," Morganen directed. "Make sure he regains full use of his limbs."

No one moved. They just stared at Morg with wide, frightened eyes.

"*Now!*" he snapped.

His shout made a third of the Council twitch. One woman and two men hurriedly picked their way down the shallow tiers, heading for Taurin, who stayed on his knees, panting heavily against the pain. Morganen looked around at the others.

"According to the laws of the Empire, if the king challenges any other mage to a duel, if that other mage wins, he or she instantly becomes the sovereign. *I* am your sovereign, now," Morganen reminded them. Lifting his hand, he summoned the Truth Stone, letting it smack into his palm. "Anyone who fails to heed my commands may have a *less* gentle taste of my power . . . and I did *not* wield my full will against Lord Taurin."

Throwing the disc up, he left it spinning in midair, flashing two clean, all-white sides to the whole of the glass-walled chamber.

"How . . . *how* strong . . . ?" Taurin gasped, peering past the Healers attending him.

"How strong am I?" Morganen finished the question for him. "My brothers may trounce me regularly at swordplay, but even as a *group*, they refuse to duel me arcanely. There is only one mage I know of in all in all the world who is my equal . . . and I only met her recently, when she came to Nightfall to help us resurrect the Convocation of the Gods. *She* will not challenge me, and I will not challenge her. We prefer to work together to attain our mutual goals.

"Now. Let us discuss, once more, *my* goals," he reminded the remaining Councilors. "Find Duke Finneg and find Hope of Nightfall. Before I lose what is *left* of my patience with you."

Blinking, the men and women nearest the surviving mirrors quickly turned back to them, evoking every possible location for His Grace in a hasty burst of magic and words. Several more rushed for the doors into the Hall of Mirrors, no doubt to use them, while others edged toward the other crystalline doors.

Morg narrowed his eyes. "I have not given the rest of you my permission to leave."

The furtive movements ceased. One of the Healers, the woman, looked up at Morganen. "Lord Taurin needs serious medical magic. You shattered his forearms and half of his fingers."

"He *could* have yielded at any earlier moment," Morg told her. "Unfortunately, he miscalculated. But I will not have him permanently injured because of his own arrogance. Take him away and give him the best possible care. As for the rest of you, *find* Duke Finneg. Particularly find Hope of Nightfall. Bring both of them to me, alive, intact, and unharmed . . . though you may have to lock His Grace in anti-magic chains," he allowed. "I doubt he will come peacefully, particularly if he finds out I am now the King of Katan—oh, and before I forget, track down Lord Consus of Kairides' bank accounts and other seized assets and ship them to Nightfall Island.

"He was *not* acting against the laws of Katan when he assisted Nightfall Island, just against the whims of your previous king . . . whims which were against the law. You have two hours to get the money transferred and sent. Above all, lords and ladies," he finished as the Healers cast a levitation charm on their former sovereign, "I have run out of patience with you.

"Do *not* make me repeat myself again."

This time, they hurried to do his bidding. Most of the Councilors headed for the Hall of Mirrors, while others set about righting the tables and chairs and gathering up the scattered papers. Only one person approached him, the Lady Samille. She stopped just out of arm's length, offering back the wire-wrapped crystal.

"Keep it," Morganen told her under his breath. "You'll be queen again soon enough, once I have completed my mission. I have no intention of staying here."

"Thank you. For not killing my husband," she clarified.

"If he had agreed to my initial request, none of this would have been necessary, and he would not have been harmed," Morg returned. "Let us hope he is capable of learning from his mistakes—you'll pardon me if I don't hold my breath, of course, but I do hope he changes."

Nodding, the temporarily deposed queen followed the Healers out of the hall.

"I think she's awakening . . . Get that other manacle on her."

"There, I found it."

Hope jerked, struggling to flail her arms, but the second application of the sleeping spell had left her even more sluggish than the first. She heard and felt the *clank* of cold metal snapping around her right ankle. The left one was already bound, as were her wrists. She struggled to open her eyes, only to realize after blinking them that they *were* open. Nothing but blackness met her straining gaze, an impenetrable visual void. She could still hear the two men as they pulled back and did things around her, the hollow scrape of something wooden, the whispering of fingers sliding over something rough, a long splash of water.

"Who's there? Where am I?" she demanded. She felt lumpy fabric under her legs and cold stone at her back, smelled fresh straw, dusty cotton, and something else, an odor reminiscent of the nursing homes she had seen in the other world, visiting elderly O'Niell relatives. The kind of bodily function scent that, no matter how much sanitizer one used, always lingered in the air at such places.

"Why, you're in Hell, of course," the voice of the first male told her, humor lacing his words. "Also known as the Oubliette. We are your tenders. We bring you fresh water and fresh food, and we are even so kind as to take away your refuse while it's still fresh, too."

"Water and food are served to your right, and the slops bucket is to your left," the second male instructed her. His tone wasn't quite as light as the first man's, but neither was it unduly harsh. "Always remember that. Water to the right, urine to the left. Don't drink out of the wrong bucket."

"Yes, that's very important," the first one agreed. "You don't want to make yourself sick. After all, once every five years, your case will be reviewed by the Department of Conflict Resolution, and you *might* be set free at that time, if the government deems you sufficiently harmless to be released back into society."

"That's usually a false hope, you know," Second Man chided. "You shouldn't give them false hope. It's almost cruel."

First Man sighed. "It's crueler to make them think they have *no* hope."

"Oh, there's *plenty* of hope, gentlemen," she corrected them. "I am *not* supposed to be here. I was kidnapped by a madman—"

"Yes, yes, His Grace did say you'd make all sorts of outrageous claims to try and get out of your sentence. He even said you'd claim to be a Seer, but that's impossible, because surely a Seer would foresee being tossed in here and take steps to avoid this place? Not to mention, Seers are national treasures, not criminals," First Man interrupted gently. Now his tone seemed more condescending than kindly. "They *all* say that they're innocent, when they're first tossed in here. 'I'm not supposed to be here!' 'I was wrongly imprisoned!' 'I *never* experimented upon those poor, magically mutilated villagers!' "

"But *I am* speaking the truth! Bring me a Truth Stone, or a Truth Wand, and you'll see it for yourselves!" Hope ordered.

Both men chuckled.

"We'll 'see' it, will we?" Second Man repeated, audibly amused. "She has no concept of life in the Oubliette . . ."

Hope sucked in a sharp breath, remembering what Consus and Morg had told her shortly after her return to this world. *The servants of the Oubliette, the guards . . .* "You're blind, aren't you?"

"Maybe she *does* have some concept of life here . . . but it doesn't matter. She'll just try to reason with us, and then plead, and then beg, and scream, and rant, and cry," Second Man related to his companion. "The crying is tedious. They're always so thirsty, afterward, begging for extra water."

"I like it when they offer sexual favors. Male or female, it doesn't matter. I just like romping on the pallets with them," First Man stated, his tone almost cheerful. "Of course, it won't get them their freedom, just maybe a nicer pallet. I don't like lumps under my knees."

"I like giving them better food. Meat for meat, as my father always said. A fair trade."

Hope flinched, protectively squeezing her thighs together. She made a quick, mental inventory of how her body felt, but didn't relax more than a fraction when she realized she was still clad in the jeans and blouse she had donned that morning, replete with the bra and underpants beneath. Even her sneakers were still tied on her feet. No bruises, no soreness, no miscellaneous dampness. No one had violated her. Yet.

Her two companions had heard the sharp intake of her breath. First Man sighed. "Oh, please. It's against the rules to rape you! And we *always* abide by the rules. *We're* not the criminals here."

"Water and food to the right, slops bucket to the left," Second Man intoned. "Try not to knock them over, or you'll have to do something *nice* for us, just to get a fresh, clean pallet."

"Do you think she'll go mad quickly?" First Man asked. "Some of them do, you know."

"His Grace did say she was clever. The clever ones usually last awhile. And if she is nice to us, polite and friendly, and doesn't kick or try to punch or bite, we could give her things to occupy her attention," Second Man added. "I like the knotted rope puzzle myself. All that lovely texture, and the trick of trying to find both ends . . ."

"I'll give her eight months to start going mad," First Man offered. "Talking to herself to relieve the boredom won't count, but seeing and hearing things that aren't there will. The usual signs."

"The usual trade, a month's worth of slops chores for the loser?" Second Man bartered.

"Of course."

"Then I'll take thirteen months. I think she's a smart one—and only two months to do something nice for us," Second Man added.

"I think you're being a little optimistic," First Man returned. He paused, sighed, and agreed. "But she might be smart about it. Two months for you, three months for me. If she does want to do something nice for us, we don't do anything until we've gotten her a birth control amulet from the Healer. It's against the rules to get the lady prisoners pregnant, after all."

"Of course, of course . . . Water to the right, slops to the left!" Second Man intoned, as if it was his holy mantra. "Don't forget it. The cells get scrubbed every half turning of Brother Moon, so if you vomit, you'll have to live with it until then."

"Slops buckets are cleaned out once a day, with food and water brought twice," First Man added, back to sounding cheerful and friendly again.

"You'll have two occasions every day to speak with someone; the rest of the time, you'll have plenty of time to contemplate your crimes," Second Man promised her. "Slops to the left, and water to the right!"

Hope heard both men moving away, and the closing of a door. There must have been a grille or something for an air vent, because when she strained, her ears still heard them shuffling away. A few heartbeats later, she heard the sound of metal on metal, the creaking of a door, the muttering of voices. But try as she did, she couldn't make sense of what they were saying to the prisoner in the next underground cell.

Oh, Gods . . . maybe I should have pretended to go along with that madman . . . Kelly would've understood the deception. It would only have been temporary anyway, just long enough for me to escape and denounce them.

There wasn't much point in wishing about what could have been, though. That was a lesson her younger self had learned, stuck in a foreign world. *So what can I do? I know they missed me when I didn't show up to take over walking the crystal for Alys—poor Morg's probably frantic by now. He'll try scrying for me, of course, but if he hasn't found me by now, then he'll not find me at all that way. Not when I'm stuck in full darkness.*

If I still needed to carry around house keys, then at least I'd have had a miniature flashlight with which to see my surroundings, but no. I had to come back home, where such things aren't necessary, she thought wryly. *Of course, if I hadn't come home, I wouldn't be in this predicament. Nauvea, Your sense of humor has certainly grown strange over the . . .*

Of course! The Convocation of the Gods! They'll be invoking it soon, Hope reminded herself. *If they haven't tracked down Finneg and forced him to return me by then, Morg and Kelly can always petition the Gods for my salvation! I only have to hold out until . . . an unknown length of days from now,* she realized, her spirits losing some of their buoyancy. She grimaced into the darkness. *Because they might put it off, treating it as secondary in importance to finding me.*

Of course . . . they could *choose to speed up the process,* she reasoned, bolstering her teetering emotions. *If I was kidnapped, it's quite possible the others were attacked. I refuse to believe Morg and the others died in such an attack—maybe they were injured, but I refuse to believe they'd all die—but I know Morg is powerful enough to hold his own. Between his powers, his brothers' and sisters'-in-laws skills, Kelly's cunning . . . yes, they'll win any battle they get themselves into. Which means they just might move up the Convocation.*

But again, I don't know *that's what they're going to do . . . and whether or not it is, I cannot affect it. So what can I do? Nauvea, any . . . ?*

Lifting her hand made the chains attached to her manacles rattle and clank, but she had enough slack to smack herself in the forehead. That also smacked some of the links into her jaw and shoulder. *Stupid . . . stupid . . . stupid . . .* Of course *there's something I can do! I can pray! Prayer empowers the Gods; if I think strongly enough of Them, They will hear me.*

Of course . . . that's presuming Kelly has Nauvea on the list of Gods and Goddesses to be formally Named . . . but I will pray that She whispers in my sister's ear, Hope told herself, rubbing her fingertips over the smooth skin of the unseen scar on her hand. *And in Morg's ear. Or maybe my fellow Seer, Milon of Natallia, wrote out a postdated note for Morg to read.*

I refuse to believe I have been abandoned here. I refuse to believe I have been forgotten. I am remembered, and I will be found . . . and to ensure my odds of success, I will pray to my chosen deity, Nauvea, Goddess of Dreaming. Because it is my most fervent dream that I will be rescued from here, and She is my chosen Goddess.

Out of habit—since in this place, it mattered not if they were open or shut—she closed her eyes, blocked out the scent and the feel of her surroundings, and began to pray. *Nauvea, Goddess of Heaven, Weaver of Dreams, I give unto You my wildest of thoughts. I offer to You my deepest imaginings. I am but the dreamer, and Yours is the Dreaming.*

I Dream of flowers in springtime . . . of cacao trees growing in the forest . . . I see myself and Morganen lying on a blanket and laughing, feeding each other food . . . I smell the forest soil, I feel the plump flesh of the grapes, I taste the wine upon my lover's lips . . . I am but the dreamer, and I give unto You my Dreamings . . .

TEN

"**V**omiting," Dominor stated in an undertone.

"That's not fair!" Trevan hissed back. "You picked vomiting last time! *I* get vomiting. Pick something else."

"Alright. Um . . . praying fervently—the sweaty and shaky kind."

"Try praying that *I* don't make you eat dirt, if you don't keep your mouths shut," Kelly growled at her brothers-in-law. "You are supposed to be *helping* the priests who come across, not betting on how badly shaken they'll be by the trip!"

Trevan and Dominor looked at each other, then Trevan tipped his reddish gold head at his sister-in-law. "She gets the catatonic ones?"

"Trevan! What did I just tell you?" Kelly demanded irritably, though her mouth kept trying to twitch up.

"Something about keeping one's mouth shut . . . which *would* qualify for the catatonic ones?" Trev offered with a grin, unrepentant.

Kelly gave them both a disgusted look . . . then furtively glanced around. Ora was seated in a chair brought for her use, wrapped in a black robe more voluminous than her usual priestly overcoat. The influx of priests and priestesses had finally slowed enough that Kelly could question them about their odd, furtive conversations; now she knew. "What's the prize, if I take the bet?"

"One point if you win. Four points gets you a chore swapped on the roster," Trevan told her. "And you don't have to clean up after the vomiting ones, if that's your bet. We thought about doing it chore for chore, but that'd be too many chores."

Ora stood, catching their attention. Her face was looking paler than when she had started, and there were hints of dark circles under her green eyes, but they were almost done. Kelly shook her head. "No, I wouldn't be able to garner enough points to make it worth my while."

Shrugging the deep hood over her head, Ora swept the folds of her robe shut. The soft wool billowed around her as she turned, sealing her in darkness. Then it bulged and the edges parted . . . and an elderly man stumbled out, clad in a white shirt and leggings that were covered in a bright yellow vest and something that looked like a cross between a sarong and a kilt wrapped around his hips. The poor man was gasping for air, clutching at his chest.

It took a moment for the three Nightfallers to realize he was gasping with *laughter*, not horror.

"Damn," Dominor muttered. "I could've *sworn* this one would be vomiting." He left the other two, moving up to orient and escort the man off to the hastily cushioned benches. Dellen, recovered from being attacked by the Mendhites, hurried to take her place by Trevan's side and await the next ones to arrive.

"I get vomiting, this time," she muttered as Ora sat down, only to stand up quickly again, resetting her robes to manifest yet another hapless cleric brought to the island via the Dark. "I had to clean up the last one."

Kelly rolled her eyes and left Trevan as he tried to charm his way out of that particular chore. Following in Dominor's wake, she pulled her notepad and pencil—product of a quick scrounge through Hope's quarters—out of her belt pouch. There were just some things that were simply easier when done the outworlder way, and note taking was one of them. At least, for her. *A year in this world, and I still haven't quite got the knack of writing on a scroll without a flat surface to set it on . . .*

"Pardon me, milord," she stated, addressing the yellow-kilted priest. He was still chuckling, an odd reaction compared to the misery most of the others had suffered during their passage to get here. But he also looked relieved to be off his feet.

"Heheh . . . hmm . . . what did you say?" His accent, as translated by the Ultra Tongue she had drunk, sounded vaguely Polynesian. It also made her ears twitch for a moment, until they grew used to hearing and translating the new dialect. The man peered at her, his brown eyes rheumy with a mixture of age and mirth. "Heh. Can you even understand me?"

Kelly smiled and wrapped her mouth around his native tongue, doing her best to match the "accent" she heard. "Of course I can, sir. I'm Queen Kelly of Nightfall, and I'm here to welcome you to our little island nation. The Convocation of the Gods will take place shortly; I just need to know your name, and which land and Deity's worshippers you're here to represent."

"Queen? A queen greets me?" He arched his sparse gray white brows in surprise. "Well, how about that . . . My title and name, young lady, is the Exarch Melulose Filomen-Amon—that's two names, joined with a *krittek* mark—of Tifrang, God of Mischief."

Kelly scribbled that down on the list of clergy that had arrived, then cross-checked the list of Names Ora had given her. "Tifrang . . . Tifrang . . . here we go. And the land is . . . the Isles of Storms?"

"Indeed. Off the northeastern coast of Mendhi," he agreed.

"Thank you very much! There is plenty of water to drink, and fruit juice," she told him after she ticked off the name on her list. Kelly gestured at the nearest of the tables spaced around the amphitheater. "Plus snacks of bread and fruit, and I think some smoked fish is still left. Once the Convocation has been invoked, the Gods Named, the initial, priority petitions offered, so on and so forth, you'll be assigned some quarters, and given a chance to speak your piece to the Gods. We're assigning everyone their time slot solely based on the order that they arrived, so I'm afraid you'll probably have to wait awhile before your concerns are addressed. At least you'll have free room and board while you wait, for this visit.

"If you have any questions or concerns, you may contact anyone wearing a Nightfall tabard—the fabric chest-drapes with the sunset horizons painted on them," she added, gesturing at the hastily assembled servants.

"Heheh," the Exarch chuckled. He eyed her in her aquamarine silks, his gaze lingering here and there, mainly over the curves accented by her laced-up bodice and the skirt flaring over her hips. "Can I 'contact' *you*?"

Kelly froze, realizing the merriment in his bright gaze wasn't just merry, it was also a bit lecherous. Pasting a smile on her face, she cleared her throat. "I'm happily married, and not interested in anyone other than my husband. But I thank you for any implied compliment you may have intended. I'll also be rather busy organizing this whole event, and wouldn't have the time to spare, even if I were interested. Which I'm not.

"Welcome to Nightfall, please heed the usual sort of polite-behavior laws you'd find in any land, try not to get into too much trouble, and I hope you have a nice stay. Excuse me, please." He cackled as she turned on her heel and strode away. Smiling ruefully, Kelly glanced around to see where Trevan had gone; the redhead was leading the latest, ashen-faced arrival to one of the still-empty bench seats.

A servant hurried over to the Exarch's side, clad in the purple-and-black tabard Evanor had hastily cut, sewn, and painted to identify the Underhall staff for their visitors. She noticed how the servant politely offered the elderly priest a mug and a plate of food, and that the priest accepted it readily. *At least one of them knows what he's doing by now . . .*

Some of the servants were still staring around themselves in wonder, taking in the carved walls and spiraling columns. They were supposed to be tending to the makeshift dignitaries the Witches had gathered from around the world. Others were struggling with their sudden duties, having been randomly pressed into service by a bout of quick questioning under Truth Stone. And still more were hastily making bedchambers ready, or turning the stark, empty kitchens into chambers that could actually produce food.

At least they *had* servants to tend the delegates. Less than an hour ago, Koranen and Danau had finished the enchantment sequence for starting up the Desalinator. The sluices had been throttled down to a minimum flow, the production of salt and algae blocks had slowed to a manageable rate, and the majority of the workers had been dismissed back to their lives. Saber had wisely recruited people under the guise that the Convocation was being invoked *tomorrow*, not today, and that the fifty or so individuals sent down to the Underhalls were here to prepare the hidden complex for tomorrow's guests.

The deception was certainly deemed necessary by Kelly. She still remembered how close she had come to *not* getting her magic-reflecting mirror lifted high enough between her and that Mendhite's rune-empowered fist. It could have been her face that had shattered during that battle up at the palace, not his hand and his forearm.

Pulling her thoughts away from the fight, she asked the latest arrival, a black-haired, middle-aged woman, for her name, country, and Patron Deity. Once that was marked down, she checked the list and blinked. *Wow . . . only two Gods left to go . . . and one of them isn't an "official" deity, at that . . .*

I'd better go to the bathroom, she realized, glancing around to make sure everyone was being well tended. *If nearly everyone is here, I doubt I'll get a chance to go once the last one does arrive.*

Hurrying out of the amphitheater, she found the nearest refreshing room. Or rather, set of refreshing rooms, a corridor lined on either side with closely spaced doors, each chamber holding a toilet and a sink, and a vein of suncrystal in the rounded ceiling for illumination. Linens and pots of softsoap had been the first things fetched down by the hastily assembled staff, raided from the spares back at the palace. The towel resting on the narrow counter was visibly dusty, but it wasn't as if anyone was going to be performing open-heart surgery after scrubbing up in here.

Inevitably, no sooner had she started to wash her hands at the sink than her cryslet chimed. Suppressing a groan, Kelly hastily finished scrubbing and rinsing her hands, blotting them quickly so she could flip open the lid. *It never fails, but that* someone's *cell phone goes off in the bathroom. Why should cryslets in the refreshing room be any different?* "Hello?"

Trevan's face filled the oval scrap of mirror. "The, um, last delegate has arrived, according to Ora. I've taken the liberty of calling Alys back from her very long walk. She should be here within . . . ten minutes? Maybe five? It's not easy to tell distance, down here."

"Make sure you get her the softest, cushiest chair to sit on. And a footstool, and something to eat," Kelly directed him. "I'll be back out in just a moment."

Closing the lid, she paused long enough to dry her hands more thoroughly, then headed back out into the main chamber. The sight that greeted her when she sought and found the last arrival was unexpected. A heavily bound, rune-warded, gagged, mumbling and struggling figure was being dragged over to a bench. Bemused, she approached the two black-robed figures hoisting the man onto the intended seat.

"Um . . . Witches of Darkhana, right? Why is this man gagged and bound?" Kelly asked, fetching out her notepad and pencil again.

"He's a priest of Mekha, from the land of Mekhana. None of

them would have come willingly, particularly if they knew who was behind the summoning, so we resorted to kidnapping one," the female Witch stated.

The male Witch nodded at their prisoner. "His name is Belaan, and he's mid-ranked at most. More than that, we couldn't say."

"Getting close to Mekhanan clergy is never a good idea when oneself is a mage," the first Witch added grimly. "Once the Gods give Their Patronage, he won't be able to act against you. Until then, I suggest he remain bound."

"Right. Um, Priest Belaan, welcome to Nightfall Isle. You're here strictly to represent your people once your Patron Deity has been summoned forth for the Convocation of the Gods. I, um, apologize for any inconvenience or discomfort this may be causing you," Kelly added, glancing at his captors, "but rest assured, we will return you unharmed to your homeland after all of this is through."

Writing his name on her notepad as she moved away, Kelly ticked off Mekha on the second list and reviewed the Names and their representatives. She didn't know the Mekhanans by anything other than their reputation, but that reputation wasn't pleasant. So long as he wasn't being harmed, she would leave him in place. After the Convocation was called to order, when there was no chance a stray shout could disrupt the proceedings, she would have his gag removed.

Only one representative left to go . . . but I haven't heard from Morg. I know he'll find Hope; he found me, after all. I just don't think he'll find her in time for this thing to get going. Squaring her shoulders, she headed toward the great stone doors dividing the tiered half circle of benches that formed the mortal half of the amphitheater from the tiered half circle of granite thrones that formed the divine half. *Which means I'll have to step up and do it for her, as her blood-sworn sister.*

Right. I can do this. Since it was cool this deep underground, she had included the underblouse of her aquamarine silk outfit. Kelly tucked her notepad back into her pouch and rolled up her sleeves, a physical preparation to match her mental one. *I am Kelly Doyle, Queen of Nightfall. I believe in Gods and Goddesses . . . as much as I can . . . but I believe even more in the right of everyone within my land to enjoy the freedom to worship whomever or whatever they want. Provided their religious practices do not harm others.*

I can definitely do this.

She heard the smaller set of doors open behind her and turned to see Alys slipping into the room. The curly-haired woman moved tiredly down the shallow steps, bulging silk backpack on her back. Beside her paced Wolfer, his golden eyes flicking around the room, alert for any signs of possible danger toward his wife. Nodding to herself, Kelly braced her gut and spoke, up, addressing the men and women quietly murmuring among themselves.

"Alright! We're about to begin, so your attention would be appreciated. Obviously, I've never done this before," she allowed as the gathered clergy and assembled servants fell silent, "but it will be done, and you will see your Deities manifest through the Gate of Heaven. First will be the Naming, as each one is called forth. Then I will request that They grant their Patronage to Nightfall as a body, formally installing us an official, independent kingdom. The second petition will be from our gracious travel agent, Priestess Ora.

"After that . . . each of you will be called forth in the order that you arrived here, presented to your Deity, and granted the opportunity to praise, worship, complain, embrace, rant, or otherwise speak with your selected Patron. Or Patrons, in the cases of those lands with multiple Gods," she allowed. "You will each have ten minutes—no complaining," Kelly added as that caused a mutter. "There are three hundred seventeen Gods and Goddesses who must be Named, and two hundred forty-nine representatives who must be given a chance to address their chosen Patron or Patrons. If we include the time needed for people to be called forth, at four petitions an hour, that's two and a half solid days, non stop, of petitioning. And we *will* be taking breaks to eat and sleep, which will stretch things out even longer."

"Your Majesty, you miscounted. I gave you a list of only three hundred sixteen names," Ora called out, half rising from her seat.

"There's one more you don't know about," Kelly returned, waving her back down with a flick of her hand.

Ora gave her a bemused look but resettled back into her chair, one of the few on the mortal side of the chamber that had a back. "Just make sure Mekha is the last to be summoned forth. As a personal favor."

There was a snort and a scoff-sounding mutter from one of the priestesses off to one side, but Kelly didn't know who, and didn't care to find out. Straightening the rolled-up cuffs of her blouse, she faced the towering stone doors that Rydan had crafted between the amphitheater and the Fountain Hall. At some point during her speech, Dominor had slipped up next to them, ready to open them at her command.

Alys approached from her left, and Trevan from her right. The redheaded mage held up a fat, flattish silver rod studded with gems and addressed Kelly under his breath. "This is a Levitator, a special kind of Artifact that non-mages can use. I modified it to be more like one of those 'remote controls' I read about in Hope's technology books, so that you'll be able to get the hang of it quickly. This white crystal button turns the rod on or off. You have to hold it for a slow count of five in order to do so.

"This green one here 'grabs' whatever you want to lift, while this yellow slider controls the distance it is levitated from you—watch out, it's very touchy," he warned her. "The slightest touch is all that is needed to send it zooming away or hurtling back. Aiming it is just a matter of pointing the rod and watching where the object itself goes. You won't need to worry about those other buttons, since it doesn't really matter which way the crystal is oriented, since the Fountain radiates in all directions.

"Now, in order to actually levitate the object, you have to touch this red crystal to the object while holding down the 'grab' button. The same with releasing it," he warned her. "But this button here, the orange one, 'pauses' the settings and locks both them and the crystal's current location firmly in place, allowing you to take away the rod and go elsewhere. You also have to hold that one for five seconds to make it work.

"To 'unpause' it, you have to press both the orange and white crystals for five seconds. That will reconnect the rod and the object grabbed, allowing you to manipulate all the other buttons once again . . . which should extract the crystal from the Gateway of Heaven and close it down," he admitted. His mouth twisted wryly. "At least, that's the *theory*. All of this was cobbled together based on ideas culled from the usual Levitator Rod schematics, your world's preferences for controlling devices, and whatever sense I could glean from the rather vague information in our copy of the Scroll of Living Glory."

"You're smart enough, I'm sure this will work," Kelly told him. At his doubtful grimace, she added, "If not, I'll just ask the Gods Themselves to pluck the two Fountains apart. The important thing is opening the Gateway in the first place. Speaking of which . . . ?"

"I have it right here," Alys said from her other side. She had unslung the silk pack from her back, and dug far enough down through the layers of silk cushioning its contents to reveal the bright-pulsing crystal. The thickly padded pack had taken the place of the original makeshift bag after the second day, allowing even a mage as weak as her to carry its power safely.

"Thank you." Thumbing the white crystal, Kelly counted slowly to five, and smiled when the rod started glowing.

Touching the red crystal at the tip to the glowing egg, she thumbed the green button until the red crystal glowed. Lifting the rod slowly up, she extracted the faceted egg, which clung to the tip of the Artifact as if it had been glued there. Light spilled from the crystal, shedding visibly like a transparent, golden-hued mist that flowed outward in all directions. Kelly felt her hair start to stand on end, as if she were touching a huge static-generator back home.

She had a job to do, and gingerly tilted her wrist. Once it was pointing upright, she gently nudged the yellow slider gem . . . and the bright-glowing egg shot up several yards, startling her. The Fountain crystal jerked to a stop when she stopped moving her thumb, stopping less than a quarter of the way to the high-vaulted ceiling, with its brightly glowing suncrystal veins.

"Touchy, indeed. You weren't kidding," she muttered as Alys moved away, escorted by her husband to the other chair in the mortal half of the chamber. Trevan bowed and moved back as well, leaving Kelly to her task. Taking the time to pull out her notepad with her free hand, Kelly flicked awkwardly through the sheets with her thumb, found what she wanted, and quickly scanned her opening speech.

Lifting her freckled chin, she called out to Dominor, speaking loudly enough to make her words echo off the stone walls of the amphitheater. "Guardian of Nightfall, cast wide the Gates of the World, that we may see what is to come!"

Bowing, Dominor turned and flicked his hands, then moved out of the way. The massive stone panels swung back, revealing the glowing, overgrown giftwrap bow that was the Fountain of Nightfall. Ribbons of energy in a hundred different hues flowed up and down, arching out from and bending around the pulsing white mass that was the heart of the singularity.

Gingerly lowering the hovering crystal, Kelly extended her arm and took aim once it was level with the pulsing Fountain beyond the doors. "Let the Gods of this world pay heed, for its people would share words with You, whom they love and support. As Queen Kelly of Nightfall, the chosen Voice of the World and the host of this Convocation, I open the Gateway of Heaven!"

Nudging the yellow crystal marginally along its groove, Kelly carefully aimed the scintillating, floating crystal at her target. The distance gave her enough time to figure out how to control the rod, though she almost hit one of the ribbon-flows with the scintillating egg. She supposed she could have moved closer, but no one was sure what would happen when the Gateway was created, so the farther away she stood, the better.

As it was, she almost jerked her arm in shock when the glowing egg shot forward the moment it passed the outer ranks of ribbon-streams. Three things happened: The slider-gem slipped out from under her thumb, the position of the controller rod in her hand stiffened as if it had suddenly attached itself to a very long invisible pole, and the Fountain exploded with light. Kelly wasn't the only one to fling her free arm over her face for protection, though she was one of only a few in the amphitheater who had a direct line of sight into the Fountain chamber.

Blinking against the eye-watering opalescence, she carefully thumbed the orange gem for five seconds. The rod dipped, losing its stiff positioning as it lost its immediate connection to the crystal containing Rora's Fountain. Tucking the controller into her bodice—somehow, she didn't think it would be wise to tuck it into the same pouch that held her magic-reflecting mirror—Kelly cleared her throat and flipped through the pages of her notebook, trying not to look directly at the light shining through the huge doorway.

"I summon forth the Gods of Heaven, calling upon each of You by Name: I summon Fate, Threefold God of Fortuna, the Weaver of Time!"

The light shifted and moved, rippling for a moment. A figure appeared in the opening, nearly as tall as the archway itself. Pacing forward, it resolved into a figure that never completely stayed the same; the long, flowing, tunic-like robes were white, then gray, then black and back again. The face was young, mature, old. The gender was feminine, masculine, and yet neither.

And the figure glowed in an odd sort of way, like a spiral galaxy glowed. Kelly felt rather . . . awed. Unsettled, as if the world no longer completely pressed against her feet. She wasn't sure if that was a good thing or a bad thing, only that it was an unsettled thing.

Determined to get on with the show, she dragged her gaze away from the God of Destiny. Blinking, Kelly refocused on the room, and gestured at the stone thrones off to her left. If she let herself be distracted by every single manifestation that appeared, she'd never get her work done. Worse, she had the distinct feeling that Fate *knew* what she was thinking . . . and that the Threefold God was amused by her. Thankfully, Fate shrunk somehow in size to fit into one of the granite-carved seats on the divine side of the hall . . . though They didn't lose Their awe-striking impact on her senses.

Carefully avoiding Fate's steady, amused gaze, framed as it was by that unsteady, shifting face, she spoke as briskly as she dared. Her voice trembled a little as she greeted the first of over three hundred Gods to come. "Um . . . welcome to Nightfall, and please have a seat while I summon forth Your fellow Deities. I'm, uh, just going to run through the list of Names, since this is going to take long enough as it is. No disrespect is intended whatsoever, just, um . . . you know, efficiency . . .

"I summon Jinga and Kata, boisterous God and beloved Goddess of Katan, Patrons of the Four Seasons of Life!"

There, that came out much more firmly, she praised herself, spotting movement in the tunnel of light that the Fountain hall had become. She looked away before she caught more than a glimpse of a man as dark as Duke Finneg and a woman as fair as Priestess Ora. *So long as I avoid eye contact, I should be fine. I can do this. I really can. I know it.*

"Please take Your seats as I continue the rest of the Naming of Names, thank you. I summon forth . . . Menos, God of Reefs and protector of Menomon!"

A figure appeared at her side, not nearly as intimidating as the blue-skinned figure that strode, overly tall and imposing, through the equally oversized doors. It was Saber, normal-sized tall and utterly relieving. She hadn't dared wait for him to finish with his work out in the city, helping Amara oversee the last of the efforts regarding the Desalinator and covertly looking for more Mendhites.

Sneaking a glance behind her, she spotted more of her family on the benches across from the Fountain door: Serina with her twins seated beside Koranen and Danau—who was staring at her Deity with wide blue eyes, the same as her two fellow Aquamancers, perched as they were on one of the benches behind her. Mariel and her son Mikor were next to Kor and Danau, equally entranced. Alys had her own eyes closed, but then she had Wolfer seated on her footstool with his back to the door, her bared feet resting in his lap and being massaged by his large, gentle hands.

Accepting the glass of water from her husband, Kelly sipped at it to wet her throat, and checked the next Name on her list. *Three hundred and . . . twelve . . . sorry, thirteen Deities to go. This is going to be a* very *long day—even if I take no more than fifteen to thirty seconds per deity, that's up to two hours' worth of summoning, and that's* not *including each priest's petition.*

"I summon Firza the Earthshaker, Guardian of Vulcana!"

"Uh, Majesty . . . I *think* I may have something."

Morganen turned away from the mirror he was currently watching. It was being panned through one of Finneg's four residences in a room-by-room check, as were three other looking glasses in the near corner of the lengthy Hall of Mirrors. The dark-skinned Councilor looked vaguely familiar to Morg. "You are . . . ?"

"Councilor Thannig of the Department of Prophecies. This comes from the Seer Pellida," he told Morg, handing over a folded scrap of paper. "Her scribe sent it across to one of my underscribes, and someone in the department wised up and realized it just might have bearing upon you—Seer Pellida is one of the Vehement Prophets, if you aren't familiar with her reputation. Apparently she was ranting about her food being too cold this morning, old age being what it is and all . . . and, well, you can read it for yourself and decide if it has any bearing on your quest."

Bemused, Morg accepted the paper. Unfolding it, he read the

neatly penned words. *"Blood calls to blood, through the darkest despair. Even the King of Katan knows you can't cook an omelet without cracking open a few heads, though some heads are utterly empty!"*

"This . . . is a Prophecy?" Morg asked, eyeing the neatly inked words dubiously.

"She has been going downhill in coherency with the increase in her age, but yes, I do believe this is a genuine Prophecy," Councilor Thannig said. "She's not a Poetic Prophet, nor a Scribal; she's a Vehement type. She'll spout the oddest of sentences in the midst of a tirade—frankly, I can't even imagine how she managed to charm anyone into marrying her, never mind the late Lord Toskin. But neither am I saying the doggerel of a Poetic would be all that appealing, either . . ."

"Has your department run an analysis of what she potentially means by 'cracking heads' and 'the darkest despair,' or is this scrap of babble all that you have?" Morganen asked the other man.

"Well, the Curse was spoken only yesterday morning, but having seen you, um, cracking a few heads together in the Council Chamber earlier," Lord Thannig offered, clearing his throat awkwardly, "and knowing that the temporal distance of their Foresight lengthens until they're at their peak of maturation, then it foreshortens again as a Seer ages . . . it seems to me that the 'King of Katan' referenced is most likely you. Seer Pellida *is* rather old, after all."

"Majesty!" The call came from one of the other groups in the Hall. "I have an agent in Orovalis City with a possible report of the Duke's activities!"

Absently tucking the paper into one of his pouches, Morganen hurried that way. Reaching the mirror, he faced the teal-uniformed guard on the other end of the connection. "Report."

"*You're* not King Taurin," the guard observed, eyeing him warily through their wood-framed connection.

"Taurin and I got into an argument this morning. He challenged me to a Duel Arcane, which I won. That makes me your new sovereign," Morg explained, quelling his impatience at having to explain, yet again, what had happened. "Report."

"Uh . . . right." The soldier glanced briefly off to the side, no doubt at whoever was the owner of the mirror he was using, then looked back at Morganen. "A man matching Councilor Finneg's description was seen entering a jeweler's shop this morning. Early enough that he had to knock heavily on the door until the proprietor came out and had words with him about the hour, before whatever His Grace said convinced the man to let him in. The jeweler says he purchased two opals, then left. The gold coins used to pay for the opals came from the Imperial Mint in Sekla County, which isn't far from the Duchy of Luichan, up in the northeast corner of the Empire.

"There have also been three reports so far of men matching His Grace's general description having taken rooms at three different inns in the city, but we haven't been able to find any of the three for a verification of their identities," the soldier reported. "Each room is still being searched for possible clues, but I should have a report on any findings soon."

"Thank you." Morganen nodded politely at the Katani soldier and turned away from the mirror. He frowned in thought, then dug out the scrap of paper the Councilor of Prophecies had given him. *Some heads are utterly empty . . . and a man matching Duke Finneg's description purchased opals . . . Of course, the memory spell! The one Alys said her cousin Barol used, back when the Council visited the island . . . Oh, no,* he groaned silently, closing his eyes against the realization. *If Duke Finneg researched the same spell Barol used and bought the opals to store his memories in, then it's most likely he's done something to Hope that he wants to forget, so that the knowledge of it cannot be forced out of him.*

Nausea welled up in him. Sick to his stomach, Morg struggled against his fears. *Seer Draganna Foresaw that we'd be married. We* will *be wed, which means she is still alive, and isn't so badly damaged by the trauma of being kidnapped that she won't want to marry me . . . Though*

*if he's touched her in any inappropriate way, I swear to the Gods I will
invent a spell to turn him inside out while he's still alive.*

Forcing his eyes open, Morganen focused on the men and
women around him. "Keep looking, people! The world isn't so big
that neither of them can hide for long, and the mangled state of the
aether limits both of them to the Katani continent and its nearest
islands. You don't have the whole world to check, just this corner of
it. So keep checking it!—Wait, what are you looking at?" he asked,
staring at the view of a bedroom one of the female Councilors was
scrying. "Is that his bedroom?

"The one for his house here at the capital, yes, Your Majesty,"
the Councilor confirmed. "I thought, if I could find a hairbrush
with some strands in it, maybe on his dresser, or in his private refreshing room . . . maybe we could make some locator pendants?

"*You* are a far smarter mage than I am," Morganen told her. "I
should've thought of that *hours* ago. Get on it, and make as many as
you can. If that helps capture him, I'll give you a rainbow pearl for
thinking of it."

"*Thank* you, Your Majesty!" Grinning, she quickly returned her
attention to her work.

*T*hree *more Names*, Kelly thought, staring at the two unchecked
deities on the last scribbled page of her notepad. *Just three more
Names, and I'm done . . .*

Her throat hurt from talking so much, her eyes burned from
the glow of the Gateway in front of her, and her nerves tingled
from the *pressure* of Divinity to her left. It wasn't a tangible pressure, but there was still something that weighed on her mind,
rubbed through her blood. Pressed against her spirit. *Like too much
sunshine, only I'm not sunburned, just soulburned.*

That was to her left; to her right, most of the priests and priestesses summoned from around the world had dropped off their
benches at the manifestation of their particular God and/or Goddess.

As had some of the island's citizens who had crept into the amphitheater. Some were still kneeling, some were standing, and a few
were flat on the floor in supplication. Some prayed, some cried, others just smiled beatifically, basking in the glow of the Divine.

Kelly felt like she was leaning against that glow, much like she
would have leaned into a stiff wind. She wanted a drink of water, but
had already drunk enough that another trip to the refreshing rooms
was going to be a good idea, soon.

"I Summon Hesten, God of Debauchery and Patron of . . .
Senod-Gra, City of Delights," she read, squinting at the fading pencil marks on the now worn sheet of paper. Arm aching, she gestured
to her left as the light from the Gateway of Heaven rippled. "Please
take a seat among Your fellow Patrons, thank you.

"I summon . . ." She trailed off, catching herself before she could
recite the last name on the list. Licking her lips, Kelly restarted the
Naming. "I summon Nauvea, Goddess of Dreaming, faded Patron
of the ancient kingdom of Nightfall."

That caused a stir of confused interest among the mortals to her
right, and an impression of bemusement from the manifested deities to her left.

"Nauvea?" Saber murmured from his place at her side, half-
emptied water goblet in his hands. Behind him, more Nightfall citizens were creeping into the room with awed expressions, taking
whatever empty spaces they could find on the benches.

Kelly raised her hand to ward off his questions. She still had one
more Name to go, but before she could read it, she had to see if
Nauvea manifested or not. *I promised Hope that I would honor her as
my sister. That includes honoring her beliefs as well as her right to hold
those beliefs. Which includes believing in Nauvea, Goddess of Dreaming.
Even if She has been forgotten by nearly everyone, Hope still believes,*
Kelly thought, staring with sore, watering eyes at the opalescent
brilliance of the Gateway. *That's good enough for me to believe, too.*

Someone laughed. It was a lighthearted chuckle, the sound of a young woman being amused by something. Expecting a ripple in the doorway as tall as any made by one of the other Gods and Goddesses, Kelly squinted at something a lot shorter. Something barely a quarter the height of the oversized doorway. It resolved itself into a woman as young as that laugh had sounded. She had golden tanned skin, brown hair swept up into a loose knot decorated with a large white flower on one side, white teeth that flashed in a grin, and a white dress not too dissimilar to the Natallian kind favored by Serina and Mariel, though hers was only slit up to the hip on one side.

For a Goddess, She looked more like a she, a normal, mere, mortal sort of woman. But She curtsied to Kelly and strode off to the left, claiming one of the few granite thrones that were still unoccupied.

"Thank you *very* much for coming," Kelly told Her, both grateful the Goddess had actually materialized and disappointed Hope wasn't back yet to witness such a miracle in person. Nauvea inclined Her head graciously, and Kelly cleared her throat.

One name left, and then I can start with the petition for Convocation-sized Patronage for Nightfall . . . and after that, I can have a pee while Ora sorts out whatever she needs to discuss. Or maybe I can wait long enough to see what she has to apologize for, she acknowledged silently. *I am lividly curious to know what sort of snaffu was so huge, she has to appear before all of the Gods to make her amends for it.*

"I summon Mekha, Patron of Mekhana, and God of Engineering!"

Kelly waited. She waited a little longer, like she had for Nauvea. Glancing sideways at her husband, she caught his subtle shrug, and wondered if her voice, rough from too much summoning, hadn't been crisp enough. Tucking her notepad into her pouch and taking a deep breath, she tried again.

"I summon Mekha! God of Engineering!" A tickle threatened to make her cough. Grabbing for the goblet, she sipped quickly from it. Before she finished swallowing, before she could get to the Patronage part, the light pouring out of the dual Fountains rippled. It resolved into the figure of a man, tall as most of the other deities, but not completely human.

Where Menos, God of Reefs, had ocean blue skin, Mekha's face and arms bore a pallid, greenish gray hue. It didn't look healthy. His features might have been handsome for a mortal man, but that skin tone made Him seem almost . . . necrotic. Adding to His unnaturalness, one of His arms was attached to His torso by bands of metal at shoulder and elbow, gears and pistons allowing it to move with close to natural grace, though it gave Him a lopsided appearance. Crystals dotted the mechanisms, empowering them, but even their golden glow seemed sickly in comparison with the light streaming at His back.

It was the sort of thing Kelly wouldn't have expected to see outside of anything other than maybe a steampunk graphic novel, back home. The kind where mad science ruled and the laws of physics were magically broken on a regular basis. Of all the Gods and Goddesses summoned through the Gateway of Heaven, this was first deity to unnerve her in an irredeemably unpleasant way.

But it's my duty to acknowledge His presence, even if something within me cannot stand Him, she reminded herself. Drawing in a steadying breath, she addressed the God of Mekhana. "Thank you for joining this Convocation. Please take Your seat with the other Patrons, so that we may begin the various petitions."

"*No.*"

Kelly blinked. Not a single one of the Gods had addressed her beyond a smile or a nod. Now one had spoken, and it was not a speech that she had expected.

Mekha raised His mechanical arm, pointing it at the blonde Darkhanan priestess seated next to the Nightfall family. His voice was gravelly, as if it had been scraped over the jagged teeth of some cog, and it had an otherworldly, almost timeless undertone, a quality which Kelly couldn't quite define. It was also rife with disgust.

"*You offend Me with the presence of that murderer. The abomination must die, before this Convocation may begin!*"

Looking more grim than tired, Ora pushed to her feet. She spared Kelly an apologetic glance. "I *told* you I'd have to be first. May I . . . ?"

Without a clue as to what was going on, Kelly was forced to bow to the request. She gestured for the priestess to take over, retreating back to the benches. Wary, Saber stayed with her, brow creased in puzzlement. Nodding in thanks, Ora moved forward, approaching the center of the amphitheater's floor.

"I am no more of an abomination than you are, Mekha," she stated calmly, chin lifted slightly and shoulders level beneath the black folds of her robe. "I have come before the Convocation of the Gods to tender my most heartfelt apologies for my part in the mayhem and destruction that ended the last Convocation, and resulted in the Shattering of Aiar—I need no Truth Stone to prove these words; You are Deities and can weigh the sorrow and sincerity of my heart at a glance. You know my words are true.

"But what was done in the past cannot be changed. This is the Law of the Universe, which supersedes even the Laws of God and Man," the Darkhanan Witch stated. "I cannot change the mistakes that were made long ago. I can only seek to correct what current mistakes I may uncover.

"When last I came before You, I petitioned for the right to address a grievous, lethal wrong perpetrated against my Guide. I requested that his sentence of everlasting imprisonment in the Dark be eased, and that I be granted the right to live a long and functional enough life to remain his wife until such time that he could regain the life that was stolen from him. Mekha challenged my petition, and did so for nothing more than the petty reason that Sir Niel was an Arbran, scion of Mekhana's nearest rival land."

"Keep your opinions out of your pleas, Daughter of Two Lands."

Kelly didn't see Fate speak, but she knew without a doubt that the eldest of the Gods had done so. How, she didn't know, but she wasn't about to stop and ask anyone. Not when that Voice was so much more supranatural than Mekha's.

Ora bowed in apology. "Forgive me. I do not know the mind of a God, nor am I a Seer, privileged to be blessed with Their thoughts. I can only speak for mortal concerns."

"But you are no longer mortal," Mekha sneered. *"You do not speak for mortal concerns, only your own selfish needs."*

"When I last stood before the Convocation, I was mortal. You challenged my petition. Tempers flared . . . and we fought. I *killed* You, Mekha," Ora stated levelly, coldly. "It was not until after my and my Guide's Goddesses granted us leave to live long enough to correct the wrongs that were done to us that I discovered what You had done. The spells You and Your priests had wrought into Your flesh were what caused the explosion that shattered the Gateway of Heaven, and gouged a huge hole in what used to be the Aian capital.

"It wasn't enough for You to be worshipped by Your people. It wasn't enough for You to be empowered by their faith and belief in You." Her green gaze was contemptuous. "Somehow, You or Your priests found a way to rip the living magic from the mages of Mekhana, augmenting Your powers unnaturally. The first ones were willing, even fanatic in their faith that You should have their power, but the more magic You took, the more You needed to take, and the spells became stronger, the thefts harsher . . . until the mages of Mekhana refused to donate their powers.

"That was when You ordered that they should be hunted down and their powers torn unwillingly from their souls . . . and You and Your priests did this *before* I came to the last Convocation hosted in Aiar." Hands balled into fists, Ora glared at the mechanized God. "One of the oldest Laws of God and Man is that the *difference* between a God and a Netherdemon is that the mortals of this realm worship—and thus empower—their Gods of their own free will!"

Grabbing the hood of her cloak, she flipped it up over her head, obscuring her face, then spun around and stepped back. The folds of her Witch robe billowed out, then parted as she moved back, leaving behind a pile of books nearly as high and broad as a twin bed. Throwing back the hood, Ora glared at her target.

"On and off, for the last one hundred thirty-seven years, I have snuck into Mekhana and questioned its residents. Of their own free wills, with their own hands wielding their own blades and their own pens, more than ninety percent of the population of Mekhana, excluding only its clergy, have signed these tomes of affidavit, and signed them *in their own blood*. More than ninety percent of Mekhanans polled, for more than four generations from all four corners of that realm, do *not* want You as their God any longer.

"*You* have betrayed the trust of God and Man by forcing Your will upon those who do not wish to give their energies freely unto You. It is not a God's place to work against the wishes of His or Her people—the only people *You* can claim as willful worshippers are Your clergy . . . and they are *less* than ten percent of the people who occupy the land of Mekhana," Ora accused. "Clergy are *not* a nation. You are *not* the Patron of the people of Mekhana.

"I may have accidentally caused the destruction of an empire, losing my temper and battling with you two centuries ago, but I *never* forced an entire nation to sustain my life. You. Are. Dead. I *killed* you. The *only* thing still keeping You alive, Mekha, is the power You are *still* raping from the people You were supposed to *protect!*" she snarled. "I call upon the Gods of Heaven to cast *this* abomination into the Netherhells, where It *belongs!*"

Gears spinning, necrotic face mottling a deeper greenish gray in the flush of His fury, Mekha raised His oversized arm, swinging it up in blatant preparation for backhanding the blonde priestess across the amphitheater. Kelly didn't wait for his arm to descend. As far as she was concerned, not even a God had the right to behave like such an arrogant ass.

"Enough!" Bounding off the bench, she strode toward both of them. Jabbing her finger first at Ora, then at the benches behind her, she ordered, "You! Sit down! And *You*," she snapped, thrusting her finger at Mekha, "if You strike down a single being *anywhere* on this island without *my* permission, I swear to all the Gods who are present, I will turn You over my knee and spank the holy shit out of you! *Neither* of you will behave like brawling children in my presence—*is that clear?*"

Mekha sneered. *"You do not give orders to a God!"*

"I *said* . . . Is. That. Clear?" Kelly enunciated, glaring up at Him.

He curled up His mechanized arm again . . . and hesitated under the unflinching force of her stare. There was a very tiny part of Kelly, deep down inside, that wondered at her sheer, brass-balled insanity for what she was doing. The rest of her was firmly entrenched in the memory of what Saber and his brothers had told her over the last year.

"The Gods of this realm *exist* because of the faith and the belief of the mortals of this realm. This was explained to me as the *sole* reason the Gods of this universe exist. It is therefore the *first* Law of God and Man, whether or not it is acknowledged formally as such," Kelly stated, fighting the urge to cough against the tickle that had reformed in her throat. She didn't blink, didn't break away from Mekha's dark gaze. *"You* cannot harm me, because I *do not believe* You can harm me. I do not give You the *power* to harm me!

"Now *sit* Your overgrown ass down—and resize it *appropriately!* Might does *not* make right. Not on *my* island."

He drew in a breath to argue with her. Kelly jabbed her finger at the granite thrones arrayed across the other half of the room. For a long moment, the God of Engineering did not move. Neither did she. Finally, He shifted toward the thrones, shrinking down to a more mortal size, though she noted He stayed large enough to dwarf His fellow Gods.

Lowering her arm, Kelly willed herself to remain calm and controlled in the aftermath of her bravado. A deep breath helped to steady her nerves. "What we have here is an accusation of unlawful conduct by a Patron God against His people. This accusation will be examined for the verification of its facts. Only *then* will an appropriate response be determined."

"You seek to claim the right to dispense justice, in this case?"

Again, Kelly didn't see Fate's lips move, but clearly They had spoken. Clasping her hands to hide their urge to tremble, she lifted her chin. "I am an outworlder by birth, and thus neutral to the politics of this Convocation by my very nature. I claim the right to be the arbiter in this matter. I admit I may have some small gratitude for Priestess Ora's assistance in assembling this Convocation, but I will *not* be swayed by that gratitude when it comes to discerning the facts of any accusation. Particularly one of this magnitude. The only things that will sway me *are* the facts."

The Threefold God studied Kelly for a long moment, then bowed Their head. *"The host of the Convocation has the right to be the arbiter in cases involving the violation of the Laws of God and Man. The Gods and the representatives of each land shall submit to your questioning."*

Now she really felt like trembling. Giving her hands something to do, she pulled out her notebook again. Flipping through the pages of names, she found the one she wanted. "I call upon . . . Veramon, Goddess of Truths, as the judge of the facts. Please come forward, or whatever it is You need to do, and ascertain the nature of these books presented by Priestess Ora," Kelly instructed. "Are they indeed the blood-inked signatures of a majority of Mekhana's citizens? And if so, were they truly marked down of each citizen's own free will as a protest against the continued Patronage of Mekha, God of Engineering?"

"You are asking a foreign God to judge the souls of My chosen people!" Mekha growled. *"Where is the neutrality of that?"*

Kelly lowered her notebook, looking at Him. Veramon was Goddess of one of the many kingdoms that had arisen out of the chaos on the Aian continent, so Her people were far enough away from Mekhana that surely they—and their Goddess by extension—could be considered neutral. But something out of the corner of her eye tugged at her attention. Glancing to her right, she looked over the priests and priestesses seated among the Nightfallers who had joined the Convocation audience.

Most of the clergy in the large hall were no longer on their knees in worshipful awe. Most had resumed their seats on the benches lining the mortal tiers of the amphitheater. Most were staring either at her, or at Ora, Mekha, or even their own deities, absorbing the revelations that had been made. Most, but not all.

Kelly flicked her gaze back and forth between Mekha to her left, and the Mekhanan priest to her right. A priest who was still bound and gagged. Narrowing her own eyes, she looked back at Mekha, then at the other Gods. Tucking the notepad back into its pouch, she planted her hands on her hips.

"You know what I find odd about this whole situation? There, Mekha sits," Kelly stated, pointing at the God of Engineering. "Casting aspersions upon both His accuser and His trial, protesting that He is innocent of all crimes, that He is, in effect, a Good God of His people . . . and *there* sits one of His own priests, bound and gagged by foreign clergy who dared lay their hands upon one of His own servants . . . and yet He has not demanded that the poor man be released!

"If *I* were a Goddess, and I saw one of *my* servants being treated like that . . . I would have snapped my godly fingers and unbound the man the moment after I stepped into the room—and don't give me any crap about You being too busy defending Your honor to have looked around and noticed the condition of Your own servant," Kelly added tartly as Mekha sat forward, scowling and looking ready to argue the matter. "You're a *God*. Or at least, You're supposed to be one. I'll bet even Nauvea, not even worshipped by more than a small handful of people at most, can tell me *exactly* what condition Her servant is currently in.

"Why don't You prove it for us, Nauvea?" Kelly asked, turning to the white-clad, flower-adorned Goddess. "Hope was Your Seer, the last time she lived in this world, under the name of Haupanea. She believed in You all the time that she was exiled to my world, and now that she is back, she still believes in You. She is still willing to be Your mouthpiece—the ultimate definition of a holy servant, because she *believes* in You. So. What is Hope's current location and condition?"

Nauvea smiled. Her voice wasn't nearly as powerful as Mekha's, let alone Fate's, who seemed to be the eldest and most powerful of the Gods, but it did hold the same immortal quality, if muted.

"She is in a dark and lonely place, but she is safe, unharmed, and currently alone. She is praying to Me. More than that . . . She has restored some of My power with her unswerving faith, and you have given Me more, but I am not a Patron Deity at the moment, just a minor godling. I do not have the power to fetch her here . . . however much you may clearly wish it."

"Thank you for Your honesty, at least," Kelly told Her. She was disappointed but not too terribly surprised. *Of course it wouldn't be that easy . . .* Turning her attention back to Mekha, she fixed Him with a chiding look. "If even the weakest and least-worshipped of Gods can tell where Her servant is, then how much more power would You have, who are worshipped by a whole priesthood at the very least? Why didn't You notice the condition of Your servant and lodge a protest?

"Veramon? Would You care to examine this pile of books for their veracity?" Kelly asked.

The dark-skinned Goddess of Truths didn't even uncross Her legs, let alone move from Her seat. *"They are filled with the blood of generations of Mekhanans, each one pledging that he or she does not want Mekha to be the Patron of their land anymore. Of the total population that have lived over the last one hundred thirty-seven years claimed by the immortal, over sixty-eight percent have been polled. Ninety point two percent of those polled signed the books of their own free will, in firm protest against their current Patronage. Seven point eight percent declined out of fear of Mekha's wrath, should He have found out about their choice, and the remainder would not sign anything brought to them by a foreigner.*

"These are the facts, and as such, are Truths." She smiled slightly, looking first at Nauvea, then at Mekha. *"I am beloved by ninety-two thousand three hundred fifty-nine Ramonai, more than enough faith to ensure accuracy."*

Mekha bristled at the accusation hidden in Her tone, but Ora spoke, drawing His attention.

"When Queen Kelly first summoned You by name, Mekha, she included the fact that You were Patron of Mekhana. Yet it wasn't until she repeated Your titles, but skipped the bit about Patronage, that You actually bothered to appear. Or perhaps it was only then that you were *able* to appear," Ora mused mockingly. "You may still be the God of Engineering . . . but You are not the Patron God of Mekhana." The priestess gave Him a dismissive look. "Frankly, given Your apparent narcissism and blatant abuses of the Laws of God and Man . . . you don't *deserve* to be a God."

"We will hear the words of the Mekhana priest," Fate directed. They lifted Their young-old-middle-aged hand. The gag vanished from the priest, though the anti-magic shackles remained. *"Speak the truth, Belaan of Mekhana. We know it is your hidden wish to unburden your soul. Do so."*

The priest worked his mouth, reddened at the corners where the gag had pressed into his flesh for the last two or more hours. "The truth . . . The truth is, I was seduced into serving by thoughts of power over others. I wanted to be one of the ones in control, not one of the ones *being* controlled. I joined the worship of Mekha so that I could be on the *winning* side. And I put it that way, because He is a God at war with His own people.

"I hunted down mage-born children, enslaving them in the name of my God. I sought out the adults who had managed to hide their powers beyond the onset of puberty, and sacrificed not only their life-energy, but their minds to His lust for living. Magic keeps

Mekha alive. I have seen His manifestations wax and wane with the amount of magic I and my fellow priests have managed to drain out of the mage-born slaves we gave to Him." Soul unburdened or not, Belaan's mouth twisted as if spitting out the truth was like spitting out the sourness of a lemon. "Either you give your powers to serve Him, as I have done, or He takes it from you to slake His unending thirst."

"*He speaks the Truth,*" Veramon stated, earning Her another glare from Mekha.

Fate looked at Kelly. "*Arbiter, you have reached your verdict?*"

Kelly shuddered. *You're in the presence of actual, living Gods . . . and one dead one. Of* course *They would know what you're thinking . . . creepy creepy creepy . . . but don't give Them cause for offense, Kelly . . . or a reason for Mekha to try and kill you anyway. Except there's no way to phrase this diplomatically, only politely.*

Clearing her throat, she moved to stand next to the pile of books Ora had deposited on the amphitheater floor. "Yes, Holiness. I have heard and seen enough to make a judgment. Mekha is *not* a Patron Deity. Not by its definition. He does *not* care for the people He claims are His.

"We have heard how a member of His own clergy serves Him more out of fear than out of love . . . and we have seen Him ignore that cleric. He steals His subjects' powers like Broger of Devries tried to steal and use the powers of his relatives." She looked at Mekha over the stacks of weathered tomes. "You know, there is an old saying from my world, in regards to certain belief systems. It went, 'As above, so below,' and it meant that Heaven and Earth should be aligned in how they behave. Mortals are encouraged to behave in Good ways, and Heaven is supposed to be the ultimate definition and repository of Good.

"But in this world, that saying works both ways. As below, so above—what we *believe*, You *become*. Broger and his son Barol both died as a consequence of their crimes, the attempt to steal the powers of others for their own use and purposes," Kelly asserted. "They killed or intended to kill others, and they died for their murderous crimes. Thus it is only fitting that Mekha suffer the same fate. He is *not* a Patron Deity . . . and he is not a God. He is nothing more than a magically enhanced, murderous thief. A bully, beating up whomever he can find for the magical equivalent of lunch money."

"He still holds great power. It is solely by Our combined will that he does not wield it during this arbitration," Fate told her, making Kelly shiver again. *"If he is to be stripped of his godhood, he would still hold that power. What would you have done with it and him, if he is deposed from his Patronage?"*

Kelly blinked, not expecting that question. A quick mental review of what she had learned in the last year about the two subjects of godhood and magic, how Gods were made and how magic circulated through the world, thankfully provided her with an answer. "Well . . . technically, he is not a living, mortal being. He is a manifestation from a time when he did actually care about Mekhanans. Or at least back when they cared about Him. But he isn't mortal flesh and blood. He's just a selfish, self-centered manifestation of group-consciousness and will."

As she spoke, the glowering, mechanized figure in the granite-carved chair shrunk. Kelly dragged her gaze away, not wanting to get distracted by the literal diminishing of a deity, particularly if she was the one responsible for his demeaning.

"So . . . um . . . he should be utterly dissolved, his energies purged of evil and purified to at least a neutral state of moral alignment, and the energy that went into creating him should be infused back into the land of Mekhana. Which, unfortunately, will lose its status as a nation with a Patron," Kelly admitted. She wrinkled her nose, thinking, then added, "Some of his stolen power should be used to break the spells draining magic from the mages of the land, and some of it should be used to destroy the authority and the power base of his clergy. Above all, his power should be used up in such a way that he can never again be manifested as a deity.

"But the rest should be infused into the land to make it healthy, and in turn make the, ah, people formerly known as Mekhanans healthy, too. But don't ask me how any of that can be done, because that's not something I know how to do. I'll defer the actual dissolution and dispersal to the experts . . . which would be You," she told the Gods and Goddesses across the hall from her. "And no weaseling out of Your duties, either, simply because *I* don't know how to do it. If Mekha was stupid enough to steal the powers of his own people, I'm sure he tried to steal mages from other lands, mages who believed in You. That means You have a duty to Your own people to end all of the damage he's done."

"*I* can stand witness to that," Ora interjected. "My Guide and I have barely escaped being drained on more than one occasion during our forays into Mekhana, and we have seen other outlanders who had been rounded up for draining and locked up in their temple dungeons. We did what we could to free them at the time, but there's no telling how many foreigners were sacrificed in Mekha's so-called Name."

"Yes . . . Anyway, that's my judgment," Kelly said, looking from the blonde priestess back to the shifting face of the Threefold God. "By his own actions, Mekha has proven he is unfit to continue to exist as a God. Dissolve his manifestation, disband his clergy, and redistribute his stolen powers in a way that will best serve the people of his former land. They'll have a rough time figuring out what to do with themselves, and who or what to worship next, but at least they'll finally be free to try."

"*You show wisdom and compassion for the people of this world, even the ones who live far from you. We concur with your judgment as arbiter.*"

Fate lifted Their hand again . . . as did every other God and Goddess, including Nauvea. Mekha lifted both of his hands, gears spinning and grayish muscles flexing as he opened his mouth to protest, but it was too late. Wordlessly, soundlessly, he disintegrated and faded within moments. There was no flash of light, no shimmering magical essence, just an image of a mechanized, jumped-up ghoul that dispersed and vanished.

Unnerved, Kelly dragged her attention away from the emptied throne. "Um . . . thank you. I wish that wasn't necessary, but, um . . . anyway . . . I have a request to bring before the Convocation, now that the, ah, first piece of business has been taken care of," she managed, gathering her thoughts. "I am an incipient queen. There aren't many full-time residents on the Isle of Nightfall—not nearly as many as worship You," she added, nodding to the Goddess of Truths, "but the vast majority of us wish to claim our independence from the Empire of Katan, and the citizens of this island have placed their faith in me to lead them.

"Given that I am adamantly in favor of each person having the right to choose to worship whomever they want—and since we've seen being *forced* to worship an unwanted deity is not a good thing," she added, "I'd like to petition all of You, on behalf of my chosen people, to grant Your joint Patronage to Nightfall Isle, making us a full kingdom in our own right and guaranteeing our various rights to worship any and all of You as we so desire.

"As proof of our desire to promote the freedom of religious belief, the people of Nightfall have gone to great lengths to resurrect the Convocation of the Gods," she stated, glancing at the priests and priestesses behind her, as well as the former Katani and Natallian and Gucheran citizens sitting on the benches with them. "It would be our delight as well as our duty under Your joint Patronage to host it again and again, for as long as we can maintain the ability to do so."

Jinga spoke up, his dark face twisting in a wry smile. "*It is customary for the hosting nation to not only go through the lengths it takes to host the Convocation . . . but to provide a special symbol of the Convocation. What is your symbol?*"

"Uh . . . what sort of symbols were used in the past?" Kelly asked quickly, her mind blanking at His request.

"*When the Empire of Fortuna hosted the Convocation, they offered up the silkworm as their symbol, stating it was fitting that the most worthy thread should be used to honor the weaving together of a hundred different faiths,"* Fate stated.

"When the Empire of Dragons hosted the Convocation," another God stated, *"they offered up the* myjii, *imported fruit from the outworld of the Fair Traders, as proof that peaceful communication with all lands would bring a greater prosperity overall."*

"When the Empire of—"

"I got it, thank you," she interjected quickly. The bit about the weird, stinky fruit that Serina's people used had given Kelly an idea. "No offense meant by my interruption, but we do have a lot of priests waiting to have their own say. My sister has brought a fruit from my world to this one, a food so holy, its name literally means 'Food of the Gods.' I, um, would like to offer *theobroma cacao*, and its most precious resulting recipe, *chocolate*, as the symbol of the Nightfall Convocation. I mean, Hope is already a Seer, and that's about as holy as anyone can get on this world, from what I understand. But she's also a *chocolatier*, an artisan who creates divine dishes out of *cacao*. That kind of makes her the High Priestess of Nightfall, since we otherwise don't have one specific organized religion . . . yet.

"So . . . what do You say?" Kelly asked, running out of steam. "Will You grant us Your joint Patronage?"

"What if We say 'no'?"

Kelly blinked, taken aback by Fate's question. "Uh . . . then I suppose we'll just use the remainder of our year-and-a-day to, um . . . convince everyone on the island to start worshipping the heck out of Nauvea, here. She *was* the original Patron Goddess of Nightfall, after all, back when the island was an independent nation, and I included Her Name to honor the history of this land as well as my sister's personal beliefs . . . but I'll still insist on everyone having the right to worship any other God or Goddess out there in addition to honoring the Goddess of Dreaming.

"Because, well, if Mekha didn't have the right to force others to worship only him, then I have even less right to demand that my people worship only Her," she finished.

For one moment, the blurred, changing face of the Threefold God solidified. Fate smiled at Kelly, looking young and happy and yet wise and knowledgeable all at the same time, all with the same face. Then the shifting resumed. In ragged groups and clusters, the other Gods and Goddesses glanced at Fate, each one nodding Their consent.

"Your petition for Our Patronage is granted. Your symbol is acceptable, and shall be regarded with highest honor all around Our world. Announce the next petitioner," Fate directed her, *"and allow the Convocation to continue, Queen Kelly of the Empire of Nightfall."*

The moment she started to bow in acquiescence, Kelly felt something shifting on her head. Hastily raising her hand to catch it before it could fall, she felt cool metal wires bent into angular, polished peaks. She didn't remove the object from her head; if this wasn't the same crown that had been floating up in the donjon since late last autumn, there was no point in fussing over its presence. Somehow, she didn't think the original would still be floating up there.

Instead, she lowered her hands to her pouch, pulling out her somewhat battered notepad. "Of course, Your Holiness. Right away. I call forth, um . . . Priest Etrechim of Fortuna. Priest Etretchim, you're first on the list. You'll have only—ah, the hell with it. Take your time," Kelly told the curly-haired man who had stood when she had called his name. "Don't bother with the ten minute rule, just don't take more than an hour if you don't have to."

Several more wide-eyed women and men were easing into the hall through the normal-sized openings, curious residents come to see the Convocation for themselves. As soon as Priest Etrechim started his petition, Kelly intended to take off for the nearest refreshing room. She hoped the influx of curiosity seekers hadn't formed a long line for them, because she really needed a potty break. But that wasn't her only reason for giving Etrechim and the others enough time to speak with his Patron. It was only fair and reasonable, given how much time she had just spent talking to hers.

"We'll figure out a way to feed and house all of you, however long this takes," Kelly added, glancing at the newcomers. "After all, it's not every day you come face-to-face with the Gods Themselves."

ELEVEN

❦

Morganen frowned, flicking his gaze repeatedly between the three mirrors arrayed in an arc in front of him. Each one was being manipulated by a Councilor who stood to one side, ensuring that the others in the Hall of Mirrors could see. Particularly the three Councilors who stood on the opposite side of the scryer, for each one held a carefully crafted locator pendant and needed to see which direction the Artifact pulled on its thong, in relation to the location being scryed.

It was a clumsy system, but it was working; the triangular wraps of wire, holding a tiny sandwich of glass panes with some of Duke Finneg's hair trapped between them, had been enchanted to react to visual proximity as well as physical closeness. That allowed them to work from the capital of Katan. So long as the aether was relatively calm, the pendants could pick up on anything within a mirror's scrying capacity.

Behind him stood three more mirrors, and six more Councilors.

The ones holding the pendants were looking for Hope; Morg had ordered the silently scrying Consus to head to his rooms, find some hairs of his missing bride-to-be, and pass them through to his former colleagues. So far, their own efforts were bearing far less fruit than the team tracking down Duke Finneg. Their mirrors showed nothing but the rugged slopes and peaks of a small cluster of mountains near the heart of the Empire, with no signs of where Hope might actually be; the aether to the south and west was too turbulent to discern actual details.

Given how calm the aether was to the east, the team in front of Morg had traced Finneg all the way to Nightfall Isle, up through Harbor City, and along a roadway that looked hastily cleared. At least, for the centermost mirror. The other two had swerved out to triangulate better, only to meet dead ends by running into solid mountainside.

Morg didn't recognize what lay at the end of that road, though considering the huge, heavily carved entryway had once been a rugged granite cliff, he could easily guess where the passageway beyond led. The citizens walking up the road, peering at the carvings of plants, animals, and knotwork vines were a second clue. He relaxed marginally, then tensed. If Finneg was somewhere down in the Underhalls, which was what the triangulation of all three pendants suggested, then the mere presence of that gateway suggested the Convocation had begun.

That was both a good thing and a bad thing: good, because it meant Nightfall was quite possibly its own independent, fully Patroned kingdom by now . . . and bad, because Finneg was lost somewhere in that crowd, with intentions and plans that only he himself knew.

Two opals for Barol's Memory Stone spell, Morg mused, studying the central image as the mage manipulated it closer to the entrance. *He's probably already used the first one to forget the first phase of his plan, whatever that had been, to avoid perjuring himself upon a Truth Stone if he's caught and questioned before the second phase can take place. But what is the second phase? He has Hope, his one legal shot at reinstating the duchy and taking back the leadership rights of the island.*

What is he up to now, though? Kidnapping Kelly? Assassinating my brothers? . . . No, he's working more or less on his own. He's not powerful enough for that, and he's not stupid enough to try it anyway . . . Finneg, what are you up to?

A flare of light splashed out of the mirror, making everyone flinch. A familiar voice followed it thundering through the looking-glass.

"You are trespassing on private property! No scrying devices are allowed beyond this point! Turn back now, or you will have your uninvited mirror shattered!"

Morg blinked to clear his vision, letting out a low whistle. "Damn, Rydan—and here I thought you'd be more subtle than that!"

"Majesty?" the mage manipulating the mirror asked.

"You heard the man. That's as far as you go," Morg told him. "Back up the mirror to the road, out of the warning zone, and open it up so I can pass through. I'll take that pendant, there," he added to the Councilor on his right. "It'll be faster from here on if I track him on foot."

"I'm sorry, Your Majesty, but that's impossible," the Councilor said. His hands automatically brushed the wooden frame to back up the intersection plane of the mirror he controlled, but his head shook, accompanying his words. "I can't open a stable Gate from this far away. Not without a second mirror to link it to! I doubt any-one can. You'll have to double-mirror it at the very least, or mirror-Gate to the nearest mainland city, and try to open a second Gate from there."

Rolling his eyes, Morg checked the pouch holding the jar of Gating powder. He still had at least three fistfuls on him, maybe more. "Then I'll do it myself."

The other mage opened his mouth to protest, then wisely shut it. Moving aside, he gestured at the mirror. "Be my guest."

Nodding, Morganen scooped out a fistful of powder and flung it at the mirror, shouting the syllables of Gate Opening. Most of the nearest Councilors yelped and hastily covered their ears, caught off-guard by his sudden spellcasting. Morg dusted off his fingers and held out his hand for one of the three Finneg pendants.

As soon as the woman handed hers to him, he started toward the mirror. Then paused and turned back to the others. Sweeping his gaze around the room, he addressed the watchful Councilors. "*Do* remember that I am the King of Katan . . . and that I *will* return. Conduct yourselves and your searches accordingly. Finneg is a weaker mage than Taurin . . . and he has earned far more of my enmity. *Don't* add yourselves to my very short-tempered list."

Turning, he hopped quickly through the cheval mirror, not wanting to give anyone enough time for the brilliant but deadly idea of breaking the frame and severing him in half. He didn't pause as he passed through the tingling-cold intersection plane, but strode swiftly toward the Underhall entrance. A few of the Nightfallers recognized him, raising their hands and calling out greetings. Morganen nodded politely to each greeting, but didn't bother to reply.

He saved most of his attention for the locator pendant dangling from his fist and the maze of corridors that lay ahead.

ell. You have landed yourself in a mess, haven't you?

Hope's daydream of cuddling up on a soft bed with Morg to help keep her warm, instead of this hard pallet with only a thin, musty wool blanket for bedding vanished. Blinking, she stared at the darkness that had consumed her world, then closed them firmly, re-building her mental haven. *I am lying on a thick, soft featherbed—twice the thickness of the one Morg sleeps on—and he's spooned behind me, arms wrapped around me . . .*

Hey. Mind paying attention when I'm talking to you?

Again her eyes popped open. Hope frowned in confusion, then pulled the thin blanket closer, huddling under its meager shelter.

I am not *going mad this early in my stay. They haven't even brought around the second round of water for the day!*

A snort startled her into pushing up onto her elbow. A moment later, a thin gray glow sprang to life, forcing Hope to squint and shield her eyes. The faint ball of mage-light wasn't bright by any measure, but it was unexpected . . . and it did illuminate the hand and face of a strangely familiar woman.

Blinking to clear her thoughts, Hope stared at her visitor. "*Giolana*? No . . . no, you're long dead . . . and I *am* going mad . . ."

The woman laughed, a soft, tinkling sound.

Hope froze. She *knew* that laugh. Eyes widening, she stared at the barely lit figure. "Nauvea . . ."

Goddess of Dreaming, and Seer made blessed,
Named, now I Am, in flesh Manifest.

"*Your sister is very clever,*" the Goddess continued, smiling as She dropped the doggerel that had always amused Her. "*She has given Me recognition at the Convocation, which in turn has finally given Me enough power to contact you—your prayers were good, your imaginings strong, but alas, not quite enough,*" Nauvea murmured. Her eyes surveyed Her Seer, taking in Hope's mussed hair and manacled wrists. "*Let us both hope she is clever enough. The same for that young man of yours. I like him. Make sure he continues to honor Me.*"

"Of course!" Hope managed, before the grey glow winked out, leaving her in pitch blackness once more. "Nauvea?"

I haven't much strength. It will grow; your sister will likely encourage your islanders to consider becoming My followers once more. Until then, I must save what little I can do for what will come.

Translation, Hope thought, *I can't save your butt, so you'll have to wait for rescue* . . . "I do understand. Um . . . just one question," Hope offered, tucking her head back down on her bicep, her only pillow in this place. "Am I still Your Seer?"

Nauvea chuckled in her mind. *When have you not been?*

"Like, when I was in another world entirely?" Hope retorted. She would have rolled her eyes, too, but it was too dark to bother doing so. "Beyond the reach of all the Gods of this realm?"

I repeat, when have you not been My Seer?

This time, Hope did roll her eyes. *Gods . . . I'd forgotten about having to suffer through all that frustrating, 'mysterious deity' crap . . .*

. . . I heard that.

Hope stuck out her tongue in the dark, then tucked her head more comfortably on her arm. Painstakingly, she built an image of Nauvea, Goddess of Dreaming—who looked remarkably like her long-gone friend and scribe—and imagined herself cuddling her Goddess. Happiness seeped all through her imaginings, warming her to her core. Again, Nauvea laughed softly. Joining Hope's daydream, She cuddled her back.

Forgiven . . . and I will have the strength to Speak through you once again, soon. In the meantime, enjoy your "vacation" from Our Prophecies while it lasts. I don't have enough power to rescue you—yet—but I do have the power to comfort you. Now, rebuild that one where you're cuddling with your man. I like the warmth and love in that particular daydream.

Feeling far happier than should have been possible in her situation, Hope complied.

Morg looked between the locator, straining at the end of its dowsing thong, and the blonde woman seated on the bench. He had slipped into the back of the amphitheater, moving along the back wall so that he could do a rough triangulation of Finneg's location. The duke *was* in this hall, and if the pendant was in the least way accurate, it *was* straining toward the blonde woman on the bench in front of him. Swinging his arm out to the side only changed the angle that the locator strained toward her.

Either we accidentally snagged hairs from a woman who used his hairbrush—though those hairs balled up between the slips of glass look dark and curly to me—or he's wearing some sort of glamour. Squinting with mage-sight didn't dispel the image of a slender woman clad in the blue linens of a castle servant. A servant Morg didn't recognize.

Definitely not one of ours, but also not an illusion—maybe a potion? No, those wear off after a set period of time. It could be a shapeshifting spell, but if so . . . I've underestimated his power. It takes a great deal of will as well as power to reshape one's gender.

It doesn't matter. There's one spell in my arsenal that will cut through any disguise, whether it's a glamour, a spellshift, or an elixir, the one I shared with Trevan half a year ago. The question is, do I unmask him here, or elsewhere?

She rose from her seat. Morganen quickly jerked the pendant down, twining the ribbon around his fist to hide it. He focused his attention on the Gods at the other end of the hall, doing his best to seem like just another respectful believer. Out of the corner of his eye, he saw her working her way toward the door . . . and saw a figure in aquamarine silk slip through the door ahead of the blonde.

Kelly. He's after her. Rising, Morganen followed both of them. He didn't bother to disguise himself, and he knew the blonde saw him, for she glanced behind her as she entered the hallway beyond the amphitheater. A glance past her showed Saber in the corridor as well as Kelly; apparently his eldest brother was being smart enough to escort his wife. *Good. She'll be protected from that side of things.*

The blonde glanced behind her again, blue eyes widening when she saw him staring straight at her. She hurried to round the corner, following in Kelly's wake. When Morg followed *her*, she frowned at him, raising her voice so that it rang clearly down the empty side passage. "Are you *following* me?" Facing forward, she hurried toward Kelly and Saber, who had glanced behind them at her words. "Excuse me! This man is following me, and it's making me very uncomfortable!"

Morg didn't waste any more time; slashing his hands through the air in an open, tapered *V*, he muttered the words that would confine "her" to her true form. Muscles bulged, the sleeves of "her" blouse ripped, but the most blatant part of the transformation came from the rapid darkening of Duke Finneg's skin. Saber jerked Kelly behind him, hand flinging up with a visibly rippling ward. Finneg spun around, but Morg didn't give him a chance to either attack or find a way to escape.

Snapping his fingers, Morg wrapped the older mage in a variation of his tendril-spell. This one engaged all of Finneg's personal shields and wards, tearing into them and forcing the older man to focus on magically defending himself. Striding forward, Morganen hauled back his arm, and punched Finneg in the jaw. A physical attack, and a very effective one . . . though his knuckles throbbed from the harsh blow.

The renegade Councilor crumpled. Kelly peered around Saber's shoulder, staring at the unconscious man on the floor. Only then did Morg realize she was wearing the crown of Nightfall. The last he had seen it, the wrought wire circlet, with its stylized, ragged peaks suggesting the north and south mountain ranges of the Isle, had still been floating over the bench-throne in the donjon of the palace. Now it perched on his sister-in-law's head.

"Gods," Kelly muttered, staring at the unconscious ex-Councilor. "Just when you think it's safe to go to the bathroom again . . . !"

Morganen shook out his fingers, soothing the sting even as the movement wrapped Finneg in a containment ward. The unconscious duke lifted up off the floor. "I think he intended to follow you to the refreshing room and ambush you. Probably to kidnap you, if not kill you outright."

"Have you found Hope, yet?" Saber asked, looking past Morg for any sign of her.

"No," Morg admitted grimly. "But I'm working on it."

Kelly shook her head. "We heard Nauvea say she's in a dark and lonely place, but I don't see how that can help you."

"Dark and lonely . . . ? Gods—of *course!*" Morganen smacked his palm against his forehead as all the pieces themselves fit together. "The Oubliette! Which is *controlled* by the Department of Conflict Resolution. He not only wanted to stick her in there, he bought those opals to literally forget what he'd done with her, and no doubt what he was going to do with you. As the head of the department, he'd have full access to it!

"He might even have the authority to incarcerate her without filing any paperwork—or at least conveniently 'losing' it! Gods—no wonder he claimed he didn't want the paperwork on his resignation to go through until tomorrow," Morg muttered, raking his fingers through his hair. "I have to get back to the Council . . ."

Saber arched one of his honey blond brows. "*You* have to 'get back' to the Council of Mages?"

"Is there something we need to know about, Morg?" Kelly added, planting her hands on her hips. "I *sent* you to Katan to be *diplomatic* about requesting their help. So help me, if you've mucked things up even *worse* with them—"

Morg's cryslet rang, startling all of them. Flipping open the lid, Morg peered through the oval, surprised to see Consus peering back. "Lord Consus? How did *you* get a cryslet?"

"Through one of the maids, who was kind enough to help me contact you. I had taken the liberty of continuing to monitor the Council after your return to the island, since I couldn't follow you into the mountain," the middle-aged mage explained. "I'm afraid they're rebelling against your rule, Your Majesty."

"Your *rule*, 'Your Majesty'?" Saber repeated, skepticism raising his voice as well as his brows.

Morg snapped up his free hand, staving off his eldest brother. "Thank you for the warning, Lord Consus. I'll return and deal them as soon as I can get back up to you. Finneg's been captured, and I think I know what he did with Hope. Do you know which mirror the Department of Conflict Resolution uses to transport prisoners to the Oubliette? Where it's located, how it's accessed, how it's warded—anything?"

"The Oubliette?" Consus shook his head. "That's another department's secret. I could tell you which department has been smuggling goods and laundering funds along the Empire's coastline, but not that. Rumor does suggest that the prisoners are held for a mandatory five years before their cases can even be looked at for a parole review. Rumor also has it that only the current department head has the power to communicate with the Oubliette . . . and if you've captured him, I doubt that His Grace would be inclined to cooperate in handing over the secrets of his office, let alone assist you in your endeavor."

Morg narrowed his eyes. "I am *not* waiting five years to rescue her. Find *another* solution—or find a happier rumor!"

The bland look Consus gave him was undoubtedly the result of decades of navigating through far worse political shoals. "I cannot. The Oubliette is well hidden, with only one known mirror connection, which is controlled by the head of the Department of Conflict Resolution. Its cells and corridors are shrouded in complete and constant darkness, which foils any attempts at scrying. It . . ."

He trailed off, his forehead creasing in a frown. Morg quirked his brow. "It, what?"

"Actually . . . that's not completely true. I was reading a book just a few weeks ago—one of the Vo Mos books, in fact. The one about—"

"Blood mirrors, of course!" Morg agreed. "I've read that one, too. In fact, that would be a *lot* faster than going back, forcing the Council back into submission, and trying to get Finneg to cooperate."

"Blood-mirrors?" Kelly asked him. "Isn't that the thing you did to track down Baroness Teretha's killer?"

"Yes, and all I have to do is . . . oh, *Gods*," Morganen muttered, grimacing. "I *can't* open up another blood-mirror! I can't do so for another half turn of Brother Moon; that kind of magic works only once a month!"

Saber glanced abruptly at his wife, gaze flicking from her to his youngest brother and back. "You cannot . . . but maybe *she* can."

"*What?*" The exclamation came from both Morg and Kelly. They glanced at each other, startled by the idea.

"What?" Saber asked as Morg eyed him warily. "Vo Mos is an entertaining writer, and we *have* been dealing with a lot of mirror-magic, lately. It only made sense to read his book."

Consus' voice wafted up from Morganen's wrist. "It would only work with a non-mage if they were a blood relative with the person they wanted to contact, and worked in conjunction with a mage . . . but a blood-mirror made by a blood-relative *should* also extend the strength of the spell, if they have anti-scrying wards set in place. Which, given the paranoid level of security the Oubliette is supposed to possess, they just might have. In fact, it would be best if both sides cast the blood-mirror, or at least opened a vein."

Kelly eyed at the bluish white scar on her palm. "Um . . . how *much* blood would be required, exactly?"

"If we're going to make a mirror big enough to safely pull her through, about a pint," Morg told her. "But no more than that. And you'll have to make the cut of your own free will, keeping your purpose firmly in your mind the whole time you're bleeding, or it won't work."

Saber laughed, a short, sharp, scoffing sound. "Trust me, if she had an ounce of *magical* power in her veins, she'd be a match for any one of us, Brother. Even you. Kelly's *will*power isn't an issue."

"What are all of you talking about?" Morganen turned, spotting the tall, pale-haired figure of his sister-in-law, Serina. Pregnancy and childbirth had added a few pounds to her slender curves, but it hadn't detracted from her sharp mind. Her amber gold eyes flicked over Finneg's floating, spell-wrapped form, and one of her platinum blonde brows arched. "Is that Hope's kidnapper?"

"She's been thrown into the Oubliette—it's a high-security dungeon for troublesome mages," Morg explained. "Kelly's going to help me open up a blood-mirror to pull her out."

"Good. Dominor's keeping an eye on the twins while I'm going to the refreshing room, so I'll just go a little farther and get my lock-picking tools." She gave all three of her in-laws a pointed look in return for their puzzlement. "If she's trapped in a high-security dungeon, she's bound to be locked up in anti-magic chains. That means you'll need someone who knows how to pick a lock. Which *I* know how to do. Those anti-magic shackles you put on the Mendhites this morning were the very same shackles I picked off of Dominor, back when he and I first met in Port Blueford."

"You have a point," Saber agreed. "But that doesn't address the problem of Hope needing to open a vein *before* her locks are picked."

"No problem," Kelly answered, drawing their attention back to her. "*Every* faction that worships a Deity or Deities has the right to petition their Patrons. Ora told me about that, back when she first asked to petition the Gods. All I have to do is petition Nauvea, acting on Hope's behalf since she isn't here to do it herself, and ask Her to assist us. I mean, if nothing else, we could ask Her to at least warn Hope that she's about to be rescued. Unless you think my blood-mirror alone will be enough?"

"Let's hedge our bets as much as possible," Morg muttered. "Serina, go get your tools. I'll get a silver tray to catch the blood—wait, I need to do something with Finneg."

"Keep him down here; I'll bring the tray as well as the tools," Serina stated, speaking over her shoulder as she walked away.

Kelly eyed the unconscious mage. "You know, I think I have an idea on what to do with him . . . that is, assuming 'Your Majesty' will agree with me on what his just and proper punishment should be. By the way, you still owe us *that* story—but not just yet, because I *really* have to pee!"

Morg chuckled, letting her and Saber hurry away. He glanced at his cryslet. "Again, I must thank you, Lord Consus. You've been an invaluable help to Nightfall. If I thought an order to reinstate you as Councilor of Sea Commerce would actually last, I'd do it in a heartbeat."

"That won't be necessary. I believe I like dealing with you Nightfallers a lot more than I ever liked dealing with my fellow Katani. *Your* style of politics are a lot more interesting, and a lot less cutthroat," Consus told him. "I've felt far more alive just in the last few days than I've felt over the last few years, and more alive in the last few months than in the last few decades. Do you think the Queen of Nightfall might have need of a bureaucrat experienced in the art of coastal and oceanic trade?"

"Ask her yourself," Morg promised, keeping an eye on the recumbent form of his prisoner. "But I'll put in a good word, if you want."

*W*ake up!

Hope jerked out of her doze, her meandering dream disrupted. Gray light sprang to life, making her wince away from it. "Nauvea . . . ?"

Wake up and get ready. Your lover is preparing to rescue you, but since I cannot help much beyond talking to you, you'll have to help both him and yourself.

Rubbing the sleep from her eyes, Hope sat up. "How do I do that?"

Nauvea grinned, then vanished, though the tiny mage-light remained. *Have a drink if you're thirsty, wash your hands and forearms in the water bucket as best you can . . . and then break your water bucket. You won't want to break the slops bucket for this job.*

She had already used the slops bucket earlier, and used a precious, small amount of water to wash her fingers. Frowning, Hope eyed the bucket. "You want me to *break* it?"

The gray mage-light zipped around her cell, revealing rounded, rough-hewn walls, the hard, dark gray basalt of the floor, the slops bucket to her left, the water bucket to her right, and her pallet.

Do you see anything other than the wood of the bucket that could form a sharp enough point? You have to create a blood-mirror, Hope. I don't have the power to rescue you; only you and your sister currently do. And that man you love . . .

"Well, he's *my* man, so keep Your daydreams about him to Yourself," she quipped, eyeing the bucket under the glow of the dim ball of light. It was sturdy, well-jointed, but age-worn; the metal bands encircling the staves near the top and bottom were rough and pitted from rust.

Nauvea chuckled.

"Right. Break the bucket." A glance at her chains showed she had plenty of movement available, enough to have almost reached the door of her cell. Shuffling on her knees to the edge of the pallet, she dipped her hands in the water, scrubbing them as best she could, then picked up the half-full bucket . . . and paused in thought. Shifting to the other end of the hard, lumpy bed, she carefully poured the contents into the slops bucket.

A wordless query tickled the back of her mind.

"If I just smashed the bucket, it would spread water all over the floor," she explained under her breath. "I need undiluted blood to form the mirror . . . I think. Either way, I'm not going to take the chance. Okay," she muttered, lifting the emptied bucket high over her head. "Here we go . . ."

CRACK! Smashing it down on the floor as hard as she could, Hope gritted her teeth against the stinging jolt of impact. Part of the bucket did indeed crack, but the tiny glow from Nauvea's gray wisp was enough to show she'd need a second hit.

CRACK!

Or maybe a third blow . . . *CRA-ACK!*

Pieces skittered across the floor. Two of them looked jagged enough to damage her wrists. Picking up the closer of the chunks, Hope hesitated. "Um . . . now?"

Yes, now.

She wrinkled her nose. "This is going to hurt, isn't it?"

Undoubtedly. But the local aether is too disturbed for a one-way mirror to reach you. Even a blood-mirror backed by the formidable will of your sister and the formidable power of your chosen man will not be enough on their own.

"His name is Morganen," Hope stated, using her own words to

bolster her courage. "And I *will* see him again, in just a few minutes—and he *will* heal me and stop the bleeding, because I have no intention of accidentally committing suicide in the middle of my escape attempt."

Nauvea chuckled. Using that familiar laugh to bolster her courage, Hope held her breath, steeled her nerves, and slashed at her wrist with the jagged piece of wood.

Kelly waited impatiently for a break in Etrechim's recital of his people's praises, good deeds, and spiritual concerns. Finally, he came to an end. Hurrying down the steps, she called out, "Um, Nauvea, if I may petition you very quickly on behalf of my sister . . ."

"*She is ready*," Nauvea stated. "*Do not delay your own duties.*"

"Huh? . . . Oh, right! The next person," Kelly realized. Hastily she dug out her notebook. "Uh, that would be . . . Priestess Saleria of Katan. Speak your piece, worship the, uh, Father Kata and Jinga as you see fit . . . and I'll be back in a little bit. Here, Lord Dominor," she added, moving over to her brother-in-law so she could offer him the notebook. "You're my Chancellor, so you get to do stuff whenever I'm busy. Just run down through the list of priest names in the order they're written if I'm not back quickly enough. Queenly business, and all . . ."

Dropping the notepad on the bench next to him, since he was holding one of his sleeping infants while Evanor cradled the other, Kelly hurried back out of the amphitheater.

Someone was trying to invade the island. At least, that was what Morg's private warding spells were trying to tell him. Unfortunately, they hadn't extracted Hope from the Oubliette, yet. *Whoever it is, whatever it is . . . they'll have to wait. Even Kelly will admit this is the priority, right now.*

He watched anxiously as Serina first levitated herself, then inverted her floating body over the crimson-filled platter. Whatever antigravity spell she used, it prevented both the panels of her tunic-dress and her knee-length braid from falling onto the edge of the visceral pool he had just cast open. Dipping through the dark red opening, she vanished down to her waist. On the other side of the platter and the inverted Arithmancer, Saber finished healing the cut Kelly had made across her wrist with her own dagger.

Unfortunately, Morg would have to wait to salve Hope's own wounds until after she came through. *First we rescue her, then we heal her, then I go take care of whoever thinks they can approach the Isle from the east side. Probably more Mendhites . . . and I've already expended roughly half my power, today.*

Serina took forever, or so it seemed. Morg stifled his impatience as he waited, but it did seem to take far too long. Finally, she pulled back. He watched to see Hope following her, and frowned when Serina righted herself without any sign of the Seer. "Couldn't you free her?"

"Oh, I freed her. I even healed her wound. *And* I set up a mage-light to give her enough to see by; it's not exactly a cheery place, over there," Serina added. "But I don't know enough about blood-mirrors to know if it will close as soon as she uses it to come across . . . and you do have a prisoner in need of a bit of tit-for-tat justice," the Arithmancer reminded him, glancing pointedly at the still-unconscious duke Morganen had moved into the room.

Kelly nodded. "You've read my mind. Let's dump *him* in the Oubliette. It might be cruel, but no worse than everything he's tried to do to us, and everything he would have done, if he could've gotten away with it."

"What about the Council?" Saber asked. "They might object to his incarceration. Not that I don't agree with you; he *was* here to capture you and lock you in the Oubliette, too, if not kill you outright. But we do have to consider the political fallout of locking him up."

"I think I can handle that part," Morg dismissed, gesturing at

Finneg's body. The unconscious mage lifted from the floor and twisted, inverting as Morg guided it to the blood-mirror. "I still have to go back and quell a certain little rebellion against my authority. I *was* going to give up the crown of Katan as soon as I had Hope back . . . but now I'm thinking a little more supervision is in order."

"Oh? What sort?" Kelly asked him.

"I'll reinstate Taurin, but only as King Pro Tem . . . a position he'll hold *only* by my will, as Regent of Katan. If I don't like the way how he and the Council act, I'll go back and—as you put it so delicately, Sister—kick their butts again. All the way to a Netherhell and back, if need be," Morg added, turning his attention to floating Finneg through the scarlet pool. A flick of his other hand levitated his own body. He might have been able to kneel on the floor and bend over the pool the magicless way, but he didn't want to brush the edges of their makeshift looking glass.

Blood rushed to his head—trapped safely inside his skin—but only as long as it took him to dip his head through the opening. A brief glance upward showed Finneg's ward-wrapped body bouncing gently against the coarse-chiseled ceiling. Smirking, he looked over at the other occupant of the cell. Hope smiled at him. She looked tired and she was still cradling her pink-scarred wrist, but she looked alive and well.

Morg glanced up at Finneg, then back down to her again. "Did he hurt you?"

Relieved to see him again, Hope almost couldn't speak. Serina had been a sight for sore eyes, but the Arithmancer wasn't nearly as important as Morganen. She shook her head, half-tangled curls sliding over her shoulders. "No . . . he just tried to convince me to marry him, and then knocked me unconscious when I refused. As if I ever would," she scoffed, not giving the duke even a contemptuous glance. "I'm in love with *you*."

"Good. Because that's probably one of the very few things in either this world or Kelly's that would make me mad enough to actually kill someone." Twisting, Morg levitated Finneg's body down to the lumpy pallet resting to one side. "Snap those manacles on him, will you? I don't want to burn my skin by touching them, since I'm using magic at the moment."

Hope nodded, shifting from her rump to her knees so that she could shuffle around the blood on the floor. The middle of the ceiling was high enough, she could have stood up, but the middle was also the location of the mirror. "Serina said I should probably be the one to do that, once you brought him through. As it was, she made them hot just from her own touch while she was floating halfway through the mirror."

"Don't dawdle. I want nothing more than to hold you in my arms and praise the Gods you're safe and well, but I can't do that until he's locked up and you're safely back home."

Nodding, Hope manhandled Finneg's limbs into position as Morganen released the warding spell around the unconscious mage. By the time she reached the fourth rune-carved manacle, Finneg was beginning to stir. Grunting, he rolled onto his side, then pushed up onto his elbow.

Morganen quickly blocked his foot from dragging through the edge of the blood-mirror, holding it still so Hope could clamp the last manacle in place, but that drew the older mage's attention. Starting, Finneg peered all around him, brown eyes wide, then focused on the two of them.

"What the—*you!*" Jerking his hand forward to cast a spell, he hissed as the magic sizzled and soaked into the nearest cuff. He quickly shook his wrist, doing his best to cool the briefly heated metal. Shooting a nonmagical glare at both of them, Finneg sneered. "Do you really think you can hold *me* prisoner? When the King Taurin finds out what you have done, imprisoning a member of his own Council . . . !"

"Somehow, I don't think the *current* King of Katan gives a damn about you," Morganen shot back. Flicking his wrist, he levitated Hope off her knees. She gasped, then *snerked* when he added,

"Particularly when you tried to lock up his wife-to-be *and* his sister-in-law in your precious little Oubliette. *Do* enjoy the accommodations. I'll get around to telling the Council of Mages what I've done with you. Eventually."

"The slops buck is to your left," Hope instructed Finneg as Morganen retreated through the mirror. "The water bucket normally sits to the right, but you'll have to wait for the guards to come back this evening before you can request a replacement. You might have to be *very* nice to them to get a new one, but don't worry. They won't rape you," she added, straightening her legs under Morganen's magical hold so that she could fit through the blood pooled on the cavern floor. "*They're* not the criminals, in this place.

"See you in five years if you pass your—sorry, *my*—parole review!" she called out quickly, before her shoulders and head vanished through the warmth of the mirror-Gate.

As soon as she floated free, Morganen left her hovering over the mirror, hurrying to seal it before Finneg got the smart idea of brushing one of his anti-magic manacles against the blood-mirror Hope had made on the cell floor. Tossing down his last fistful of powder and shouting the words that closed the portal, he added an extra phrase at the end. The scarlet pool curdled, browned, and dried in the space of three heartbeats, leaving a dark, flaky mess.

Only then did he pull Hope down to her feet and into his arms. Hugging her close, he buried his face in her hair, allowing himself a shudder of relief that she was safe. "Please let Nauvea know how much I honor Her," he whispered into her ear. "She heard all of my fervid dreams of getting you back, safe and sound, and She helped me to fulfill them."

I told you I liked him. Natua does, too. She worked with Morganen, acting through Her Seer, Milon, Mariel's late husband, until both you and I could return, Nauvea whispered in Hope's ear. *Now that I'm back, We'll be able to help shape and guide the world that is to come, thanks to you, and him, and that odd but endearing sister of yours . . .*

Well, that's good and fine, Hope thought firmly at her Goddess.

You can spy on my daydreams and night-dreams all You want, and use me as Your Seer when the timing is once again right, but I'd really prefer a bit of privacy—or at least a lack of commentary—whenever I'm snuggling in my Morganen's arms. He's mine, *dammit.*

Unoffended, Nauvea chuckled as She left. Or maybe She just fell silent. Hope didn't know which was which, but then that was just one of the many things she would have to cope with again, now that she was a Seer with a Goddess once more.

Breeeeeeedeeeeng! Breeeee—

Reacting quickly, Saber snapped open the lid of his cryslet. "What is it? Dellen? Why are you calling?"

The maid's voice came through loud and clear. Or rather, loud and strident. "*First* of all, there's a huge fleet massing on the eastern horizon. *Second*, the Mendhites have gotten loose and they're trashing the palace! And *third—I QUIT!*"

Saber flinched back from the Artifact on his wrist, wincing at her vehemence.

"This is the *third* time I've been attacked today, and I am *not putting up with it anymore*! Unless you plan on tripling my salary and replacing my clothes, you can *forget* it! I'd rather work in an inn!"

"Replacing her clothes?" Kelly asked, puzzled.

"Finneg's outfit. He must have attacked Dellen," Morg offered.

"Dellen, calm down," Saber ordered. "We'll round up the Mendhites. Just get yourself out of the palace and somewhere safe; we'll be up there shortly."

Kelly caught his hand, swinging the mirror of his cryslet over to her. "Dellen, just calm down, make sure you're safe, and take some time to cool off, okay? You're very good at your job, and you definitely should be able to work in a safe environment. Once everything's settled down, we'll discuss safety wards and hazardous duty pay, bonuses and recompense, and we'll see what sort of reasonable compensations and precautions we can make for the future, alright?"

The woman on the other end of the mirror connection muttered something uncomplimentary-sounding.

"Would you at least *think* about staying?" Kelly asked. Dellen grumbled something, and Kelly nodded, closing the lid of her husband's cryslet. She gave Saber a defensive look. "What? Good employees are hard to find! And we really do need to implement some sort of hazardous-duty pay system."

"We have an invasion to worry about," he countered. "I don't know how they got out of their manacles, though."

"What, did you think I'm the only one in the world who can pick a lock?" Serina asked, rolling her amber eyes.

"Be that as it may, we need to round them up fast, or we won't have a home left," Saber said. "We're going to need Rydan and Dominor, Koranen—"

"I'll do it," Morg interrupted. "I can do both, no problem. Three Mendhites aren't a challenge, and all I have to do with the ships is shove them back across the ocean before they can land any troops." That earned him a hard, assessing look from his eldest brother, but Morg didn't flinch.

"Bring the Mendhites down here once you've captured them," Kelly instructed Morg. "They're really only here because of the second Fountain. If they *see* that the Convocation has already begun, then maybe that'll knock sense into them and they'll stop acting up. I'll sentence them later when I have the time for it, but I want them to stop fighting against us now."

Over the ocean the Mandarites roam
Tell them to send all the holies back home

Saber, Kelly, Serina, and Morg all stared at Hope. She blinked in confusion, then flushed with embarrassment. "Did I, um, say anything just now?" They nodded, and she winced. "Um, sorry. Nauvea likes to pretend She's a poet."

Laughter filled the back half of Hope's mind, relieving her that her Goddess wasn't mad.

Morg hugged her. "We'll get used to it, I'm sure. I'd like you to come with me," he told her. "That might seem to put you in danger, but I don't want to let you out of my sight again, at least for a while."

Hope squeezed him back. "Relax. I *know* I'll be safest with you— no offense to the rest of the family."

"None taken," Saber agreed. "Now get upstairs and stop them from wrecking our home, Brother, or I'll take it out of your hide."

Morg flipped him a mock-salute, thumping his fist across his chest. Hope caught his other arm, dragging him out of the room. "This way; I know a shortcut . . ."

The Mendhites were still wearing their anti-magic shackles when Morg captured them. It was only their nonmagical bonds they had broken, and the destruction they were wreaking was nothing more than the results of brute force. That explained why Dellen got away so easily a second time. Actually, only two of the Painted Warriors were breaking into locked cabinets and tossing around papers in the rooms of the north wing. The third man still had one arm wrapped in a cast from knuckles to elbow, supporting the bones the Healers had spell-knitted back together.

Capturing them simply required the same spell Morganen had used on that Katani Councilor, the one who had stolen away Queen Samille's warding-crystal. Their feet trapped in bonds of stone and their wrists, ankles, or throats wrapped in magic-draining runes, they literally had no way to fight back, let alone run. Leaving them there, Morg escorted Hope over to the east wing, aiming not for his quarters on the second floor, but the third floor and Consus' door.

He opened it a second before they arrived. "Finally. You have a lot of damage-control to do," Consus told Morg. "The Council of Mages is now debating whether or not to declare war on Nightfall, citing the legal precedent of 'harmful interference in the governance of their former nation' as an act of rebellious terrorism, not an act of rebellious independence."

"They have no legal grounds," Morg dismissed. "Taurin challenged me fair and square—I even gave him an opportunity to back out of his challenge, but he didn't. But they can wait. We have a fleet approaching from the east, and I wanted to use the mirror I left with you to get a good look at them."

Consus waved his arm at the mirror lying flat on the table, and moved back to monitor the one in the cheval stand that Morganen had salvaged from his home. "Help yourself—I sincerely hope you were not harmed by your kidnapping, Your Grace," he added to Hope. "Duke Finneg lost his mental stability some time ago, and I regret that he took out his imbalances on you."

"I'm fine. A little tired of being knocked unconscious, but I'm safe and sound. What is *that* thing?" she asked, pointing at the figure-eight frame hung on the wall of his sitting room. The twin ovals of silvered glass had captured her attention the moment she entered the room. Hope couldn't look away.

"Uh . . . just a dual mirror. It . . . What are you doing?" the ex-Councilor asked her warily.

Compelled by her instincts, Hope crossed to the wall and lifted her hand. The moment her fingers brushed against the silver frame, faces filled both mirrors, fluttering and shifting. Voices babbled in snippets of conversation. Curious, she trailed her finger up along the outer right edge, and stopped when her instincts said to stop.

As the two mages in the sitting room stared, she studied the moon-round faces, tanned and vaguely familiar. Mendhites. They were talking back and forth, something about ship deployments. Instinct brought up her other hand. Spreading her index and middle fingers, Hope touched both panes of glass simultaneously. The images rippled, and the Mendhites blinked with shock.

"Who are you? How did you break into this scrying?"

Well? Talk to them! You know who they are, Nauvea prodded her. *They have twenty of these ships, each one linked to the next by a relay of*

mirrors just waiting to be opened in sequence, and each one scattered in a line from here to the Bay of Mendham.

"Uh . . . gentlemen. I am the Seer Hope of Nightfall. I am bidden by my Goddess to have you spread these words among your little fleet of twenty ships," she stated, carefully matching her accent to theirs so that her dose of Ultra Tongue would ensure she was understood. "The Convocation of the Gods has been reinstated, and the Gods have given Their joint protection to Nightfall.

"Any further attempt on your part to steal away the components needed for opening the Gateway of Heaven will be considered an act of war, and dealt with appropriately—and by 'appropriately,' gentlemen," she warned them, "I *do* mean that my Goddess will step halfway around the world, turn you over Her knee, and spank the holy spirit out of you.

"Furthermore," Hope continued as they gaped at her, "your three agents caused a great deal of property damage and even some personal injury, here on Nightfall. Your government will be fined an appropriate amount for the physical damages by Her Majesty, Queen Kelly of Nightfall . . . and my Goddess has bidden me to tell you that your fleet and their mirrors are to submit to being commandeered."

"*Commandeered?!*" the man in the left-hand oval protested. "You have no authority to dare such a thing!"

Oh, for the love of Us . . . !

Mid-splutter, the man's eyes snapped to the side, widening until a ring of white surrounded the brown of his irises. "*Goddess . . .*" he whispered.

The man in the right-hand oval was also staring to the left, equally shaken.

"As . . . as the Goddess wills it," the man on the left said after a long pause. He cleared his throat and looked out at Hope again. "I apologize profusely for any damage our agents may have done . . . and we *will* accept our charge of giving safe transport home to the holy emissaries of the world. So swear I, Dakim Leje!"

"Um . . . just one question," the man on the right offered hesitantly. "What was the, ah, fate of the three Puhon brothers?"

Morg moved up behind Hope, resting his hands on her shoulders. "They have been captured and given medical treatment. Once our queen is no longer busy with the immediate needs of the Convocation, she will pronounce sentence upon them, giving them an appropriate punishment for their crimes. Expect to be fined very heavily in coins and trade goods. We know the Puhon brothers, as you called them, were offered a contract to kill Her Majesty. It was offered by a Katani official turned renegade—oh, and don't look for any further help from Katan. There's been a change of leadership in the Empire, and with it, a change in policy."

"We'll contact you when the Convocation is over, when we know which priests and priestesses will need your assistance in returning home again," Hope said. She double-touched the mirrors again. The images of the Mendhites rippled, dissolving back into a reflection of Consus' sitting room.

"Fascinating," Consus muttered. "Now, tell me *how* you made that mirror work in all of our presences, when up until now, it has only ever worked when someone was completely alone with it?"

Hope shrugged, turning to face him. "Instinct. Just . . . instinct. I saw the mirror, and just knew I could do things with it."

Morg exchanged a look with Consus. "Fascinating, indeed. She's a Seer, not a mage . . . but then that's not a normal scrying-mirror, is it?"

Consus opened his mouth, closed it as he reconsidered, then let out a sigh of resignation. Giving Hope a gracious bow, he said, "Even I can see the hand of the Threefold God in this matter. Not only in allowing the creation of it, but in arranging for it to come to your attention, Lady Seer. You may consider it your wedding gift."

"Thank you . . . though I honestly didn't know any of that would happen until it actually did. So . . . um, shouldn't we be looking at that fleet?" she asked, glancing up at Morg.

"Right. The fleet." Returning to the mirror on the table, Morg activated it, stroking and tapping the frame to adjust its view over to the eastern half of the island.

It didn't take long to find the fleet. Sixteen ships, all crafted in variations of a foreign but familiar design, met the mirror's questing focus. Morg frowned and shook his head slowly, pulling the mirror's viewpoint outward again to see their exact positions in relation to the Isle. They weren't quite within longboat distance of the shore, yet, but when Morganen focused closer, he could see the longboats being made ready for deployment.

Panning over to the largest, fanciest boat, he searched the faces of the crew. The one he wanted, he almost didn't recognize, for it had picked up several long scars around the mouth. Tightening the focus with a few more strokes of his fingers, Morg sighed roughly. "It figures . . ."

"What figures?" Hope asked.

"Hope, meet Lord Kemblin Aragol, Earl of the Western Marches of Mandare," he introduced, though he didn't bother to open the mirror for any actual communication between the two of them. "And what looks like a sizeable chunk of the Mandarite fleet."

"Charming," Consus muttered. "What brings them here, in such great numbers?"

"The usual," Morg dismissed. "Revenge, conquest, and rampantly arrogant misogyny. Dominor told me he had cast a truth-speaking compulsion upon Lord Aragol, right after Serina freed him from his shackles. From the looks of his scars, whoever bought him off the Natallian slave-block didn't appreciate his honesty. This isn't going to be pretty."

"There are sixteen of those ships," Consus pointed out. "I know personally how you can shove one ship halfway to the mainland, but sixteen?"

"I could shove sixty ships in a single day before breaking a sweat," the younger mage dismissed. "No, I meant that if we just shove them away, they'll just sail right back here, still intent on conquest and vengeance. We need to figure out a way to discourage them permanently from returning."

"Did their God not manifest?" Hope asked. Her query earned her a puzzled frown from both men. "You told me several months ago, after Dominor's return, that he explained how they had managed to break away from Natallia, declared themselves an independent kingdom, and even managed to manifest a Patron Deity.

"If so, that God has been Named down at the Convocation, and is therefore *our* Patron Deity as well. And it says quite clearly in the Laws of God and Man that no two kingdoms that share the same Patron Deity may go to war with one another," she reminded him. "That's one of the biggest reasons *why* it's such a big deal to be the host-nation of the Convocation. All Kelly has to do is request to the Mandarite God to manifest and send His Mandarites back home again, before they can break the Laws of God and Man."

Both men stared at her, but it was Morg who started laughing first. He laughed breathlessly hard, tickled by the irony of it. The puzzled look of his woman and his sort-of friend forced him to gasp out an explanation of why that was so amusing. "Gods! Kelly—the ultimate, rabid equalist—demanding that the God of the *Mandarites*—the ultimate misogynists—!"

He didn't even have to finish, which was good, because he couldn't. Hope grinned, and even Consus chuckled. Wiping at his eyes, Morg struggled to control his mirth. It didn't work. Helpless with laughter, all he could do was gasp for breath between spasms and try to stay upright.

Hope quickly guided him to one of the chairs at the table so he could collapse onto it, rather than onto the floor. With her own cryslet still missing, she flipped up the lid of Morg's gilt-and-crystal bracelet and punched the glittering buttons, dialing Kelly's cryslet. *Don't forget to encourage Him to act on our behalf, Yourself,* she thought at Nauvea. *I don't want the technicality of Kelly being a "mere female" to*

stay their Patron's hand in this matter. If He balks, I'll tell her to threaten Him with dereliction of His duty.

Oh, trust Me, none of Us are going to challenge her reasonable requests, today. Not after what she did to Mekha! And this is a very reasonable request, so long as she doesn't demand they be harmed. He wouldn't go for that.

Trust me, neither would she, Hope reassured Her, as Kelly opened her cryslet, answering the call.

TWELVE

❦

Morg rubbed at his temples, fighting against the headache
that was building. King Pro Tem Taurin just went on and
on and on, barely stopping for breath. Morg couldn't even make
sense anymore over what the other man was trying to tell him, other
than it *might* involve the budget. But he wasn't completely sure. The
other mage gestured, trying to make some point, but Morg couldn't
really care right now.

More than two weeks had passed since their duel, and Taurin's
casts had long since been removed. Morg was grateful the other
man's arms hadn't been permanently damaged by his powers—he
honestly didn't like hurting others—but despite Morg's repeated
shows of massive magical strength intermixed with equally great
restraint, the other man was still a belligerent pain in the . . .

"And that's why I need *your* decision now, to have time to prepare!" Taurin finished, glaring through the mirror, hands planted
on his hips.

To have time to . . . ? His skull throbbed. Narrowing his eyes,

Morganen glared through the mirror separating them. "Do you mean to tell me that you have to have this decision *today*, for something you could've asked about *two days later*?"

"I told you! The Council needs time to prepare!"

Morg closed his eyes. "What day is today?"

"The second of Mars, of course!"

"*No*, what day, *in specific*, is it today?" Morg repeated, opening his eyes for another pointed glare. Taurin frowned back. "Today . . . is my *wedding* day. You *knew* that today was my wedding day. You knew it last week! And you give me an unnecessary headache on my *wedding day*?"

The pro-tem king folded his arms across his chest, defiant.

Gritting his teeth, Morg turned away from the mirror and rummaged through a collection of papers Hope had left on her outworld vanity table. Extracting one of them, he spun back to the mirror and brandished it. "Do you know what *this* is? This is a copy of an agreement signed by the Duchess Haupanea of Nightfall. She finally tracked down her prophecies cupboard and recovered this. *This* is a binding indemnity scroll.

"It says that, *if* the closing of the Portal on Nightfall turns out to be necessary, and *if* any delay in its closure leads to the harming of Nightfall property, income, or personnel, the Empire of Katan will reimburse Nightfall for its losses," Morg told him. "Two hundred years ago, a Councilor of Katan *delayed* closing the Portal, and in doing so, triggered the Curse of Nightfall and damaged the production rate of the Desalinator, ruining the island's inhabitability.

"Now, I *could* hold this over your heads," Morganen warned him. "Not only did the actions of a Katani government official lead to the disruption and economic destruction of the duchy of Nightfall, but the government of Katan has been *stealing* what meager profits were left over from the damaged desalination plant, for two hundred *years*. That's a *lot* of indemnity to have to pay.

"But *have* I held this over your heads? No. Not until you disrupted my *wedding day*."

Councilor Thera, head of the Department of Taxation, snorted audibly, visible behind Taurin's shoulder. "That scroll isn't worth the ink that was used to scribble on it! *That* indemnity is for the *Duchy* of Nightfall, and *you* are now a kingdom."

Morg lost his temper. "That does it! I am siccing my *sister-in-law* on you! I don't care *what* Kelly tells you to do about this so-called budget problem, you are going to *do* it, to the letter *and* the spirit. And you are going to *like* it, or I am going to throw *you* in the Oubliette!"

Taurin's jaw dropped. "You can't do that! That harridan has no authority, in Katan! *You* might, but *she* doesn't!"

"On the contrary, I may be the Regent of Katan, *your* superior, but I am also *her* loyal subject . . . which puts her over *me* in the chain of command," Morg told him. "The Gods Themselves confirmed it when They said she was the Queen of the *Empire* of Nightfall . . . and you *only* get to be an empire when you rule over two or more kingdoms. Now, you sit there in that Council Chamber, and you think about what you've just unleashed on yourselves, because you *will* be hearing from Queen Kelly tomorrow—*after* my wedding is over!

"Good day!"

Snapping his fingers, Morg shut off the connection between the two mirrors. He glared at the silvered glass for a few more seconds, then raked his hands through his hair, muttering dire threats under his breath. Only when he had calmed down again did he head back into his bedroom.

On his bed lay his wedding finery, trousers and sleeveless tunic stitched from robin's egg blue silk, and embroidered with green and gold knotwork. But he didn't put it on. Tucking the folds of his dressing robe tighter over his chest, he picked up his cryslet and punched in the number for his sister-in-law.

Kelly appeared in the oval scrap of looking glass after a moment. "Morg? I'm kind of in the middle of something."

"I know you're getting ready for the wedding," Morg apologized,

"but I just got pestered by Taurin about some stupid budget crisis that could've been handled in a few more days, instead of today. And he *knew* that today was my wedding day!"

"Ah—hold on," she muttered, shifting her arm so that he had an awkward view of her ear and part of the ceiling. "Aren't you finished with that diagnostic spell, yet?"

Mariel's voice floated across the connection. "I told you, it takes two full minutes! Have some patience. We're almost ready . . ."

Kelly shifted her arm, putting her face back into view. "Sorry. So they've been demonstrating that they're a pain in the ass. What else is new?"

"I told them I was siccing *you* on them. Tomorrow, could you please get Dominor to help you call them up, and give them a piece of your mind about whatever it is they were trying to bother me with?" Morg asked

"Oh, sure, make *me* the 'bad cop,'" she muttered, though she grinned as she said it.

"Kelly, Saber, look—it's purple!" Morg heard Mariel exclaim. "It's *purple*!"

The view of Kelly's face jerked off to the side. The minor tracking-spell controlling the mirror's focus lost all control as the view jiggled and jostled wildly. "*Purple*? Are you sure? Oh my god— Saber, it's *purple*! WOOOOHOOO!—*Chocolate for the win!!*"

Hastily averting his gaze so that he wouldn't be nauseated by the gyrating view, Morg frowned in confusion. *Chocolate for the . . . ? Oh! Chocolate . . . and purple for a positive pregnancy diagnosis! Congratulations, Sister!*

Grinning, Morg tried to catch her attention to congratulate her out loud, but the mirror was now showing nothing but a bunch of rustling honey gold hair, and the sounds of laughter intermingled with kisses.

Giving up, he closed the lid, ending the connection. Morg tossed the cryslet back onto his nightstand and rubbed at his temples, soothing his stress headache. One day, it would be himself that

Hope hugged and kissed in her euphoric glee. But in order to get to that point, he had a wedding to attend, the last wedding of Seer Draganna's last Prophecy. His wedding. Still grinning, he quickly stripped and reached for his clothes.

Wherever the land, whatever the people, the wedding of a Seer was invariably treated as a national celebration, with the prophet's happiness believed to be a portend of blessings to come for the whole of their home kingdom. This wedding was made all the more momentous, for Hope was not just marrying Morg—who had become the sovereign of the very land that had once exiled him to her home island, ironically transferring some of those blessings to Katan as well as Nightfall—but she was also marrying him in front of all of the Gods Themselves.

It had taken two weeks to wade through all of the petitions of the various priests and priestesses fetched to Nightfall Isle, and it had been suggested by Nauvea Herself that their wedding be the last official act of the Convocation. Or, as Nauvea had whispered to Hope, *I never could resist all those daydreams people have about their "perfect" wedding . . .*

But once she was in the amphitheater, dressed in a gown that incorporated both local and outworlder flair in its elegant design, Hope didn't really pay much attention to the Gods. They radiated both warmth and approval against her senses, but didn't do much more than sit in Their seats and watch as she faced Morg on the amphitheater floor. Nor did They need to, not with a ceremony so simple and elegant.

Kelly, dressed in new silks of her own, nodded in approval as Morg and Hope clasped each other's hands. Opening the scroll in her own hands, she began her part of the ceremony as officiator. Each time she paused, Hope and Morganen spoke in unison, reciting their vows. Together, recital-and-response flowed like free-verse poetry.

"Marriage is a privilege . . ." Kelly read.

"I will not take the rights and responsibilities of marriage for granted," Morg and Hope responded together.

"And a commitment."

"I will make this marriage a priority in my life," they vowed in unison.

"Marriage requires patience . . ."

"I will strive to listen to and acknowledge my spouse's point of view."

"And compromise," the redhead warned them.

"I will strive to find ways wherein both of us win, or at least that we take fair and reasonable turns." That one was a bit of a mouthful, and Hope rolled her eyes. Morg bit his lip, struggling not to laugh.

"Marriage is filled with tragedies . . ."

"I will be there to support and comfort my spouse in times of sorrow."

The urge to laugh faded from Morg, a promise taking its place in his steady aquamarine gaze.

Hope blushed, warmed by his determination to protect her.

"And triumphs."

"I will be there to encourage and cheer for my spouse in times of joy." Her brown eyes sparkled back, reminding him of rich, liquid chocolate ganache.

"Marriage is a sharing of resources . . ."

"I will be generous in times of plenty, and share fairly in times of scarcity."

"And a nurturing of family."

"I will help my spouse to care for our children, and will treat their relatives with the courtesy I would give my own kin." Unable to resist, Morg quickly stuck out his tongue at Kelly. She rolled her eyes—and then stuck out her own, before resuming her solemn duty.

"Marriage is a sanctuary . . ." she intoned.

"I will strive for harmony in our relationship."

"Built on a foundation of caring."

"I will aid and comfort my spouse in times of illness and injury, to the best of my ability."

"Marriage is a union of two hearts . . ."

"*I will faithfully honor my spouse as both lover and friend.*" Lifting her hands to his lips, Morg kissed Hope's knuckles.

Kelly cleared her throat, returning his attention to the final vow. "Pledged before the Gods Themselves."

"*I take this person to be my lawfully wedded spouse, until life dies or love ends, and it has been proven upon a Truth Stone that either cannot be revived,*" Hope and Morg recited. Both snuck glances off to the side, to the divine half of the amphitheater.

"Of those who are gathered here, in the understanding that you represent—or actually *are*—the eyes and the ears of all the Gods in Heaven," Kelly stated, amending the final phrase of the ceremony, "have you witnessed these vows in good faith?"

"*We indeed have,*" Fate stated, answering before anyone else could. The other Gods nodded, and the witnesses on the mortal side of the room cheered. Morg and Hope blushed at each other.

"Well, you heard it from the Gods Themselves," Kelly told them, dropping her solemnity in favor of a grin and a flip of her hand. "They now pronounce you husband and wife! And in the tradition of *my* old world . . . you may now kiss the bride."

Morg didn't even have time to pull her close; Hope threw her arms around his shoulders and claimed his mouth most thoroughly. Wrapping his arms around her, he returned the kiss with enthusiasm and relief that she was finally *his*, as was Prophesied.

Rising from Their seat, the Threefold God moved gracefully down the tiered steps lining the amphitheater. Reaching the bottom, They gave the kissing couple an indulgent smile, nodded to Kelly, and turned to walk back up through the Gateway of Heaven. In twos and threes, the other Gods rose and followed, finished with Their attendance at the Convocation.

It took more than ten minutes for all of the Patron Deities to file out of the amphitheater, but by the time even Nauvea had left, fluttering Her fingers in farewell as the last Goddess to leave . . . Morg

and Hope were still exchanging slow, succulent, tender kisses. Kelly cleared her throat. Then cleared it louder.

Giving up, she bapped them lightly on the upper arms with the rolled-up marriage scroll. "Hey! You can stop the kissing now. Honest."

Sighing, Hope reluctantly pulled away from Morg's lips. "No, I can't . . . He's better than chocolate."

Morg tugged her lips back into range, devouring them with greater hunger than before.

Kelly rolled her eyes. "Well, *I* have to see if this levitation gizmo of Trevan's can close the Gateway, and *you're* in my way."

Fluttering her hands—and poking them with the scroll when that didn't work—she got them to move off to one side. Once they were out of the way, she pulled out the levitator rod, thumbed the orange and white buttons for five slow counts, and then nudged the distance controller with her thumb, pulling the sliding button back toward herself, separating Fountain from Fountain.

Instantly, the shimmering, opalescent brilliance of the Gateway imploded, closing the Gateway of Heaven. The crystal came flying back, forcing Kelly to lighten her touch so that the glowing egg of energy didn't smack her in the chest. Backpack in his hands, Saber stepped up and neatly caught it, insulating it in layers of silk.

Deactivating the rod, Kelly tucked it into a side pocket, then helped her husband shoulder the pack. They would have to establish a trustworthy priesthood at some point, hopefully soon. But for now, it was his turn to resume the task of "walking the dog." Tucking her arm into her husband's elbow, Kelly glanced at her sister and brother-in-law . . . who were still kissing each other, oblivious to the crowd of Nightfallers making their way back to their city.

Nor did they pay any attention to the clergy of two hundred and forty-eight nations, who made their way toward either Priestess Ora and the Darkhanan Witches for a trip back home through the Dark, or for the first of the twenty Mendhite ships, mirror-Gates ready and waiting to speed their return to their homes. At the very least, she would've thought Morg would remember that his own twin was leaving tomorrow with his wife, Danau, and the three Aquamancers she had arrived with, for they were headed back to Menomon to build their own version of the Desalinator.

But no. They're still playing kissy-face with each other. She waited a few moments more, then gave up. *Oh, for the love of . . .* "Get a room, you two!"

They didn't respond—at least, not to her. They certainly responded to each other. Sighing in mock-disgust, Kelly gave up and let Saber lead her into the rest of the Underhalls, leaving the happily married couple alone.

Not until they were alone did Morganen and Hope bother to come up for air; only then did they smile at each other and stroll, arm in arm, back to their suite.